# ARABESQUE

"is a novel full of interesting characters and unusual locales, told with an air of casual sophistication and absorbing reading."
—*Library Journal*

"spins silky strands of love and loves lost, gliding over the parqueted floors of elegant houses in the world between wars."
—*Kirkus Reviews*

"is an elegantly romantic mature love story, brilliantly portrayed."
—*Publishers Weekly*

*also by the same author*

**Fugue**
**Of Love and Wars**

# ARABESQUE

## THERESA DE KERPELY

STEIN AND DAY / *Publishers* / New York

FIRST STEIN AND DAY PAPERBACK EDITION 1985

*Arabesque* was first published in hardcover
by Stein and Day/*Publishers* in 1976.
Copyright © 1976 by Theresa de Kerpely
All rights reserved, Stein and Day, Incorporated
Designed by Ed Kaplin
Printed in the United States of America
STEIN AND DAY/*Publishers*
Scarborough House
Briarcliff Manor, N.Y. 10510
ISBN 0-8128-8111-7

*For Oliver G. Swan*

*Special Acknowledgment*

To Mary Solberg, an inspiring editor whose genius lies in her ability to see below the surface that she is helping to shape and polish, my gratitude and admiration.

T. DE K.

# Contents

### Part One

1   Joanna and Julian   11
2   Old Browne   37
3   Sybil and Maximilian   76
4   Nicolai and Lucrèce   108
5   Amanda   193

### Interlude   211

### Part Two

6   Fricka   221
7   Joanna and Keres   268
8   Joanna and Julian   290
9   Joanna   301
10   Sybil and Consuela   305

# Part One

# 1

# Joanna and Julian

I

I had never experienced cold of the kind that set in that day. Not that it was ever very warm. Julian and I, with our English passion for being by the sea in all weathers, had rented a waterfront villa in Scheveningen for the off-season, only to discover that even English standards of warmth were impossible to achieve with an angry North Sea raging on the doorstep and winter gales constantly battering casements designed to let in the sun rather than keep out the wind. And that winter, the winter of 1922, the storms were exceptionally violent.

But on this particular day the cold was different. The wind had stopped its incessant assault for the first time in weeks. Under a pallid sun, row after row of little white-frilled waves were following one another across the level sands as peaceably as they did in summer. Indoors the potbellied iron stoves were burning red-hot, yet the windows were heavily crusted with ice on the inside.

The girl who came every morning to help with the housework had not yet appeared. Luckily, the door-to-door vendors, who thought us slightly mad—like all foreigners—but worth holding onto as customers, came as usual; the baker and the milkman and the greengrocer with covered horse-drawn wagons, and the fisherman from the wharf with a barrow drawn by a dog. I bought a haddock for Julian's supper and a slender brown-skinned sole for the children's lunch. The fisherman scooped out its entrails in one virtuoso movement, and I put it quivering fresh from the freezing sea into the hot fry pan, which shocked it into a postmortem leap that landed it, flapping, on the floor. Cissy, the baby, was frightened out of her wits, but my four-year-old son, Pip, was amused and tried to catch it.

Nothing amused me.

It was one of those waiting days when what hasn't happened yet stops everything else from happening. Only the gutted fish completed its final dance on the kitchen floor. Pip's amusement lasted no more than a moment, and the sole cooked could not hold his attention either; he kept running upstairs to his grandmother's room to see if she was back, and her stomachache gone.

Her bed was still unmade, and so were the children's cribs and the double bed that I slept in with Julian—who hated unmade beds, undusted rooms, unscoured bathtubs, all disorder, but would have to put up with it for once; not because the girl hadn't come, but because the sheets had refused to be smoothed, the pillows had fought to retain the hollows of last night's sleepless heads, and the rooms had shut their doors on their private dust.

Julian came back from the chancery in midafternoon.

"When the Old Man heard what had happened he told me to take the rest of the day off. He's not such a stick as I thought. He's pretty decent, in fact. He asked his wife to come over this afternoon and stay with the children so that we can go together to visit your mother."

"I'd rather go alone."

"But I want to go with you."

"Why? You don't love her. You don't even like her—you've never got along with her."

"That's not true. Who asked her to come and live with us after your father died? Who offered her a home?"

"You 'offered her a home,' as you call it, because you're sentimental. I knew it wouldn't work. She didn't like you any more than you liked her—whatever you say."

"Then why the hell did she come?"

"Because she loved *me*."

But the quarrel was stopped, like everything else, in the indecent act of happening; I suddenly heard myself using the past tense. Julian said, "You'd better go and get ready—Lady G. will be here any minute now."

I went upstairs to put on my warmest coat and my strongest suit of armor. It was a long walk from our end of the seafront to where the tramlines from The Hague looped and the trams made a five-minute halt before going back the way they had come. I was pulling my rubbers on over my shoes in the hope of keeping my feet warm, when I heard the front doorbell ring. A black Rolls-Royce, with a uniformed chauffeur standing beside it, was parked on the icy esplanade, carless for months until yesterday, when the ambulance had come for my mother; and the sight of it cut through my armor with lightning ease, bringing all the sensations and feeling of yesterday back in a single rush of anguish.

From downstairs in the hall came the voices of Julian and Lady G., wife of the chargé d'affaires. Their tones were low enough to suggest conspiracy, but it was hard to imagine Julian in conspiracy with the titled owner of a Rolls-Royce.

I looked in on the children taking their afternoon naps in their tumbled cribs, and hurried downstairs to interrupt the muted conversation, which had moved into the living room, and accept, *force majeure*, a favor I hadn't asked for and didn't want, from a woman I had met only once, at an official reception. She appeared more simple and motherly now than she had then, but I found her kindness condescending. And used as she was to the orderly surroundings created by a large staff of servants, she would not fail to notice what I had left undone, undusted, unwashed. But she would never understand why. She might even try to tidy things up for me out of pity.

"My *dear* Mrs. Crest. . . . I can't tell you how sorry I am about your mother. But please set your mind at rest with regard to the children. Your husband has told me what to do when they wake, and what to give them for tea. My chauffeur will drive you to your destination, and wait for you there until you are ready to leave."

The thought of that sleek black car upset me so much I forgot to be polite. "I would rather go by tram," I said without thanks.

"But the car will get you there sooner, my dear."

I failed to grasp her meaning. I thought we had to use her car because we were using her time. And even when Julian said, "Joey . . . it's important that we should get there with the least possible delay," my mind still refused to accept the true reason for haste.

The chauffeur touched his peaked cap and opened the car door. Julian had to push me inside. "Where to, sir?" the chauffeur asked.

The Rolls glided off. It motion, creamy and rich and flowing, like that of the ambulance, brought back the anguish again. Julian touched my hand, but I turned away and looked out of the window. The woods, the little woods between Scheveningen and The Hague, were pure Hans Christian Andersen; the leafless trees were all made of glass, which the reddening sun was too cold to break, and the wind, far out to sea and dying, too remote. Under the tinkling branches the winter children bobbed in and out like balls of bright-colored wool. The cyclists homing along their special track flew their rainbow scarves against the distant wind like pennants.

Julian spoke through a tube to the chauffeur, giving him directions. The car turned gracefully out of the crystal woods and advanced at a wary pace into alien terrain, into uncleaned streets where tatters of newspaper rustled along the gutters or, caught by the nose of the car, swirled up and fluttered like rags against the windshield.

The hospital visiting hours were over, but we were admitted. When we entered the wing where my mother was, I heard a peculiar sound that reminded me of an animal plaint I once heard as a child, tried not to hear, then prayed to hear again when the crack of a shotgun had stopped it.

A matter-of-fact head nurse received us, "Mynheer ... Mevrouw," then, changing to stilted English, "It is good that you have come. We have placed the mother alone in a small room, but please to wait a short time before you enter. She receives an injection to ease her pain."

We sat down to wait on a hard bench. Young nurses came and went, their voluptuous bodies starchily cased in blue-and-white cotton. I had seen them all before, less clothed, on the walls of the Mauritshuis. "How jolly they all look!" Julian said. "Did you know that Lady G. was a nurse before she was married?"

"No."

"Well, she was. She told me about it today, and it put her a long way up in my estimation. And the Old Man too. She worked in the London nursing home where he went to have his appendix out. That's where they met."

"Was that what you and she were talking about when I came downstairs?"

"That—and other things."

An older nurse, tall and rawboned; emerged from a half-open door and came over to us without smiling. After apologizing for her inability to speak English, she took us into a pure white cell with a floor like an indigo lake. My mother, gray against white, seemed scarcely to breathe, but her eyes were open. She said in a clear, pale voice, separating the words as if the pronouncing of each cost her an immense effort, "It's . . . getting . . . dark."

"I couldn't come any sooner, Mother dear. But you needn't have worried, they said we could see you outside of visiting hours."

Julian explained, "Joey had to wait until I got home. The girl didn't turn up—just when we needed her most: The Old Man's wife is with the children now. We came here in her car."

"The woods are beautiful, Mother. All frozen. I wish you could see them, you'd write a poem about them."

But my mother had closed her eyes.

The head nurse appeared at the door and motioned us out. "Please not to talk too much. It is better that she sleeps. I have informed the doctor that you are here, and he instructed me to inform you that the end is not far off. He thought you might desire to stay with her."

"I'll stay," I said.

"Perhaps we could both stay. . . ."

"The end may not come until late in the night," the nurse said, then moved away to attend to something else.

"In that case," Julian said, "I suppose I'd better go home now and take over from Lady G. But I'll find someone else to sit with the children, and then I'll come back."

"No. Stay at home with the children—please."

"But . . ."

"*Please!* Can't you understand? I want to be alone with her."

"I understand that. I just want to be here to take you home . . . afterward."

"I'd rather come home by myself."

After a moment's silence he said, "I see." He took out his wallet. "Here's the money for a taxi. Even if the trams are still running I want you to take a taxi."

We went back to my mother. Julian sat down beside the cot and took her hand in his. He said very low, as if he didn't want me to hear, "I'm sorry. I'm sorry for everything. Can you forgive me?"

She made no answer, but I saw her fingers curl around his palm in a weak attempt at pressure. After a minute or two, he said, "I must say good-bye now—I have to get back to the children." He bent and kissed her forehead, then lifted her hand to his lips, laying it down on the coverlet afterward with extreme care, as if its fragile flesh and bones were already turning to dust. He rose and stood looking down at her with an expression on his face that I had never seen there before, an expression of reverence. "How beautiful you are," he said, with a strange kind of wonder in his voice, "how very beautiful. . . ."

I took his place at the bedside.

"I . . . want . . ." my mother began, her voice now paled to a whisper. I waited, but no more words came, though her lips were moving. I put my face close to hers, which had always been so fragrant, and I thought how much she must now loathe the smell of herself.

"What is it that you want, Mother? Please try to tell me." But her lips stopped moving. Again, she seemed scarcely to breathe. I called the nurse.

"My mother wants something, but she can't tell me what it is, she can't speak," I said in my faulty Dutch. The nurse bent over her, sponged her face, moistened her lips. The nurse had beautiful hands, tender hands.

Watching, I stepped for a moment outside of myself, and perceived the immaculate scene—each burnished object in its appointed place, long shafts of winter light from the high-set window, deep reflections, the peaceful, bending form of the nurse, the white wings of her cap—all in exquisite balance, as Vermeer might have composed it.

The nurse put one of her big bony hands on my shoulder. "Keep the mother calm. She must go to sleep before she begins to feel again."

I considered her grayish profile against the white of the pillow. Julian was right. She was beautiful. Old and dying, she was far more beautiful than I was, young and fully living. We were not unalike; we had the same clear blue eyes, the same fine skin and fair complexion, and to some extent the same delicately cut features; but her planes were purer than mine, and her eyes reflected lights not visible to me.

I laid my hand lightly on hers, which would never again pick up the little gold pencil with which she wrote down her poems—the gentle, devotional poems for which she had so much wanted appreciation from me. It was still a shapely hand, blue-veined and fragile, an old hand, but undisfigured by age. At my touch, she opened her eyes and looked anxiously into mine. Once again her lips moved inaudibly. I tried to read them. They seemed to be forming a single word—*love*. Yet I failed to respond. I said, "Rest now, Mother. We can talk later—I'm not going to leave you."

There was a long, deep silence. I thought she had finally fallen asleep, but she had merely skipped a few beats of time, for she suddenly said as if there had been no interval, and quite clearly, "But *I* am going."

The nurse came in at my sudden cry and felt her pulse again. "She is still here. Listen. . . ."

But although she still breathed I knew she had slipped out of reach for good and all. I should never know for certain what it was that she wanted to tell me.

The room darkened. The nurse put on a light behind a screen. Through the half-open door I could hear the subdued clatter of supper trays being distributed. The nurse brought one in for me.

"You are very kind," I said, "but I cannot eat now."

"Eat. You have to be strong."

She left the tray on the table. I looked at the food with a mixture of nausea and longing. I had eaten nothing since yesterday. I pushed the tray from me. A moment later I pulled it back and ate everything on it. When the nurse returned I was so ashamed I couldn't look at her.

"Good," she said. "The mother would not wish that you should starve."

The doctor came. I had seen him for the first time yesterday, before the emergency operation. He was known as the best surgeon in The Hague. "If anyone can save her, he can," they had said when we brought my mother in. But he had told us bluntly not to expect a miracle, all he could do was try.

"I am glad that you got here while she was still able to speak," he said. "When I came to see her at noontime she was repeating your name over and over. There was something she wanted—or wanted to say—and she knew she was going. So I called the

17

legation and told your husband that there was no time to lose."

He was feeling my mother's pulse as he spoke, then he turned up her eyelids. Looking back at me, he said gently, "There is nothing more that we can do—except relieve her pain. But I do not think she will feel any more pain. The end will come in a matter of hours. Do not be surprised if she begins to breathe harshly. There is a house physician on call, and Sister, here, will stay on duty for as long as she is needed—and she is a good, motherly woman as well as a good nurse." Turning to her, he said in Dutch, "I told Mevrouw that you are good like a mother."

A blush spread all over the nurse's homely face, up to the roots of her straw-straight hair and down to the tip of her long nose.

The night watch began.

In commanding me to eat, the nurse had said, "You have to be strong," an admonition that I had not taken literally. But in that austere setting there was no concession to physical weakness in anyone but the patients. I thought of a print called *The Vigil*, given me by my mother when I was a young girl to hang on my bedroom wall. It showed a crusader knight in a coat of mail kneeling bolt upright before a stone altar with his hands clasped on the hilt of his sword; and I, curled up on my warm bed, would imagine him purging his heart of dross before tomorrow's battle, and enjoy a vicarious triumph of mind over matter. Now, sitting bolt upright on a straight wooden chair beside my mother's deathbed, with my heart brimful of dross, all I wanted to do was stretch out somewhere and sleep.

Behind the screen, the nurse, sitting bolt upright on an equally hard straight chair, seemed, like the knight, above all human weakness. Overcome by mine, I slumped forward and rested my head on the cot. But my mother's breathing, now grown raucous, kept me awake. Obsessed by my longing for sleep, and half over the edge, I felt angry with her for making so much noise.

The big, bony, tender hands of the nurse reached down to the bottom of the well in which I had finally found oblivion and brought me back up to the surface. The raucous sounds had stopped. All sound had stopped. Then my mother gave an infinitesimal sigh. The nurse echoed the sigh. "*Het is voorbij*," she said, It is over, and went out with great delicacy. I stayed for a few minutes looking down at my mother who wasn't there anymore. I felt numb.

It was five o'clock in the morning.

"Can I get a taxi at this hour? I live out in Scheveningen."

"They will answer a call to come here at any hour," the nurse said, "but the fare will be double."

While she was calling the taxi I put on my things.

"The driver says it is terribly cold, over forty degrees of frost. You should cover your ears, Mevrouw."

I turned up the fur collar of my coat.

"Good-bye, and thank you, Sister."

She took my outstretched hand and held it, looking at me as if she were trying to make up her mind about something. "It is hard to lose the mother," she said. Then she did what I hoped she would do. Her embrace was as big and bony and tender as her hands.

The taxi man, speechless with cold and muffled up to the eyes, drove like a demon along the tattered streets and through the Hans Andersen woods, where the winter children were fast asleep and the cyclists' pennants folded and no wind blew.

About fifty yards from our door I told him to stop. He took the double fare, and the triple tip I gave him by mistake, without a word, and like a demon departed.

The moon was down and the darkness intense. I could barely discern the long white lines of the sea, and I could not hear it at all. I let myself noiselessly into the house, took off my rubbers and shoes, and stole upstairs in my stockinged feet. At the top of the stairs I paused to listen. The bedroom doors were open, and the house was so still that the children's thistledown breathing was as clearly audible as the deeper, slower sounds of their father's sleep. When no one stirred, I went to my mother's room and knelt down by her unmade bed and told it what I hadn't told her. Then the longing for sleep overtook me again. But I couldn't stay there, in that empty room, so still, so cold. Even though it seemed like a last betrayal of the dead, I had to seek the warmth of the living, to go where I belonged.

When I crept in beside the sleeping Julian, he stirred, "Joey . . . ?" Only half awake, he groped across the gap that I had purposely left between us and moved over against my back. "My God! You're frozen!"

"Everything's frozen."

"So it's all over. What time did it happen?"

"At about five o'clock."

"Did she go peacefully?"

"Yes."

"Was she able to tell you what it was that she wanted?"

"No."

He was silent. I started to tremble. He put his arms around me. I felt no more than the animal comfort of being enclosed by another body.

"I shouldn't have allowed you to come home alone ... I should have gone back and waited for you...."

"I didn't want you to come back. I was quite all right. The nurse got a taxi for me."

He pressed closer against my back and nuzzled the side of my head—a familiar gesture of reconciliation. But I couldn't respond. My heart was covered with ice. After a while he began to caress my shivering body with his warm hands and mouth. He believed that all ice could be melted by physical warmth.


When the children's voices woke us the sun was up and the starry patterns of frost on the windowpanes glittered. "We've overslept," I said, but I didn't spring out of bed as I normally would have. I felt an extraordinary lethargy, an utter indifference to time and daily duty.

"It doesn't matter," Julian said. "I'm taking a week's leave as of today. There's a lot to be done. I have to go to Rotterdam about taking your mother home on a British cargo boat."

"Home?"

"Yes. Back to England. I'm sure that's what she wanted."

"She wanted more than that."

"What do you mean?"

"Nothing. It doesn't matter."

He pulled on some clothes and went downstairs. I could hear him raking the ash from the stoves and putting on more coal. Evidently the girl had again failed to turn up. But I still made no move. In the next room Cissy set up a wail. Pip came in, "Cissy's crying. She's wet."

"All right. I'll come."

"Granny hasn't come back yet."

"I know."

"But when . . ."

"Don't worry me, Pip—I've got a bad headache. Let's get dressed now and go downstairs."

Julian had put on the kettle for tea and was making toast.

"If my mother is going home, I want to go with her."

"Of course you'll go with her. We'll both go."

"But how can we both leave? What about the children?"

"Lady G. knows someone, an English girl, who would be willing to come and stay with them while we're away. We spoke of it yesterday."

"I want to go home with Granny," said Pip, starting to cry.

"You can't," said his father shortly. "Go and play in the other room, your mother and I want to talk."

An obedient child, he ran off, and from where I sat I could see him climb up on a chair to play with the patterns the frost had drawn on the window and scratch little peepholes through them with his fingernails. Julian lighted a cigarette and smoked for a minute or two in silence. I felt his eyes on me, but I wouldn't look at him.

"You hate me, don't you?" he said.

"I don't want to talk, that's all."

"You hate me because I didn't believe in her aches and pains. Well . . . neither did you. But you won't admit it. You want to put all the blame on me."

Pip came running in. "Get out!" his father said.

He stopped in his tracks. "What is it?" I asked him.

"The sea's stopped moving!"

"Don't tell lies," his father said.

Pip's face crumpled. "Don't cry," I said, "we'll go out and see for ourselves, shall we?"

Smiling again, he pulled at his father's sleeve. "You too," he said.

We put on our coats and went out into the sun, and a cold so bitter that it was inconceivable how the two could exist at the

21

same time. We crossed the road to the beach. Far out, where the water was deep, there was movement. But the shallow waves had been caught as they rolled in over the flat sands, and turned, like the woods, to glass.

Before I could stop him, my winter child went bobbing over their crystal crests like a ball of bright-colored wool. "Look at me! Look! I'm Jesus!"

## II

The deep frost lasted for two more days. Then a wind came up, brought snow, sleet, rain, and then died down, leaving the sea sullen and sluggish and the waterlogged land in a state of raw suspension.

Julian and I left for England with our feelings in much the same state. On the train to Rotterdam we sat face-to-face on either side of the clouded window, grim and raw as the landscape, not speaking, not meeting each other's eyes, but watching, through patches of glass rubbed clear by our woolen-gloved fingers, the ghostly forms of cows and windmills and ships loom up through the mist that hung motionless over the meadows.

At Rotterdam, we took a tram down to the docks. On a square close to the river the tram made its terminal loop and we got off. Julian led the way down a cobbled street that brought us out on the quay. There he insisted on taking my arm, and we walked along together, but still apart, trying not to trip over the hawsers, or get in the way of the longshoremen loading and unloading cargo, or get caught by one of their swinging hooks and hoisted into the air that resounded with shouts and curses in half the languages of the world from the polyglot ships' crews.

"There she is!" Julian said, pointing to a dumpy little freighter painted with the inappropriate name of *The Swallow*. A crane was lowering tire-sized cheeses into her hold. Watching the operation, a little apart from the scurrying, shouting crew, was a lanky ship's officer slightly bent at the waist, like a stalk of tall grass broken in the middle. He wore the modestly braided uniform of the mercantile marine, livened up by a bright red muffler. But his bearing was more like that of an undertaker keeping an expert eye on the final phase of his professional services from a discreet distance.

"That's the captain," Julian said, adding in a low voice as we went up the gangplank, "he's doing us a favor, so be nice to him even if you don't feel like it."

A seaman drew his attention to our arrival. He shook hands with me solemnly but without any words of condolence, which I thought was tactful of him, seeing that I was not wearing black. "The cabin is ready for you, ma'am," he said with the air of an admiral greeting a royal guest on his flagship, "and I hope that you will find it comfortable. Weather permitting, we shall weigh anchor in half an hour, after which the evening meal will be served."

"Are we likely to run into stormy weather?" asked Julian.

"A fog bank," the captain said, "that's what we're likely to run into—unless the wind changes, and then it could be a heavy crossing. But you needn't worry about your piano. It's firmly wedged in between the cheeses—even a hurricane wouldn't budge it."

"If you'll excuse me," I said, "I'd like to go to my cabin now, I have a slight headache."

The cabin boy took our bags and conducted us to the ship's only passenger cabin. It wouldn't hold all three of us at once, so we let him put the bags down and leave before we went in ourselves and shut the door. We were still crowded, and the enforced physical contact with Julian upset me because in a way I wanted it, which seemed almost indecent under the circumstances. I escaped to the only possible distance, the upper bunk, from which I asked him, "What was all that about a piano? Am I going dotty? Or are you?"

He took off his raincoat, hung it up on a peg, and took his cigarettes out of the pocket before he answered, "I'm sorry I let you in for that. I wanted to tell you on the train, but you were so cold and distant that I couldn't."

"Tell me now."

"Well . . . Seamen are superstitious. They're afraid of the dead. If the crew of this ship, or even the captain, had any idea that your mother's remains were on board, they'd refuse to sail."

"Do you mean to say. . . . Oh, my God!"

"Shh, keep your voice down."

I started to laugh. I could hear my own laughter in the way

that one hears one's own voice after a few drinks—as if someone else were producing the sounds.

"Joey! Stop it! You can't afford to have hysterics in this tub, you've got to keep up appearances no matter what."

I took several deep breaths, as I used to do as a child when seized by a fit of giggles in church. The spasms stopped. A few quiet tears came out of my eyes. I wiped them away with the edge of the clean, coarse pillowcase under my head. When I thought I could speak in an even voice, I asked, "Does anyone know?"

"The shipping company knows, of course, and the fellow in the consulate at Rotterdam who helped me arrange it with them."

"I don't understand why you didn't tell me what you were going to do—after all, she's *my* mother."

"I didn't tell you at the time because I was afraid you wouldn't agree."

"And I always thought that *you* were the sentimental one!"

"That's where you're wrong. Sentimental people have no sense of proportion. I knew how important it was that your mother should be taken back to England and be buried next to your father—so important that it didn't matter how it was accomplished, short of committing a crime. And all I've done is pull a few strings and tell a few lies and keep you in the dark."

"There must have been some other way."

"Every other way would have cost us money that we simply haven't got."

"If the captain doesn't know, how is he doing us a favor?"

"We're guests on his ship. And with what we save on the trip to England and back we can go to Clovelly for a night—afterward. You'd like that, wouldn't you?"

We had spent the first night of our honeymoon at Clovelly.

The boat began to throb. I felt as if I were inside a drum. Bells rang. "That's for supper," Julian said. "Coming?"

"No."

"You'd better eat while we're still on the river. You'll be sick as soon as we hit the open sea—even without a storm."

"I'm sick now."

"Look here, you needn't eat much if you don't want to, but do me the favor of putting in an appearance, will you? And try to look as if you were going to England for a few days' holiday. Please."

24

I got up. "Where's the lavatory?"

"Next door."

I washed my face, tidied my hair, and sat on the toilet seat for an age in the hope that Julian would go into supper without me. But he banged on the door and told me to hurry up.

Before we went into the dining saloon, I said, "You'd better tell me why you're taking the piano to England. If the captain mentioned it once, he may mention it again."

"It's a birthday present for my sister—I got it from a colleague who's being transferred to a hot climate and doesn't want to take it with him."

"Your *sister?* What sister?"

"The musical one who has hopes of becoming a professional pianist. Do you know enough now?"

"More than enough. I had no idea that you were such a good liar."

"That's not lying, it's harmless invention for a good cause. Don't look at me like that, Joey, I did it for you . . . be nice to me, kiss me. . . ."

"Not now."

"Come on, just once to show that you don't hate me, please. . . ."

"Later."

"Is that a promise?"

It was a safe promise. "Later" was indefinite. And the time would eventually come when I could kiss and be kissed without feeling guilty. At least, I hoped that it would.

The captain and three other officers were already seated on bolted-down chairs around a bolted-down table, shoveling food into their mouths as if they were stokers feeding the furnaces below decks. When they saw us they put down their knives and forks and stood up with their mouths still full. I could see the food convulsing their Adam's apples as they swallowed it. The captain introduced the engineer, middle-aged, bulky, bald, bespectacled; the first mate, lean, dark, seamed; and the third mate, little more than a boy, with bright eyes, curly hair, and an impudent grin.

A place was reserved for me on the captain's right, next to the first mate, and for Julian on his left, next to the engineer. The galley steward plunked down before me a plate filled with boiled beef, potatoes, and cabbage, and a big thick cup full of milky tea sloshed over into the saucer. I picked at the food, swallowing a few morsels with difficulty.

"Delicate stomach, ma'am?" inquired the captain.

The last thing I wanted to discuss was stomach trouble. "No," I said, "it's just that I'm a poor sailor, even the throbbing of the engines is enough to make me feel queasy."

"It's better to eat well. You need something to throw up when the time comes. There's nothing worse than the dry heaves. I speak from experience."

"I can take liquids," I said, hoping to shut him up by drinking down the strong, sweet tea with a show of gusto—though I hated sugar in my tea. But it made me feel so much better, morally and physically, that I asked for a second cup, in place of the suet pudding.

The captain shook his head.

"Tea comes up much more easily than suet puddding, Captain."

"I grant you that, ma'am, but by the same token there's a good chance that some of the suet pudding will refuse to come up. And if it weren't for what refuses to come up, I'd die of starvation. Look at me! Six feet two and thin as a topmast. Before my stomach dropped I weighed nineteen stone."

"Surely something can be done?"

"That's what you'd think. After all, a stomach's only a sort of bag. It shouldn't be so difficult to haul it up and sling it in the right position."

An odd snort, like a suppressed laugh, came from the first mate. I turned and met his eyes. They tried to hold mine, but I looked away. Just then the captain abruptly rose, excused himself, and left like a man who has suddenly remembered that he has to catch a train. The first mate followed him out, with a gesture that seemed to imply, "Sorry, but I have to keep an eye on him."

Now, I thought, was the time for me to escape. Julian was happily talking politics with the engineer. The third mate was finishing up a second helping of suet pudding with the inward look of a child bored by adult conversation and thinking only of his own mysterious child's concerns and of getting back to them as quickly as possible.

I shifted in my seat, preparing to leave. My movement caught the third mate's attention. He looked across the table at me. "I don't know nothing about politics and that. I never was one for book learnin'," he said, not apologetically, but scornfully, and as if he and I were two of a kind, both equally uninstructed, and the same age. We probably were about the same age, but because I was married and had two children I felt older than my twenty-three years, although on my good days my looking glass told me that I didn't look more than eighteen, and on his good days Julian told me the same thing. And now the third mate's bright eyes were telling me that too, despite the fact that I felt like an old hag. I warmed to the third mate, even though he and I were farther apart than he seemed to think.

"Where do you live?" I asked him, just to be friendly, "In London?"

"At sea. That's where I live," he said.

While I was wondering just what he meant by that, he got up. "Duty calls," he said, and gave me his impudent smile like a personal gift.

When he had gone, and I had, so to speak, put his smile away out of sight, I got up to go. Julian rose too, still haranguing the engineer about the desirability of a Socialist government. "Don't let me break up your conversation," I said, "I'm going to try to get a little sleep while I can."

"I'll join you later, then," Julian said, sitting down again. "But my dear fellow! Can't you see. . . ."

If duty did not call the engineer, I thought, I could count on being left to myself for quite a long time.

I felt the need for some fresh air before going to the cabin. At the risk of running into the captain, I went up on deck. There was no wind, only the current of air caused by movement, and *The Swallow's* movement was slow and cautious, she was feeling her way through patches of dense fog. I leaned over the rail at the stern of the ship, watching its sluggish wake. I could hear the captain talking on the bridge and the first mate answering him. Then I heard descending footsteps. I made a dash for the companionway, but I wasn't quick enough. The captain's tall, bent-in-the-middle figure cut off my escape. "Getting a breath of fresh air before turning in, ma'am?"

"Yes. But I'm going below now—I want to get some sleep while we're still in calm waters."

"Don't worry, ma'am, you'll have plenty of time to sleep before we get out to sea."

His tone was at once resigned and wistful; I interpreted it personally, as signifying a desire to talk to me about his dropped stomach, combined with the realization that I wasn't going to stay and be talked to.

"Goodnight, Captain."

"Goodnight, ma'am. Sleep well."

I went down the companionway without looking back, but I could feel him standing at the head, watching me go and wishing that I would stay.

The cabin was so stuffy that after trying unsuccessfully to open the porthole, which I suspected had never been opened since *The Swallow* was built, I propped the door ajar instead and lay down on the top bunk without undressing. I tried to sleep. But sleep had perversely deserted me ever since I had allowed it to overcome filial piety. I might just as well have stayed up on deck, I thought, and talked with the poor old captain. What was wrong with me? Why did I find it so difficult to be kind, to be warm?

For the past few days I had been cruelly cold to Julian, who had shown what was, for him, extraordinary control. His physical lovemaking on that bitter night, that frozen early morning, had been more than anything else an attempt to bring me back from the dead, to warm and comfort me. And in a way it *had* comforted me, and would comfort me now if I could allow myself to accept it without feeling guilty. But I was ashamed even to think of it, as I had been ashamed of my hunger for food when my mother was dying.

So when Julian entered the cabin and shut the door, I feigned sleep. He came close, and, unbelieving, began to caress me, alienating my soul from my body by overwhelming the one with desire and the other with guilt. "I hate you," I said, and pushed him away. At any other time this would have started a love-fight, a not entirely mock battle that would have ended in peace and satisfaction for both of us. But now Julian said, "I'm sorry. I'll go up on deck for a while."

After he had gone I wished him back. I felt exhausted; not peaceful, not satisfied, but spent. It was the culmination of a much longer strain and conflict than that of the preceding few minutes, and it achieved what the will had been impotent to achieve—the capitulation of sleep, which was so abrupt that it was only when I awakened, equally suddenly, and sweating, that I was aware of it.

I had no idea of how long I had slept. It was pitch-dark—no lights of any kind were to be seen through the porthole—and unnaturally still. It took me a few moments to realize why; there was no more throb in the drum, the engines had stopped. The sudden hoot of a foghorn made me start. It was answered by another, farther away. In the silence that followed I heard Julian catch his breath, stir, and turn over in the lower bunk with a little dreaming whimper. I lay still for a while, then I lowered myself cautiously to the floor, felt for my coat and shoes, and left the cabin.

Emerging from the companionway onto the deck was like stepping up into a cloud. All lights, all forms—of bridge, funnels, lifeboats—had vanished. At the sound of footsteps I stood very still. They passed and repassed me, heavy but soft in rubber boots. They were not the captain's footsteps. This man was not bent in the middle. I couldn't see him even as a shadow, but I could tell from the way he walked that he held himself erect.

Foghorns called to and answered each other from near and far, but in between were periods of silence so eerie, so enclosed, that it was difficult to believe I was on a real boat on a real river. Even the footsteps pacing slowly back and forth on the wet surface of the deck had a muffled, dreamlike quality. Coming alongside me for the fourth time, they halted. My presence had been felt—or recognition of it had been decided upon. They moved closer, and stopped again. I heard a rustle of oilskins, then a groping hand encountered my shoulder. I remained motionless. The hand moved, the fingers lightly pressing, feeling the stuff of my coat, and the contours beneath it. There was a moment of suspension, of waiting. Then the hand was withdrawn and the footsteps moved away.

The next time I awakened, it was as light as it was ever likely to be in that cell of a cabin with its single porthole up against an impenetrable white wall. The boat was still lying idly at anchor, the foghorns were still lowing like a herd of lost cattle. But I felt better. I even felt hungry. I had no watch, and I wondered what the time was. Julian had left the cabin.

I washed my face, and applied powder and lipstick for the first time in five days. I brushed my long hair and piled it up neatly on top of my head. Then I replaced my crumpled dress with a skirt and sweater—the only change of outer garments I had with me, except for the black that I had insisted on bringing for the funeral.

I went in search of breakfast. Sounds of talk and laughter came from the dining saloon. Julian, the first mate, the engineer, and a sullen man who was introduced as the second mate were sitting around the table, but they were not having breakfast. The table was strewn with bottles of Dutch gin, and in the middle of it like a circular centerpiece, a gigantic artificial flower made of red-and-yellow wax, bloomed one of the tire-sized cheeses.

Julian jumped up. "Come and join the party," he said with six-o'clock-in-the-evening-at-the-British-Club-bar joviality. "I thought you were never going to wake up—you've been asleep since about nine o'clock last night."

"What time is it now?"

"Three o'clock in the afternoon. And we're still stuck in the same bloody fog bank." He cut a wedge of cheese and presented it to me on the point of the knife. "Have some breakfast."

I recalled the facsimiles of the centerpiece being lowered into the hold—padding for the piano—and shuddered.

"Come on, Joey, take it . . . it's damn good cheese, and you needn't be afraid of throwing it up, we'll probably still be stuck here this time tomorrow."

"That's right," said the engineer cheerfully. "I'm going to miss my wife's birthday."

The first mate gave his odd snort. Julian poured out a tot of gin and held it out to me. "Have a drink, it'll do you good."

"I can recommend it," the engineer said. "It's the finest quality, like the cheese. Gin and cheese, that's what the Dutchies are good for."

"I can think of something else," said the first mate.

"Not in front of my wife if you don't mind," Julian said, ready to pick a quarrel.

The first mate got up and left. "No one can stop me from thinking," he said over his shoulder.

"Swine," muttered Julian under his breath.

"Don't fash yourself, Mr. Crest," said the engineer, "he's out of sorts, not enough sleep. In this sort of foul-up he always stays on duty—no matter whose watch it is. He's the kind that doesn't trust anyone's judgment but his own."

"That's him all over," the second mate said.

The engineer pointed to my untouched glass and pantomimed lifting the glass and tossing the gin down his throat.

"That's right," said Julian, "drink up, Joey, you're too sober."

I did as he said. I knew I had to lessen the gap between his devil-may-care mood and my guilt-ridden sobriety. The gin burned my gullet all the way down and tasted like castor oil. But its effect was euphoric and almost instantaneous. "Now eat," Julian said, "or it may knock you out."

It had already severed the mental connection that had made the cheese seem abhorrent, and increased my hunger to the point where scruples disappear, and caution as well. I ate two wedges of cheese in succession and held out my glass for a second tot of gin. "Good girl!" said Julian. Our eyes met as they had not met for days, and he suddenly pulled me to him and kissed me on the mouth. The engineer roared with delighted laughter and slapped Julian on the back. "That's what I like to see! Real, honest-to-God conjugal love that isn't ashamed of itself. Doesn't happen like that where I come from."

"Where do you come from?" I asked him as soon as I could speak.

"Glasgow. Well, I suppose I'd better go and see what's happening in the engine room. These fogs are unpredictable, they lift when you least expect them to."

Julian and I went to the cabin. The boy was there, making up the bunks. Frustrated, we went up on deck into the cloud—white now, but just as impenetrable as it had been in the night. "I think I know a quiet spot where we can sit down," Julian said, "if we can find it." Groping in what he thought was the right direction, we stumbled on the protruding edge of something and fell together onto the rough wet surface of a stretched tarpaulin. When I tried to get up, Julian pressed me back and pinned me under him. Protest was impossible—but I didn't want to protest.

The violence of our swift, wordless lovemaking cleared my

head, and I realized that we were lying on the closed hatch of the cargo hold. I felt as if I had just committed an act of sacrilege. But I couldn't blame Julian for it, I had given myself up to it willingly, with only a fleeting sense of impropriety. Quite suddenly, and from very close by, came the revolting sound of dry heaves.

We sat up and began to talk about the weather. Then Julian said, "I don't seem to have my cigarettes with me, I must have left them in the cabin. Shall we go below now—or do you want to swallow some more fog? For my part, I've had enough."

"Just a little more," I said. "I'll join you in a few minutes." It seemed more politic not to go down together, but I left the hatch and found my way to the rail.

"Good afternoon, ma'am," said the captain's gloomy voice right in my ear. "I fear this fog is cutting your holiday short. It's one of the worst I can remember. But there's nothing to do but wait. It's an act of God, and there's no arguing with the Almighty."

"It will cut short your time ashore, won't it?" I asked him.

"Yes, ma'am, it will. But that doesn't matter to me. I'd just as soon be at sea. There was a time when I couldn't get home fast enough. But that was years ago, when I was a young man like your husband, and had a young wife like you—pretty and kind, like you, ma'am, if you'll pardon my saying so."

He knows, I thought, he heard.

"Yes," he said, "those were happy days. . . . Excuse me, ma'am."

He moved quickly away, and a few moments later I heard the sound of dry heaves.

From surprisingly close at hand came the first mate's derisive snort, and his disembodied voice. "Why doesn't the old fool retire while he can still walk off the ship?"

Not sure whether I was being addressed, or someone else whom I couldn't see, I remained silent. The voice moved away, giving an order. Another voice said, "That's him all over. Bloody cruel bastard."

"It's a lovely fog, isn't it?" said a third voice.

"Yes," I said, "it's a lovely fog."

"You and I know what's what, don't we?"

I said, "Are *you* sorry for the captain?"

"I don't see no reason to be sorry for him. He lives at sea, same as I do, and he'll die at sea, same as I hope to, and that's all there is to it. We're two birds of a feather."

"I think I know what you mean," I said. "I didn't yesterday, but I think I do now."

" 'Course you do. You're a sharp one. It don't take book learnin' to understand things like that."

"I've got to go below now—but I'm not sure if I can find the companionway."

"I'll give you a hand—but first I got to find yours."

We laughed. His hand found mine without the least trouble, as if he could see just where it was placed on the railing. He took it in a firm, unequivocal grip. "Rightyoh! We're off!"

And we were off. At a fast trot. "What are you doing? Where are you going? We'll run into something!"

"Oh no, we won't! I got sea eyes, and that means eyes that can see in a fog, and underwater, and in the dark too. Three turns around the deck, and you'll have had your constitutional."

When he came to a stop suddenly and accurately at the head of the companionway, I was breathless and glowing. "Thank you," I said.

"Duty calls," he said. "More's the pity—I could've done with another three turns."

Luckily for me, Julian had fallen asleep. If he had come up to look for me and found me running around the deck hand in hand with the third mate, almost anything could have happened. The last thing I felt was sleepy, but I climbed into my bunk because there was no other place to sit—the narrow padded bench was taken up by our bags. Very soon the bells rang for supper, and Julian woke up. "Joey? Are you up there, Joey?" I reached down with my hand and he took it and nuzzled my fingertips with his lips. "I fell asleep. I'm sorry—I meant to make love to you again—properly."

"You mean less improperly."

"I suppose it was rather improper. But you didn't mind, you liked it—I know you did."

"We'd better go in to supper now. If we're late a second time, the captain will be offended."

"A fat lot you care . . . but you're right." He leaped out of the bunk stark naked, and put on his clothes very fast, combing his hair and knotting his tie with the aid of his shaving mirror, which he hung on one of the coat pegs. "You don't think the captain guessed what we were up to, do you? He couldn't see us, of course, but he might have heard something."

I thought that he wasn't the only one who had heard something. "He might have—but I think he's past being outraged by that sort of thing. After you'd gone below, he came and talked to me . . . you know, I think he's dying, and determined to die at sea and not in a hospital bed."

"You're bloody perceptive all of a sudden. . . . Oh! I'm sorry, I'm *sorry!* I shouldn't have said that. Please don't cry. . . . Darling, please . . ."

But the floodgates were open at last, and I couldn't close them.

"My poor darling," Julian said, "my poor darling . . . I didn't know, I didn't realize. . . ."

I whispered between sobs, "Go in to supper without me. I promise to cry quietly."

He did as I asked. There was no longer any barrier between us. But I needed to be alone. To be still. Not to spoil the lovely fog with words or even with thoughts. An act of God, the captain had called it, and maybe it was. My soul and my body were floating in it together, blissfully reconciled. Only an act of God could accomplish that.

A knock on the cabin door was a jarring interruption that I tried to ignore, but when it was timidly repeated, I said, "Come in." The cabin boy entered with a bowl of soup and some soda crackers on a tray, "Compliments of the captain, ma'am, and he's sorry you're feeling poorly."

I drank the soup and ate the crackers as if the meal were all part of the act of God.

Much later, Julian looked in. "Asleep?"

"No."

"Are you all right now?"

"Yes."

"Really all right?"

"Yes, *really* all right."

34

"Then do you mind if I don't come to bed just yet? We've got a poker game going."

"No. Go ahead. And thank the captain for sending me in a tray—tell him I ate everything."

"I've got something else for you, compliments of the engineer," he said, producing an unopened bottle of Old Jenever. "You seem to have made quite a hit with the engineer."

I put the engineer's gift away in my suitcase. There might be a moment in England when it would come in handy. Then I lay down again, and after a time I must have fallen asleep, for I didn't notice when the drummer began drumming. The ship was pitching and tossing out on the open sea before I emerged from the lovely fog, and the cheese and the gin and the soup and the crackers all came up together.

In reconstructing the figures and the patterns of an arabesque that took shape in that strangely distant period between the two world wars, I have only a collection of old letters and photographs and a few pages from a diary to confirm memory. And memory is capricious about what it chooses to retain.

From my mother's burial, shrouded in drizzling rain, it has preserved the illumination of a single moment—the moment when I threw the first handful of earth on my mother's coffin. I knew as I did it that I was burying both symbolically and actually an innocence I would never encounter again.

On the following morning, when Julian and I awoke in the little hotel on the beach at Clovelly where five years earlier I had been given my first lesson in love, the sun was shining on the light blue water of a calm sea, and the air was soft and mild, like spring.

"I hope this weather keeps up," Julian said, "but anyway I've decided to take the regular boat back to the Hook. I can't risk getting stuck in another fog bank on the Maas."

I looked at him in surprise. "But I thought we couldn't afford to take the regular boat—and come here as well?"

"We can now. While you were being seasick I was winning at poker. I took the shirt off that bastard of a first mate."

"But he might have taken the shirt off you!"

"I knew he wouldn't. He's a good player, but his eyes give him away every time. I found that out on our first night aboard, when he was sitting next to you at supper. He was looking at you while you were talking to the captain, and his eyes gave away quite a lot that I didn't like. But I got even with him all right."

Less than a year later, we were taken away from the steely waters of the North Sea and set down by a glittering human stream iridescent with decay; the Calea Victoria, main thoroughfare of the city of Bucharest, capital of Rumania. A legendary country, associated in my mind with Gypsies, werewolves, and vampires, and in Julian's with rich oilfields, feudal landowners, a corrupt society, and a poverty-stricken peasantry. But it was there that I learned how to recognize the many disguises of love, and to look beneath them.

# 2

# Old Browne

I

Trains. Before the coming of air travel, trains were as emblematic of life in the foreign service as caravans are emblematic of life in a traveling circus.

The train that was taking me from Bucharest down to the Black Sea for the summer was gathering speed as I lurched along the corridor and entered the compartment where the children were settled with their Fräulein and the younger of our two maids.

Cissy was pleased to see me, she was afraid I'd been left behind. Pip, six years old now and embarrassingly observant, inquired gravely, "What were you and Father doing behind the kiosk?"

"We were saying good-bye."

The maid grinned, and the Fräulein pursed her lips.

Julian and I were standing together on the platform, uneasy at leaving each other for a whole month but doing our British best not to let anyone see it, when the guard started slamming doors and warning all passengers to get on the train. Julian bestowed on me the hasty public kiss of an English gentleman seeing his wife off on a summer vacation, then suddenly gripped my arm, rushed me down the platform to a newspaper kiosk, and pulled me behind it.

The guard blew his whistle, but Julian wouldn't release me, and the train was already moving when he boosted me onto it, three long, swaying cars away from my little domestic clutch.

I went and stood in the corridor beside an open window, to

avoid more questions from Pip, and to cool down after Julian's embraces, frustrating and unsettling as a last-minute prelude to four weeks of chastity—for we were still physically faithful to each other despite the efforts of the enterprising and attractive Rumanians to enlarge our experience, which made our yearly summer separations a sort of endurance test. But they couldn't be avoided. The Bucharest of those days was too unhygienic a city to be safe for children in the hot weather, when the diseases that flourish in dirt and dust would flare up into murderous epidemics. The British and American wives and children all went off to the sea or the mountains for July and August, where husbands with cars would join them on weekends. But Julian had no car, and he could only get away for one month.

For our first summer in Rumania we rented a little white-washed cottage with no conveniences, grandiloquently called a villa, in the Danube port of Constanza. It belonged to the Turkish consul, who invited Julian down to see it before taking it. But Julian, bedazzled by the Turk's two ravishing and emancipated daughters, had failed to notice the cockroaches and the bedbugs and the smell in the outhouse.

We were wondering where to go next time, when Old Browne came to the rescue. Passing through Bucharest on his way to somewhere else, he dropped in at the legation, as everyone in the service did when they happened to be in town, and got to talking with Julian about the little port on the Black Sea where he was posted. He could find us a nice clean villa there, he said, for less money than we had paid in Constanza, and he would be only too glad to be of help.

"I think we can rely on him," Julian said, when the arrangement was made. "He's a decent old boy, and he'll take good care of you while I'm not there."

It was unlike Julian to consign me so confidently to the care of another man, no matter how "decent," but I found an explanation for that in the Foreign Office List, where Old Browne's birthdate showed him to be fifty-two years of age, twenty-seven years older than I was—old enough to be a father to me. In Constanza, an American vice-consul named Johnson, who was about my own age, had been more than willing to take good care of me in my husband's absence, but not like a brother. Keeping him in line had been difficult. Old Browne might be less fun than young Johnson, but old bachelors were easier to handle than young ones.

I also learned from the Foreign Office List that Old Browne had been in the same post for an unusually long time. "And the chances are," Julian said when I brought it up, "that he'll stay there until he dies, or retires—unless the port expires first, which may well happen, it's moribund already. According to Granby-Smith, who knows all about Old Browne, or says he does, he was well on his way up when he made a fatal mistake, and he was lucky not to be sentenced to some hellhole in the tropics."

I wanted to know what Old Browne's mistake had been—I had reasons of my own for worrying about what sort of mistakes were regarded by the Foreign Office as fatal, but Julian thought it wouldn't be fair to tell me. "For one thing," he said, "I only have that bastard Granby-Smith's word for it, and even if the poor old blighter did make an ass of himself, it's nobody's business but his own."

Julian's sympathies always lay with the makers of mistakes, the rebels, the losers. His dislike of Granby-Smith, a recent arrival in the chancery, was, for the moment, more generic than personal; a natural dislike of the would-be winner who always supports the winning side.

The journey across the monotonous, fertile plains to the mouth of the Danube was slow and sweltering. The train had left Bucharest before sunrise, but what with delays at customs and bad connections, the sun was going down when we finally reached the Bulgarian side, whose landscape resembled that of the moon. A fellow passenger, a Bulgarian woman who understood English, was reassuring. "Have no fears! The resort is a paradise!"

We stopped at a wayside halt. Our fellow passenger said that we would be there for twenty minutes, so we left our stuffy compartment for an exploratory stroll in the evening air, and she told us where to find what we were looking for. It turned out to be a smelly, circular pit, designed for males, with sloping guttered footholds around its rim. We decided on a nearby clump of bushes instead, and found that others had had the same idea before us. *"Pfui!"* said the Fräulein, holding her nose, *"Was für ein ekelhaftes Volk!* Hopefully the resort will be more civilized."

As we got nearer the coast, the volcanic landscape changed.

Flattening out, its rusty surface developed patches of green, and a few isolated trees made their appearance. "You see!" the Bulgarian woman said, triumphantly pointing them out. "Forests!"

Leaning out of the train window as it rolled slowly into its final stop past the crowds of people waiting on the platform to greet the passengers, I identified Old Browne without any difficulty. Rather frivolously dressed, for an Englishman, in a cream-colored suit with a blue-and-yellow-striped tie that matched the band on his panama hat, and light tan shoes, he was nevertheless unmistakably British. In the foreign service one soon learns to recognize the subtle trademarks that betray nationality without benefit of speech. In Old Browne it was a certain restraint of movement and manner that distinguished him from the more impulsive Europeans surrounding him on the platform.

He introduced himself to me with the formal courtesy of a generation accustomed to toasting *ladies* and running after *women*.

He had brought his car, but it wouldn't hold us all, not to mention the piles of cardboard boxes containing the necessities for civilized living that were not to be found in economy villas; so he packed the affronted Fräulein into a broken-down cab with the maid and the luggage, and led the way with me and the children in his shiny blue Fiat. "Italian cars take the rough Balkan roads better than English cars," he said, excusing his failure to support the motor trade of the country he represented.

He unlocked our villa for us and gave me the keys. Set out on the kitchen table was a cold roast chicken, bread, milk, and a bowl of fruit. "I thought you might be hungry," he said. While he helped the smiling maid and the sulking Fräulein to bring in the baggage, I wandered through the four rooms of the villa. They were very barely furnished, but they looked and smelled clean, and in each room there was a vase of fresh flowers. "From my garden," Old Browne said when I asked him where they came from. "I thought they would liven the place up."

He wished us a good night's rest—"You won't find any bedbugs here!"—and said he would get in touch with us next day.

Too exhausted to miss Julian's body curved around mine, or even to think of it, I lay listening for a while to the sound of the sea; then, drifting into sleep with the scent of verbena from Old Browne's garden in my nostrils, I dreamed of Clovelly.

Early in the morning, one of those indispensably polyglot office factotums employed by British representatives in foreign countries delivered a magnificent bouquet of roses, still fresh with dew, and a note from Old Browne requesting the pleasure of my company at dinner that evening:

I will call for you at a quarter to six, and, if the idea appeals to you, we will drink an apéritif at the Café Sofía before coming back to my house for dinner. In the meantime, please don't hesitate to make use of the messenger, who speaks English, in any way you wish—he will find some excuse to take the rest of the morning off anyway.

I wrote an equally formal note of acceptance, and asked the messenger where the market was and how to get there. He drew a rough diagram for us on which he wrote down the street names in both Cyrillic and Roman lettering so that we could recognize them when we saw them. The maid gave him a melting look, and he immediately offered to accompany her to the market. "I will show where to find the most young hens and the most fresh fishes," he said, "and every time that my good friends see Miss . . ."

"Ileana," the maid said, smiling, ". . . Miss Ileana coming to buy food for Madame, they will give her the best goods without cheating, for my sake."

It took us all morning to get settled in. In the afternoon I went with the children and the Fräulein for a walk in the Sea Park, a shady promenade on a bluff overlooking the bathing beaches and the pier.

I was proud of my children, of the well-behaved little boy and his pretty, gold-ringletted sister, and I was very conscious of the impression we made as a group; the two children in spotless white, their Fräulein, bulky but neat in blue with starched white collar and cuffs, and their young mother in an elegant pink linen frock that nobody would have guessed was homemade. It was the impression of well-bred unostentatious British superiority that we were expected to give, but that I was obliged to create and sustain on my own because Julian would have no part in it.

The Fräulein came to a sudden standstill. "*Um Gottes Willen! Was geht hier vor!*"

"The ladies aren't wearing any clothes," my son said with an air of giving her information.

"The policeman is cross with them," said my daughter reasonably.

But the naked ladies seemed to be much crosser than the policeman, who was clearly trying to pacify them rather than reprimand them for their nakedness. I overheard a passerby remark casually in German, "Their clothing must have been stolen from their cabin," as if neither that nor their appearance was anything out of the ordinary.

"*Was für ein ekelhaftes Volk!*" said the Fräulein, her worst fears about the resort confirmed, and probably surpassed.

"Where do you go to sunbathe and swim?" I asked Old Browne as we sat on the terrace of the Café Sofía sipping straight vodka, suggested by him as the most suitable prelude to his dinner.

"I dive into deep water from some rocks near my house. I'm not a sun worshiper. But the municipal beach is all right. It's clean and safe."

Was it really all right? I wasn't so sure about that. But I was embarrassed to speak of naked ladies to this courtly middle-aged man whom I scarcely knew. "I don't much care for town bathing beaches," I said. "I don't like the crowds, and I don't like the clammy cabins. In Constanza, we used to hire a droshky and drive to a quiet little beach where we could change in the shelter of our own umbrella."

"There are plenty of beaches here, within walking distance, where even the shelter of an umbrella is superfluous," Old Browne said, "but I wouldn't advise you to go there without your husband. The town beach is more suitable for a lady alone, or with children, because of the rules that the men and youths stay on one side of the pier and the women and children on the other." He hesitated, coughed, plunged, "You see . . . it's the custom of the country to swim and sunbathe in the . . . er . . . nude."

"Oh!" I cried. "Now I understand!" And I told him as discreetly as I could about the incident of the naked ladies in the park.

"They were certainly not *ladies*," he said, "Bulgarian *ladies* would have stayed down on the beach and left it to the manager of the cabins to go up and get the police. They were probably nightclub girls. I can't tell you how sorry I am, Mrs. Crest, that you should have been subjected to a shock like that on your first day here. I am very much to blame. It was most remiss of me not to warn you about the local customs."

"That's all right," I said. "I wasn't shocked, I was just puzzled. Maybe they were nightclub girls—they had very good figures."

Old Browne's silence, and his slightly disgusted expression, accused me of being unladylike. He glanced at his watch, and I hastily swallowed the rest of my vodka. "If you would really like to see my garden before dinner," he said, "perhaps we had better be going. My cook is a tyrant, but also a genius—which makes it worthwhile to submit to the tyranny and be punctual."

I was to become very familiar with the walk past the harbor to the quiet old street on which Old Browne lived, and it usually took about twenty minutes to get there; but on this first occasion Old Browne was so anxious not to be late that we did it in less than ten.

The ocherous wall of his house, and the ten-foot-high garden wall that was an extension of it, stood flush with the narrow sidewalk. The windows, like those of the neighboring houses, were protected by wrought-iron grilles and closely shaded against the intrusion of even a passing glance. On the other side of the road was the sea, and Old Browne pointed out the rocks from which he dove into deep, swirling water. Bulgarian style? I couldn't imagine that without an inward giggle.

I said, "You must be a good swimmer."

"Not as good as I used to be, I'm afraid. I can't do more than a mile without getting blown."

Taking this as a oblique boast, I didn't produce the compliment that I thought he was fishing for. But I did have the tact not to tell him how many miles my husband could do without getting blown.

We stopped before a narrow but massive door in the garden wall. With the air of a man about to reveal some glittering treasure, he unlocked it, threw it open, and revealed a luxuriant garden completely enclosed by the wall and by the arcaded facade of the house, which suggested a cloister, and gave me the feeling of being nefariously introduced into a monastery. But the atmosphere was more like that of a Turkish potentate's harem; flooded with the last golden light of the day and the almost palpable perfume of roses, it was so sensual that I suddenly wanted Julian. How splendid it would be to make love with him there in that orgiastic tangle of flowers and warm light and intoxicating fragrances! Old Browne, bending over the rim of a sunken pond in an effort to lure a pet goldfish out from under the waterlilies, presented no obstacle to this momentary daydream—his plump, middle-aged figure could easily have been that of a guardian eunuch.

"My friend won't come out, I'm afraid," he said, straightening up and bringing me back to my senses. "Well, what do you think of my garden?"

"I think it's enchanting!"

"It's as good as any garden in England, isn't it?"

"Better. It has something that no English garden could possibly have . . . an Arabian Nights quality."

"How interesting that you should say that! As it happens, that's just what I've tried to achieve, a blend, I mean, of East and West, of the familiar and the . . . er . . . exotic. I wonder what you'll think of my house—shall we go in?"

From the outside it had the mysterious charm of all old and secretive buildings, especially those of an alien culture. Inside it was dark and cool, but airless. In excluding the curious glances of strangers, Old Browne had also excluded the clean, incurious wind from the sea. Most Englishmen, faced with the choice between privacy and fresh air, would manage to find a compromise or, failing that, would choose the fresh air and take care of the privacy by surrounding themselves with an invisible aura of isolation as with an insect repellant. But with Old Browne, the East had won over the West in this matter, and in his interior decoration as well.

The room in which we awaited the "tyrant's" summons to dine was furnished only with two low divans, covered with silky Oriental rugs and rich, soft cushions, and two equally low tables on which were great shallow bowls of intricately worked silver filled with red roses. Two splendid porcelain jars in a deep, strong shade of blue stood on the floor holding sprays of jasmine, whose perfume, mingled with that of the red roses, hung in the close air like incense. The polished wood floor was bare. But the white-washed walls were adorned with Oriental rugs and hangings too ancient and frail to survive being put to any other use, and a collection of antique scimitars and daggers.

The only touch of England hung on the narrow strip of wall between two windows, guarded by the sickle blade of a scimitar; it was an innocent aquarelle of the willowy reaches of a river, and I could imagine it being sketched on a summer day by a lady wearing a wide-brimmed straw hat—Old Browne's mother, perhaps.

Through an archway that led to another room, partially concealed by an embroidered hanging, I could see an immensely wide, richly covered divan, heaped with cushions, that seemed to take up almost the whole floor space. From behind a screen masking a second archway came the flicker of lighted candles and the muted sounds of deft-handed, soft-footed service.

"Count," said Old Browne, when a good-looking young manservant wearing a white linen jacket folded the screen back and announced in French that dinner was served, "I want to present you to a lady who will, I hope, be a frequent guest at this table."

The young man bowed. Uncertain whether to treat him as count or butler, I offered him my hand, which he kissed in the aristocratic manner, scarcely touching it with his lips.

Except for the first course, a huge mound of fresh caviar piled on a bed of ice, with slices of lemon and thin, buttered toast to go with it, the beautifully cooked meal was French. Served by the elegant count with one epicurean dish after another, I congratulated Old Browne on having secured a French chef who would grace an embassy kitchen.

"The count is the chef," he said, "but he isn't French, he's a White Russian. And a very capable fellow. Astonishingly versatile. I discovered him in a nightclub in Sofia, doing Russian dances for a mere pittance. He doesn't live in, he has a room in a house farther down the road with some other White Russians. Which suits us both—I like my privacy and he likes his freedom."

I wondered how he had found out that the performer of Russian dances could cook, and why he had given me the far less interesting and totally irrelevant information that his tyrant, and treasure, did not live in.

Indolent after the excellent meal and two different kinds of wine, I accepted a Turkish cigarette and curled up on one of the divans with my silk-stockinged legs and bare arms disposed to the best advantage; it was the period of very short sleeveless dresses and very long cigarette holders—which was the only reason I smoked; it gave me an opportunity to make graceful gestures. I remarked idly that Bucharest was full of Russian émigrés, trying to live on their accomplishments, and creating a temporary fad for everything Russian—except Bolshevism—and even giving the Rumanian Gypsy musicians stiff competition in the field of dinner music, which they had always had completely to themselves.

"Singing is another of Dimitri's accomplishments," Old Browne said, referring to the count by name for the first time, "and he's given me a new appreciation of Russian music of all kinds. . . . Would you care to listen to a few things now? Yes? Are you sure? Well then, just a moment . . ."

I was expecting to see the count come in with a balalaika, but instead the awesome voice of Chaliapin as Boris Goudonov rose from the room with the big divan. As reverently as if he were in the singer's presence, Old Browne tiptoed back and settled himself on the divan facing mine. When two Chaliapin records had been played through, he put on Rimski-Korsakov's *Scheherazade*.

The quiet in the house suggested that the count had already departed to his own quarters, and the sense of intimacy, inherent in the surroundings and accentuated by the sensuous music and the final fragrance of the now fully opened red roses, was overpowering. Wary, I got up before Old Browne had time to put on another record. "It's been a delightful evening. . . ."

"I'm sorry you have to leave so early. . . ."

"So am I, but we're not quite settled yet—I still have some unpacking to do."

Walking me back to our villa, he asked, "Do you play tennis?"

"Yes, we play a lot—almost every day."

"Then you're probably out of my class," he said politely.

"Oh no! My husband plays a pretty good game, but I'm no champion."

After an overlong moment of silence, he said, "In that case we might have a game one afternoon if you'd care to. Some Bulgarian friends of mine have a tennis court at their summer place a few miles up the coast, and I have an open invitation to use it whenever I wish. They don't play themselves. Let's see . . . today's Tuesday. . . . How about Friday, at five o'clock?"

I agreed, suspecting that the two-day interval was his way of punishing me for my tactlessness. It certainly taught me to value his attentiveness. Without a reputable male escort there was nothing for a woman in my position to do when the beach day was over but go to bed and read, and by Friday afternoon I had had enough of that to make me very pleased to see Old Browne drive up in the Fiat, prepared to play tennis.

His outfit, immaculate white "flannels," open-necked shirt, and dark blue blazer, was almost too faultless—like the perfect English of a foreigner whose only mistake is never to make any. But he disarmed even this private criticism by telling me how nice I looked in my tennis outfit, how well white suited me. "I can see you've been down at the beach," he said. "You've already got quite a tan. How was it?"

"Sandy and safe—but the ladies are awful."

He smiled as if he had expected as much.

His Bulgarian friends were an old countess, who didn't put in an appearance, and her colorless, thirtyish daughter, who was playing the flute when we arrived. Old Browne suggested that she should come out and umpire our game, but she said she had to practice her part in a Mozart quintet, and when we had finished play we should come in for tea.

"Nice place, isn't it?" Old Browne observed on the way to the tennis court. His tone made me think that he was proud of his intimacy with these people, and had brought me here as much for that reason as for the tennis. With its spreading wings and flowering courtyards, it was an intensely romantic place, stamped with the quiet dignity of the old aristocracy, built with taste and lived in with taste for many generations, but allowed to deteriorate physically for lack of money.

Between the house and the sea was a terraced garden with stone steps leading down to a tiny private beach. Old Browne took me down there after four sets of singles, of which I let him win three to make up for my tactlessness. "You play a jolly good game," he said. "I must confess that I didn't expect such a smashing serve from such a gentle little lady."

Poor Old Browne, I thought, with a glimmer of understanding, but with more youthful condescension than anything else, I'm glad I let him win.

The tepid sea, calm and clear as a lake, and the total seclusion, were invitations to tear off sticky clothes and take a Bulgarian swim. If only Julian were here with me instead of Old Browne! Or even young Johnson ... well, no, that would have caused complications; but at least the idea wasn't repulsive.

Back in the shaded, sun-slatted hall of the villa, the pale flautist was waiting to refresh us with glasses of pale tea and spoonfuls of rose-petal jam—which I liked so much that in the course of these ritual refreshments after our almost daily game of tennis I must have consumed an entire rose garden.

I have forgotten the name of the pale flautist—let us call her Irina—but I see her very clearly; a vague, Pre-Raphaelite figure, willowly, melancholy, fading, and hopelessly in love with Old Browne; always courteous and welcoming to me, exhibiting no vulgar jealousy, yet persistently asserting her intimacy with Old Browne by subtly emphasizing their long acquaintance, and addressing him by his first name, Adrian. Old Browne treated her less like an old friend than like a first cousin, whose consanguinity is a barrier that makes it safe to indulge in a little mild flirtation. Which made me wonder, fleetingly, what the real barrier was.

When Old Browne asked me, "Do you dance?" I said yes, without adding any tactless remarks about my husband's skill as a dancing partner.

"There's an open-air 'dancing' here which is rather fun—we might try it one evening if you'd care to. What about Saturday night—that's tomorrow—after a little dinner at my house? Are you free?"

It was part of his code of good manners to pretend that I wasn't entirely dependent on him for my recreation.

The open-air "dancing," a primitive garden enclosure with strings of colored lights and a Gypsy band, was the only respectable place of amusement in the resort. The sign written over the entrance in Bulgarian said, Old Browne told me, *Boris Popovich's Select Dancing*, but it was generally known as Popo's— a double entendre that needed no explanation. Frequented on Saturday nights by the residents of the little town as well as by summer visitors, it revealed the extent of Old Browne's acquaintance. Yet the impression I got was not so much that Old Browne knew everyone, as that everyone knew Old Browne—and was speculating about me. He did nothing to help them out. No one

48

was introduced to me, either then or on subsequent Saturday nights. No one was ever asked to join us at our table. Even at his home we were always tête-à-tête—as if he were courting me.

But despite our daily meetings, and all the little attentions he paid me—the flowers, the gourmet dinners, the new records bought to entertain me afterward—his behavior remained as impeccably "correct" as his attire. He devoted all his spare time to me, without ever demanding anything in return beyond what he called the pleasure of my company. And, at the time, this seemed to me to be a perfectly fair arrangement.

He put me so much at ease that I no longer felt it necessary to leave early after the exquisite little dinners prepared for us two or three times a week by the versatile count. We dined late, and I would stay on until after midnight, smoking Russian and Turkish cigarettes, sipping Balkan liqueurs, listening to the phonograph, talking. Old Browne did most of the talking himself; recalling his boyhood, regilding his golden days at Oxford, describing his experiences in Bulgaria, but never touching on his career "before the fall," which must have encompassed the years of the 1914 war. It was as if he had leaped straight from Oxford to where he was now. And he couldn't be in a place that he liked better, he said; it suited him perfectly, and he felt himself very lucky to have been left there in peace for so long—it had become home to him.

Listening, I recalled what Julian had said, and I wondered what would happen if the port were to die before he did, or before it was time for him to retire. Would he get a letter telling him to "proceed forthwith" to one of the tropical hellholes? Or would he be recalled to England and chained to an insignificant desk in Whitehall? Somehow I could not see him complying with either order. My romantic guess was that he would dive into the sea from the rocks near his house and let the Foreign Office repatriate him in a long wooden box.

During the first hour or so of these platonic evenings with Old Browne, the count's presence in the house provided a sexual note that was faintly but pleasurably disturbing. I was very conscious of him as an attractive young man, and I was pretty sure that he was conscious of me in the same way. Whether or not Old Browne was aware of this, didn't seem important. But I don't think he was aware of it until the evening when he asked the count to perform for Madame. The way in which he made this request reminded me of myself cajoling the children to show off their accomplishments to a guest. But the count needed no cajoling, he was clearly delighted to be asked.

When he brought in his balalaika he had exchanged his white jacket and black trousers for a loose embroidered blouse and baggy pants tucked into high, soft-leather boots.

He sat cross-legged on the floor and sang song after tender song in the Russian language; the tenderness came through in the music and the voice of the singer; and the inflections expressive of love, or sadness, or longing that he gave to the words, made the literal understanding of them seem unnecessary. And when he danced, the spell of his physical grace, of his sensuous movements, revived the Arabian Nights illusion of my first entrance into the enclosed world that Old Browne had created for himself.... *Behind the embroidered hanging, in the secret chamber of the immense divan, Scheherazade is awaiting the moment when her lover, the dancing slave, shall elude the vigilance of the guardian eunuch....*

"Thank you, Dimitri, that was a fine performance," Old Browne said, suddenly cutting it short as if the count were a child whose antics were getting tiresome.

The count picked up his balalaika and said goodnight. The look he gave Old Browne was hard to interpret—I had nothing in my previous experience to compare it with. Disdainful, cold, it seemed to convey the mixture of contempt and resentment that a young and gifted aristocrat might feel for a middle-class, middle-aged failure who was in a position to give him orders. But that was not all. There was something else that I couldn't define, and that made me feel sorry for Old Browne.

On the last weekend before Julian joined me, Old Browne and I were invited by the countess to dine with her and her daughter after our Saturday afternoon tennis. I met the old lady for the first and only time that evening. She suffered from a bad heart, and kept to her room for most of the day. She was a tall, heavy, imposing woman, an aristocrat of the old school. She treated Old Browne like a family friend of long standing but of slightly lower social status. He treated her as I could imagine him treating his own mother, with a mixture of tender familiarity and respect.

She must have been aware that her daughter loved him, but she gave the impression of not even considering him as a possible son-in-law. He seemed to know this, and to accept it, but not without regrets and uncertainties. There were times when I caught him looking at Irina rather wistfully, as if he could almost fall in love with her, or wished that he could allow himself to do so. I couldn't make up my mind whether he had considered the idea of marrying her and rejected it because he didn't love her enough, or whether in view of the mistake that had stunted his career he felt he was not in a position to propose marriage to the daughter of a former ambassador, or whether it had never entered his head to marry her or anyone—he had many of the characteristics of the born celibate. Or had the countess intimated to him that his lack of rank made him unacceptable as a husband for Irina?

I pondered these things while the four of us made desultory conversation and ate minced lamb rolled up in vine leaves, eggplant salad the color of milky jade, and yogurt with cherry jam.

After dinner, over syrupy Turkish coffee and homemade apricot brandy, the countess recalled her diplomatic past. Most of her anecdotes were familiar to me, but I enjoyed comparing her discreet versions with those recounted by Julian. Old Browne seemed less amused. I sensed an uneasiness in him, and between stories I came to his rescue. "It must be getting late," I said.

Without looking at his watch, Old Browne said, "It's half past ten."

"That is not late," the countess said. "In my young days I used to stay up every night until the small hours. Alas, I am obliged to retire early now, but that is no reason why you should not stay on and keep Irina company."

Old Browne's face fell. "I really think we should be going," I said. "I hate to drag Mr. Browne away, but frankly I am feeling rather tired after all that tennis."

Old Browne drove back to the resort at a breakneck speed. "Not nervous, are you?"

"Not a bit."

"Are you very tired?"

"Not very—the fresh air has livened me up." The canvas top of the car was down, and the salt wind was tangling the curls of my bobbed hair.

"In that case we might look in at Popo's—if you'd care to."

Popo's was crowded, but a table was found for us immediately. Old Browne must have reserved one on the off chance. Among the couples on the floor dancing a slow tango, one pair seemed like professionals. As they came nearer I saw that the man was the count. The girl had unfashionable hair, long and piled up on the top of her head. When the music stopped they both joined a group sitting around a long table—the count's Russian friends, no doubt. I had never seen him at Popo's before. And Old Browne didn't look too pleased to see him there now.

Old Browne and I danced the next dance, a foxtrot, and the count sat it out with his friends. Then came another tango, which Old Browne knew he was not very good at—he was too portly, for one thing. The count came over to us and bowed. "Is it permitted," he inquired in French, "to request the pleasure of dancing this tango with Madame?"

With an exaggerated courtesy that would have sounded ironical in any other language, the count was asserting his rights as a gentleman, and Old Browne was in the sad position of having no rights to assert. The power lay with me. Whatever I did, I was bound to offend one or the other of them, and I wanted to dance with the count. After three Saturday evenings of sedate circling with a plump poker, I wanted to feel again the magic of real rhythm, of perfectly coordinated, concerted movement that produces an illusion of levitation. So I said to Old Browne, "Will you excuse me?" and took off on a flight that both I and the count knew—I was sure that he knew—left Old Browne grounded in an agony of jealousy; but only, I thought, of youth and supple limbs and the not yet lost power to fly without wings. And this, I reasoned, was a form of jealousy that older people just had to get over.

"Madame dances like an angel," the count said softly, pressing my hand ever so slightly. The dance over, he returned me with a bow to Old Browne, like a daughter to her father.

The furious look that Old Browne now gave the count more than equaled the look of disdain that the count had given Old Browne when his command performance had aroused his employer's jealousy, and again I thought how stupid it was to get upset over not being able to compete with the young. But my conscience told me that just because Old Browne was, compared to us, *old* Browne, I should have resisted the invitation to the flight, especially when in a few days' time I would be taking off on a nonstop flight of one kind or another with Julian, who was due to arrive on Tuesday evening.

The band started up again with a foxtrot. I got up and held out my hands to Old Browne. "Come on," I said when he put on a diffident air, "this is one of my favorite tunes." He rose at once, but his dancing expressed his feelings as clearly as any words. It was only when the group of Russians got up and left, and the count with them, that his taut muscles relaxed and he recovered his temper. But he was taciturn for the rest of the evening.

"Well," he said, when we left at closing time, "so here we are at the end of our last Saturday night at Popo's."

"Why? Is the place closing down?"

"No, no. I only meant that this is the last time that I shall be your escort."

"Next Saturday, you and I and Julian will all come here together, I hope."

"Thank you," he said.

"Perhaps Irina would come too. . . ."

"Perhaps."

Next day, Sunday, he took me and the children, but not the Fräulein, for a long drive inland, to the lunar landscape, and he explained to Pip how the oddly shaped hills had come into being. This was the first time that he had taken the children out riding in his car, and I felt that it had some significance, but I wasn't quite sure what.

On Monday night he invited me for dinner, alone, as usual. The meal was perfect. The count had reassumed his role of the discreet manservant, and Old Browne had two new records to play for me. Yet something was wrong. There was a tension in the atmosphere that had not been there before. Ill at ease, I got up to go earlier than usual, and Old Browne didn't protest.

Walking me back to my villa, he was unusually silent. When we stopped at my door, he said, "Well . . . here we are," as if we had come to the end of a long journey.

I said, "Thank you for another delightful evening."

"I'm glad you enjoyed it," he said. "I'll be here at half past nine tomorrow evening to take you to the station."

He shook hands with me in his usual formal way, but he held

my hand in his for a fraction longer than usual. He seemed to be sad, and because I was happy I felt like giving him a kiss to cheer him up. But before I had time to make a fool of myself, he had lifted his panama hat and was walking briskly away.

On the drive to the station, I was too excited by the prospect of being together with Julian again to notice what sort of mood Old Browne was in. There were a lot of people waiting to meet the train, which wasn't due for another twenty minutes. "If you will excuse me," Old Browne said, "I shall leave you now. With so many people around, you will be quite safe."

I thought he was afraid of being in the way, which he would have been, but out of politeness I asked him to wait. "I'm sorry," he said, "but I can't. I've made an appointment for ten o'clock that I have to keep, I'm afraid." This would have struck me as odd if I hadn't been so blinded by my preoccupation with Julian and our reunion.

When Julian got off the train and advanced toward me with open arms—nobody knew him here, so he didn't have to be discreet—I felt shy, as I always did after a separation. "We'll have to take a cab," I told him. "Old Browne brought me here in his car, but he couldn't stay—he had an appointment."

"Thank God," said Julian. As we went through the ticket barrier to the cab stand I caught sight of Old Browne driving away. So he *had* waited. He had wanted to make quite sure that I was safely with Julian. How sweet, I thought. Good Old Browne! Then Julian blotted him out of my mind again as thoroughly as if he had never existed. We were no sooner in the cab than I was in Julian's arms, and for the next thirty-six hours I was out of them only for brief intervals, and Old Browne never once entered my mind.

On the second morning after his arrival, Julian said, "Let's go swimming."

"Shall we go with the children to the town beach?"

"No! Do you think I want to be segregated with a lot of bloody males?"

"Do you think I've enjoyed being segregated with a lot of sagging females?"

Julian wasn't sure how to take this, and for a moment I thought I was going to be consigned to the municipal harem with the children while he went off alone to ogle the pretty girls on the unrestricted outside. "We could take the children with us to the free beaches and let Fräulein have the day off," I said, not without cunning.

"Foxy, aren't you? We could, but we won't. Not today. Today I want you all to myself."

So we set out together for the unsegregated beaches that Old Browne had not thought it proper for me to visit alone. On the first one we came to, the scene was domestic; whole families—grandparents, parents, children—were spread out to dry in the sun wearing nothing but straw hats, placed over their faces. Farther on were some young couples, close but decorous, their only intimacy the sharing of one hat. A group of young men attired only in their glasses, or sunglasses, which gave them the appearance of absent-minded students, were playing with a huge rubber ball. "Don't look," Julian said.

Beyond a cluster of rocks we discovered an uninhabited stretch of white sand. "Here?" I asked.

"Seems like a good place," Julian said.

I had nothing on under my beach coat, which I slipped off when Julian wasn't looking, and before he had recovered from the shock of my unexpected nudity—in a public place—I was in the water. But he was not to be outdone, and he punished me for outdoing him by half drowning me. Then the uninhibited intimacy of the sea began to take effect, and turned us into a pair of dolphins joyously mating underwater.

Back on the warm sand, lying naked in the sun on an open beach for the first time in my life, I had a sense of Paradise regained, and so, I think, did Julian.

In the late afternoon we got up from a long siesta temporarily cured, by satiation, of our reunion fever, and ready to fulfill our obligation to Old Browne by taking some notice of him. "Let's go and see him now," Julian said, "and ask him out for a drink. It's only a quarter to five, he'll still be in his office."

"We should have done that yesterday—he's probably very hurt by now."

"Nonsense. He knows better than to expect to see us on the first day of our reunion."

It occurred to me then, for the first time, that our reunion might in itself be a cause of pain to Old Browne.

He seemed quite pleased to see us, and there was nothing in his manner to suggest that he had expected to see us any sooner. But the tension that I had felt on my last evening at his house was even stronger now. As courteous as ever, he was subtly withdrawn from me. And it soon became apparent—sooner to me than to Julian—that he meant to keep us both at a distance.

He was sorry, he couldn't come out for a drink, he had made an appointment to see someone after hours. "What about dining with us tomorrow?" Julian asked. Unfortunately that was not possible. He was leaving for Sofia in the morning, he would be away for several days. "But I hope that you will both come and have dinner with me at my house when I return. I'll get in touch with you as soon as I get back."

Free to forget him without feeling guilty, we went to Popo's that evening and danced together with just as much expertise, I thought, as the count and his partner with the unfashionable hair. I looked for them, but they didn't come in—the count was probably packing Old Browne's valises for him. And because it was a weeknight, and the clients were all summer people, I didn't have the satisfaction of arousing more speculation.

But on Saturday night I could almost hear the tongues wagging. The count was there, dancing with the same girl. I pointed them out to Julian. "That's Old Browne's manservant. He's a Russian count, and he's an incredibly good cook."

Julian gave him a long look. "He's probably good at a lot of other things, too."

"Well, yes, actually he is. He sings Russian songs to the balalaika, and does Cossack dances. That's how Old Browne happened on him—he was performing in a nightclub in Sofia."

"I see," Julian said. "Who's the girl?"

"She's one of a group of White Russians trying to make a living here—he has a room in the same house."

"Oh. Well . . . she's a damn pretty girl, whatever else she may be. And her hair is gorgeous. I wish you'd let yours grow again."

Swimming and dancing and making love and running about

with the children kept us healthily tired without tennis. But Julian was hoping to play on the countess's court when Old Browne came back from Sofia. He was disappointed. In the note that we got from Old Browne inviting us to dinner there was no mention of tennis. Julian wondered why.

"He's afraid you'll beat him," I said, "and he's not about to risk it."

This made sense to Julian, who always played to win. But I knew it wasn't the whole explanation.

There were five other guests at Old Browne's dinner party: an elderly Englishwoman with big teeth and a small title, who was probably there thanks to a letter of introduction that could not be safely ignored, a fat Bulgarian official and his fat middle-aged wife, and the slim Rumanian consul with his slim young wife—who made eyes at my husband across the table while her husband made love to my feet under it.

Old Browne's manner to me was as formal as if he had only just made my acquaintance. The Rumanian couple had seen us together at Popo's, and had doubtless jumped to Rumanian conclusions. But aside from them, no one would ever have guessed that Old Browne and I had spent the latter half of every day in each other's company for a month, much less that night after night we had been alone together in this secret, shuttered house for hours after the count had gone off to his lodging.

Sauntering back to our villa, Julian and I talked about the party; the food, the wine, the guests, the house, and Old Browne himself. "He's not as friendly as he was when I met him in Bucharest," Julian said. "I wonder what's the matter with him."

"I think I know. I think he's jealous."

"Jealous? Of whom?"

"Of you."

"Of *me!* Why in hell should he be jealous of me?"

"Because now that you're here he can't have me to himself anymore, and he's in love with me—I've just realized it."

"In love with *you* . . . but that's impossible."

"Why is it impossible? He's not *that* old!"

"Why? Because Old Browne's a. . . . Old Browne doesn't fall in love with women."

Long after Julian had gone to sleep I lay awake, thinking about all that he had been telling me about Old Browne, and trying to reconcile it with what my intuition had suddenly told me about Old Browne's feelings for me. His behavior with respect to the count could certainly be interpreted to fit in with what Julian had said, yet I was convinced that he had fallen in love with me, and that I would have perceived it sooner if I hadn't been blinded by my image of him as the stereotype of the kindly old bachelor who finds pleasure in the company of the young but makes no demands on them, and whose jealousy is as impersonal as his affection.

The conflict remained unresolved. I was still too inexperienced, too unversed in the quirks and complexities of human behavior to realize that they overlap, coexisting in the same person, swaying the balance now one way and now the other. And Julian, though not intolerant of sexual deviation, was too single-minded by nature to understand ambivalence in any form.

Uncertain who was to blame for the distance that had somehow established itself between us and Old Browne, we made several attempts to bridge it, but he didn't meet us halfway, so we gave up, thinking that on the whole it was his loss. But I felt vaguely guilty—if only for having upset his equilibrium through lack of understanding.

II

Back in Bucharest, I forgot all about Old Browne until someone from the British legation in Sofia sat next to me at a dinner and we started talking about the resort, where he too had spent a summer, and he remarked that there was so little activity in the port that it was going to be reduced to a noncareer post. So it had happened.

I asked Julian, "What will poor Old Browne do now?"

"He'll survive, don't worry. He's a decent old boy, but crafty—they all are."

About six months after that, one day in June, a little less than a year since Julian had confidently consigned me to the care of the "old bachelor," he came home with the news that the old bachelor had turned up at the legation with a wife, whom he was showing off to everyone before proceeding to his new post in a busy Western European port.

"Well!" I said, "that *is* news! What's she like?"

"Top-drawer, thirtyish, spinsterish, may have been prettyish once. . . ."

"*Irina!*"

"No, this woman's English. He met her in Sofia, at one of those mixed-bag legation lunch parties. It turned out that they were staying at the same hotel—he was there on short leave and she was just seeing the Balkans, so I suppose he took it upon himself to help her see them. Anyway, they got engaged, and they were married in London a couple of weeks ago—he was back in Bulgaria just to wind things up and hand over the office."

"Do you think he's in love with her?"

"I should say it's just a question of expediency."

"What about her? Do you think she loves him?"

"Maybe. Maybe she just wanted to get married—though she must have been pretty desperate to choose a man with Old Browne's leanings. Unless she's a bloody innocent. Come to think of it, that's probably just what she is."

"How long are they staying? We could ask them to lunch. . . ."

"I did—for tomorrow—but she said they were leaving first thing in the morning. Which I thought was rather funny, because earlier, when she was talking to Granby-Smith, I could have sworn I heard her say that they were staying for two more days."

"Perhaps she doesn't want to meet me."

"You may be right. She had a funny look on her face when I was telling her how kind her husband had been to you and the children last summer . . . you know, all the polite rot one has to say."

"Maybe you'd better not have said it."

"Maybe he was glad that I did."

I thought that might well be true. But I didn't like the idea of having been made use of as a cover—or was decoy the better word?

A couple of days later, I ran into Old Browne and his wife on the Calea Victoria. She was nearer forty than thirty, I thought; not unhandsome, but rather faded—like a piece of good-quality furniture left too long in a shop window. Her outfit—shantung dress, brown alligator handbag and pumps, leghorn hat trimmed with brown velvet—was tasteful and obviously expensive, but she wore it without any flair. She was the kind of upper-class

Englishwoman whose conception of elegance is to wear good clothes as if they were old rags. When Old Browne introduced her, she gave me the coldest look I had ever had from anyone.

I said, "I thought you had left already."

"We should have been in Brussels by now," Old Browne said, "but there was a muddle about our wagon-lit reservations. . . ."

"Why didn't you let us know—we could have lunched. . . ."

His wife looked at her wristwatch and said, "We're going to be late for our appointment, Adrian."

But whatever else Old Browne had sacrificed for the sake of expediency, he had kept his good manners. "That's all right, my dear," he said. Then, turning to me, "I suppose your husband told you that I'm leaving my beloved little backwater—the port was practically dead, there was no justification for keeping a career man there any longer."

"You had been there much too long as it was," his wife told him. "I know it was what you wanted, but you were wasted, and Uncle Gavin realized it."

"My wife's uncle has recently been made a division chief at the Foreign Office," Old Browne explained.

She put her hand on his arm, "We really must go. . . ."

"And so must I—I'm already late for *my* appointment," I said, holding out my hand. Old Browne shook it, pressing it a little. His wife chose that moment to blow her nose. I hailed a droshky and jumped in, leaving Old Browne agape on the sidewalk, raising his panama hat while his wife tugged at his arm.

And there I would like to leave him, while I fill in some other designs in the arabesque that were interlacing with mine more closely than his was at that particular time. But he won't let me. He insists that I continue to follow his pattern to the point where it breaks off—as far as he is concerned.

To do this, before going back two years to the beginning of our sojourn in Bucharest, I must take a three-year leap into the future.

After a year in South America, a difficult year for Julian, in a chancery where it seemed he could do nothing right, he had been transferred to Rome. We returned to Europe on an ocean liner that docked in the busy port to which Old Browne had been promoted at the time of his marriage. Our train to Italy would leave the same evening, but we had booked two rooms in a hotel for the interval between arrival and departure. After settling in the two children and their Fräulein—a different one this time—Julian and I went out for a walk.

"What do you think?" Julian asked as we strolled past a building crowned with the British flag, slap-slapping in the sea wind. "Shall we look in on the old boy?"

"Why not? We have nothing else to do."

Mr. Browne, the secretary said, was about to leave for a luncheon engagement. Just then he emerged from his private office, very much the British government official, in a dark suit with a white shirt, starched wing collar, and plain tie, black shoes, an umbrella hooked over his arm, and a pair of chamois leather gloves in his hand.

He greeted us with expansive cordiality. Whatever had troubled his relations with us during those last weeks at the resort had obviously passed, and either he knew that his wife's animosity toward me had passed too, or he had forgotten it, for he said, "How long are you staying—I'd like to have you come to my house for a meal. What about dinner this evening? My wife would be delighted...."

We told him that we had to catch a train at nine o'clock, which meant getting back to the hotel by eight at the latest. He looked disappointed. "Well ... that does make dinner rather impossible. How about joining us for cocktails earlier?"

Julian glanced at me. "We'd love to," I said.

"All right, then, that's settled, I'll pick you up at the hotel at a quarter past five."

He left the building with us. "You looked in at just the right moment," he said. "A minute or so later, and you would have missed me, and I don't expect to get back to my office much before it's time to leave again—I'm going to an official luncheon honoring the new French consul general, you know the sort of thing, speeches and all that."

Julian and I went to a restaurant on the wharf to eat crayfish. "We may as well have a good meal now," he said. "We'll have no time for dinner."

"We can fill up on cocktail snacks."

"I wonder if there'll be other people there."

"If he lets his wife know in time, I'm sure there will be—she'll want to dilute us."

"Oh well, I don't really care one way or the other—as long as she doesn't dilute the whiskey."

That was something I had taken to doing. "I'll be interested to see what his house is like," I said, "what effect that woman has had on his taste."

"You mean how successful she's been in suppressing it, or changing it," Julian said, "and not only as regards interior decoration."

I was, in fact, very curious as to how Old Browne's marriage had turned out sexually. But for the moment my curiosity was rather clinical. Aside from my appreciation of Old Browne's genuine kindness to me, and my respect for his unfailingly "correct" behavior under stresses whose nature I hadn't fully realized at the time, the basis of my still unrecognized affection for him had been pity. But he was no longer an object for pity. He had managed to turn his failure into what looked like a brilliant success, he was the very image of the man who has "made it" against all odds.

His friendliness, his obvious pleasure at seeing us, had put Julian into a good mood, and I was grateful for anything that reassured Julian, and made him feel that he wasn't disliked by everyone in the service. On the way back to the hotel, he bought a gingerbread man for Cissy, a package of foreign stamps for Pip, who was in the collecting stage, and a bunch of spring violets for me. As he pinned them on my lapel he gave me one of the humble, pleading looks that always touched me to the heart. "It will be all right this time, Joey. I'll be good. I swear I will." He was talking, of course, about his new assignment.

For the cocktail party I unpacked an emerald-green dress that Julian liked—emerald green was his favorite color. It was plain but very chic—the sort of dress that adapts itself to the unexpected. I put it on and surveyed myself in the long wardrobe mirror. I still looked younger than my age—I was almost thirty, but the difference was not as wide as it used to be, and took more artifice to sustain.

Beyond my own image I could see Julian's, reflected in the small dresser mirror as he changed his tie and brushed his hair. At thirty-five, he was still a handsome man, but he looked older than his age. Too many late nights, too many drinks, too many violent emotions had somehow blurred him—and hardened me, I thought, looking once more at myself, veneered me with an air of blasé sophistication that was not natural to me.

We went into the next room to tell the Fräulein to take the children down to the dining room early, without waiting for us. "We'll be back by eight," Julian said, "and we'll leave for the station almost immediately, so it would be a good thing if you can be all packed and ready to go when we come."

"Where are you going?" my son asked. "You're all dressed up."

"To a cocktail party. Do you remember Mr. Browne—who took us out in his car that summer we spent in Bulgaria?"

"Of course I remember him. He was the old man who was always inviting you out to dinner and giving you roses. I didn't like him."

"Good heavens, you do remember him well, don't you? But why didn't you like him?"

"Because."

"That's a silly answer," Julian said. "You had a perfect right to dislike him, but you've got to have a sensible reason."

"Oh go on, Julian," I said, "*you* don't always have sensible reasons for disliking people."

"Well, if I haven't got one, I make one up."

Pip grinned at that. He could sense what his father expected, when things were all right and when they weren't.

The reception clerk phoned up to say that Mr. Browne was awaiting us in the lobby. "You go down," I told Julian. "I'll join you in a minute. I forgot to put on my earrings. . . ."

Pip followed me through the connecting door into the other room. "I *had* a sensible reason," he said. "Father didn't understand, that's all."

"You said *because*, and that isn't a reason."

"I meant because he—Mr. Browne, I mean—was always asking you out to dinner and tennis and rides in his car without us."

"Cissy was too small—she was only a baby."

"*I* wasn't a baby," he said. "I was six and a half."

"But even now that you're nine. . . ."

"Nine and a half."

63

"All right, even now that you're nine and a half I don't take you everywhere. I can't take you to grown-up parties, you know that, darling."

"That's different," he said. "And there's Father."

He looked at me with a kind of benevolent wisdom. It was such a grown-up look that I said, as I would have to an adult, "If you felt like that about my going out so often, why didn't you say so? If I'd known that it was making you unhappy, I wouldn't have done it."

"That's why I didn't say so. I didn't want to spoil your fun."

I felt my pseudosophistication cracking—if I stayed another minute I would burst into tears, and Julian would be furious at being kept waiting. I gave Pip a quick hug. "I must go now. I wish I didn't have to, but I must."

"I know," he said. "May I sit in here while you're out? I want to sort the stamps Father brought for me, but Cissy won't leave me in peace."

"As you see," Old Browne said, "I've got an English car now. My wife prefers English cars. She has a little Morris of her own. She goes out to a lot of lunch and bridge parties—you know the sort of thing—and it became too inconvenient having only one car between us." He said it with satisfaction. "My wife has a few other people coming for cocktails," he went on, and I nudged Julian. "You probably know some of them. Whitt Elliott, the American consul, was in Bucharest at the same time as you, wasn't he? And then there's Granby-Smith. He's in Brussels now. He wasn't happy in Bucharest, so about six months ago he got himself transferred. We see quite a lot of him, he comes down to visit the Elliotts—he and Elliott play golf together. He's spendng this weekend with them."

This reminded me that the day was Friday—a natural day for a cocktail party. I always lost track of the days on board ship. We knew and liked the Elliotts; Julian always got along well with Americans. But he didn't like Granby-Smith any better now than he had liked him three years ago. They were like two hostile dogs of the same breed but attached to very different masters. Julian recognized in Granby-Smith all those values that he had rejected in his own family background, and opposed politically. And

Granby-Smith saw in Julian the "gentleman Socialist," a renegade and a traitor to the class from which they both sprang. As for me, I had my own private reasons for not thinking much of Granby-Smith.

Julian and Old Browne gossiped about mutual acquaintances—who had been moved recently, who had been promoted, who had been consigned to one of the well-known hellholes and why (as if Old Browne had never been in that danger himself)—while we crawled with the heavy traffic of late afternoon through the business district. We picked up speed on a seemingly endless boulevard that eventually brought us to an old part of the city, a sleepy residential district with hardly any traffic and no visible inhabitants.

"We're nearly home," said Old Browne, turning down a sycamore-lined street where the houses were uniform only in their reserved dignity, which suggested inherited wealth and well-preserved dowagers. We stopped before one with the slightly frivolous distinction of bright green window boxes filled with spring flowers. It was also the only one with cars parked in front of it.

Old Browne sounded his horn, and a heavy door at the side of the house was opened to let the car pass through into a cobblestoned entryway, an old porte cochere leading into a covered courtyard originally intended to shelter horse-drawn carriages. Through an open arch at the other end of it I caught a glimpse of green grass and lilacs in flower.

Old Browne took us into the house by a side entrance. "The kitchens and servants' quarters are down here," he said. We went up a short flight of stairs carpeted in serviceable drugget and through a swing door at the top—covered in green baize, like the doors that separated the under world from the upper in the homes of our rich relations in England. And the upper world to which we were introduced by Old Browne, talking all the time, was that of England—dogs and all. Two cocker spaniels lavished affectionate greetings on Old Browne, who had no pets when I knew him before. "We were lucky to find a place like this," he was saying, "we heard of it through a friend, a relative of my wife's, as a matter of fact. The owner of it lost his young wife under tragic circumstances and couldn't bear to live in it after her death. But he didn't want to sell it, so when we came along he was only too pleased to lease it to us. We persuaded him to store most of his furniture in a part of the house that we don't need, but my wife has been able to use a few fine old pieces that go with her own things."

A maid took our coats, for although it was near the end of April the air seemed cool to us, after living in a subtropical climate. Old Browne ushered us into an elegant, high-ceilinged room that was really two rooms connected by folding doors that were folded back, allowing the light to flood in from windows at both ends. It was too full of people for me to take in the details of its decor, I only knew that it was wholly English, with an Englishness of the very highest quality, subdued and expensive, yet, in some indefinable way, casual.

Old Browne took us up to a woman whom I did not at first recognize, in fact I don't think I would ever have recognized her if Old Browne hadn't said, "Of course you've both met my wife . . . Almira, you remember the Crests, who so kindly asked us to lunch when we were passing through Bucharest?"

"Oh yes," she said. "So nice of you to come—my husband tells me you're on your way to Yugoslavia."

I was just about to tell her that we were on our way to Italy, not Yugoslavia, when a silver tray appeared before me, borne by two white-gloved hands, on which was a choice of martinis and sherry. I hesitated for a moment between them, and a man's voice said softly, "If Madame would prefer something else . . ."

I knew that voice. But I knew better than to betray my recognition of it, still less my shock at hearing it in this room. I was not a diplomat's wife for nothing. So, without looking up, I said, "I'll take the sherry, thank you," and continued my conversation with Almira Browne.

Another silver tray appeared, borne by another pair of white-gloved hands, this time those of a woman. The tray was covered with canapés, some of them spread with the tiny salted globules of caviar that seem to have no relationship with the belly of a sturgeon, but to be the eggs of the little jars in which they are sold.

New arrivals claimed my hostess's fluttering attention, and I joined Old Browne and Julian, who were at that moment being served with Scotch and soda by the count.

Old Browne said, "You remember Dimitri, don't you, Mrs. Crest?"

"Of course," I said, smiling at the count, who bowed slightly in response. "I'll never forget your marvelous dinners," I told him.

"As a matter of fact," Old Browne said, "you two ate one of the last dinners Dimitri cooked for me that summer. What about another glass of sherry, Mrs. Crest?"

The count went off to get it, and Old Browne edged us away from the crowd and toward the window. "You must see Almira's garden—she's a great gardener."

The casements were open, and a pleasant smell of humus and new-mown grass came up from the long walled garden. A copper beech shaded one side of the well-shaved lawn, and a curving flower bed edged the other with irises, tulips, and jonquils.

"It's a herbaceous border, really, but Almira plants bulbs between the perennials so that we have something in bloom for almost nine months of the year. But the roses don't do so well here as they did in Bulgaria—not enough sun."

The count brought the sherry. When he was out of earshot, Old Browne said, "Yes. Shortly after that dinner party at my house, Dimitri decided to leave my service and go back to his old profession of cabaret dancing and singing—this time with a female partner, one of the group of White Russians he lived with. But he and the girl soon quarreled. When he wrote to me from Paris last year, saying that he was sick and tired of the life, and broke into the bargain, I told Almira about him. She was going to Paris for a few days to do some shopping, so she got in touch with Dimitri and engaged him—as a sort of majordomo, really. And he's proved invaluable. He supervises the running of the house, he cooks for special dinners, he acts as my valet and my wife's chauffeur, and looks after everything when we're absent. And of course his fluent French is very useful here."

I was wondering whether he now "lived in," when Old Browne volunteered the information—as he had once before.

"We've given him what amounts to a private suite, a couple of rooms and a bath, away from the other servants, at the top of the house."

There was a moment of silence, a rather long moment, in which Julian and I avoided looking at each other. Then Old

Browne said, "Well, I suppose we'd better mingle—or Almira will be after me for monopolizing you."

It was obvious that he had drawn us aside not so much to show us his wife's garden as to give us a weatherproof explanation of the count's presence in his household before we had time to inadvertently say the wrong thing. He needn't have worried. I knew when to keep my mouth shut, and even Julian, who wasn't noted for his tact, could be counted upon to be diplomatic in a situation that didn't touch him personally. He drew a sharp distinction between diplomacy and tact, which he considered a form of insincerity in personal relationships.

He demonstrated this a moment later by simply walking away when Granby-Smith came toward us, smiling. Julian being what he was, he had probably taken the wisest course, but I felt a flare of anger at being put in the position of having to be ostentatiously friendly to Granby-Smith to cover Julian's ostentatious rudeness, and not only get no thanks for saving a social situation, but inevitably be reproached by Julian for publicly siding with an enemy. My conversation with Granby-Smith was the acme of the insincere politeness that was the approved currency in the Foreign Service. I automatically trotted out all the diplomatic cocktail-party clichés while I looked over his shoulder at my hostess, who was saying the same things to another one of her guests.

No wonder I hadn't recognized her as the woman I had met on the Calea Victoria two years earlier; marriage had transformed her. For one thing, she looked ten years younger. And this was more than an illusion created by clever makeup, the latest style of hairdo, and a dress that could have come only from one of the most exclusive Paris houses. It was fundamental; she had the confident air, even the radiance, of a woman who knows that she is sexually attractive to men. And she obviously was. The glint in Granby-Smith's eyes when she left the group she was with and came to join us told me that.

The count approached with another tray of martinis and sherry. My hostess and Granby-Smith took martinis. I knew from experience that I had better stick to one kind of drink, and I regretted my original choice. I felt like getting slightly drunk, but to mix martinis with sherry would only make me sick.

"You know, Almira," Granby-Smith remarked in his well-bred

voice, "that Russian of yours manages to convey the impression that he's not a real butler, but only acting the part of one in a play."

"In a sense, he *is* only acting the part of a butler," Almira said, "but I think he does it very well, don't you? Dimitri is a White Russian, Mrs. Crest, he was born into the old Russian aristocracy."

"All White Russians were princes or princesses in their own country," Granby-Smith said. "The capitals of Europe are simply crawling with royal émigrés—the Romanovs must have been quite extraordinarily prolific."

"Dimitri has never pretended to be anything more than a count," Mrs. Browne said with a faint note of reproach in her voice, "and he prefers that we don't even mention that. He wants to be known simply as Dimitri. But he *is* an aristocrat, the other servants respect him and defer to him naturally. And the household has been running much more smoothly since he came to take things in hand."

He had changed very little, I thought. He was still slender and lithe and graceful in all his movements, his dancing had seen to that. And there were no new marks of deprivation or struggle on his face, no signs that his experience with the girl—the girl with the long hair?—had left him sadder or wiser. He had always had an air of secret superiority, conferred no doubt by his blue blood, for whatever his real title may have been, he obviously came from the former ruling class in Russia. Almira was right there. I knew a lot of White Russians, and I could distinguish between the real and the imitation aristocrats. If there was any change in him now, it was a slight intensification of his self-assurance.

More guests arrived. Almira went to greet them, and I got away from Granby-Smith by responding to a wave from the Elliotts, on the other side of the room. Whitt, cordial and full of martinis, beamed at me from behind his glasses and told me how well I was looking, and his wife, full of the enthusiasm that absence generates for almost any former acquaintance, kissed me and cried, "Joanna! How *good* to see you! You're looking just *wonderful!*"

"So are you, Amanda," I said, thinking that she looked younger than when I had last seen her, over a year ago. But the change in her was not so much physical, I thought, as psychological. Her good looks—for she was good-looking rather than pretty, with the warm, wide smile, white teeth, clear skin, and generally "wholesome" air characteristic of many young American women—were no longer marred by the air of dissatisfaction characteristic of many young American wives. Yet their husbands were always so nice; more faithful and more domesticated than their European counterparts, and not half so domineering as English husbands tended to be.

"That's such a cute dress you're wearing," Amanda said. "Don't tell me you made it yourself—it looks like Paris."

"Thank you," I said, telling her nothing.

I still made most of my own dresses. Even if our improved finances—improved by a raise in pay that went with Julian's grudgingly given promotion, and by a legacy from his grandmother, who was the only member of his family alive or dead from whom he would accept anything—had allowed me to buy Paris models, Julian's principles wouldn't have allowed it. I copied them instead. But when Julian bragged about it I could have killed him. He joined us now, too late to say the wrong thing. Whitt was telling a joke, and he and Julian were soon exchanging stories that either Amanda or I had heard too often already.

"Let's go and sit down over there," she said, indicating an unoccupied sofa in an alcove. "My feet are killing me, they always do at cocktail parties. And I want to talk to you."

I wondered what it was that she wanted to talk to me about—her tone was confidential, but although we had seen a good deal of each other socially when we were both living in Bucharest, we hadn't been particularly close.

We sank into the deep, downy sofa, and Amanda eased her feet out of her high-heeled shoes with a sigh of relief. "Oh! Does this feel good! I know it's very unladylike—but you don't mind, do you, Joanna?"

While she wiggled her toes, her eyes roamed around the room as if seeking something. "What a lovely setting Almira has made for herself," she said. "How nice it must be to be able to buy whatever you want, no matter what it costs."

I looked at her in surprise. It hadn't occurred to me that Old Browne's expedient marriage had brought him money as well as professional rehabilitation.

"Oh yes!" Amanda said. "Didn't you know? Almira is the only

daughter of a shipping magnate. It's a mystery why she married Adrian. . . . Not that I've anything against him, I think he's a sweet guy—but they do say. . . . But you knew him quite well before he was married, didn't you? I seem to remember that he found a Black Sea villa for you one summer. . . ."

It was strange to hear her refer to Old Browne as *Adrian*. "I didn't know him all that well," I said cautiously, "but he did find a villa for us, and he was very helpful. It wasn't easy to be in a place where we couldn't even read the letters of the alphabet, let alone speak the language. And he spoke it fluently."

"Well, he'd been there for a good many years, hadn't he? Charles Granby-Smith says. . . ." But Almira was coming toward us.

"What are you two doing over here in a corner all by yourselves?"

"Admiring your taste," said Amanda, speaking for both of us. "This is *such* a lovely room!"

For me it had less appeal than the exotic interior of the little cloistered house by the Black Sea—of which it bore not the smallest trace. It was less crowded now, the guests were thinning out. At the far end I could see Old Browne closing the casement windows against a sudden shower. Murmuring excuses to Almira and Amanda, I got up and went over to him. "We'll have to be going very soon," I said, "and I haven't really had a chance to talk to you."

"My dear Mrs. Crest . . ."

Implicit in both my words and his was the recall of that brief period in which we had seen so much of each other. "There is something I want to say to you"—the words were unpremeditated, they came from some part of my being that I didn't know existed—"something that I should have said long ago, but didn't— perhaps because then I didn't know how to say it."

He smiled. "Now what *can* that be?"

"Just 'Thank you.' I never thanked you properly for all your kindness to me that summer, never told you how much I appreciated it, how much I valued your company, how much I enjoyed those marvelous evenings of good food and good music and good conversation with you in your little Arabian Nights house."

A moment of silence. A barely perceptible sigh. "That's how I

71

used to think of it myself," he said. "My Arabian Nights house— and that's how I still think of it."

"Do you ever miss it?"

"Not really. I have my nostalgic moments, of course, but I don't really miss it. I have everything that I want here. And a lot that I didn't know I wanted. I'd been so long in one place that I'd lost sight of the fact that change gives one a new lease on life. For me it's been almost a rebirth." He was looking down the long room at Almira as he said it; but his gaze encompassed the count too, unobtrusively performing his duties, and I had no sense of discord. It seemed to have all fallen into place.

"I wish you weren't leaving quite so soon," Old Browne said. "I have some fine new recordings that I'd like to play for you, and a better machine to play them on than the one you used to listen to. Would you like to see it? It's in my study."

So that's where he keeps his treasures, I thought. But I was wrong. In the replica of an English country-house library that Old Browne called his "study," the only object that I had seen before was the innocent aquarelle, which looked much more at home here than it had among the scimitars. "I remember this," I said. "It was on the wall between the windows. And I had an idea that it had been painted by your mother. I imagined a lady wearing a wide-brimmed straw hat sitting at an easel set up on a green lawn."

"How extraordinary! It *is* my mother's work—it's a view of the Thames from the garden of the house that I lived in as a child. You must be clairvoyant, Mrs. Crest! Even the straw hat . . ."

"But where are all the other beautiful things? The rugs, the collection of ancient swords, the silver bowls, and those splendid blue jars . . . I hope you didn't sell them."

"How well you remember!" he said with undisguised pleasure. "No, I didn't sell them. I brought them along and stored them in the attic, and now I've furnished Dimitri's rooms with them—he always liked them."

I had a sudden vision of the enormous low divan with its silky Oriental cover and its heaped cushions, and Dimitri lying among them, stretching his limber body like a young puma.

The Elliotts drove us back to the hotel. We were late, and we had to scramble to get the children and the Fräulein and fourteen pieces of luggage onto the train in time. The beds were already made up in the sleepers. I undressed and lay down. Julian stayed out in the corridor for a while, drinking Scotch from the flask that he always carried with him. He was slightly drunk when he came in, but affectionately drunk. We made love, which was not very good in the narrow bunk on a hurtling train—the rhythm of whose wheels didn't coincide with the rhythm of our bodies. But it was better than quarreling about Granby-Smith.

Later, when Julian had retired to the top bunk, I said, "Old Browne's marriage seems to have turned out very well—for both of them. It's taken ten years off her."

Julian snorted.

"Don't you agree?"

"Do you want to know what I really think?"

"What?"

"I think that bloody Russian gigolo fucks them both."

We had been in Italy for about three months when we heard that Old Browne had been accidentally drowned while swimming. The news upset me more than it upset Julian, who said, "Poor old bugger. But it's not a bad way to die, and at least he had his day in the sun."

It distressed me because I knew now how fond of him I was, and because of my intuitive guess three years earlier that he might end up being repatriated in a long wooden box—by his own choice.

I wanted to know exactly how it had happened, and I thought that Amanda might be able to tell me. So I wrote to her.

When her answer came, I took the letter upstairs to read in the privacy of my room.

He took off for the weekend alone [she wrote], driving his car himself. And he went all the way to Scheveningen (that was where you lived when Julian was posted at The Hague, wasn't it?) and put up at a posh hotel on the seafront. They say he dined there—alone—the night he arrived, had breakfast brought up to his room next morning, and then went out. When he left his key at the desk he told the clerk that he expected to be back by six, in case there were any phone calls for him.

There was a call—from Almira. But it was the next morning. Isn't that terrible? I mean, calling him too late—when he wasn't alive anymore.

Of course the clerk just said that he was out. But when he had been missing for twenty-four hours, the management notified the police. They found his clothes on a lonely stretch of beach where there were no lifeguards or bathing huts—he must have walked there because his car was still in the hotel garage. His body had been recovered earlier, by some fishermen—it had got tangled up in a trawling net, but they had no way of knowing whose body it was until the alarm went out.

As everyone says, it was the sort of accident that could easily happen—the English mania for privacy, an unguarded beach, a riptide, or just plain exhaustion. Especially with a man of Adrian's age.

What isn't so easy to explain is why he didn't take Almira with him to Scheveningen, particularly when he had returned only the night before from a trip to London, which he had wanted to cancel when Almira got an upset stomach at the last moment and didn't feel well enough to go with him. But of course she wouldn't let him change his plans. She told me this at the time, just before he got back from London, when we were having our hair done. And she was feeling quite well again then.

She's in England now. I saw her briefly before she left. She looked terrible, and she couldn't talk, she was still in a state of shock. But the servants are talking (Almira's personal maid is related to my cook), and they say—Whitt would be furious if he knew I was telling you this, so please keep it strictly under your hat—they say that Adrian came back from London a day earlier than he was expected—classic, isn't it?—and caught Almira and Dimitri in bed together up in that top-floor suite of his, which they say is like something out of *The Thief of Bagdad*. . . .


I didn't read any more. I knew better than she did what Dimitri's rooms looked like. And I knew where Old Browne had entered the sea—Julian and I used to go there to escape the vigilance of the lifeguards, who wouldn't let Julian swim out as far as he wanted. I thought of Irina. I imagined her, still hopelessly in love with Old Browne, interrupting her practice of Mozart to look at the morning paper and reading there of his death. Did she play a requiem for his soul on her flute? Did he think of her, and her glasses of amber tea, and her rose-petal jam, as he walked out to meet his death in the gray North Sea?

I wept. Through an open window Pip heard me, and came to see what was wrong, "Why are you crying, Mummy?"

I was crying for so many things that I couldn't tell him about. But I told him a truth, the simplest one. "I'm crying for Mr. Browne," I said. "He got drowned."

"Do you think a cup of tea would make you feel better?" Pip asked in his grown-up way.

I said that perhaps it would, and he went off to get it.

Since that summer by the Black Sea I had learned a lot about human nature and human suffering, and I was able now to feel a deep, genuine pity for Old Browne. But it was only much later, years later, that I really understood what had made him want to die.

Eventually, of course, I went back to Amanda's letter and read the rest of it.

That day at the Brownes [she wrote], I wanted so desperately to talk to you, really talk to you—I've always felt that I could trust you—but I never got a chance to say what was on my mind. It's divorce. I want to leave Whitt. I'm in love, Joanna, seriously in love with another man, and deeply involved with him. Don't speak of this when you write me—I show your letters to Whitt. I'll tell you about it in September, when (if I can hold out that long) I'll be coming to Italy with Whitt for a short visit with an old friend who's posted in Venice, and I'm pretty sure that we can fit in a couple of days in Rome, but if Whitt can't make it I'll come on my own.

In a postscript she added,

Did you hear about Maximilian Gavriolesco and the awful thing that happened to him?

And in a P.P.S.,

Better not mention that either when you write.

# 3

# Sybil and Maximilian

In the Bucharest that I knew, the Calea Victoria, where I wanted
to leave Old Browne standing in the sun with his new wife, was
more than the city's principal thoroughfare; it was the effervescing
mainstream of its dissolute life. And in order to get anywhere, I
had to go up or down or across it. We lived on its bank, so to
speak, about midway between its source and the point where it
merged into a Rumanian version of the Champs Elysées. On the
day when I ran into the Brownes I was walking briskly along its
most fashionable stretch at the hour of the noon "promenade"—
when the chances of getting one's bottom pinched were high—on
my way to have lunch with Sybil Gavriolesco at Capsa's.

Capsa's was the oldest-established restaurant in the city.
Outwardly unpretentious, it had something of the prestige of an
exclusive London club. The waiters were as respectfully familiar
with the regular clientele as old club members, and the food they
served was as strictly Rumanian as the food in a London club is
strictly British; even the menu was in Rumanian only, although
the language of fashionable society was French.

Capsa's was also clublike in that above the restaurant there
were suites for the convenience of clients whose homes were in the
country but whose business and pleasure lay in the city. Maximilian Gavriolesco was one of these. His business activities,
vaguely described as import and export, often kept him in town
late, and social life only got into its swing around midnight, so he
maintained a couple of rooms on the second floor of Capsa's
where he and his wife could spend what was left of a winter's night

after a party, when to ride for an hour or more in an open sleigh, with the temperature well below zero, would have been more than an inconvenience.

Rumania in the twenties was a country of painful contrasts. Its blazing summers and bitter, snowbound winters were paralleled in its society. Glittering balls would be held in glittering salons while an army of ragged men and women shoveled the snow in the streets outside, a sight that made Julian rage.

On the roads leading out of the city, the snow would accumulate layer by frozen layer, making the horse-drawn sleigh the safest means of transport in winter. Covered with snow, the flat countryside around Bucharest looked like the Russian steppe. "I expected to see lean wolves slink out from the shadows at any moment," said Sybil Gavriolesco, describing her first Rumanian winter.

She had already lived through four of them on that day in early June when I entered the gloomy dining room at Capsa's and found her awaiting me at a small table set for two. Which was unusual. I had expected to find her with Maximilian, and both of them surrounded by what we called the Gavriolesco entourage, a group of young Rumanians, male and female, relatives, hangers-on, and unclassified individuals vaguely connected with Maximilian's business, who took advantage of his lavish hospitality, or were, perhaps, rewarded by it for extracurricular services.

Sybil was drinking mineral water, and told me that she didn't want anything to eat, but that I should go ahead and order whatever I wanted. "Start with caviar and champagne," she advised. "It will all go down on Max's monthly bill, which he never checks, so you may as well splurge."

"But why aren't you eating?" I said. "Don't you feel well?"

"Not particularly. But that isn't why I'm not eating. I'm going to see my doctor this afternoon, and he told me to fast—he's going to take some tests. It's nothing serious," she added. "I simply don't go in for being serious—least of all with my beautiful, *beautiful* body."

The last three words were in quotes, and there was a vaguely familiar note in the mimicry that I couldn't quite place. I wondered if she was pregnant, and if so, by whom. For Maximilian was reputed to be impotent, a rumor that gave rise to a lot of speculation about his marriage to Sybil seventeen years after his first wife's death in childbirth, due, so rumor said, to the congenital disease from which he suffered, along with a lot of his countrymen, before the cure was discovered.

"Where's Maximilian?" I asked.

"In Paris—I hope."

While I ate the little lake crayfish that were one of Capsa's specialties, Sybil sat twisting her glass of Vichy water in silence, and I wondered why on earth she had asked me to sit on the other side of a table for two and eat at her expense, or rather at Maximilian's expense, a meal that she couldn't share. I had never seen her in such a mood. She was one of those women who have to shine. If she had her dark moods, she never let anyone see them. No one, but absolutely no one, must ever say that Sybil Gavriolesco was boring, and no one ever did. But there were times when for me her brilliance didn't ring true, and the cruel wit that was part of her stock-in-trade seemed forced, and I would have liked to tell her not to force it, that the laughter it provoked was uneasy. Her chief butts were her compatriots, the British Colony bigwigs who sycophantically followed the lead of the legation in snubbing her and her husband.

In this, as in many another situation, Julian was an opposition minority of one. When the "Old Man's wife" suggested, after seeing us in the Gavriolescos' company, that we would do well not to be seen in it too often, he said, "To hell with the Old Man's wife! We'll see as much of the Gavriolescos—or anyone else, for that matter—as we damn well like."

Actually there were not many opportunities. We had a standing invitation to share their box at the opera, but we were seldom free on the right evenings. As for social gatherings, we met the Gavriolescos only at those semipublic affairs, charity balls and dinners, to which Maximilian's money was a passport, and where, as wealthy contributors, they were accepted for the occasion by people who wouldn't dream of inviting them home. The only reason given for this ostracism was that Maximilian had a shady reputation. "But that's nothing out of the way," Julian said. "This is a shady country. The only honest people are the peasants."

Over our one-sided lunch it was I who tried to amuse Sybil, and I wasn't very good at it. She seemed incapable of responding; I

78

doubted whether she was even listening. She had invited me, I realized now, because for some reason she was afraid to be alone.

Out on the street, she said, "Are you doing anything special this afternoon?"

"No. Later, when Julian gets back, we're going to the country club with the Elliotts for tennis, but now I'm just going home."

"Then would you do me a favor? Would you come to the doctor's with me? I shan't be there very long."

I didn't want to go with her, but I saw panic in her eyes. "All right," I said. "I'll come."

Maximilian's car was parked on the other side of the street, but Sybil hailed a droshky. She gave the fat eunuch driver minute directions in her fluent Rumanian that was tinged with a faint North of England accent. We clip-clopped down the Calea Victoria to a district near the river, the real river, a muddy stream whose sloping banks were splashed with the garish colors of handwoven peasant rugs spread out for sale, and turned into one of the little uneven sidestreets whose charm lay in their lack of uniformity; for although the houses presented an unbroken front, it seemed as if each one had been built at a different time by a different architect and fitted into whatever space was available, either by squeezing or by stretching, until no gaps were left. Sybil stopped the driver before a door without any nameplate, paid him, gave him a large tip, and told him to come back at four o'clock, "And if we're not already out here, ring the doorbell."

Our own ring was answered after a wait of several minutes by a very pretty, very slatternly girl, who admitted us into a narrow hallway smelling of food cooked with garlic, and then disappeared through a door on the right. From a door on the left a youngish man came out, wearing an ordinary business suit. He addressed Sybil as "Madame" and she called him "Doctor"; neither used the other's name. He looked at me, rather anxiously, I thought, and Sybil said, "This is an English friend, where can she wait?" He opened the door on the right. There was a little flurry behind it and the sound of another door closing. "In here," he said, "if Madame will excuse the slight disorder . . ."

The disorder was more than slight. The room was a private sitting room, and the divan was so tumbled that I guessed he and the girl had been making love on it when the doorbell rang.

Through the other door he shouted an order for coffee, then he said, "If Madame will excuse me . . ." and left me alone.

I felt very uncomfortable, and not only physically, though the stuffiness of the room soon made my head ache. The windows, which were on the street side of the house, were closed, imprisoning a variety of stale smells, among them the unmistakable smell of bedbugs, and although I knew that bedbugs only came out at night, I began to feel a nervous all-over itch that made me get up from the comfortable rug-covered divan that was surely the doctor's bed, and sit on a hard chair.

The girl came in with a brass tray on which was a Turkish coffeepot, a tiny cup and saucer, and the usual glass of cold water. Smiling, she put the tray down on a table still cluttered with the remains of the meal that had, no doubt, preceded the lovemaking. But the state of the table concerned her less than the state of the divan. Two of the pillows were on the floor; picking them up, she disclosed a pair of panties that she kicked out of sight. Still smiling, she turned to me with a shrug and said something to the effect that gentlemen were not very tidy. While she cleared away the dishes, I sipped the strong, sweet coffee. She asked me in the polite third person if there was anything else I would like. I said that I would like to have one of the windows opened. Her smile disappeared. I said, "It does not matter." Smiling again, she left the room before I had time to ask for any other impossibility.

My headache got worse, and the hard chair made the rest of me ache too. I went back to the divan and lay down with one of the heavily embroidered pillows under my head. To hell, as Julian would say, with the bedbugs. There was nothing to read, and the coffee kept me awake, so I started to think about Sybil, and what might be happening to her in the room across the hall, and if it was what I thought it was, why had she chosen me—one of the group that looked down on her—to hold her hand in a situation with which Rumanian women were more familiar than most Englishwomen. She had never confided in me; she had made a point of treating me as a hopeless innocent, too naive for words. "God! Joanna, you're so easy to fool!" or, "All that romantic idealism of yours makes me sick. Come off it, for God's sake." Which may have been her method of finding out how much I really knew and perceived, how shocked I would be by the truth, and how capable of helping her.

My thoughts went back three years to our first meeting.

We had arrived in Bucharest a month ahead of the first snowfall. Apartments were scarce, and we had to live for a few weeks in a hotel. The only one in the city recommended for foreigners, it offered French food and the sound of British voices in the bar. But it was not free of bedbugs, and the smell of the kerosene that was used as a weapon against them, nor was it above asking single men when they checked in whether they wanted a room with or without a girl—of which there were quantities drifting along the corridors in their peignoirs.

When Julian and I got bored with the French food and the British voices, we went to eat at the Cina, a fashionable restaurant where the voices were international, and you could dance between courses, with hostesses wearing blouses made of transparent material with nothing underneath them.

But none of this seemed to be the real Rumania, and a Rumanian acquaintance told us to try Capsa's if that was what we wanted.

We were wrestling with the menu, guessing aloud what each dish might be, when a waiter handed Julian a visiting card with the name *Maximilian Gavriolesco* engraved on it, and a penciled note, "I see you are having difficulties with the menu. If you and Madame would care to join us at our table, my wife and I would be delighted." We looked up and encountered the smiles of a couple two tables away; a heavy, middle-aged man, very dark, and a young woman with bright red hair.

Julian and I looked at each other. "Why not?" Julian said, but before he could send his penciled assent back with the waiter, the man at the other table had risen. It didn't occur to me until much later that he knew just who we were, and that Sybil had prompted the invitation, for reasons other than the ostensible one.

"My wife is English," Maximilian said, "and she remembers her own difficulties with the language when she first came to my country."

At close quarters, the difference between their ages was more apparent. I placed him in the middle fifties, but his wife, I thought, was probably about my own age. In fact, she was twenty-seven and he was sixty-four.

They recommended this and that specialty of the house, including what Maximilian translated as "savage duck"—irritating his wife, who said, "Don't try to be funny, Max, you're no good at it," and suggested fresh red caviar to start with, but before that *tuica* with ripe olives. The menu settled, Sybil took over the conversation, telling us nothing about herself, but a number of startling things about people we knew, or had thought that we knew.

While Sybil was making her witty jibes, I was forming that swift first impression, habitual with Foreign Service people on meeting strangers, that would go into a kind of mental dossier, labeled *Gavriolesco, Sybil*, for future reference. *Money, audacity, piquancy* were the key words in my mental notes. Another word suggested itself—*perversity*, conveyed by a deliberate contradiction in Sybil's appearance. Her flaming red hair was cut very short in a style called the "Eton crop," which gave her small, pointed face the look of an impudent boy's. But her heavy makeup, and a pair of long jade earrings that intensified the green of her eyes and matched her cigarette holder, were flamboyantly feminine, and her fashionably boyish figure was curiously accented by the deep scoop of her black sleeveless dress that revealed almost to the nipples a pair of childishly small, unsupported breasts. When she knew me better, she told me that Rumanian men didn't go for girdles and bras. "When they dance with you," she said, " they want to feel the three Bs." "The what?" I asked stupidly. "Brahms, Beethoven, and Bach," Sybil said, and seeing that I was still puzzled, "Breasts, Belly, and Buttocks, in the English translation—really, Joanna, you're past belief."

In view of this verbal coarseness, I was amazed to discover that she had, like me, been brought up in an English country parsonage, where she had, in her own words, "only just escaped being fucked by the curate" when she was sixteen years old. A startling statement that shook my faith in the fundamental innocence of the clergy, because the same thing had very nearly happened to me, although I didn't realize it at the time; I had no idea why my father's curate—who looked like an overgrown choirboy—was chasing me all over the parsonage in my parents' absence, only to end up on his knees before me, thanking God for saving his soul through my blessed innocence. Julian had enlightened me.

At the age of twenty-three, Sybil had escaped, still intact, from curates, the country parsonage, and her widowed father, and had taken a "position," as ladylike jobs were called then, in Switzerland, at a finishing school for the daughters of gentlemen, rich gentlemen, where she taught the young ladies to speak the English language. One of her pupils was the seventeen-year-old daughter of Maximilian Gavriolesco, Consuela, who had developed a crush on her English teacher and had invited her to spend a few weeks in Rumania during the summer vacation.

Of all this, the only thing that I learned that first night at Capsa's was contained in Maximilian's brief explanation of how he had met his wife. "She came to visit here as my daughter's teacher and friend, and she stayed to become my wife." The other details were given me piecemeal by Sybil herself, as our acquaintance deepened into a rather prickly friendship. But her reminiscences always stopped short of that fateful visit to Rumania; they went back, like Old Browne's, to before the fall, to an earlier and more innocent part of her life. And I suspect that I was the only person to whom she could talk of her country parsonage childhood in England and be understood, or even believed, and that her trust in me was based on our common background.

When we excused ourselves that evening on the ground of an after-dinner engagement, Sybil looked put out. Maximilian was suave. "You will hear from us," he said. "It would be a great pleasure if you would do us the honor of visiting us at our country house—for a weekend, perhaps." And when we said we would enjoy that, he turned to Sybil and remarked, rather strangely, I thought, "That will be very interesting, will it not?" This remark, with the peculiar emphasis that he gave to it, left a curious, almost a sinister impression. "I wonder what he meant by that," Julian said. "He's an odd fish."

"So is she. But I rather liked her."

"I can't say that I liked either of them," Julian said, "but I did find them interesting."

We soon forgot them, however. We found the apartment on the Calea Victoria, and we didn't go back to Capsa's—we were sick to death of restaurants.

Domestically, life was easier for me in Rumania than it had been in the far more civilized country of Holland, which we had just left. Here, wages were so low that we could easily afford a Fräulein for the children and a mother-and-daughter team for the housekeeping. This inequity made the Socialist-minded Julian feel guilty. But he was told that to pay any more than the going rate would spoil the market for underpaid Rumanian officials who could barely live on their salaries but had to have at least one servant in order to maintain their dignity.

One day in spring I was surprised to get a letter from Sybil Gavriolesco, reminding us of our promise to visit them in the country and asking us to spend the Orthodox Easter weekend with them en famille. This had an innocent sound, and conjured up visions of Sybil and Maximilian as benevolent landowners joining their peasants first in worship and then in feasting and dancing the hora, rather like Christmas Day at the manor house.

I showed Julian the letter. "Shall we go?"

"Why not?" Julian said. "I'd rather like to find out what that old scoundrel meant by 'interesting.' "

It was agreed that Maximilian should pick us up in his car on Saturday afternoon. But instead of Maximilian, a beautiful, languid young man appeared who introduced himself as Maximilian's son-in-law, Mircea Maniu. "But everyone calls me Micu—it's the logical contraction."

He had a small open car whose back seat was only a dickey, which meant that we would all have to sit together in front, and I could see that Julian, who knew by now that Rumanian men were not to be trusted an inch, were, in fact, experts at making a sexual pass of the crudest kind right under a husband's nose, didn't like the idea of having me sit so close to such an obvious specimen of moral decadence as the elegant Micu. But it couldn't be avoided. So I squeezed in between Julian, who put his arm possessively around my shoulders, and Micu, whose sensual lips curled in a smile that expressed both appreciation of another male's precautionary measures and a determination sooner or later to circumvent them.

The squalid thoroughfare that was, Micu said, the only way out of the city to our particular destination, took us past the slaughterhouses and the wholesale meat market—half a mile of open stalls where the carcasses hung exposed to sun, flies, dust, and the marauding dogs that fought over the offal thrown into the street by the bloodstained butchers. Neither the perfume that emanated from Micu's elegant person on one side of me, nor the smell of Julian's cigarette smoke on the other, was strong enough to disguise the nauseating reek of blood and offal.

Farther on, it was Julian's turn to be sickened, morally sickened, by the condition of the peasants, men and women incredibly beautiful in face, form, and costume, living in habitations unfit even for the animals with which they apparently shared them. "One day," Julian said to the imperturbable Micu, "there will be a revolution here as there has been in Russia, and your holy peasants will cut your unholy throats."

Micu laughed. "They won't cut mine. I shall be in Paris."

"I wasn't being personal, my dear fellow," Julian said. "I meant your collective throats as a class."

But I knew that Julian would have cut Micu's throat with pleasure if he had met him face to face in a revolution, and not entirely from revolutionary motives.

On the edge of one of the poverty-stricken villages, Micu stopped before an iron gate in a high, whitewashed wall, and sounded his horn. The gate was opened on the inside by a lad in peasant dress, and we entered what I can only call the Gavriolesco compound. There was no "big house," only a series of low buildings completely detached from one another. Micu stopped the car in front of one of the buildings, and we got out. "I wonder where Sybil is," Micu said.

Just then she appeared, almost unrecognizable in Rumanian national costume, with a scarlet kerchief hiding her cropped hair. She was walking a pair of enormous dogs on the leash. At the sight of us they uttered savage growls. Micu yelled in English, "Get them away!" But they were too powerful for the slight Sybil to control physically, and at this moment their will seemed to be stronger than hers. Julian started to go to help, but Micu stopped him. Then two peasants with sticks appeared, and, mastering the dogs, took them away.

Micu went close up to Sybil in such a threatening manner that for a moment I thought he was going to hit her. "You fool!" he said in English. She answered him in Rumanian, telling him to go to the devil, that much I understood. "I apologize for this scene," she said to us. "I had no idea that the dogs would behave like that—they are usually quite docile."

"Docile?" said Micu. "Really? I should hardly describe them as docile. But you know them better than I do, since you've taken to walking them every day."

The look that Sybil gave him then was a very strange look, an intimate look—in the sense that a knife is intimate with the flesh it enters. Julian remarked to me later, "There's something funny going on between Madame Gavriolesco and that young man."

Micu went off to park his car somewhere behind the buildings, and Sybil took us into what she called "the drawing-room pavilion." "*Pavilion* is *my* word," she said. "It suits the place, the whole arrangement is so Chinese."

There was nothing Chinese about its physical appearance. The "drawing-room pavilion" consisted of one long, oval room with a vaulted ceiling—patched with damp where rain or snow had seeped through the roof. It was dank and chilly and smelled of mildew. The tile stove at one end of it was evidently unlighted, and the narrow windows at the other were so overgrown with vines that they admitted no sunlight and couldn't be opened to let in the warm outside air.

There were rugs everywhere, on the parquet floor, on the mildewed walls, above and around the windows, and, of course, on the divans. Their colors were exquisite. Not garish like those of the new rugs on the river bank, but soft and rich, in the subtle shades of rose and purple and cream that one sees in a bed of zinnias. "They are very old," Sybil said, "and Max is very proud of them, so be sure to admire them. They were made before the invention of aniline dyes, when the peasants concocted dyes of their own from plants. Would you like to take a walk in the grounds before it gets dark? Max is sure to be late, he always is."

I was glad to get out into the sweet-scented evening air; there were lilacs in bloom, and syringa, and some cherry trees. The church was on the grounds, in an English manorial way, but this place was more like a farm than a manor. There were chickens scratching in the flower beds, and a tethered goat was trying to get at a syringa bush just beyond its reach. An army of barefoot serving girls attired in picturesque national costumes of the same type as Sybil's, but less ornate, were scurrying from building to building with pails and mops and brooms, as if a grand Easter cleaning had been undertaken at the last minute. Which it had. But I didn't know then that before a Rumanian party of any kind, the cleaning was begun only when the guests were due to arrive; Rumanian guests knew better than to arrive on time.

A young girl emerged from one of the pavilions and came toward us. She was dressed like the others, but the sandals on her feet told me that she was not a servant. "Oh, there's Consuela," Sybil said, "my stepdaughter, Madam Maniu—isn't that absurd?"

"What is absurd?" the girl asked, joining us.

"That you should be my stepdaughter," Sybil said.

The girl smiled, and I thought I had never seen a more lovely smile or one that was so openly seductive. Very small and soft, with downy skin and what Julian described as "bedroom eyes," she had an extraordinary face; a perfect oval, with exquisitely drawn features and a curving, sensuous mouth, it was at once childish and corrupt—like the face of a child that has lost its innocence without being aware of it.

"Where's Micu?" Sybil asked her.

She shrugged, without answering. The shrug conveyed indifference to her husband's whereabouts rather than ignorance of them. Sybil told her that we were going for a walk, and she said, with another lovely smile directed impartially at both me and Julian, that she would come with us.

Just then a motor horn sounded outside the gate, which was opened to let in a car driven by a woman. "Ah! C'est Lucrèce qui arrive," Consuela said, then, explaining, "She is my husband's cousin. She has a car of her own, she is very ... enfin, elle est très libre."

newcomer, who I thought must be English or American, for at that time Rumanian women were seldom to be seen alone at the wheel of a car.

"She has no parents," Consuela informed us. "They are dead. She has only her brother. He will come also, but later."

As Sybil brought her over to us, she was unwinding the long

gauzy scarf that she had worn in the car to protect her hair from the wind and the dust, and I saw that she was free from the slavery of fashion as well as of convention. Her blond hair was braided in two thick braids, like a peasant girl's, and in taking off the scarf she had loosened the pins that held them up, so that they slipped down, theatrically long, like those worn on the stage by Marguerite in *Faust*, and she allowed them to hang loose, without showing any embarrassment, while Sybil introduced her as Princess Aman.

"No," she said, "not Princess Aman. Lucrèce. I am Lucrèce."

She shook hands with me and with Julian, saying "How do you do?" with no foreign expectation of being told how we did. "I can feel that my face is covered with dust," she said to Sybil with a little grimace, "and I should like to wash it off. I don't like to have a dirty face."

"She has been driving for hours," Consuela told us as Lucrèce went off with Sybil. "She has come from her home in the mountains. She and her brother are fortunate, they have two houses, one in Bucharest for the winter, and another one in the mountains for the summer. . . . Ah! *Voilà mon père.* . . ."

A sleek closed car glided in through the iron gate. Maximilian emerged from it speckless, with every oiled hair in place. He threw up his hands with delight on finding us there—as if it were a surprise to him—and apologized profusely for his lateness. He brushed the back of my hand with his black moustache, put his arm around Julian's unresponsive shoulders—only for a moment, but with a shade too much familiarity—and kissed his daughter on the lips. "*Comment ça va, mignonne?*"

"*Très bien, Papa.*"

They spoke as if French were their own private language, but, remembering his manners, Maximilian said quickly to us, "Of course you understand French?"

"Of course," Julian said.

Micu appeared on the scene as if by magic, his footsteps so soft that I hadn't heard him coming. "The dogs should be kept chained up," he said to his father-in-law, "or one day they will kill someone."

Maximilian drew his heavy eyebrows together. "But they *are* kept chained up—the servants have orders never to let them loose. What happened?"

"Ask Sybil."

"*Rien n'est arrivé, Papa ... mais rien!*"

So Consuela had been watching. She seemed so distressed that I intervened. "It was really nothing, Monsieur. We arrived unexpectedly when your wife was walking the dogs on the leash, and they growled at us because we were strangers, that's all."

"I could have calmed them down," Julian said, "if Monsieur Maniu hadn't restrained me."

"I was afraid for you, and for Madame," said Micu, but I saw in his eyes that he was lying. His fear had been for himself. Julian regarded him coldly.

Sybil joined us. "Hullo, Max. What's the matter? You look cross."

"Something happened with the dogs. What was it?"

"*Papa! Ne te fâche pas, je t'en prie....*"

"*Tais-toi.* What happened, Sybil?"

"I'll tell you later," Sybil said. "I suppose Micu's been exaggerating, as usual. Don't let's bore the Crests with family quarrels—or they'll never come to see us again."

"*Mille pardons!*" cried Maximilian. "In my concern for you, Madame, I forgot myself. Rest assured that the dogs will not get loose again."

"My wife and I are not afraid of dogs, we're accustomed to handling them. All English people know how to manage dogs," Julian said.

There was so much implied contempt in this remark that all Maximilian could do was ignore it. "What about some refreshment?" he said, as though struck by a brilliant idea.

I murmured to Sybil that first I would like to wash my hands—a British euphemism that in Rumania didn't always get you where you wanted to go. But Sybil led me straight to an earth closet in an outhouse. The lock on the door was broken. "I'll stand guard outside," Sybil said, "in case Max comes along—he's always wanting to pee."

I emerged red in the face from holding my breath. "I expect you'd like a real wash now," Sybil said. "I'll show you your room in the guest pavilion."

It made me blink. "Amusing, isn't it?" Sybil said. "One of Max's bright ideas." Its walls and ceilings were completely covered with mirrors, and the huge divan bed was placed squarely in the middle of the room to ensure maximum reflection for its occupants. The "real wash" was provided by a singularly incongruous piece of furniture: a marble-topped washstand, complete with pink china basin and ewer, and on its lower deck a waste-water pail and two chamber pots. To make love on that divan-bed with the washstand reflected from every angle would be like making love with Queen Victoria watching, I thought.

While I tidied myself up before one wall, Sybil postured before another, swinging her tightly swathed hips and crossing her feet in the steps of a hora. But although the steps were correct, her movements were not those of a real Rumanian, and the beautiful national costume looked, on her angular figure, like something she had borrowed to wear at a fancy dress ball.

I said, "What is it like to become a Rumanian?"

"You can't become a Rumanian," Sybil said, "you have to be born one."

When we returned to the drawing-room pavilion, a gramophone was playing a slow tango. Julian was dancing with Consuela, and Lucrèce with a young man who could only be her brother, so great was the resemblance between them. Lucrèce had changed into a strikingly handsome national dress, with the same wide-sleeved embroidered blouse as those worn by Sybil and Consuela, but with a pleated, plum-colored skirt richly encrusted with silver; heavy and full, it opened and closed like a fan as she danced, disclosing the red-embroidered hem of a narrow white underskirt, which gave the effect of conscious modesty, like the long pantalettes of Victorian days.

Micu was sitting talking to Maximilian. He got up as soon as I entered, and asked me to dance, stopping, as we tangoed past the gramophone, to put back the needle. Sybil took Micu's place beside Maximilian. They talked in low tones while making a pretense of watching the others dance. Sybil's expression was confident and contemptuous. Whatever Micu had been saying about her, his wife was on her side against him, that had been perfectly clear. And she was lucky to have Consuela on her side, I thought, recalling Maximilian's not entirely fatherly kiss.

The music was little more than an aphrodisiac throbbing, and dancing with Micu was only a little less than actual lovemaking. I could see that Consuela was inviting Julian to go to the same lengths, but however captivated Julian might be, he always kept his weather eye on me, so when Micu wanted to replay the record for the third time, I wouldn't let him.

Lucrèce brought her partner over. "My brother Nicolai," she said, and we exchanged "How do you do's" without waiting for answers.

Nicolai spoke English fluently and idiomatically, with a cultured British accent that could only, I thought, have been acquired in England. Perhaps he had been educated at Oxford or Cambridge.

Paris was the Mecca of most Rumanians. But it turned out that Nicolai Aman was an ardent Anglophile who knew London well and preferred it to any other city. "My sister and I spent a couple of years there," he said. "I was reading international law at London University."

Lucrèce was less communicative than her brother. But in response to my genuine interest, she told me, rather diffidently, that she was a painter, and had gone to London with her brother to study at the Slade School of Art. "We felt very happy in London," she said, in her slightly stilted English. "We made many English friends." Which didn't surprise me. With their coolly courteous manners, their cultured accents, and their reserve, they were the acme of British "good form."

In Bucharest, their title as well as their attributes must have put them on the invitation list for diplomatic parties—though I couldn't recall having seen them anywhere, and they were not the sort of people who remain unnoticed. In addition to their striking resemblance to each other, their whole appearance was arresting. Both equally tall, they moved with the athletic grace of classical statues come to life, and their coloring was extraordinary, a combination of ash-blond hair and brown eyes and the matte, slightly sallow skin associated with brunettes. Rumanian men were inordinately dandified, but I couldn't imagine this very masculine, very Anglicized young man dyeing or bleaching his hair, and there were no dark roots at Lucrèce's center parting. Later in the evening, I couldn't resist asking Sybil whether or not their unusual coloring was natural. She laughed. "That pair," she said, "would no more think of dyeing their hair than a pair of tigers would think of bleaching out their stripes."

Micu put on a foxtrot. This time I had Nicolai for a partner, and Lucrèce danced with Julian—as formally as she had with her brother. He permitted himself no liberties with me, which made him all the more interesting; Rumanian dancing partners were boringly predictable in their pursuit of the three B's.

In the intervals of conversation between the dances, Julian discovered that Nicolai was interested in politics, but his mistrust of Maximilian, and the peculiar ambiguity that hung in the air like a faintly unpleasant odor, kept him more discreet than he usually was on the subject. And I had the impression that Nicolai, too, was not speaking freely.

Lucrèce did not join in their talk, but her attention was focused on them; she listened to what they were saying with an occasional half-smile, a slight upturning of the corners of her mouth, which was more subtle than Consuela's, and suggested a seductive power of the mind rather than of the body—a power that was already influencing me, and captivating me. Her insistence on being called Lucrèce, *tout court,* had seemed at first like affectation, but now I thought that she might well be one of those rare and unique beings whose genius or beauty, fame or ill-fame, bestows on them a singularity that makes titles and second names superfluous.

There was no mention of dinner, and I was beginning to feel light-headed on too much to drink and too little to eat when the church bells started to ring. "It's time to go," Sybil said. "Have you got a scarf to put over your head—or shall I lend you one?" I had put one in my overnight bag. Julian and I went to get it and "wash our hands" on the way. "Wait till you see the room that we're going to sleep in," I said.

He was unimpressed. "It's the sort of thing that they have in high-class brothels."

"How do you know that?"

"Hearsay . . ."

"Come on now, the truth!"

Sybil's voice at the door interrupted a promising love-fight. "Are you ready?" "Damn," said Julian under his breath. "Just a moment, Sybil," I said, and she laughed.

At the church door we were each given an unlighted candle to hold. The tiny church was tight-packed with peasants in their best clothes. The conflict of incense, garlic, perfume, and perspiration was overpowering. There were no seats; everyone stood at uncomfortably close quarters with his neighbor. Julian and I were next to each other. On my left, Micu had insinuated himself between his wife and me and was so close that his thigh was crushed against mine. I couldn't see Sybil and Maximilian, but Nicolai and Lucrèce were immediately in front of us, and I was struck by their reverent attitude, their involvement in what was going on.

Up at the high altar two voices, one bass and one tenor, chanted unfamiliar, unintelligible prayers. The congregation genuflected, bowed, and made the sign of the cross at intervals. I followed suit, but Julian stood upright and motionless through it all, like one of the Guardsmen outside Buckingham Palace.

The stifling atmosphere, the monotonous chanting, the concerted movements of the crowd, of which I was a part willy-nilly, had a hypnotic effect on me, and my thoughts wandered back to the past, and to the very different Easter services of my childhood. The tinkle of a bell at a moment of breathless silence brought me back to where I was. The tightly packed worshipers fell to their knees on the damp stone floor like a flock of settling birds, and I knelt with them, pulling Julian down too. Now I could see the priest elevating the Host. And it was during this solemn act, in which I felt myself almost forcibly involved by a power too strong to resist, that Micu's profligate hand crept under my skirt.

With dramatic suddenness a great collective cry broke out from the congregation, and Micu, unperturbed by the kick on the shin that I had given him as soon as it was practicable, whispered, "They are saying, 'Christ is risen!' "

Then we all made way as best we could for the black-bearded priests and their acolytes, who lighted the candles nearest to them as they went by, and the flame was passed from one candle to another until the whole church was alight with moving flames that followed the priests in solemn procession around the outside of the building. "We go around three times," Micu said, "and we have to keep our candles alight all the time."

"We have to keep them alight until we get back indoors," Nicolai said. "In Bucharest, people carry them all the way from the church to their homes."

"What happens if your candle goes out?" I asked.

"It's bad luck," Micu said with a laugh, edging up close to Sybil. A moment later her candle went out.

At the end of the third circumambulation, the triumphant cry of "Christ is risen!" went up once more from the people and was repeated three times, like a cheer, before they dispersed, each carefully guarding the flame of a wish or a hope. Among the eight of us on our way—so Consuela told me in French—to the dining pavilion, it seemed that Sybil would be the only one cheated of luck, but as she led the way arm in arm with Maximilian, his flame was extinguished too, without any apparent cause, for the night was completely windless.

Once over the threshold, we whose candles still burned blew them out. Then we all embraced one another, exchanging the kiss of peace on each cheek and exclaiming, "Christ is risen!" In this mood of religious euphoria I forgave Micu his dirty little misdemeanor. And outwardly, at least, the enmity, if enmity it was, between him and Sybil was submerged in the joy of the Resurrection.

The dining pavilion was, like the drawing-room pavilion, a single room, and even colder and damper than the one into which we had first been introduced. On the mildewy walls there were neither rugs nor mirrors, only hunting trophies: a bearskin, antlers, the stuffed heads of stags. Now I knew what the dogs were, and why they were dangerous. They were boarhounds, trained to deal with the formidable wild boar. But when I admired the trophies and congratulated Maximilian on his prowess as a hunter, he said, "Those days are over for me now. I leave the chase to the younger generation." And Sybil said, "Max goes in for spectator sports only."

The meal we sat down to, at two o'clock in the morning, was a banquet. It began with borscht, brought in from the kitchen pavilion in a silver tureen, from which Sybil ladled it out into silver bowls that were carried around to the guests by two barefoot serving girls. After the soup came stuffed carp, tasting through all its spices of river mud. Of what came after that, I remember only the principal dish: a young lamb roasted whole. My glass was constantly being replaced by one of another shape, filled with wine of another color. Small wonder that I have forgotten not only what we ate but what we said as well.

At a certain point, not very far along, my memory stopped recording speech and gave itself up to receiving visual impressions; the epicene, decadent beauty of Micu, the equivocal offers in Consuela's eyes as they fluttered from Julian to me, and the watchful expression in Maximilian's, as if he were trying to gauge the effect of his daughter's charm; Sybil, laughing too loudly, talking too much, her small boyish head free of its kerchief and seeming not to belong to the rest of her body—still trapped in an alien disguise; and side by side, immediately opposite me across the table, Nicolai and Lucrèce, in sharp relief against the candlelit wall, like imperial images stamped on gold coins. But Slavic rather than Latin. High cheekbones, very wide; straight, blunt noses; large mouths with very white teeth, but rarely smiling, expressive most of the time of a brooding melancholy. I perceived them now as personages of a past era, human enigmas that no amount of piecing together of correspondence can fully solve.

Julian and I didn't have an opportunity to make love among the mirrors after all. The night was already over by the time we got up from the dinner table, and Nicolai and Lucrèce, who had to leave, offered to drive us home.

I think that I rode with Nicolai in his car, and that Julian rode with Lucrèce. But I am not absolutely sure. Through the haze of wine and fatigue, I could no longer distinguish between the brother and the sister. They had become one.

Waiting for Sybil at the doctor's, I was recalling this hallucinatory meeting with Nicolai and Lucrèce when the doctor came in, looking sweaty and strained, as if he had just brought his patient through a difficult childbirth. He told me that "Madame" would soon be ready to leave, she was just resting. "She is all right," he said, "but when she gets home she should go to bed and take the pills that I shall give her. If there are no complications, she need not see me again. If there are"—and he furtively crossed himself— "here is my telephone number." He obviously thought that I was going to stay with her.

The doorbell rang, and he gave a little start. "That must be our droshky," I said. He looked relieved and went to get Sybil, who came out into the hallway looking very pale and vague, as if she had just come to after an anesthetic. She didn't talk in the droshky, she still seemed half asleep. But at a terrace café on the Calea Victoria, about a block away from Capsa's, she woke up, told the driver to stop, and paid him off with a note that included another large tip.

"I need some black coffee to pull me together," she said.

"You're not thinking of driving out to the country now, are you?"

"No. I'll stay in our rooms at Capsa's until tomorrow. Max won't be back for another two days—I hope."

When the waiter had brought her black coffee, she took out a cigarette. "Don't try to smoke now," I said. "It will only make you sick. Wait for an hour or so until the effects of the ether have worn off."

She looked at me sharply. "So it has happened to you too," she said, adding with a gleam of her usual malice, "Who would ever have thought it?"

I was furious with myself for having inadvertently given away to Sybil, of all people, something that was nobody's business but mine and Julian's; and not what she thought it was, either, for I was pretty sure that she was crediting, or discrediting, me with an extramarital pregnancy. She said, "Don't look so upset. I'm glad to know that you're human. Now I can be more honest with you."

We were silent for a minute or two. I felt that she was on the verge of confiding in me, and I wasn't quite sure whether I wanted her confidences. She was sitting with her back to the entrance, so she didn't see Charles Granby-Smith come in with a girl, but she saw me acknowledge his gesture of recognition when he saw me. "Who is it?" she asked.

"A colleague of Julian's, and not one of his favorites. His name is Granby-Smith, he came last year. You must have met him," I added, knowing how sensitive she was at not being invited to the houses where she was likely to meet legation people.

"Oh yes," she said, "I know him, I've met him several times. He's quite a charmer. Is that what Julian has against him?"

"Julian's not jealous of him if that's what you mean. He knows that he has no reason to be. It's just that he and Julian rub each other the wrong way, and he's Julian's superior—as far as rank's concerned."

She let the subject drop. But the presence of someone she

knew, even though several tables away, had a bad effect on her. She went back to her most flippant tone, and talked too loudly, and although I no longer needed to worry about being told too much, I felt cheated in some way, as if an offer of serious friendship had suddenly been withdrawn without any reason.

Leaving the café, we passed Granby-Smith's table. He half rose as we went by, and before we were out of hearing, the girl he was with was asking him who we were. On a side street near the café were several waiting droshkies, and Sybil must have thought I intended to take one, for she said, as abruptly as earlier she had asked me to go with her to the doctor's, "Can you spare me a few more minutes and come in with me?"

Julian was probably home and wondering where I was. But I felt that I couldn't refuse. As we were going in at the side entrance of Capsa's, Micu came out. "What a pleasant surprise!" he said, gallantly kissing the tips of my fingers.

"I persuaded Joanna to come with me to see Charlie Chaplin," Sybil told him.

"I was looking for you," he said. "I thought you could drive home with me and leave Max's car here so that he can have it as soon as he gets back."

"I'm afraid not," Sybil said. "I'm going to a party at Joanna's this evening, and if it ends late I'll stay in town overnight."

"It will end late," I said. "Our parties always do."

Micu shrugged. "See you sometime tomorrow, then, Sybil. *Au revoir*, Madame."

His tone to me was noticeably colder than before, which wasn't surprising; I had openly underlined our intentional failure ever to invite him and Consuela to our house.

The upstairs rooms at Capsa's were Eastern European versions of rooms in a London "family hotel," with heavy nineteenth-century furnishings. The only bathroom was at the end of the passage and was shared by the occupants of the dozen rooms on the floor. It was hardly the place for Sybil to stay in her vulnerable physical condition, and I felt rather cross with her for not doing the thing properly while she was about it, and going to a private sanitarium—which could always be arranged if one had enough money. But that was probably the reason Sybil had risked the hole-and-corner method; Maximilian was generous with charge accounts but stingy with cash, and presumably he didn't have an account to which such a thing could be charged without his checking up on who had charged it.

Sybil's room smelled of kerosene and cosmetics. She locked the door. Maximilian's room adjoined hers; it, too, smelled of kerosene and cosmetics. She checked to see that no one was there, then she locked the communicating door, leaving the key in the lock. "God only knows how many people have a key to Max's room," she said. "That little rat Micu certainly has one. Thanks, by the way, for backing me up in that absolutely necessary lie. It was decent of you."

"That's all right. But I'm afraid I'll have to tell Julian—at least I'll have to tell him something. Luckily we weren't intending to go anywhere this evening, but we're not having anyone in, either. It's Fräulein's evening off, and we're going to play games with the children."

Sybil didn't answer. She was looking at herself in the dressing-table mirror, inspecting herself with extraordinary intensity.

"I look like a whore, don't I? An expensive whore."

Now I didn't answer. I didn't think she expected me to, I thought she was really talking to herself. But she turned on me truculently, as Julian sometimes did when he'd had too much to drink and wanted to pick a quarrel.

"Well, why don't you say something? I know why! It's because you're thinking that's just what I am—and you're damn well right."

I wasn't demonstrative with women. To touch another woman always made me feel awkward. But I knew that this was a moment when words were of no use at all, when a physical demonstration of affection was the only thing that would convince Sybil that I didn't despise her. I said, "Don't talk rot," but at the same time I put my arm around her shoulders. I turned her away from the mirror. "You should lie down now. Let me help you undo your dress at the back."

She allowed me first to take off her necklace and pendant earrings, and then to unhook her dress and pull it off over her head.

"Kind Joanna," she said, and stood there in her slip without moving while I put her dress on a hanger. She seemed not to know

98

what to do next, not to be able to act on her own. I led her to the bed and she sat down on the edge of it while I knelt on the floor and removed her shoes. There was something touching about her helplessness that took away my embarrassment and made me feel as if I were putting Cissy to bed when she was too tired to protest. Then I peeled off Sybil's silk stockings, and something changed. I became acutely aware of her and of my position in relation to hers. I looked up. Her greenish eyes met mine for a second, then shifted. But when one has long suspected something, if only subconsciously, a second is quite enough to confirm its existence.

She got in between the sheets and pulled the covers up over her. "I'm cold."

I hoped that she wasn't running a temperature; that, I knew, was a highly dangerous symptom in her case. I asked her if she had a thermometer, and she said that she had one and would take her own temperature later.

"And if it's up will you promise to call the doctor?"

"Yes, yes," she said impatiently, as if now she wanted to get rid of me, and there was nothing that I wanted more at that moment than to get away from her. But I hesitated to leave her alone. If all was not well, the next few hours could be crucial.

"If you'd like me to stay, I can easily call Julian and tell him to find another partner. . . ."

"No, please go."

"All right. When I get back from the country club I'll call you."

She made no response. She had buried her face in her pillow, and if she had been any other woman I would have thought that she was crying.

It was lucky that Julian and I were playing with the Elliotts, and not, for example, with Granby-Smith and one of the numerous girls with whom he was so popular, for my anxiety about Sybil made me play badly, and we lost the first three sets out of five, winning the last two only because Julian played a savage game at the net, volleying every ball that came within his long reach before I had a chance to miss it.

After he had redeemed, at least partially, his reputation as a first-class tennis player, we all went into the clubhouse for drinks.

Granby-Smith was there, with the girl who had been with him in the café, and whom he now introduced as a friend on a visit from England. "By the way," he said to me, "what was the name of the rather remarkable-looking lady with you this afternoon—her face was so familiar, I know I've met her somewhere. . . ."

"That was Madame Gavriolesco," I said, not entirely surprised to hear that he didn't know her name—she was capable of saying that she had met people to whom she had never been introduced, or of pretending to know someone much better than she actually did.

"She was very striking," the English girl said. "Is she a well-known actress—or something like that?"

Granby-Smith smiled, rather unpleasantly, I thought, and I felt impelled to defend Sybil against his unspoken sneer.

"She is the English wife of a rather well-known Rumanian," I said, "and she's one of my best friends."

At that, Julian gave me a look of approval. I had redeemed my failure as a tennis partner.

After one round of drinks, the Elliotts said that they had to leave, they had a dinner engagement, and Granby-Smith offered to give us a lift back to town if we felt like staying on for a while. "Thanks," said Julian curtly, "but I think we'll leave with the Elliotts."

From mixed motives, I softened Julian's rebuff by saying, "We really can't stay any longer, we've got some people coming in for dinner."

I hadn't had a chance to tell Julian about my afternoon; when I got back from Capsa's the Elliotts were already at the apartment. Now, as soon as they had dropped us off, Julian said, "Why on earth did you make up that story about our having people to dinner? I *wanted* to snub Granby-Smith."

"I had to make it up because of Sybil. Max is away, and she's staying in town tonight, and a party at our flat is her alibi."

"Alibi! Look here, Joey, I'm not against Sybil, and I liked the way you stood up for her just now, but I'm damned if I'm going to get involved in her intrigues, or let you get involved."

"I'm already involved," I said, and I told him everything.

He took it very seriously. If anything happened to Sybil, he said, I might find myself in a pretty awkward position, and it suddenly struck me that she had deliberately maneuvered me into taking this risk—for her own devious ends. Then I thought how cynical I was becoming, and I was feeling ashamed of my suspicion, when Julian confirmed it. "You should know by now," he said, "that Sybil is completely unscrupulous, and I'm very much afraid that she has made a fool of you. For some reason she wanted you as a witness."

"I promised to call her as soon as I got home."

"By all means call her—it's in our interests to keep her alive," Julian said grimly.

The phone rang several times before Sybil answered it, in a rather faint voice. "Hello?"

"Sybil . . ."

"Oh, it's you."

"How do you feel?"

"Bloody awful."

"Is your temperature up?"

"It's a hundred and three—and I'm having terrible cramps."

"Have you called the doctor?"

"No."

"Then I'm going to call him."

"No, don't. I don't want him to come here. . . ."

"I'll be with you in ten minutes," I said, and hung up.

"Well?" said Julian.

"She's very ill, and she hasn't called the doctor—she doesn't want him to go and see her there."

"Call Mavrescu," Julian said, "and tell him it's an emergency. If he bucks I'll speak to him . . . no, wait, I'll put in the call and tell him that you want to speak to him, that's better."

Mavrescu was my own gynecologist, in fact it might be said that he was the diplomatic corps gynecologist; all the diplomatic wives went to him, and he had a reputation for being an exceptionally honest Rumanian as well as a good doctor.

He was having dinner when Julian called him to the phone. I told him briefly the story that was later to be the official version of what had happened; that I had lunched with Sybil, who had complained of stomach trouble and hadn't felt like eating. But we had gone to see a film together, and later to a café, and she had seemed better. As Maximilian was out of town I had invited her to spend the evening with us and some of our friends, but she had just called from her room at Capsa's to say that she felt too ill to come.

He said, "What are her symptoms?" I told him without comment, and he immediately agreed to meet me at Capsa's in twenty minutes' time. He must have guessed what was up, but the fact that the call came from me and Julian was enough to absolve him of any complicity in what had gone before, and at the same time obligated him to do something about it. Already I was proving my value as a witness. Without waiting to change my clothes, I took a droshky down to Capsa's. I wanted to talk to Sybil before the doctor arrived.

She appeared alarmingly ill, and she had obviously been crying. I cursed myself for having left her. She didn't seem to mind my having told Julian everything, and she smiled when I recapitulated what I had told Dr. Mavrescu over the phone.

"I have one more favor to ask of you," she said. "If I die . . ."

"You're not going to die."

"I may—I'd rather like to, as a matter of fact—and if I do, there's someone who has to be told the truth. Will you do that for me, Joanna?"

"That's asking a lot, Sybil."

"It's my last will and testament," she said, with a touch of her usual flippancy, or an attempt at it, "to the man I love I bequeath—the truth. You can't refuse the last request of a dying woman, can you?"

Dr. Mavrescu's arrival temporarily rescued me. While he was examining Sybil, I waited outside on the landing. There was no one around, and no sounds came from behind the doors that opened off the landing, but I had a sense of eyes and ears at keyholes. The doctor came out in less than five minutes, looking very grave. He said for the listening doors, "We'll have to get her appendix out immediately. I'll have an ambulance here in fifteen minutes. I'll warn the management—you help her to get ready." Then he put his hand on my shoulder and said in a low voice, "You did well to call me, Madame."

I helped Sybil into a robe and slippers. Her skin was hot and dry, and her eyes were wild—but with something more than fever.

"Will you do what I asked, Joanna?"

Her would-be flippant words about the last request of a dying woman had been a more effective shaft than she knew. "Either Julian or I will find a way of doing it," I said, thinking that we might have to descend to writing an anonymous letter.

"Is that a promise?"

"Yes."

I thought I saw a flicker of triumph in her wild eyes, even of wicked amusement. She took a small velvet jeweler's box from under her pillow. "And see that he gets this. It's a ring."

I slipped the box into my handbag. The ambulance men were already knocking on the door, and I was hoping that she would forget to give me the name of her lover, but she caught at my arm and whispered it to me while the men outside knocked for the second time, and I knew why she had withheld it until the last possible minute. It was Charles Granby-Smith.

Six days and several light-years of anxiety later, I went to visit her in Dr. Mavrescu's private sanitarium. Up until then, only Maximilian had been permitted to see her, and then only for a few minutes. I found her lying back on her pillows, waxily pale and surrounded by flowers, almost as if she were dead.

"People have been so kind in sending flowers," she murmured in the hearing of the nurse, "but if you hadn't had the sense to suspect appendicitis they might have been piled on my coffin."

As soon as we were alone, she said, "Well, I saved you and Julian some embarrassment by not dying, didn't I?"

"Frankly, yes."

"I suppose you waited to see what happened before telling Julian about Charles?"

"Yes, I did."

"I'm glad. Now that I'm still alive I'd just as soon Julian didn't know."

"Do you wish you hadn't told *me*?"

"No. But I probably wouldn't have told you if I hadn't thought I was a goner. And if I hadn't seen Charles with that girl just when he knew that I. . . ." She broke off in midsentence, but I didn't let her get away with it.

"So he knew all the time."

"Of course he knew—he paid."

"Then why on earth did you make me promise to tell him the truth if anything happened?"

She had the grace to blush. "I owe you an apology, Joanna. I was beastly to you. I tricked you into coming with me to that awful doctor—but that was chiefly because I was frightened to go alone and I couldn't trust anyone else not to talk. I was frightened because I'd let things go on too long, out of some lunatic hope, I suppose. Anyway, I knew that what I was going to have done was more dangerous than usual, and so did the doctor—poor devil, that's why I didn't want him to be seen at Capsa's. And then, after you'd been so decent to me, I worked on your sense of loyalty and friendship to make you promise to do something that I wanted done out of pure revenge. Seeing Charles with that girl just at that moment made me want to die just to spite him, and made me want to humiliate him as well. And when you told me that he and Julian disliked each other, I saw just how I could do it. As for the ring . . . sending him that was like spitting on something to make it worthless."

I had the ring with me, but before I could give it to her, Maximilian came in. Slipping the box back into my handbag, I got up to go. Maximilian pressed my hand emotionally, "But for you, Madame . . ."

"You mustn't go without seeing the criminal," Sybil said. "Show it to her, Max."

From among the bottles of eau de cologne on the bedside table he brought forward a test tube with a healthy-looking appendix in it. "Here is that small criminal," he said, and wagged his finger at it as if to say, *Naughty, naughty.*

A few days later I got a message from Sybil, asking me to come over and see her that morning if I could manage it. This time I found her sitting up in bed and looking much better. "Max will be taking me home this afternoon," she said, "and then it won't be so easy to see you alone."

My eye lit on the test tube, which was now in a prominent position—on display, as it were, for visitors.

"That appendix . . ." I said.

"It's mine, my very own. There's nothing wrong with it at all—it's a perfect specimen—but that angel doctor of yours thought I'd better have it out—for lots of reasons—so as soon as the other thing was under control, out it came. Have you seen Charles lately?"

"I've seen him one or twice at the club."

"With that girl?"

"Yes."

"Who is she?"

"A friend from England, a Lady Betty Something-or-other—I didn't catch the last name when he introduced her. She's here on a short visit."

Sybil asked no more questions. There were tears in her eyes. And I thought, not for the first time, what unworthy objects women weep for. "Forgive me for howling," she said. "It's just weakness. Find me a clean hanky, will you? They're in one of those drawers."

When I gave her the handkerchief, she took my hand and held it for a moment, as if it were a lifeline. "I love Charles," she said. "I really love him. I want to divorce Max, or have our marriage annulled—I could, you know, he's been impotent from the start. But Charles says that a scandal like that would ruin his chances of ever becoming an ambassador, with me as his wife, and I suppose that's true. But he wants to marry me, and he's promised to marry me, after what he calls a 'decent interval,' when Max dies—which *could* happen at any moment—he's getting on for seventy, and he's got all sorts of things wrong with him—but probably won't. It's just the people who ought to die, the really evil people, who hang on the longest."

*Evil* . . . a strong word, coming from someone as cynical and sophisticated as Sybil. But even if Maximilian *was* evil, her unconcealed wish for his death chilled me.

"If we lived in another age," she said, looking down and tying her tear-soaked handkerchief into knots, "we'd hurry things up a bit. But we're too civilized—at least Charles is. I'm not so sure about myself. Have you ever felt like murder, Joanna?"

"I've never hated anyone quite enough for that," I said, "but I understand those people who assassinate tyrants."

"I don't hate Max. Hatred's too good for him. I *loathe* him."

"I can't imagine why you ever married him—unless it was for money."

"Being married to a rich man isn't having money—I can assure

105

you of that. But I didn't marry him entirely for his money. My motives were mixed. Motives usually are, aren't they? I was, believe it or not, naive. I didn't grasp just what Max's social position was, I saw myself making an entrance into society, with a capital *S*, forming some kind of *salon*—'that witty and charming hostess, Madame Gavriolesco'—and all that rot. And then, of course, I was in love. Oh, not with Max! With Consuela. At that time I thought I was a lesbian, in which case what could be more convenient than an old, impotent husband with lots of money who didn't ask too many questions. You must admit, the situation was appealing."

"It wouldn't have appealed to me."

"Well, it doesn't appeal to me anymore. It lost its appeal when Max brought Micu onto the scene."

There was a long silence.

"It's hell," she said at last. "I never used to believe in hell, but I do now. I'm in it. And I'm still clear-eyed enough to know where I am and to want to get out of it. But I've got to get out of it soon, or I won't want to—I've noticed that people get used to their hells, and then they really are damned."

There was another long silence. What she had said was unanswerable. And painful, for reasons unconnected with her. I looked around me in search of something—a book, a magazine, even a bouquet of flowers—to bring us back again to the ordinary physical world. What I did find was a little icon, propped up against a vase of flowers and partially hidden by a big bottle of eau de cologne. I picked it up. It represented a *mater dolorosa*, and I knew enough about icons to recognize it as an antique, and a gem of an antique at that.

"You'll never guess who sent me that," Sybil said. "It's priceless."

Uncertain of just how she meant that phrase, I said nothing. I had already guessed that Lucrèce had given it to her. I put it back on the cluttered table. I didn't want to talk about Lucrèce.

"Let me give you back your ring before someone comes in," I said.

Sybil took the box, but she didn't immediately put it away.

"Did you look at it?"

"No."

"Honest Joanna. That's what I like about you, you still have scruples. Would you like to see it?"

"Yes—if you want to show it to me."

She took the ring from its dark blue velvet pad and handed it to me. Made of silver, and wrought with the delicacy and detail of the old Italian craftsmen, its broad circle was formed by three nude bodies, two female and one male, obscenely linked together. I felt that Sybil was watching me closely, waiting for my reaction. "Look on the underside," she said softly.

There, engraved in minute letters, were three names: *Sybil, Micu,* and *Consuela.*

"Max had one made for each of us...."

Speechless, I handed it back to her.

"You don't know the half of it yet," she said. "There are things that I don't suppose you've ever even imagined. But you needn't look so alarmed. I'm not going to tell you about them—I still have some sense of decency left."

And here I shall leave her for the time being. There was nothing I could do to help her out of the hell she was in. The only person who could do anything to save her was Granby-Smith, and he had no intention of doing it. But I couldn't tell Sybil that. And she wouldn't have believed it. She had to have hope.

# 4

# Nicolai and Lucrèce

## I

To trace the patterns of Nicolai and Lucrèce from the beginning, I must go back again to our first Rumanian spring, and that Easter Sunday morning when they brought us home after celebrating the Feast of the Resurrection at the Gavriolescos' country estate. The Calea Victoria was so deserted that the policeman on traffic duty, who knew us, rushed across the road to give us the kiss of peace from under moustaches whose waxed ends were several inches long. Nicolai and Lucrèce, driving away, saw it and made forbidden U turns behind his back, with a wave to us.

Our apartment was on the top floor of an old and ramshackle building in a large courtyard, where most of the dwellings were the humble homes and workshops of independent craftsmen of all kinds—shoemakers, tailors, stonecutters, carpenters—who worked in their doorways or out in the yard when the weather was fine. They were Julian's chief reason for taking the apartment. He felt more at ease among these simple artisans, who took so much pride in producing a well-fitting shoe or a nicely carved tombstone, than he did among people of his own class.

At this hour—it was almost seven o'clock—on an ordinary morning, the court would have been humming with talk and the sound of tools, but now all was quiet; everyone was asleep, getting over the joy and excitement of the Resurrection.

On parting with us, Nicolai and Lucrèce had said that they hoped to see us again before very long.

Climbing the three flights of stairs up to our apartment, I asked Julian whether he wanted to see them again.

"I'm not sure. Do you?"

"I'm not sure, either."

We were too exhausted to discuss the weekend before we went to sleep. And I, for one, didn't want to. My feelings were too mixed. In addition to the physical strain of being up all night, and eating and drinking far too much, I was conscious of an emotional strain, a sense of having been put to some sort of test, and not only by our hosts, but by the Amans as well.

Yet their attitude to us had been perfect. In a country where everyone wanted something—if only to go to bed with you—and people asked the most personal questions on first acquaintance, and reserve, even on such things as the size of your income, was considered unfriendly, it had been a relief to meet people as reserved and self-contained as this brother and sister, who had given no sign of wanting anything from us, and who had no social advantage to gain from knowing us.

Why, then, was I so ambivalent about seeing more of them— what was I afraid of? And what was Julian afraid of? But as time went by and we heard nothing from the Amans, I wondered why they had said anything about seeing us again in the first place.

These questions were still unanswered when I left Bucharest for our first Rumanian summer by the sea, at Constanza, in the unhygienic villa Julian had rented from the Turkish consul. And it was there, on the little secluded beach that I went to every day with the children and their Fräulein, that I next encountered Lucrèce.

It was almost time for us to leave and drive back to our villa for lunch and a siesta. While the Fräulein was getting the children dried and dressed, I went for a walk to some rocks at the other end of the cove. There, sitting all by herself at the edge of the water, was Lucrèce. One-half of her immensely long hair hung shining and loose, and the other half she was braiding.

Intent upon what she was doing, she didn't see me. I sat down on the sand at a little distance from her and watched her plaiting the pale-gold strands in and out. I wanted to go and speak to her, but her evident self-absorption, and the fact that she and her brother had made no effort to renew their acquaintance with us, made me afraid of intruding where I wasn't wanted. I decided on a childish solution; I would walk past her, and if she didn't recognize me I would say nothing.

She was so close to the water that to pass in front of her I had to enter it and wade through the shallows. I was within a yard of her when a child, a little girl, bumped into me, upsetting her pail of water. I stooped to help her refill it, but she cried and ran away from me to Lucrèce, who looked up, and recognized me with her haunting half-smile. I sat down beside her while she comforted the child and sent her off again, bucket in hand. "That is my little niece, Marioara," she said.

It never occurred to me that the child might be Nicolai's daughter, I didn't think of him as having been married. Lucrèce, I thought, had probably confused *niece* with *cousin*—a common Rumanian error. She asked where we were staying, how we liked Constanza, how long we expected to be there. "We are only here for the day," she said. "We drove down last night, and we are leaving again in a few hours. Nicolai had a client to see in the port—I must drive back very soon and pick him up."

Pip came along at that moment to tell me that our droshky was waiting. I introduced him to Lucrèce, and he shook hands with her and said "How do you do?" like a grown-up person. But for all his good manners, he stared at her hair. "It's very long, isn't it?" she said, flipping the finished braids back over her shoulders.

Encouraged, he asked her, "Are you a mermaid?"

"Yes," she said gravely, "I am. I live on a rock far out to sea."

"I thought so," Pip said.

He asked me no questions about her. But next day he said, "She's not here. She must have gone back to her rock."

A couple of days later, Julian arrived. "We saw a mermaid on the beach," Pip told him. "She was doing her hair. . . ."

"Don't tell lies!" Julian said.

"But she *said* she was a mermaid—didn't she, Mummy?"

I hadn't intended to tell Julian of my meeting with Lucrèce, but now I was obliged to. "You see," Pip said to his father, "I wasn't telling a lie."

"Lucky for you," said Julian, "you're saved this time."

But in backing up Pip's story, I had conjured into being a cloud that hung between me and Julian all day, held there by our mutual secretiveness about our feelings for Nicolai and Lucrèce, which was hard to explain. There was nothing to hide, except, at least in my case, a vague troubling of the emotions that I didn't define as sexual because it emanated from both of them equally, although my meeting with Lucrèce had told me that it was not unconnected with their enigmatic physical beauty.

I had avoided questioning Sybil about them, but she had volunteered the information that although they were in the topmost layer of Bucharest society, they lived reclusive lives. "They never go to parties," she said, "and they never give any. They have a mania for privacy. They sometimes go to the theater or the opera, but they sit by themselves—wild horses wouldn't drag them into our box. And they spend much more time at their country place near Brasov than they do at their town house."

But it was at a party that I next encountered them, a grand ball at the legation, given as a farewell to the first secretary and his wife. He had been in the post for several years, kept there longer than was customary because of his popularity with the Rumanian royal family. But now he was being promoted and sent to a Scandinavian capital as chargé d'affaires. I was dancing with him when I saw Lucrèce come in, followed by Nicolai, and even in this brilliant crowd their appearance was striking, and in a regal way. The other women were dressed in the sleeveless, knee-length evening dresses fashionable at the time, but Lucrèce was wearing a floor-length, tight-fitting dress of black velvet with a high neck and long sleeves, her only ornament a pair of gold pendant earrings. Her thick golden braids were arranged like a halo, giving her a Byzantine look.

"Oh, there are the Amans!" my partner said.

And I said, in spontaneous response to the note of pleasure in his voice, "How splendid they are!"

"Splendid? Well, yes, now that you draw my attention to it, I suppose they are rather splendid. I knew their father very well. He was quite a prominent man at court, very popular with the royal family. He was killed in a car crash not long after I came here, but I had known him for years before that. He left his children with a couple of houses and quite a lot of land but precious little hard cash, so Nicolai had to put his law training to practical use and I've recommended him to a few people I know. He's a bright young fellow and well up on international law. His sister is considered to be quite a good painter—though I'm no judge of that."

He obviously assumed that I knew them better than I did. "I met them only once," I said, to correct this impression, "at the Gavriolescos'. A relative of theirs is married to Maximilian Gavriolesco's daughter."

"Ah yes, Maximilian Gavriolesco. His wife's English, isn't she."

It was a statement, not a question, and the tone in which it was made added an unspoken rider to the effect that in marrying Maximilian, Sybil had not only changed her passport, which was forgivable, but had also discredited her unchangeable national heritage, which was unforgivable.

As the music came to a stop, we found ourselves close to Nicolai and Lucrèce. My partner shook hands with Lucrèce and touched Nicolai affectionately on the shoulder. "I'm so glad to see you both here, it was good of you to come. . . . I believe that you and Mrs. Crest already know each other. . . . Oh dear, my wife is making frantic signals—one of the princesses must be arriving. . . ."

"How have you been," asked Nicolai, "since we saw you being kissed by a policeman on the Calea Victoria?"

"That was an experience," I said, and Lucrèce smiled her subtle half-smile, conveying the impression that she understood the wider implications of my remark.

"Mrs. Crest and I have met since then," she said, "on the beach near Constanza, and her son took me for a mermaid."

"Oh yes," said Nicolai. "I remember your telling me about that."

"We had hoped to see you again before this," Lucrèce said, "but the time passes so fast that one does not observe where it goes, and I have been getting ready for an exhibition of my paintings."

"Oh, how exciting! When is it going to be?"

"Sometime in the spring," she said vaguely.

"What will be sometime in the spring?" Julian asked, joining us.

"An exhibition of my sister's paintings," Nicolai said.

"Really?" said Julian, turning to Lucrèce. "How interesting! Do let us know when the exhibition opens, I'd love to see your work."

"We both would," I said.

Lucrèce looked at us for a moment, as if she were trying to separate the truth from mere politeness.

"In that case," she said, "I shall send you an invitation to the opening."

"My sister is very modest," Nicolai said. "She sends invitations only to people she believes really want to come."

"It is not modesty," said Lucrèce. "I am proud of my work. But I do not want to put my friends into the position where they have to make an excuse. That is such an uncomfortable position."

The music started again, and Julian asked her to dance. I danced with Nicolai. In these high-toned surroundings his formal restraint was less remarkable than it had been in the Gavriolesco atmosphere. But now it affected me more strongly and less agreeably. I felt as if I were dancing with one of those classical statues that he and his sister had called to mind when we met for the first time, with a figure in the form of a man, but cold and inaccessible as marble.

We didn't dance together, or even speak with each other, again that evening, but he and Lucrèce kept coming into view, perhaps because I was looking for them. I observed that they were acquainted with almost everyone there, including the royalty, and it was obvious that their connection with the Gavriolescos was purely accidental, the result of their cousin's marriage to Consuela, which was probably a calculated exchange of rank for money—or at least expectations. All of which made their air of aloofness during that weekend understandable, but didn't explain why they were there. But even here, in their native waters, so to speak, they seemed aloof and detached, and in some way unreal; they were like two golden galleons of a past era that appear, in certain lights, to haunt their former seas.

The engraved invitation to the *vernissage*, the private opening of Lucrèce's show in a little gallery on the Calea Victoria, was in French, and requested the honor of our company from four to six in the afternoon. When we arrived there, at the midway point of five o'clock, it was immediately apparent that Lucrèce had meant what she said about limiting her invitations to those who were really interested. Not more than a dozen people were present, and most of them turned out to be artists or art critics. The exceptions were a stately middle-aged woman in black, wearing a string of what I was quite sure were real pearls, whom Lucrèce introduced as her aunt, and a very old Englishwoman, eccentrically dressed in a heavy tweed coat and skirt of a past fashion, with a Tyrolean hat crammed down over a head of untidy white hair, whom Nicolai introduced as "Our dear Miss Godwin, who came from England to be our nanny when we were children and has stayed with us ever since because she knows that we couldn't live without her."

"You lived without me all right when you were in England," Miss Godwin said, a trifle tartly.

"And you had the time of your life without us, Nana, you can't deny that."

"I don't deny it. I did what I'd always wanted to do. I went on a world cruise."

"And what did you think of the world?" Julian asked.

The old woman looked at him keenly, out of pale blue eyes overhung with bushy white eyebrows. "Are you making fun of me, young man?"

"Not at all. I've seen a lot of the world myself, and I've formed my opinion, and now I'd like to hear yours."

"There's nothing wrong with the world," Miss Godwin said. "How could there be? God made it and saw that it was good. It's the people who live in it that I don't think much of."

"God made them too, Nana," Nicolai said softly.

"But the Devil put his finger into *that* pie," Miss Godwin said, "as you very well know."

"Miss Godwin read to us from the Bible every Sunday when we were children," Nicolai said.

The conversation was interrupted by the arrival of one of the royal princesses, who embraced Lucrèce and the stately aunt, had her hand kissed by Nicolai, and exchanged a few polite words with us in English—we were the only people there connected with the British legation, or any other legation, for that matter. Accompanied by Nicolai and Lucrèce and the aunt, she made a tour of the gallery, commenting on the exhibits in French. Before one, an impressionistic watercolor of the Summer Palace at Sinaia, she stood for a long time. "*Ça, c'est mon enfance,*" she said, "*plus belle que toutes les beautés de la Grèce. Gardez-la pour moi, ma chérie.*"

After she had gone, Micu and Consuela came in with Sybil and Maximilian, and I suspected that Micu had been told to see to it that the Gavriolescos didn't appear until after the princess had left; perhaps the aunt had made a point of this, for her manner to Sybil and Maximilian was so cold that it was almost insulting. And she was only a little warmer to Micu and Consuela, who had—I'm sure she thought most unfortunately—got connected with her by marriage.

Maximilian bought two paintings, and talked with the critics as if he could buy them as well, which, of course, he could have if Lucrèce had allowed him to. There was no question of our buying any of the paintings, they were priced far too high for us, but over in a corner there was a little drawing that I coveted. It was a sketch of Nicolai, reading, seen in a mirror with Lucrèce behind him making the sketch of him and of herself. It was a beautifully composed drawing, and it conveyed their essential unity, which went deeper than mere physical resemblance and conferred singularity on both of them at once.

"Do you think we could possibly afford to buy it?" I asked Julian, rather timidly and without much hope, for although it was not as far out of our range as the paintings were, it was priced very high for a small drawing.

"Of course we can't afford it," Julian said. "If we buy it we'll have to do without something else. The question is, what are we willing to sacrifice for it?"

It was a shock to realize that he wanted the drawing as much as I did.

When we told Lucrèce that we wished to buy it, she said, "But that drawing is not for sale! That is why I put that big price on it."

"My sister is very illogical," Nicolai said. "She doesn't want to seem so proud of a little self-portrait that she must exhibit it even though it isn't for sale, so she puts a ridiculously high price on it instead."

"I am sorry," Lucrèce said. "It was misleading."

"It was positively fraudulent," Julian said. "Joanna and I have spent the last half hour trying to decide which of our needs to sacrifice for this work of art. . . ."

"And arguing over where to hang it," I said, carrying on the banter to conceal a disappointment that was out of all proportion to the actual value of what was being denied me.

"Oh," said Lucrèce, "I am so sorry. . . ."

"They could sue you," her brother said, "for offering something for sale on false pretenses, or for causing extreme mental anguish—I can think of half a dozen plaints."

"I'll know whom to consult when I want to sue someone," Julian said, "but it's more likely to be my landlord than your sister."

Sybil came up. "What's the argument?"

"No argument," I said. "We wanted to buy this drawing, but it isn't for sale—unless the artist changes her mind at some future date."

"You'll never get that," Sybil said, "never. What are you people doing this evening—shall we all have dinner together at Capsa's?"

But Nicolai and Lucrèce were dining with the aunt, and we were going on to a cocktail party given by the military attaché and his wife, who had snubbed Sybil unmercifully at a recent charity tea. I was now so irritated by Sybil's remark about the unattainability of the drawing that I told her just where we were going.

"Enjoy yourselves," she said, "I wouldn't be caught dead at that woman's house." And I thought rather spitefully that she would never be given the opportunity.

Julian was thoughtful as we left the gallery. He said, "It was rather an oddly assorted gathering, wasn't it? And so small—I felt that we were rather out of place. But I suppose that we made it practically impossible for Lucrèce not to invite us."

"I don't think so," I said. "If Lucrèce hadn't wanted us there, she wouldn't have sent us the invitation."

He was silent for a minute or two; then he said, "You wanted that drawing very badly, didn't you?"

"Yes. But so did you."

"You're right," he said. "I did. But I'm damned if I know why."

When we were walking up the driveway to the military attaché's villa, he said suddenly, "If we were to invite them to dinner, do you think they would come?" And he didn't have to tell me whom he meant.

It was rather like inviting two shy forest animals to dinner. To reassure them, I said in my note to Lucrèce that there would be just the four of us.

When five days passed and I got no answer, I didn't know what to think. Then Nicolai telephoned. My letter had been forwarded to them in the country, he said, where he had left Lucrèce that morning, but she would be joining him in Bucharest in a few days, and they would be very pleased to dine with us.

I said, "I hope that seven o'clock is not too early for you, but I want you to see my children before they go to bed."

"I would like that," he said. He sounded tired and depressed, and I thought that perhaps he had just lost a case.

On the day of the dinner I didn't tell Pip who was coming. Both children were in the sitting room with us when Nicolai and Lucrèce were shown in. Cissy sat solemnly staring at them, but Pip stood up.

"Do you remember me?" asked Lucrèce. "We met on the beach last summer."

"Yes, I remember," he said. "You're the mermaid." He didn't seem in the least surprised to see her in our sitting room, fully dressed.

"This is my brother Nicolai," she said.

Nicolai held out his hand. "How do you do, Pip? I think I'd better tell you at once that I am not a merman."

"I see," said Pip. "You're just a man."

Cissy scrambled up from the rug and went up to Nicolai. "I like you," she said. He laughed, and picked her up and put her on his shoulder, from where she looked down on Pip in triumph.

Unlike most of our other guests, who would give the children only a minute or two of perfunctory attention, Nicolai and Lucrèce gave all of theirs to Pip and Cissy until the Fräulein came to take them to bed. This interest in my children flattered me, fed my maternal pride, but I could see that Julian rather resented Lucrèce's absorption with Pip, to whom he said a noticeably curt goodnight.

"They are beautiful," said Lucrèce when the door had closed behind them and the Fräulein, "and your son has such perfect manners. I am very fond of children, and so is Nicolai."

"Wait until you have children of your own," Julian said. "Being a parent changes one's viewpoint a bit."

"In what way?" asked Lucrèce.

"When you see so much of them, and are responsible for everything connected with them, there are times when you think of them as a bit of a nuisance."

"I would never think of my child as a nuisance," Lucrèce said.

"Nor I," said Nicolai.

"Just wait," said Julian, "just wait and see what you say when you're in a position to speak from actual experience."

There was a moment of silence, the kind that follows a blunder. Then Nicolai said slowly, "I will tell you something that is not generally known outside of my immediate family. I am already in that position. The little girl who was with Lucrèce on the beach near Constanza is my daughter. But as you must have discovered by now, my compatriots are incurably inquisitive, and if I were to let it be known that I am a father, my sister and I would be plagued with questions, and if we didn't answer them all chapter and verse, the most ridiculous romances would be invented about me."

"I understand perfectly, my dear fellow," said Julian, "and I appreciate your confidence in our discretion."

I, too, appreciated that. But what he had told us upset me. And I sensed that Lucrèce was distressed by her brother's admission—after all, they hardly knew us. She said nothing, but her expression was grave, as if she had been reminded of something painful. Fortunately, the moment of all-round embarrassment was cut short by our little Transylvanian maid, who shyly announced that dinner was served.

At dinner the conversation was carried on chiefly by the two men. Lucrèce was very quiet. She was attentive to what was being said, as she had been before at the Gavriolescos', but now her habitual expression of brooding melancholy was lightened less often by her enchanting half-smile. The talk was on impersonal subjects: life in England, the possibility of another war, the justice or injustice of the Versailles treaty from the Hungarian and Rumanian standpoints. Socialism. And finally the plight of the peasants in Rumania and their intrinsic worth, as opposed to the intrinsic corruption of Bucharest society, and the inevitability of a revolution.

Finding a member of the landed aristocracy in complete agreement with him on these points took the wind out of Julian's sails. Cheated of what he enjoyed more than anything else—an argument with the "other side"—he tried to provoke one by saying aggressively, "That's all very well, my dear fellow, but theoretical agreement isn't enough. As a landowner, with virtual power of life and death over your peasants, what are you doing about it?"

"All that it lies in my power to do," Nicolai said equably. "One day you must visit us in the country and see for yourself."

Then Lucrèce asked Julian very quietly, but unexpectedly, "And what are you doing in practical support of your beliefs?"

"I think," said Nicolai, "that the question is rather, What are you, as an ardent Socialist, doing in an elite body chosen from among the wealthy upper classes to further the interests of a capitalistic empire?"

"That's a fair question," Julian said, "and one that I often ask myself. I'm not at home in what you call the 'elite body,' in fact I'm a thorn in its side. It would love to eject me, and probably would but for the fact that its nature is changing. The man who has just replaced your father's old friend is a factory worker's son with no private income, a man who earned his own education by winning scholarships and who speaks with a Lancashire accent. He's the new diplomat—the man of the people."

"How romantic you are," Nicolai said. "It's easy to see that you're an aristocratic idealist—exactly as I am."

"What else can we be? We can't alter the fact that we were born into the so-called upper classes. We can only repudiate them ideologically. But I'm not all that aristocratic. I've got a common strain in me, thank God. My maternal grandmother, bless her, came from what you would call 'peasant stock.' "

"I wasn't questioning your sincerity," Nicolai said, "and I don't think Lucrèce was, either—to do that would be impertinent of us, considering what we are, and where we stand in the public eye. What we were challenging was your right to challenge us from your particular position. As for the common strain, there's probably peasant blood in us too. So we're pretty much in the same boat—although you, as an Englishman, will be safer than we will be when the storm breaks. Here, even those of us who have tried to effect some change will be wiped out."

"Our sins have been too great," said Lucrèce. "We have earned annihilation."

Julian looked at her rather sharply, as if he suspected irony. But her expression was deadly serious, serious to the point that it inhibited all further speech; and once again the four of us hung suspended in an unnatural silence, so intense this time, so heavy, that when I finally broke it with a suggestion that we should move, that coffee and liqueurs were awaiting us in the other room, I felt as if I had interrupted the minute of national silence on Armistice Day by blowing on a tin whistle.

Julian put on a new dance record, a Boston, and said to Lucrèce, "Shall we dance?"

Nicolai looked questioningly at me, but I said, "Not just now," and we sat sipping cognac and coffee, and watching the slow, dreamy dance of the other two. Glancing at Nicolai, I saw that he was gazing with extraordinary intensity at Lucrèce, and looking from him to her, I saw something in her expression that chilled me, something that I hadn't noticed before, and that corresponded to her brother's marble inaccessibility. She *is* a mermaid, I thought, an Ondine, cold as the sea, able to strangle a man with a single braid of her long hair, and pull him out with her to her mythical rock, and drown him.

It was a hot night. The Rumanian spring was so short that it could hardly be described as a season. After the first thaw would come a few milky days, still smelling of snow while the almond trees burst into blossom, and cool, damp evenings, and then it would be summer. But through May and most of June the heat was not unbearable, and after the unrelenting cold of the winter months it gave one a feeling of freedom to stretch and unwrap oneself. So after our guests had left, Julian and I took off all our clothes and lay down on our bed naked because the night was hot rather than as a prelude to making love. All the same, it wasn't like Julian to be so remote, so passive, so silent.

"Julian . . . are you asleep?"

"No. I'm thinking."

"What are you thinking about?"

"Those two. How strange they are."

"In what way do you think they are strange?"

"I'm damned if I know. They're just not like anyone else I've ever known."

There was a long silence. A troubling silence. At last I put out my hand in a tentative caress. His flesh felt cold to my touch. I abruptly withdrew my hand, as if I had touched something slimy.

"What's the matter?" Julian asked.

"Nothing. I was only saying goodnight."

"Goodnight," he said, moving out to sea.

## II

It was from the windows of a train that I first saw the wild, romantic landscape in which Nicolai and Lucrèce lived their real lives.

The train was the fabulous Orient Express, on which I traveled for the first time when we moved from Holland to Rumania. Its ultimate destination was Istanbul. On the way it would stop at Vienna, Budapest, Bucharest; names charged with the magic of the unknown, and with intriguing labels attached to them. Vienna was flighty, Bucharest frivolous and corrupt, Budapest wicked—the wickedest city in Europe. The train arrived there at midnight and stayed for about twenty minutes in the murky, glass-domed depot, where I longed to leave the train, so great was the fascination of wickedness.

By morning we were traveling through the land of werewolves and vampires, Transylvania, where the blue Carpathians rose tier upon tier from fold upon fold of pine-covered slopes.

Isolated from the world in an upland valley between the dark folds and the high blue distances was the true home of the Amans.

On a Friday afternoon in September, soon after we got back from our Bulgarian summer, Julian called up to say that Nicolai was there in the chancery. "He's driving up to their country place tomorrow morning, and he wants to take us with him. He has to be here on Monday for a court case, so he can drive us back with him on Sunday night. Have we any engagements that we can't get out of?"

"We're supposed to be dining with the Elliotts tomorrow evening, and we're invited to Mrs. Winthrop's at-home on Sunday afternoon."

"*That's* easy enough to skip," Julian said, making it clear that he wanted to accept Nicolai's invitation.

"I think I can get out of the Elliotts' dinner without offending them," I said.

"Good! Hold on a moment, Nicolai wants to talk to you."

In the four months since he and Lucrèce had spent the evening with us, months of total silence on their part, my imagination had worked on the impressions that evening had left me with, and had built up around Nicolai's fatherhood precisely those absurd romances that he wanted to avoid. His matter-of-fact tone on the telephone washed them away like a cold shower. "Hello! How are you? I'm so glad you can come. I just wanted to tell you to be sure to bring some stout shoes—we'll be doing a lot of walking."

I told Amanda Elliott the truth. She was a new enough arrival in Rumania, and naive enough, to regard an invitation to stay with a prince and princess in what she imagined to be their Transylvanian castle as something that no one in his right mind would turn down. "How thrilling!" she said. "Of course you must go! But you must promise to tell me all about it when you get back—and look out for vampires!"

"Those two really are odd," Julian said. "It's a year and a half since we first met them, and in all that time they've never invited us to their town house. Yet now, after making no effort to get in touch with us for nearly four months, we're asked to go and stay with them on the spur of the moment as if we were old friends."

"If you didn't want to go, you could have refused off your own bat, without calling me. You knew that we were invited for dinner at the Elliotts'."

"If I *had* refused off my own bat, you would have been furious," he said shrewdly. "If Nicolai were like all the rest of the bloody little aristocrats crawling around this town, I would have refused without a moment's hesitation—I'd have taken the short notice as a piece of damned impertinence. But Nicolai is different. He interests me. What he said at dinner that night was very interesting indeed."

Not a word about what Lucrèce had said.

On the drive up to the mountains, I sat in the front seat of the open car between Julian and Nicolai. Julian, who had objected so strongly to my sitting next to Micu, didn't seem to mind how close I was to Nicolai—as if their political brotherhood made them brothers in fact. After a little three-sided talk about our stay in Bulgaria, and a lawsuit that Nicolai was hoping to win, and the disfiguring of the landscape by the oil derricks at Ploesti—which brought up the evils of big business and capitalism—the two men drifted into a political discussion in which my opinion was not asked for.

Letting go, as it were, of my mind, I allowed my senses to take over; and the rough texture of the mountains, now so close, the pungent scent of the pines, the sounds of water falling over rocks from a great height, and racing over stones alongside the road, served as a defense against the troubling proximity of a surrogate brother for whom my feelings were not those of a sister.

We stopped at the fashionable mountain resort of Sinaia, to stretch our legs and drink Marghilomans—strong black coffee laced with rum and named after its inventor. "You know," Julian said, "if we could find a reasonable pension, it might be a good idea to spend next summer up here instead of at the sea. I like mountains, and it's near enough to Bucharest for me to come up on weekends."

"That's an excellent idea," said Nicolai, "and you'd be near enough to our place for us to see something of you."

Julian looked skeptical. "Nice of you to say so, my dear fellow, but we live much closer to you in Bucharest and we don't see much of you there."

"We don't really live in Bucharest," Nicolai said. "We own a house there, that's all." His tone was rather curt, as if he resented Julian's remark. We finished our Marghilomans in silence. Nicolai looked at his watch. "We'd better be on our way," he said, "if we don't want to keep everyone waiting for dinner." Midday dinner was the norm in Rumanian everyday life. But I wondered who "everyone" was—relatives, guests?

Before reaching the medieval city of Brasov, we turned off the main highway and drove for about twenty kilometers along a dirt road through the forest that finally brought us out into a small, high valley, richly cultivated. On the opposite side of it, under the northern slopes, protected by the forest from the blizzards driving down on the north wind, was a tiny hamlet, its whitewashed buildings clustered around a church with touches of gold on its roof that gleamed in the sun.

"That's our village," Nicolai said, "our real home."

We stopped in front of a house that was set a little apart from the others and surrounded by fruit trees and vines, but that seemed very small for a nobleman's country seat.

Lucrèce came out to greet us, dressed in the same national costume that she had worn at the Gavriolescos'. Her manner was warmer and less aloof than on previous occasions, and I had the feeling that we had finally been accepted as friends and that what Nicolai had said about seeing a lot of us if we spent a summer in Sinaia had been sincere.

"I am so happy that you have come," she said. "There is no telephone here, so all I could do was wait and hope."

"How soon will dinner be ready?" Nicolai asked.

"Very soon. But you have time to change."

He excused himself and went off. "If you wish," said Lucrèce, "I will show you your room."

We followed her down a trellised arbor, where heavy bunches of grapes still hung on the vines, to a turreted wing of the house that we entered directly by a side door. "This was my father's private retreat," she told us, "the place to which he escaped when he wanted to be alone. I hope that you will feel comfortable in it. If you want to wash, here is a bathroom—the fire has been lighted under the heater since early morning, so there should be plenty of hot water. I shall come back to get you in about twenty minutes— if that is convenient—and show you the way through this complicated house to where we shall eat."

The room in which she left us was complicated only in the implications of its extreme simplicity. "What a contrast," Julian said, "to that godawful room at the Gavriolescos'!"

This room was without any mirror, like a monk's cell. The whitewashed walls were bare but for an icon. The bed was an old-fashioned country bed, rather small for two, piled high with the huge, square goose-feather pillows that served as eiderdowns in cold weather. An old carved chest, an oak wardrobe, a table, and a straight chair completed the furnishings. On the polished floor beside the bed was a peasant rug in the beautiful mellow tones of the past. It all smelled very sweet, of beeswax, of bed linen laundered with homemade soap and stored in a cupboard with aromatic herbs, of chrysanthemums growing below the open windows, of the hot varnish of the water heater in the bathroom and the lingering smoke of the pine logs now blazing under it. "Do you mind if I use the bathroom first?" Julian said, going in and shutting the door before I had time to say yes or no.

He had thrown his dusty car coat over the back of the chair. I took mine off and hid them both away in the wardrobe like sins. The room seemed almost too clean for human use.

Julian was slow. I banged on the bathroom door. He was taking a bath, I could hear him splashing. "I had to," he said. "I didn't feel clean enough for this place."

Obscurely annoyed by this echoing of my own feeling, I told him to hurry up and get dressed, Lucrèce was due back in five minutes.

"Don't worry," he said, "I'll be ready. I wouldn't keep her waiting for the world."

The house, which had seemed so small and unpretentious from the front, spread out at the back, where it resembled a monastery, with its many outbuildings and its cloister-like arcades that enclosed numerous courtyards. In one of these, facing southwest and flooded with sunlight, was a long trestle table covered with a gaily embroidered cloth and set for a dozen persons. Flagons of wine, great loaves of brown bread, and bowls full of purple and amber grapes were arranged at intervals down the middle. But the guests for this feast, whoever they were, had not yet arrived. Only Nicolai was there, playing with his daughter. He had changed into peasant clothes and looked so different from his Bucharest persona of an urbane, Anglicized young lawyer that for a moment I didn't recognize him.

His daughter had grown several inches in the fourteen months since I had seen her for the first time, and had undergone that subtle change from child to little girl that takes place with the loss of the first milk teeth. She was shy but self-possessed, and more than ever like her aunt. Who was her mother? And what had happened to her? These were questions that I could never ask, and I had the feeling that no matter how well I got to know Lucrèce she would never volunteer the information. But Nicolai might. Or the old Englishwoman, who had lived with them since they were children, and whose appearance at that moment gave rise to the thought. She was dressed exactly as she had been the first time we saw her, and the heavy tweed coat and skirt with the Tyrolean hat squashed down over her white hair seemed more eccentric then ever, now that she was at home.

"Nana thinks she will catch a cold in her head if she ventures outdoors without her hat," said Nicolai. "Nana, you remember Mr. and Mrs. Crest, don't you? They were at Lucrèce's show. . . ."

"Well!" exclaimed Miss Godwin. "Well! Wonders will never cease!"

"You are our first visitors from the outside world for more than five years," Lucrèce explained.

"And they are here, Nana," Nicolai said, "because they are in sympathy with our ideas."

The old woman pursed her lips tightly together over her false teeth, which should have been long and protuberant but instead were small and even, so that her mouth had caved in, and looked at us with a "more fool you" expression in her pale eyes.

"Nana isn't in sympathy with our ideas," Nicolai said. "She's a dyed-in-the-wool conservative, aren't you, Nana?"

The little girl said something to her father in Rumanian about a cat. She addressed him as *Nicu*, and disapproval of this familiarity was written all over Miss Godwin's face, but all she said was, "Speak English, Marioara—where are your manners?"

"Yes, Mimuka," Nicolai said, "tell Joanna and Julian in English what you have just told me in Rumanian."

"My cat . . ." Marioara began.

Nicolai interrupted her, "*Our* cat. You know very well that the animals here belong to us all."

"Our cat has nine kittens. I found them in her basket this morning. I would like to keep them all, but Nana says no, that would be a men . . . men . . ."

"A menagerie?" I said.

"Men-ag-erie . . . Would it be a men-ag-erie, Nicu?"

"It would be too many cats for one little girl," he told her, "there are other children here who would like to adopt a kitten. But you may adopt one—whichever one you like best."

Miss Godwin frowned. "That will make two cats, one puppy, six rabbits, five goldfish, and a pony. How many more animals are you going to let her adopt?"

"As many as she can take care of properly, Nana. Taking the responsibility for animals is as important a part of her education as learning to read and write."

A bell was being rung, and two men and three women, all wearing national dress, came out of the house and stood by the benches around the table. "I shall introduce you when we are all seated," Nicolai said, "and if you have no objection I shall present you quite simply by name without any reference to your position. I am trying to encourage a sense of equality, of respect for the individual regardless of rank."

He sat at one end of the long table, and Lucrèce at the other. Julian and I sat facing each other in the middle. A young girl brought out an enormous soup tureen and placed it in front of Lucrèce, afterward sitting down on her right. Then Nicolai stood up and said in Rumanian, "I want to introduce to you our English friends, Joanna and Julian Crest. They understand Rumanian, so do not be afraid to talk with them." He then introduced the men and women to us by name, but without reference to their occupations. We exchanged smiles and greetings in Rumanian.

Lucrèce ladled the soup, which had meatballs and dumplings in it and turned out to be the main dish of the meal, into bright, glazed pottery bowls which were passed from hand to hand down the table. The loaves were cut into huge chunks, and the wine poured into beautiful Bohemian glass goblets that seemed, like the master and mistress of the household themselves, to be anachronisms, not in relation to the actual period but to the dream of the future, or rather of an ideal future, that was being enacted.

The wine, which tasted of muscatel grapes, released a torrent of uninhibited talk of which, at first, I understood very little and Julian even less because everyone at the legation spoke English and the language of society was French, whereas I had the advantage of being obliged to speak Rumanian with my two peasant maids. But my vocabulary was limited to the subjects of food and housekeeping, and the maids were too respectful to correct my mistakes. Now, Marioara, who had seated herself beside me, giggled at everything I said, and Miss Godwin threatened to send her away from the table if she couldn't be more polite. But I told the little girl that I wanted to learn to speak Rumanian properly and that she should teach me by correcting me and telling me the right words and the right way to say them. So she helped me to converse with the middle-aged woman sitting next to me on my other side, whose name was Marie and who turned out to be the wife of the man sitting next to Nicolai and telling him of all that had taken place on the farm during his absence in Bucharest.

"My husband is responsible for the farm when the master is absent," she told me, using a respectful Rumanian designation for Nicolai which I was sure that he would consider a relic of serfdom but which he probably didn't know how to replace without offending the sense of fitness in people for whom his family had been "the masters" for generations. "And when the mistress goes away," Marie went on, "I am responsible for the household, and my sister—she's sitting over there by the mistress—looks after the little girl because Miss is not young enough anymore to go everywhere with a child."

Miss Godwin said in English, "I am responsible for the child. I and no one else. That silly young girl over there is only a pair of legs."

Julian grinned, and I knew what he was thinking.

"But she can't run as fast as I can," said Marioara.

After dinner Miss Godwin took Marioara indoors for a nap. The others quickly cleared the table and went off to their various occupations. "Tomorrow," Nicolai said, "they will stay and talk. The *popa*—the priest—will be here, he always has dinner with us on Sundays, and the people who run the mill and bake the bread will be here too. Everyone who was at the table today is a member of the household living under this roof. Shall we go out now and take a look at everything? There is so much that I want to show you!"

He addressed us both, but I knew it was Julian's company that he really wanted, and that Julian would just as soon go with him without me. So, when I realized that Lucrèce wasn't going, I decided to stay with her.

"What would you like to do?" she asked me. "Would you like to see the house—or would you prefer to take a siesta?"

"What do *you* usually do at this time of day?"

"Nothing."

"Would you mind very much if I kept you company while you are doing nothing?"

I had no sooner said it than I knew I had been tactless, intrusive. I should never have elected to stay behind with her in the first place; she had wanted to be alone. But she said, with her inbred good manners, "On the contrary, I would very much like to have your company—I am only afraid you will be bored."

And I thought that this fear had prevailed when, instead of

remaining quietly in the now deserted courtyard, she took me across a walled garden where the younger of the two men who had been at the table was gathering melons, and told him as we went by, "I am going to show my English friend our beautiful church."

It stood by itself at the very edge of the forest, below the highest mountain, and its beauty, or rather its kind of beauty, was unexpected in that wild place. Lavishly embellished with wood carvings, gilded icons, and frescoes in rich, deep hues of crimson and blue, it was a far cry from the rude Saxon fortress which had housed the God of my childhood.

"My father and mother are buried here," said Lucrèce, "and my grandparents and my great-grandparents, and there is a place beside them in the vault waiting for me and Nicolai. . . ." She fell silent, and stood looking down at the stones engraved with the family names. Through a window above them a sunbeam disclosed the dust on the wings of a wooden angel—guardian of sleep and ready guide on the day of resurrection. "But neither of us will be laid in it," she said finally.

Abruptly turning away, she preceded me up the empty nave, paused to bow to the holy icons above the high altar, then took me out through a small back door. The forest smelled sweet and alive. "Shall we walk a little?" she asked. "There is a place in the woods where it is very agreeable to do nothing."

For about a hundred yards we followed a track rutted by bullock cart wheels along the edge of the forest, then we turned in among the trees on a narrow, sharply ascending path that soon became too indistinct for me to perceive. But invisible as it was to me, Lucrèce seemed able to see it. She threaded her way in and out of the pines that grew more and more densely together, and I thought there might be trail marks on their trunks that I didn't recognize. When the incline was steep she turned to give me a helping hand. But she didn't speak and neither did I, the silence around us was too intense to break.

I felt the shiver of mingled fear and excitement that deep woods, even in England, aroused in me. If Lucrèce were to fall and injure herself, I thought, I should never be able to find my way back for help. I felt like the blindfolded child in a game of blindman's buff after having been turned around three times, but without the recourse of tearing off the blindfold.

My sense of time and distance were lost with my sense of

direction. We seemed to have walked, or climbed, for hours, for miles, when a glimpse of daylight appeared through the trees like the light at the end of the Simplon tunnel. We had reached the summit of a ridge, and the edge of a precipice; a sheer fall of rock into depths where the pale green, feathered crowns of young spruces wavered like seaweed fathoms down.

Looking across the ravine at the vista of peaks retreating into the farthest distances, I felt trapped, lost in the multiple folds of their black skirts. One could grope among them for years, I thought, and never find a way out. I was at my companion's mercy, dependent upon her knowledge of her surroundings, her sureness of foot, her goodwill toward me—Ondine might have taken the form of hamadryad intent upon losing me. I felt her hand on my shoulder and stiffened, instinctively bracing myself. "Do not stand so close to the edge," she said. "It can cause vertigo in those who are new to the mountains."

We lay down to rest on a gentle slope from where we could see the mountains but not the ravine. I felt exhausted. I could have fallen asleep, but I didn't want to sleep. I wanted to talk, and induce Lucrèce to talk. I was aware that my fantasies of her as cold and treacherous mermaid or mischievous hamadryad were projections of my own jealous fears of a woman whose charm, or power, I could not analyze and so could not combat, and to whom I myself was irresistibly drawn.

Alone with her in what was for me a dangerous wilderness, I thought how little I knew about her and her brother, and how full of riddles and contradictions that little was. Our first meeting with them was a riddle. Thinking back to it, I realized that it was almost certainly their first visit to the Gavriolescos'; neither of them had shown any familiarity with their surroundings, and from remarks let drop by Sybil later, I gathered that it had also been their last. What had induced them to accept Sybil's invitation? Particularly for Easter—a festival that they would naturally want to celebrate in their own home, in their own church, with their own peasants, and above all with the little girl, Nicolai's publicly unacknowledged but clearly beloved daughter by a woman whose memory, I romantically believed, stood between him and other women, including myself.

I was now so far from the drawing rooms of Bucharest that I

broke all the rules of the diplomatic game, and my own code of good manners, by asking Lucrèce outright, "What on earth made you come to the Gavriolescos' that Easter?"

She answered equally directly. "We came because Nicolai wanted to meet Julian—what he had heard about Julian's political opinions interested him."

"But Maximilian and Sybil knew nothing about his political opinions at that time. . . ."

"Maximilian knows more than most people imagine he does— and Sybil, a good deal less. But we didn't hear it from him. We heard it from my father's old friend in your legation. I do not think I am betraying his confidence—you must be aware that Julian is known as 'The Bolshevik in the Chancery'?"

We were both aware of it, and it worried me; both the paraphrase and its original were only too accurate. But Julian was proud of it.

"There are times," said Lucrèce, "when Nicolai feels very lonely. He needs to speak with men of his own kind who do not think him mad."

"And what about you? Are you never lonely?"

"Of course I am. But I have chosen it."

"And Nicolai hasn't?"

After a long silence which made me feel guilty of prying, she said, "Nicolai is not as strong as I am."

Strong. Yes, that was it. Her strength was what drew me to her—quite apart from her resemblance to Nicolai. My mother had been a woman of great spiritual strength, and although I had never been able to get along with her, she had nevertheless supplied the female support that I needed. I was continually searching for someone to replace her in my life. I don't know whether I fully realized all this at that moment, or only as the result of a self-knowledge acquired later. But I accepted Lucrèce's definition of herself as strong, and recognized spiritual strength as the indispensable quality in a friendship of any real value between me and another woman. In Lucrèce it seemed to be combined with a lot of other attributes that in my mother had compelled my admiration and at the same time irked me: religious belief and observance, dignity, modesty, reserve, and that rarest of all Victorian virtues among Rumanian society women, chastity. All of which made up a personality so far removed from that of an Ondine that the fantasy seemed unjustified to the point of absurdity.

I asked Lucrèce another direct question.

"If Nicolai knew that Julian's political ideas were the same as his own, then why, after going to so much trouble to make our acquaintance did he make no effort to develop it—until now?"

"We waited because we had to be sure that we could trust you."

"In what way? Politically?"

"As human beings."

Only a short time ago I had been debating whether or not I could trust her. Now she was showing me what it felt like to be trusted by another human being whose demands were an unknown quantity. For an instant my fear of her returned. There was something almost inhuman about choosing new friends only after examining their credentials over a long period.

I said, "You are strange people. When your father's old friend spoke to me of you and your brother, he didn't convey the impression that he thought you different from other people, or that your way of life was different."

"He doesn't really know us. He sees us as the children of our parents—their reflection. He loved our parents. He used to visit here often when they were alive."

"But he has never come here to visit you and Nicolai..." I said, recollecting her observation that we were their first guests from the outside world in five years.

"We never invited him here. He would not have understood. He was even unhappy over what we did with our town house—he had been to so many balls and parties there. But at least that wasn't communism—which would be his word for what we are trying to do here. He didn't know, of course, that this was our reason for, as he put it, 'sacrificing the family palace,' he just thought we were short of money."

"Did you sell the family palace?"

"Oh no. Nicolai wouldn't do that—even though he believes, as I do, that sooner or later it will be taken from us. And anyway, it's more valuable to us now as property. We have converted it into flats and rented them, all but the little one on the ground floor where the caretaker used to live in my parents' time. I'm surprised that Sybil didn't tell you that, or Micu."

I could guess why Sybil hadn't told us. Aside from Micu, the Amans represented her sole claim to social acquaintance with aristocrats, and she wouldn't want to devaluate them in our estimation. And Micu, as an aristocrat himself, would be ashamed to admit to foreigners that a cousin of his, however distant, could not afford to keep up his town residence. The impoverished English nobleman who cheerfully conducts tourists around his ancestral home was still on the far side of a cataclysmic war.

"We never see Micu. And we don't see much of Sybil."

"*We* see as little as possible of anybody—except our people here. So giving up our town house was not really a sacrifice. But it's a paradox to become a town landlord in order to start a socialistic experiment in the country—and Nicolai isn't comfortable about it."

"It's the old question of whether or not the end justifies the means," I said, wondering what had finally convinced her and her brother that we were to be trusted. Politically, the dinner table conversation at our apartment could have done it. But humanly, the decision must have been taken before that or Nicolai wouldn't have told us when he did what was known only to his "immediate family."

Ashamed of my inquisitiveness, I tried to compensate for it by volunteering some information about myself. I told Lucrèce that I was an only child, and had lost both my parents within the same year. "So what with my having no close relatives and Julian's having repudiated his, he and I are very dependent upon each other. We have plenty of acquaintances, but the constant moving from one post to another makes it hard to form close friendships, and it's harder still to keep them up from the other side of the world. The only people one can be sure of running into again are colleagues, and colleagues are like neighbors, somehow it's better not to get too intimate with them. Especially in our case."

It occurred to me while I was saying this that with Nicolai and Lucrèce our transience was probably in our favor; if they regretted becoming too friendly with us, the British Foreign Office could be depended upon to break up the unwanted tie before very long.

"My parents used to say the same thing," Lucrèce said. "My

father was in our diplomatic service for several years. He was posted in Stockholm and Paris and London. Nicolai and I were born in London. Perhaps that is why we are both so fond of England. Then my father was offered a government position at home, and we came back to Rumania." She paused. I sensed in her a struggle between her almost abnormal reticence about anything personal and a desire to communicate with me on a personal level. After a short silence she went on, "Nana came with us because of Nicolai. He was a very delicate child, and she couldn't bear the idea of giving him over into anyone else's care—she didn't trust even my mother to look after him properly. She thought of him as *her* baby. And now that he is a man, she has transferred her possessiveness to his child."

I waited, thinking that she might go on to tell me of the marriage, or love affair, from which the child had sprung. But she said nothing more. I looked across at her. She had closed her eyes. I recognized this as a gesture of withdrawal. She had not told me much, but to her even that small confidence must have been an effort, and I knew from my own experience the odd sense of diminishment, and of irritation against one's interlocutor, that follows what a naturally reserved person regards as a surrender to weakness.

She lay on her back, within touching distance, but as untouchable as if she were surrounded by an electrified fence. Her hands were clasped behind her head, her raised arms lifting her full breasts, and for an instant I saw her as I believed a man would see her, as Julian probably saw her, sensually and aesthetically attractive to an almost painful degree—intensified by her utter inaccessibility.

The September sun was in process of falling behind a mountain. A slanting ray caught me full in the face, dazzling me. I turned my head to one side and saw the ray gild for a moment the gray face of a rock, on which something seemed to be carved. I stood up, and, shaking the pine needles off my clothes, I moved nearer to the rock. A primitive cross had been cut out on its face as if it were a tombstone. A memorial to a lost traveler? To someone who had fallen, or leaped, over the edge of the precipice? Lucrèce must know, I thought. It might be the reason she frequented this spot. But she said nothing about it and neither did I.

I wanted to leave. The distances were still sunlit, but the ridge had already dropped into deep shadow. I said, "How dark it is getting!"

"I do not need light to find my way through these woods."

We made our way back in silence, as we had come. Near the edge of the woods, where the path was again visible, we saw Marioara scrambling up the slope toward us. Magda's voice could be heard in the distance, calling her. "You see!" she said triumphantly. "I *can* run faster than Magda!"

"But you must not run away from her, that is very naughty," Lucrèce said, kindly but severely. "And you are not allowed to come into the woods, you know that, Mimuka."

"But you come here every day," the child said.

"Who told you that?" Lucrèce's voice was suddenly cold and sharp.

Marioara began to cry.

"Answer me, Mimuka."

"Nana . . ."

Down on the cart track Magda was running up and down, calling and wringing her hands—a gesture that I had thought was peculiar to opera singers. She came to meet us with tears in her eyes.

"Tell Magda that you are sorry you ran away from her," Lucrèce said to the equally weepy Marioara.

The child threw her arms around the girl's neck. "My pigeon," Magda said in Rumanian, "my precious little pigeon . . . you gave me such a fright."

In the walled garden Miss Godwin was furiously scolding the young melon picker for distracting Magda from her duty. Now she turned on Magda. "Good-for-nothing baggage!" she said, adding a word in Rumanian that drew a rebuke from Lucrèce.

"Now, Nana, you mustn't say things like that."

Magda fled toward the house, weeping. "Trollop!" Miss Godwin said. "And as for *you*, Marioara, you're a wicked, disobedient child. And you're going straight to bed."

"No! No! I'm *not*!" cried Marioara, bursting into tears.

Lucrèce put her arms around the child. "That's enough, Nana," she said very quietly. "You're forgetting again."

Miss Godwin stumped ahead of us, muttering to herself. As we crossed the courtyard, Nicolai and Julian came out of the house. Marioara broke away from Lucrèce and rushed to her father, followed by the furious Miss Godwin.

"What are you muttering about, Nana? You look ruffled, your feathers are all up. . . ."

"Your daughter," Miss Godwin said, "is a self-willed brat—just like her mother."

Nicolai took the old woman by the arm and led her into the house.

"Poor Nana," said Lucrèce, "she is getting very old. She is beginning to confuse the generations, to mix up past and present."

"I hate her," said Marioara.

"Please don't use that word, Mimuka. We do not hate anyone."

"Nana does, she hates. . . ."

Lucrèce cut her short. "Nonsense. Nana loves us all very much."

Marioara's face showed signs of crumpling again, but Julian, more patient with other people's children than with his own, diverted her by asking her to show him the litter of new kittens. And I asked Lucrèce to show me the geography of the house.

Rambling passages led to several different wings in which suites of rooms had been assigned to different members of the household. "Nicolai believes that even in a communal household each member should have some private territory, in addition to a bedroom," Lucrèce explained. "We have done a lot of remodeling, pulling down some walls—to make my studio, for example—and putting up others. The original furniture, rugs, pictures, have been distributed equally—everyone has something beautiful to live with. But there is no luxury. People so often confuse beauty with luxury."

Which was just what I had done, I thought, with the Bohemian glass goblets.

Where doors were ajar we stopped and looked in for a moment as we went by. In one, a little sitting room, Marie was sewing by the window. I noticed that she did not rise, respectfully, on seeing us, as the housekeeper in any ordinary Rumanian household would have done, but just smiled at us and made a remark about the sunset.

Lucrèce opened a door and told me, "This is *my* special territory." The long studio was flooded with cool north light, and was uncompromisingly professional and functional, except for a grand piano in one corner, its top propped up for playing. "That was my mother's, it used to be in the drawing room of our Bucharest house. My mother was an excellent musician. I play just well enough to amuse myself and accompany Nicolai and his violin, but no more than that."

Beyond the studio, connected with it by double doors, now wide open, was a bedroom. Monastically bare, totally devoid of luxury, even comfort, it had one great beauty: a magnificent, glowing icon, hanging on the wall that faced the doors, as if Lucrèce wanted to be able to see it even when she was working.

The immaculate cleanliness that Julian and I had thought was almost too rarefied for ordinary mortals to live in, extended to the whole house, and intensified the general impression of air, light, and space. The sparsity of the furniture showed up the individual characteristics and beauties of handcrafted objects that would have been lost in more crowded company. Tables, chairs, chests, cupboards—all were handmade, some of them by the master cabinetmakers of a past era, others by peasant carpenters with a natural sense of design. The stuff of covers and curtains had been woven, like the rugs, on hand looms, and the stitchery embellishing them had been done by fingers performing extempore, so to speak, within a broad framework of tradition, so that although there was no mistaking the ethnic origins of the patterns, nothing was ever repeated twice in exactly the same way. In England, I thought, an attempt at such a decor would have been self-conscious; here it was natural, and as naturally harmonious as the landscape outside.

Did the human element match it? At dinner I had felt that it did—except for Miss Godwin, but her age and her nationality had made her dissonance seem like comic relief, a musical joke. Since then, however, it had manifested itself as a powerful discord with vibrations strong enough to destroy the whole harmonic texture.

A clock chimed the half hour. "Oh!" said Lucrèce, "we are late for tea.... Of course, it's long past teatime by English standards, but everything happens later here."

We found Nicolai, Julian, and Marioara waiting for us in a

large room that Lucrèce said was the communal living room, "Where we eat together in the winter, and work, and talk, and make music." At one end was a long refectory table, and at the other, grouped around a tile stove, were deep wicker armchairs with loose, embroidered cushions. "My parents brought these back with them from England," Nicolai told us. "They had flowered chintz cushions, my mother loved them, but my sister has Rumanianized them."

Against the wall was a small upright piano, its rosewood case recalling the one in my own home as a child. A couple of flutes and a violin were lying on top of it, and a double bass was propped up beside it. "That's an English piano too. They told my mother that it was called a cottage piano, so she couldn't resist bringing it back to her cottage in Transylvania. We've recently had it rewired and refelted, it was getting awfully tinny."

The tea was good, strong English tea with milk, and there was a plateful of Huntley and Palmer's Mixed Biscuits to go with it. No one joined us. Miss Godwin was lying down—Nicolai took a cup of tea to her in her room. Now, with just the four of us sitting in English basket chairs, drinking English tea and eating English biscuits, while the little girl watched her cat suckle its new kittens, I felt completely at ease with Nicolai and Lucrèce for the first time. I sensed the early warmth of a friendship coming to life, a friendship uncomplicated by emotional undercurrents that I couldn't explain. The familiarity of teatime had disarmed me.

After tea, Lucrèce sat down to the cottage piano and played Rumanian folk songs which Nicolai made us sing along with him. Then I played English and Irish songs, and Magda and her young man came in to listen.

Nicolai suggested that later on in the evening we should go to a tavern in Brasov where we could get something simple to eat and could listen to a Gypsy band. Julian, who loved such places, agreed enthusiastically. Magda, eager to atone for her fault of the afternoon, said that we could leave for Brasov at once if we wanted to, she would give Marioara her supper and put her to bed and stay beside her until we returned. Lucrèce thanked her, but said we were in no hurry to go, and she would give Marioara her supper and put her to bed herself.

"Little bird," Nicolai said, when the child kissed him good-night, "you won't upset poor Nana again, will you?"

She shook her head and buried her face in his shoulder. He kissed her hair, the same color as his own but softer, silkier. His expression was tender, but sad, as if he were thinking of her mother.

"Come, Mimuka," said Lucrèce, "say goodnight now to Joanna and Julian."

But first she had a question. "Nicu, what is a daw-ter?"

After a moment's hesitation, Nicolai said, "A little girl who is very much loved."

"Very much loved by us all," said Lucrèce, with a touch of wistfulness in her voice. Marioara went off with her obediently but reluctantly, much as Pip and Cissy went off with their Fräulein at bedtime.

"Nana's becoming a problem," Nicolai said. "She used to be the soul of discretion. But now that she's nearly eighty she's losing control. I suppose I made a mistake in ever letting her know that Marioara is my own child."

"You're in a predicament now," Julian said, "unless you don't mind the rest of your people here knowing it."

"I'm not concerned about that—even though they don't actually know it, I'm sure that they take it for granted. It's the likeliest explanation of why she lives with us, and so natural that they wouldn't think it worth talking about. This isn't Bucharest, thank God! No, it's the child I'm worrying about. . . . How about going into my study and having a glass of *tuica* while we're waiting for Lucrèce?"

The atmosphere of the study, or library, was heavier, darker than that of the rest of the house because of the books that lined three walls from floor to ceiling. On the one free space, between the windows, hung a large oil painting, a portrait that caught my attention immediately because it didn't seem to go with the room.

"That's Lucrèce's portrait of our father," Nicolai said. "She put it in here because most of these books were his and she thought he might like to be with them. A couple of years ago she exhibited it, but nobody liked it, not even his old English friend. *Everyone* came to see it, but they had all known him too well, or imagined they did, to agree with Lucrèce's idea of him. It's too abstract. Distinguished political figures are expected to appear fully fleshed and decorated, even on canvas."

In this remarkable portrait the flesh and decorations were

noticeably absent. Indeed, there was something ghostly about it, as if Lucrèce had tried to paint a disembodied spirit.

Nicolai brought a bottle of *tuica* out of a cupboard. "Made here on the farm from our own plums. A hundred proof and a hundred percent pure. Cheerio!"

"Cheerio!" said Julian, draining his glass at one gulp, as did Nicolai. "Good stuff! It warms the cockles, all right."

Nicolai refilled Julian's glass and his own—I had taken only one sip from mine, and already my cockles were on fire. Julian and I were sitting on the only two comfortable chairs in the room; low but armless, covered in black petit point with a medallion of roses, they were Victorian in style and added to the feeling of density in this room, as did the massive bureau-desk placed at right angles to one of the windows. Nicolai pulled out the desk chair for himself. Its seat and back were also covered with petit point. "My grandmother's work," he remarked. "She was half English and half Russian—like Queen Marie. Lucrèce and I very much resemble her, though we have the dark eyes of my father's side of the family. Here is a miniature of her, done when she was a young girl in England—*her* mother was a lady-in-waiting to Queen Victoria."

As in all nineteenth-century miniatures, the subject seemed to be made of porcelain. But the physical characteristics of this woman, whose mixed Russian and Anglo-Saxon blood, together with the cross-strain of Rumanian, had resulted in the remarkable physiognomy and coloring of her two grandchildren, and her great-grandchild, were far too strong to be annulled by the pink-and-white inanity of the miniaturist's art. Very fair ringlets and china blue eyes were contradicted by wide, high cheekbones, a blunt nose, and a large, sensual mouth whose Slavic formation had resisted the prunes and prisms of Victorian reformation.

After putting the miniature back on the desk, Nicolai poured himself a third *tuica*. "I'd like to ask your advice," he said. "You have children of your own—your son must be about Marioara's age. If you were in my position, how would you go about answering the question implicit in what Marioara asked me just now?"

"If a client were to ask for *your* advice in such general terms, you would withhold it on the grounds of insufficient data," Julian said dryly.

Nicolai smiled. "Of course I would. But I'm not asking you for legal advice, only for your opinion as a father—and for yours, Joanna, as a mother—regarding a child's capacity for understanding. I don't know how much, or how little, to tell her."

"What *have* you told her?" asked Julian. "Does she think she's adopted, or what?"

"I haven't told her anything. She has been with us ever since she was a few months old, and she accepts us as two people, named Nicu and Lucrèce, to whom she belongs in the same way that the other children in the village belong to two people who are called something in Rumanian that no one has translated for her as *mother* and *father*. As it happens, none of these children is old enough to give her what you English call 'ideas'—it's a young community, and the children are still quite small. But I realize that even if Nana hadn't precipitated an explanation of some sort, I couldn't have put it off much longer."

One of the windows was open. It was already dark outside, and a cool night breeze had sprung up. It fluttered the papers on the desk. Nicolai gathered them together, and closed the window. "Actually," he said, "I've been worrying about it for some time. That was why I told you the truth that evening after seeing you together with your children. I needed advice. But I couldn't ask for it from anyone closely connected with me—though I feel terribly guilty over having thrust on you, precisely because you are English, and therefore discreet, the kind of confidence that embarrasses English people more than anyone else."

"You needn't worry about that, my dear fellow. I could tell you a thing or two that might embarrass *you.*"

"You are fortunate not to have to explain them to your son."

"He'll have to be told some of them sooner or later, but they don't touch him closely enough to do much damage, whereas what you decide to tell or not to tell Marioara may affect her whole life."

"I know. That's why I'm asking your help."

"Children are very good at accepting the truth," I said. "And Marioara has virtually accepted half of the truth already—you just have to teach her the English word for the role that you have always played in her life. And explain Lucrèce's relationship to her and to you, teaching her the word *aunt* and its meaning."

"But what about the other half of the truth? What about the word *mother*? Can I tell her that her mother is dead—without harming her emotionally?"

"What does *death* mean to her?" Julian asked.

"Disappearance. Until we all arrive in Heaven—Lucrèce has told her of Heaven, but not of Hell. She knows nothing of evil—yet."

Except what Miss Godwin has taught her, I thought.

"If you are ever going to tell her anything, this is the time to do it," I told him. "Before someone destroys her innocence."

"Joanna is right," Julian said. "She knows more about innocence than I do. I lost mine much earlier in life than she lost hers."

"I shall try to follow your advice," Nicolai said.

"But before you tell Marioara anything," I warned him, noting that he had said *I* and not *We*, "you should talk it over with Lucrèce. The image of a mother waiting for her in Heaven may appeal to Marioara's imagination so strongly that she may reject Lucrèce—unless Lucrèce is the one to tell her, or at least share in the telling."

Nicolai looked at me as if he were really seeing me for the first time. "You are very wise, Joanna," he said, then abruptly changed the subject. A moment or two later, Lucrèce came in, all ready to leave for Brasov. Nicolai must have heard her footsteps before we did.

On the drive to Brasov, we were all very silent. Lucrèce, who sat in the front seat next to her brother, was moody; perhaps she sensed that something had taken place among the three of us while she was not there, and resented it. Or perhaps she had seen Miss Godwin again, and something had taken place between the two of them. Miss Godwin was confused, but exactly where her confusion lay was hard to guess. Whom did she hate? Lucrèce? Or Lucrèce's mother, who was also the mother of Nicolai—*her* baby? Or the mother of Nicolai's child? Or all three of them? Did she love, as devoted nannies often did, only the males of the families in which they acted as surrogate mothers, and in that case had she expressed her true feelings toward Marioara that afternoon in her fit of senile temper?

Julian reached for my hand under the car rug that the cool night air in the mountains made necessary in an open car. The gesture, or rather its moderation, told me a lot. Julian's physical appproaches were a barometer of his emotions that I had learned to read pretty accurately over the eight years of our married life. It told me now that Lucrèce's shadowy form on the front seat, the tilt of her head swathed in its gauzy scarf, the occasional silhouette of her profile as she turned to say something to Nicolai, and the sound of her low-pitched voice with its faintly exotic inflections were more exciting to him than the proximity of my only too well known body on the seat beside him. But it also told me that I had nothing to worry about; he was attracted, yes, but his friendship for Nicolai automatically put Lucrèce "out of bounds"—which he assumed to be Nicolai's attitude with regard to me. It was not only his political thinking that set Nicolai apart from the run of Rumanian aristocrats in Julian's estimation. Julian believed him to be a man of honor in every respect.

Being at the tavern with Nicolai and Lucrèce was rather like being at Popo's with Old Browne. It was obvious that everyone knew who they were, and were just as astonished to see them there with a foreign couple as the habitués of Popo's had been to see Old Browne there with a young woman. And, like him, our hosts discouraged everyone who stopped by our table for a word of greeting by deliberately failing to introduce us. But it was done, or rather not done, so gracefully that they gave the impression of conferring a favor on the would-be intruders merely by deigning to recognize them and say good evening.

We were on our third flagon of wine when the Gypsy band started playing a hora, and a group of young people, probably students, got up to dance it, forming a ring. "Come on!" said Julian. "Let's join them!"

He might have been a magician saying abracadabra! All the aspects of Nicolai and Lucrèce that we had thus far seen or imagined were shed in two minutes, along with an unknown number of years. The lively, crisscross movements of the dance shook the pins from Lucrèce's hair; flushed, laughing, bacchic, with her braided coronet all askew, she looked like a peasant girl of eighteen who has just been rolled in the hay, and I could see Julian falling madly in love with this new Lucrèce right under my eyes—not recognizing it as an illusion.

When we sat down again at the table, she said, "We are mad.

Quite mad. We haven't danced the hora in a tavern since we were students. I don't know what possessed us."

"It was my fault," Julian said. "I got you into it—but you enjoyed it, didn't you? I know *I* did."

She began to wind her long scarf around her disordered hair. "It's past midnight," she said. "I think we should leave now if you don't mind. Tomorrow is Sunday."

I knew what she meant. And again she brought my mother to mind, knocking on my door before it was light, telling me to get up at once, or we would be late for "early Communion." Julian knew what she meant too. I could see the respect in his eyes. Yet early in our marriage he had ridiculed me for the very observances that he now respected in Lucrèce. I thought now, for the thousandth time, how contrary men were, and how maddening.

We were silent again on the drive back to the farm. The moon was high, and under its pallid light the landscape was eerie enough for the legends of vampires to seem less unbelievable than they did by daylight. As soon as we arrived, Lucrèce said goodnight and went off to her austere bedroom, so out of keeping with the bacchic persona released, or brought up from the past, by the rollicking national dance. Nicolai, reverting to his most urbane, most Anglicized persona, politely offered us a nightcap in his study. Which I refused, but Julian accepted. "Just a quick one, do you mind, Joey? I'll join you in ten minutes."

"Sleep as late as you like," Nicolai said. "Breakfast, especially on Sunday, is a movable feast and completely informal. If you don't find us somewhere around the house or garden, just go to the kitchen and ask whomever you find there for whatever you want. We eat dinner at noon."

I didn't hear Julian come in, I was already asleep. But before that I had lain awake for a long time, trying to sort out the emotional transitions brought about in me by the continually shifting aspects of their personalities that our hosts chose to let us see—or was it the other way around? Were they being continually metamorphosed by our subjectivity, our reactions to their secretiveness? Only one thing remained constant: their political idealism. Which almost everyone I knew would label *communism*, and dangerous, but which they themselves would call the practical application of Christian principles to life in the twentieth century.

I wondered how far and how stringently they applied these principles to their personal lives. Perhaps they were members of some strict Third Order, vowed to chastity while living in the world. I could well imagine this to be the case with Lucrèce, but not with Nicolai. I saw men as inescapably sensual beings. My marriage to Julian, and the way other men acted toward me, and toward women in general, had convinced me that a man's love for a woman was synonymous with sexual desire. For my part, I could not conceive of feeling sexual desire for a man without loving him, an equation of love with sex that made me perceive infidelity as the death of love. There was another kind of love, and I longed for it. But I called it friendship, and I looked for it only in women, women whom I believed to be spiritually strong—like Lucrèce.

I was awakened very early by all the country sounds, far less blatant than those of the city, but unfamiliar. Julian was still fast asleep when I got up and went into the bathroom, taking my clothes with me. When I was dressed, I went straight out into the garden. The air was almost sharp, its clarity and glitter resembled that of a frosty winter's morning, but the chrysanthemums and the marigolds and even some late roses were blooming untouched by frost, and the only hint of fall was in the slight yellowing of the leaves.

The church bell was ringing for early Mass. I decided to go. There was nobody about. Whole flocks of birds were peaceably pecking at seeding plants and overripe fruit in the walled garden. Beyond it, crossing the meadow, were Nicolai and Lucrèce. They were about fifty yards ahead of me, but I didn't try to catch up with them. For one thing, I thought they would rather be alone—they had had so much of our company on the previous day—and for another, I wanted, though I couldn't have said exactly why, to observe them without their being aware of it.

They walked sedately side by side, quickening their pace when the bell stopped ringing. Under the arch of the door, Lucrèce put her hand on Nicolai's arm, and they stood still for a moment, looking at each other. Touch, pause, and look were a single gesture, at once natural and enigmatic; suggestive of warning, reassurance, or encouragement, and in any case of closeness, of a spiritual intimacy that makes words unnecessary.

I waited a few minutes before I followed them in, as quietly as possible, and stood at the back in the shelter of a column. There were only half a dozen worshipers, including Nicolai and Lucrèce, who were up in front near the sanctuary, where the richly vestmented priest, with his long black beard and his stately, ritual steps, looked like the figure of an apostle in an icon moving about against its gilded background.

The services in my father's Saxon church had been as simple and unadorned as the building itself; the *Book of Common Prayer* without any popish frills. Visiting cathedrals in Europe after my marriage, I had occasionally happened in on a Roman Catholic Mass, but in cathedrals the elaborate was the norm. I had thought the pomp of the Easter Mass in the little church on the Gavriolesco estate something special in honor of the Resurrection. Yet here, at six o'clock on an ordinary Sunday morning, in an isolated Carpathian village, a celebration was going on that for sheer aesthetic beauty was equal to any that I had witnessed in great cathedrals, and was all the more striking because of the almost empty church and the grouping of the worshipers; the two tall, beautiful figures in front and the four peasants behind them, like characters in a mystery play at which I was the only spectator.

I slipped away just before the end of the Mass, and returned unnoticed to the house and to Julian, who was still in bed but awake. "Joey! Where have you been?"

"I've been to church."

"With Nicolai and Lucrèce?"

"No. They were there, but I didn't go with them."

"Then what made you go?"

"I don't really know. I woke up very early and went outside and the church bell was ringing ... and somehow it pulled me toward the church."

"As it did when you were a child."

"I suppose so."

He was thoughtful. "Joey, tell me ... do you miss your religion? Did going to church this morning do something for you?"

"Yes ... it gave me a marvelous aesthetic experience."

"Is that all? Don't you believe in God anymore?"

"I do believe in God ... but I can't find Him in churches the way I used to."

"I suppose I'm to blame for that."

"Partly. But it probably happens to most people sooner or later."

"It hasn't happened to Nicolai and Lucrèce."

"How do you know? How do you know that they aren't holding on to something they've lost, hoping that if they hold on long enough it will come back?"

I had no reason for saying this, other than to challenge Julian's certainty. But the moment I had said it I had an intuition that it might be true.

"I don't think they are," Julian said, "but in any case I would admire them for having the strength to hold on."

He was silent for a while. I had taken off my jacket and was sitting in the sun on the broad sill of the open window. It disturbed me a little that he didn't ask me to come back to bed. Not that I wanted to, but it bothered me that he didn't seem to want me.

"You know," he said, "you should never have let me talk you out of your religion. It was partly what attracted me to you in the first instance."

"Then why did you make fun of it all the time?"

"I wanted to see how strong it was, I suppose—how strong *you* were."

He got up and went to the bathroom. When he came out, he said, "Come back to bed with me, it's still much too early to get up."

I said, "I don't feel like it," but he came up close to me and started to undo the front of my blouse, and through my skirt I could feel him getting hard. I responded, as usual, but less warmly than usual. I couldn't help feeling that I was a substitute for the unattainable Lucrèce.

Afterward, he said, "You're jealous of Lucrèce, aren't you?"

"No. Not really."

"Well, you needn't be. I'm not the sort of man who wants to fuck a nun."

"She didn't look much like a nun last night when she was dancing the hora."

"She looked like a schoolgirl, and I'm not in the habit of fucking schoolgirls, either."

"I was a schoolgirl when you married me."

"But I didn't try anything before we were married."

"You never had an opportunity. Mother saw to that."

"I didn't want to. I fell in love with you because you weren't the sort of girl that men fool around with."

What bothered me when Julian said things like that was not so much what he said as the fact that he seemed to be unaware of what he had said, and its implications. And I perceived in that lack of awareness a gulf between us that no amount of physical love could bridge. I said now, "Let's get up and go for a walk."

There were twenty people at dinner, which was served as before in the sunny courtyard. Miss Godwin looked grim, and rather sour, as if yesterday's bile was still coming up in her throat. I was glad not to be seated near her. I had taken a strong dislike to her.

The priest, as the spiritual father of the whole company, was placed at the head of the table, and Lucrèce and I sat facing each other on his right and left—like handmaidens. But he had stepped out of his icon, and his black stovepipe hat had no halo attached to it. Genial, and probably sensual, his teeth very white and his lips very red in the bush of his black beard, he devoured the good food and wine with childlike gusto. Lucrèce treated him with deference, and his manner to her was a subtle mixture of fatherliness and respect. A respect that I supped to be both personal, for an exceptional woman, and general, for the class to which she belonged; an attitude bred by a lifetime of dealing with the nobility, and of human, if not spiritual, subservience to them. But once or twice I caught him looking at her with a curious expression in his eyes, an expression of pity. Which seemed to me to be the last thing that anyone would feel for Lucrèce.

The general conversation, in which the priest joined with his booming but not unmusical bass voice, was country talk, about crops and weather and plans to buy more livestock, about the need to repair the church roof before the first snows, and about the possibility of persuading a physician to join the community. I listened, but I didn't say much. While I was searching for the right words in Rumanian, the conversation would get ahead of me. I was so quiet that the priest asked me in French whether I understood what was being said. I replied in Rumanian that I understood perfectly. I also understood—as he did—that the language of Bucharest society, the language that distinguished the educated from the uneducated, could not be spoken at that democratic table.

During dinner a wind had sprung up, bringing with it a smell of rain and masses of low clouds with torn edges. While the table was being hurriedly cleared before the imminent downpour, Julian and I exchanged a few words with the priest in French, and discovered that he was the son of a university professor who had tutored the father of Nicolai and Lucrèce in Latin and Greek.

"Prince Gheorghe and I were the same age," he said. "We were good friends. It was he who arranged for me to be the priest of this church, when the old one died. I have been here for twenty-five years. When I came here, Nicolai and Lucrèce were little children—*les innocents*."

"And now...?" said Julian, perceiving, as I did, a note of regret in his voice.

"And now..." The priest sighed. "Now...they are big revolutionaries."

Julian smiled. "Innocent revolutionaries," he said, "the kind that you, as a priest, should approve of. Followers of Christ rather than of Marx."

A rush of heavy rain interrupted the conversation and drove us indoors. We spent the wet afternoon in the communal sitting room, where Julian and I and the priest were the audience for music made by the others; the man who ran the mill strummed on the bass fiddle while Magda's young man piped haunting minor melodies on a flute; Nicolai and Lucrèce played Rumanian dances together; the whole group sang folk songs.

When the church clock struck five, the priest, who had seemed to be half asleep, woke up and said it was time for him to go. And one by one the others bade us good-bye and went off to their evening chores.

"We should soon be leaving for Bucharest," Nicolai said. "I have work to prepare for tomorrow's court hearing."

"Before you go we shall have tea in my studio," said Lucrèce.

Miss Godwin, who had retired to her own rooms after dinner, did not reappear, so the final image that I carried away with me from that first weekend was one of domesticity undisrupted by passion, senile or otherwise, and somehow exalted by being united with art. For me a painter's studio was still a mysterious place, where one walked on tiptoe for fear of disturbing a muse. But here, in the midst of brushes and palettes and paints, surrounded by canvases, finished, half-finished, or stretched and ready for the brush but still untouched, still virgin, was set the symbol of home that had done so much to reassure me the day before—the familiar English tea table; and in the background a child picking out a nursery tune on the piano with one finger.

Close to me, propped on a shelf against the wall, was the drawing that Julian and I had both wanted so badly, and I realized that this was its context. Nicolai in the drawing was seated in the chair that he occupied now, with an oval mirror behind him, reflecting his profile and the upper part of his body and Lucrèce too, her hands now busy with teapot and teacups instead of with paper and pencil, and I felt as if I were inside the coveted picture rather than outside it in the reality it portrayed—although even that was reality reflected in a mirror.

It was raining again when we left, but Lucrèce threw a cape over her shoulders and came to the gate to see us off. "You must come and visit us again very soon," she said.

This time I chose to sit by myself in the back seat of the car. The hood was up, and what with the rain and the rapidly falling dark there would be nothing to see but the lighted patch of road immediately in front of us. So I might as well sleep, and let the two men talk between themselves. Nicolai began by politely directing remarks to me over his shoulder, but after a while I pretended not to hear. "She's asleep," Julian said. They tried to speak softly, but I caught fragments of their conversation.

"It's a beautiful experiment, I don't deny that, but it isn't far-reaching enough. You'd have accomplished more by using your father's reputation to get yourself into a position of political power and working from there to change things on a big scale."

"My father achieved his reputation by working for the existing system, not against it. If I were to step into his shoes and pull down everything he believed in, I would feel even more guilty toward him than I do now."

"I don't see that at all. You would be tearing down only to rebuild. And there's no earthly reason why you should feel guilty now—you are using your inheritance only for good."

Nicolai's reply was lost in a peal of thunder, and the cloudburst that followed it obliterated both their voices for as long as it lasted. Then the rain slackened off, and at the same time Julian's voice rose.

"Balls!" he cried. "There's no such thing! Good and evil are purely subjective definitions of human actions."

"And I assume that there are some human actions that you would condemn as evil...."

"Right."

"But you would qualify your condemnation as being purely subjective."

"Of course."

"Julian!" I said. "Don't talk rot! You'd do nothing of the sort."

Julian turned sharply around. "I thought you were asleep."

"How could I sleep with you shouting like that?"

He didn't answer. I expected Nicolai to make some tactful remark that would ease the tension, but he said nothing. Both men stayed silent, willfully silent, it seemed to me, for so long that at last I did fall asleep and awakened only when we reached the Calea Victoria.

"You must come and see us again very soon," Nicolai said when we thanked him for the weekend. "The mountains are beautiful in the winter."

But we didn't go again until the spring.

At Christmas, Lucrèce sent us a pen-and-ink drawing of the view from her studio window, to remind us, she said, that she and Nicolai still existed. "We hope to see you here again very soon," was written in Nicolai's hand above their two signatures. The absence of a definite invitation disappointed us, but now that we knew them better we could accept their withdrawal as part of the rhythmic pattern of our relationship with them; and inevitable, since they had renounced the world in which we were obliged to live and despised the social vortex that we were still naive enough to enjoy.

Then one day in early March, when the snow piled up in the streets was turning to slush, I ran into Nicolai unexpectedly on the Calea Victoria.

I saw him before he saw me, and I thought he looked drawn and worried—an impression that his sudden smile of recognition instantly dissipated. "What luck to meet you!" he said. "I just called your flat, after trying to get hold of Julian at the legation and not finding him there."

"Julian's in Galatz," I told him. "He won't be back until tomorrow."

"And I'm going back to Brasov this evening. What about having some tea with me—or are you on your way somewhere?"

I was on my way home. The idea of inviting him back to the apartment crossed my mind and was rejected. "I'd love to have tea with you," I said.

"Do you mind a short walk? I haven't got my car with me, I came down by train. The road to the farm is still impassable by car, even the main road is pretty bad."

I fell into step beside him, not asking where we were going, not even bothering about it. "How's Lucrèce?"

"She's doing a lot of painting. She likes being snowed in. But of course we both ski."

"And how's Marioara . . . and Miss Godwin . . . and that delightful *popa* . . . ?"

While he was answering my questions we left the Calea Victoria and walked a long way down a quiet residential street, named after a general, where the slush on the sidewalk was several inches deep. We stopped at a wrought-iron gate which Nicolai unlocked with a cumbersome key like that of a prison and stepped into a courtyard with a spreading tree, now bare of leaves, growing in the center of it. The pinkish stone house enclosing it was one of those ancient, secret dwellings that, like Old Browne's house by the Black Sea, resemble convents or harems. It had tall, narrow windows barred with wrought-iron grilles, and an imposing arched entrance with a coat of arms carved in stone above it.

"Behold the former palace of the Amans," Nicolai said, "and enter this way, if you please, the present dwelling of the heir who has willfully squandered his substance on a chimera. 'Your poor dear father would turn in his grave'—that's what my aunt says, my father's sister whom you met at Lucrèce's show. Poor lady, she talks in clichés, like most people. The bigger the tragedy, the bigger the cliché."

The former caretaker's flat was close to the gate, with a separate entrance. It consisted of two rooms, opening into each other, and a kitchen. The front room had a window facing the street and was fitted up as an office, with a divan in one corner; the back room, whose window looked out on the courtyard, was more comfortable, furnished with a few beautiful antique pieces that looked out of place under the low ceilings and the uncovered water pipes that ran along the wall and up to the floor above. Now, late on a winter's afternoon, the flat was dark and chilly. A small tile stove was built into the wall between the rooms, and I automatically went up to it as one does to a fireplace, but it was cold.

"I'm sorry," Nicolai said. "I didn't bother to light it. I've been out all day, and the hot-water pipes are enough to keep the temperature bearable. Make yourself as comfortable as you can while I get the tea. This sheepskin will keep you warm."

I curled up on the divan in the back room and pulled the sheepskin that was lying across the end of it up over my knees. Now that I was alone, undiscoverably alone with Nicolai, the disturbance that I usually felt in his presence had gone, as if it had depended upon his unavailability. I merely felt curious as to how he would act toward me in these circumstances that were of his own choosing. I asked him, calling through the open door of the kitchen, when the train left for Brasov—for at that time and in that country trains ran infrequently; it wasn't a question of catching the ten-fifteen if you missed the seven-fifteen, you caught the one and only or waited twelve hours for the next.

"It leaves at six-thirty," he said, "but to get a seat I should be at the station by six o'clock."

Which meant that we had less than an hour. A limitation that might be lucky, but was all the same disappointing.

He came in from the kitchen. "Please excuse me for a moment," he said as he went through the front room to the entrance. "I'll be back in a jiffy." His upper-class accent gave the expression, which he must have picked up in London, a comical sound. He went out just as he was, without putting his coat on, and I wondered where he was going. Perhaps the WC was outdoors. Then I heard the gates clang shut.

Left by myself, I prowled around the two little rooms, trying to get the feel of them. On Nicolai's desk stood a framed photograph of his father in diplomatic court dress. To impress clients? To distract their attention from the makeshift quality of the office, the water pipes going through the ceiling? There were no other photographs, but a couple of Lucrèce's paintings decorated the plain whitewashed walls.

In the back room was a tall cupboard similar to the one in which I had hidden away our dusty car coats in the immaculate guest room at the farm. A key was in the lock. On an impulse I turned it, and the door of the cupboard swung open. At one end hung half a dozen dresses, including the long black velvet dress that Lucrèce had worn at the legation party, and below them was a row of high-heeled shoes. At the other end hung three dark suits, a tuxedo, and a "tails," and a set of neatly treed shoes to go with them. On an upper shelf, hats, gloves, lingerie, shirts were arranged in exquisite order. A series of costumes and masks ready to assume at a moment's notice. It was like the wardrobe of two vaudeville actors, a team sharing the same dressing room and performing nightly a joint burlesque of high society life.

Just as I was relocking the wardrobe, Nicolai opened the outside door, making me start as if I had been caught stealing. He had been out to buy milk for my tea.

"But how ridiculous! I could easily have taken my tea plain!"

"Not easily. Not without making a face as if you were swallowing a bad medicine."

He had brought some *madeleines* too, from the delicatessen. He asked me to pour the tea. I felt constraint setting in. And perhaps he did too. Anyway, we were both silent. Then the water pipes started to gurgle loudly.

"That means that someone upstairs is taking a bath," Nicolai said. "The boiler for this wing of the house is just next door to us." After a moment, he added, "You can see now, can't you, why we never invited you to come here."

"Not really . . . I mean, I can see the superficial reasons, but I don't think they hold good with people like us."

"How could we know, how could we be sure, what sort of people you were?"

"You had some idea before you even met us," I said. "Lucrèce told me that."

"I know," he said.

"And anyway, one sometimes has to take a risk on people."

"We took an enormous risk when we asked you up to the farm."

"Aren't you exaggerating? After all, you knew that Julian and I were in sympathy with your ideas—you told Miss Godwin that was why we were invited."

He didn't dispute that. He couldn't. He held out his cup for more tea without saying anything. The pipes had ceased to gurgle, and the room was very quiet. I could hear the faint tick of the little traveling clock that stood on a table beside the divan. It showed exactly five-thirty.

"Political sympathy isn't everything," Nicolai said. "It doesn't necessarily spell friendship."

"The diplomatic life doesn't spell friendship, either. Lucrèce and I talked about that when we went for a walk in the woods while you were showing Julian the farm."

"I know. She told me."

"Do you tell each other everything?" I asked.

"We couldn't hide anything from each other even if we wanted to," he said. "We can read each other's thoughts."

"That must be because you're twins—you *are* twins, aren't you?"

"Yes. And freaks too, in a way."

I waited for him to explain what he meant by that. He seemed uneasy, as if he had said more than he intended, and wished he could take it back.

He said finally, "It's freakish for fraternal twins to resemble each other physically as we do. We were so much alike when we were born that the midwife thought there must be something wrong with the sex of one of us—that nature had meant us to be identical, both girls, or boys. But we turned out to be normally male and female. So really it's only our physical resemblance that's freakish."

The alarm of the little clock suddenly and unexpectedly went off. Nicolai jumped up and stopped it. "I forgot that I had it set for twenty to six to be sure of not missing my train."

"I must go," I said. "I'm sure you have things to do before you leave."

"I have nothing to do but shove a few papers into my briefcase and turn off the lights. We can leave together—you'll need a droshky—it's raining—and so will I. There's a droshky stand just around the corner."

Any other Rumanian man would have managed to subtly convey the impression that catching the evening train had ceased to be important. Rumanian men were very good at putting themselves gracefully at a woman's disposal. If Nicolai had done that I would have despised him, but I thought that he might have at least expressed regret at having to leave so soon.

I began to gather up the tea things. "Let me do that," he said.

"No, please. You collect your papers. I'll wash the cups."

The tiny kitchen had a wood-burning range, and on top of it was a gas ring. Everything was immaculate. Everything was in order. I washed the cups and hung them on their hooks, and emptied the tea leaves into a tin strainer. "What shall I do with the *madeleines?*" I asked Nicolai.

"I'll eat them on the train," he said.

He helped me on with my coat. Any other Rumanian man would have taken this opportunity to press my shoulders. But not Nicolai. When we were both ready to go, he opened the door and switched off the light—at which point any other Rumanian man would have kissed me, or tried to kiss me, as a matter of principle. But Nicolai stood aside to let me go ahead of him into the courtyard.

The droshky stand was quite literally just around the corner. Nicolai told two of the drivers to pick up their reins. Then he put me into the cab with the sleekest horses. All this time we hadn't said a word to each other. He asked me now where I wanted to go, and I told him, home. He tucked the rug, supplied in all droshkies, around my knees.

"Give my greetings to Julian," he said, "and tell him I'm sorry I missed him."

I held out my hand, and he took it. But instead of giving me the conventional English handshake, he leaned forward and kissed me full and hard, on the mouth, drawing away very quickly, almost with panic, as if my cold, rain-wet lips were live coals.

I told Julian about my meeting with Nicolai, and about having tea with him in his office apartment. I said nothing about the wardrobe full of masks, nor, of course, about that desperate, last-minute kiss, so suggestive of a modern St. Anthony, which had been my first intimation that Nicolai wore a mask all the time.

A few weeks later, I got a letter from Lucrèce, inviting us up to the farm for Easter.

Fortunately, the Orthodox Easter didn't coincide with ours, for Pip and Cissy, who looked forward to Easter egg hunts as much as they did to Christmas, were not included in Lucrèce's invitation. And I could understand why; you couldn't bind children to secrecy.

The Elliotts were going to spend that weekend with American friends at Ploesti, and offered to drive us as far as Sinaia, where we wanted to complete our arrangements for the summer. They had a big American car with plenty of room in the back seat, where I sat with Amanda and listened to her prattle about clothes, parties, the iniquity of Rumanian servants, and other people's marital problems—since with Whitt there she couldn't discuss her own. Which was a good thing. I knew too much already about Whitt's shortcomings as a lover. She was always telling me of the advances made to her by Rumanians, and of how they thrilled her. But she never gave in to any of them.

She belonged to a breed of women now rapidly becoming extinct; a virgin when she married, she was at once puritanical and sensual, responding to sexuality, yearning for it, in fact, but believing adultery to be sinful, and terrified of the slightest physical contact with the inhabitants of a country where the worst of what she called the "unmentionable diseases" was passed on from one generation to another like a national characteristic. Fear of it kept many an English wife faithful to her husband, and not enough fear of it had got many a naive young Englishman into trouble.

As we drove through the burgeoning forest, pooled with bluebells, purled with icy streams, Amanda was telling me in a low voice, because Whitt didn't like her to gossip, of a rumored affair between a middle-aged diplomat's wife and a boy who was almost young enough to be her son. I said that I didn't believe it.

"But it's true," Amanda said, lowering her voice still further. "I know it for a fact."

"You can't know anything for a fact that you haven't seen with your own eyes," I told her sententiously. Just then, as if they guessed what was being whispered about behind their backs, Julian and Whitt stopped talking, and Amanda, always ready for such contingencies, changed the subject with so much expertise that I found myself talking of something quite different without the smallest break.

Half an hour later, when she and I were alone in the ladies room of the hotel in Sinaia, sitting in smelly adjoining cubicles, she went on as if there had been no interruption, "Whitt saw it with his own eyes. He caught them doing it at a party."

"Behind a potted palm?" I inquired sarcastically. The parties of those days, especially diplomatic parties, didn't spill quite so freely into the bedrooms as they do now.

"Behind a potted palm is right," Amanda said. "Whitt was out on the terrace, looking for someplace to . . . well, he had to go and the bathroom wasn't free, and there she was with his you-know-what in her mouth. Whitt was terribly shocked. He said only whores did things like that."

I decided not to disillusion her.

She jerked the chain. "No water," she said, "as usual. You'd think that at least in a hotel as big as this . . . I hope you lined the seat with paper, Joanna."

"No paper," I said.

While we washed our hands under a trickle of rust-colored water in a dirty washbasin, she added her rider, "And it wasn't even a clean, decent, American you-know-what!"

I would have liked to tell her about the Amans' immaculate house. But I knew that the only way to keep their confidence inviolate was not to mention them at all. When Amanda had pressed me to tell her "all about" our first weekend in the mountains, I had taken refuge in the diplomatic trick of talking a lot and saying nothing, of magnifying inessentials to the point that they totally conceal the essentials. For although Amanda was as well-intentioned as Sybil was malicious, the two were equally dangerous when they had something interesting or unusual to tell.

In Sinaia, Julian confirmed his reservation of three rooms in a pension for the summer, although privately I was a little apprehensive now with regard to Nicolai. A whole world of passion, guilt, and desperation had been concentrated in the single leap from behind his mask that Nicolai had allowed himself. And it frightened me, threatened me with the possibility of an emotional demand that I couldn't cope with.

But the Nicolai who came to pick us up and take us on to the farm made me doubt my own senses, wonder whether I had really glimpsed the man behind the mask, or only imagined him.

## III

The Resurrection of Christ, which we had come to celebrate with these two of his twentieth-century disciples, was perfectly synchronized with the spring resurrection of their particular corner of the earth. All life was in bud or blossom. The light was pale and soft, the air scented with fruit trees in bloom, with violets and narcissus, with fresh-plowed earth, with fecundity. Even the black pines had that pale, green-fronded look of new growth. And the people of the farm all seemed to be touched by the glow of the imminent Resurrection as they moved around, preparing for its celebration.

Lucrèce worked with the other women of the household like some medieval mistress of the manor; baking the Easter cakes, turning the lamb roasting on the spit, setting the table for the midnight supper, piling colored eggs into woven baskets. She was dressed in the same style of national costume she always wore, but one so splendid, so exquisitely embroidered, that a queen might have worn it. "It's an heirloom," she said. "It first belonged to my great-great-grandmother, who bequeathed it to her eldest daughter, and so on down the line to my mother, who bequeathed it to me. It's very fragile. I put it on only once a year—for Easter."

"What is bee-queethe?" Marioara asked.

"It is to leave something to somebody in your will," Nicolai said.

"What is a will?"

"It's a letter of instructions to a lawyer—someone like me."

"Did my mother write you a letter of instructions? Did she beequeethe me a beautiful dress?"

"Yes," said Lucrèce, "she did. But you mustn't ask any more questions about it now. You must wait until you are twenty-one years old."

"Why?"

"Because that is the law," her father informed her gravely. "And now you had better take a nap if you want to be wide awake for the Resurrection."

She went off with Lucrèce quite happily; evidently the new relationship had been successfully established.

Later, Julian said to Nicolai, "So you told her about her mother?"

"Lucrèce and I told her together, as Joanna suggested. I'm grateful to you for that suggestion, Joanna. As you see, she is closer to Lucrèce now than she was before. Lucrèce has a new importance for her, a new place in her life. But she's getting more and more difficult with Nana. There are times when I wish that poor Nana had somebody in England who wanted her. I feel what you English call a 'cad' to be saying this after all her years of devotion to us, and of course the question wouldn't arise if it weren't for Marioara. But Nana's getting too old and crotchety to be with a young child, and too mixed up in her mind. She puts all sorts of crazy ideas into Marioara's head—without meaning any harm, of course."

I wasn't so sure of Miss Godwin's good intentions. "Will she come to the Resurrection?" I asked.

"No. In all the years that she's been here, she's never once entered our church. She's a stiff-necked Protestant. But she'll be at the supper, even though she thinks it a pagan feast, and subversive at that—with the slaves all sitting at table with their masters. Poor old Nana. She doesn't see any link between resurrection and revolution."

There was a curious and paradoxical difference between this Easter celebration and the one of two years earlier, at the Gavriolescos'. There was greater simplicity here, but more elegance; even in the church service, whose ritual was, of course, the same, there was less pomp and more true grandeur. And there was an added dimension, in which the congregation became as much a part of the ritual as the celebrating priest, and it seemed to me that this was because the dominant personalities of Nicolai and Lucrèce were, in a way, sacerdotal, diffusing their own spirituality on their people, and influencing us. At the Elevation, Julian dropped to his knees without being pulled down by me.

"Christ is risen!"

The victorious cry was a paean of bells ringing over and over around the church and all the way back to the house; the kisses of peace, a flight of birds brushing our cheeks as they passed.

We put our still-burning candles into the holders provided for them at the supper table, and ate by their flickering light. The supper was not the elaborate feast offered by Sybil and Maximilian, but a simple, almost ritual, meal of roasted lamb, bread, wine, and Easter cakes.

When it was finished, Miss Godwin, tight-lipped with disapproval, took Marioara away to bed, and I was invited to help Lucrèce and the other women clear away the dishes and wash them. Finally accepted as one of the community, I felt immensely happy; and at the same time acutely aware of the spiritual exile in which we normally lived.

Before saying goodnight, we went out to the courtyard and walked there arm in arm with Nicolai and Lucrèce, reluctant to end so perfect an experience, even though I felt that it was actually the start of a lifelong friendship. Looking up at the clear sky, where the stars were already beginning to fade, Nicolai said, "Tomorrow will be another good day, and if you agree, we will go for a long hike in the mountains and take our lunch with us."

Lucrèce presented us with the holders in which our candles had guttered down to the last puddle of wax. "Take these as a keepsake, to remember us by, to remember this Easter by, wherever you are next year."

"We shall never forget it," we said simultaneously, voicing a truth that had yet to be proved.

"Christ is risen!"

"He is risen indeed!"

Alone in our room with the cooling predawn air pouring in through the open windows, we lay awake for a long time without touching or speaking. Then Julian said, half under his breath, as if he were talking in his sleep, "How beautiful . . . " And again, "How very beautiful . . ."

He could have meant the whole Easter experience, but I was sure that he was thinking of Lucrèce. And suddenly I remembered when, and of whom, I had heard him use those words before, in that same tone of wonder. Did he remember? I told him.

"I had forgotten," he said, "but now that you've brought it back to my mind, I see a resemblance . . . it's a sort of radiance."

That made me cry.

The sun of Easter morning was just coming up when a soft but urgent knocking on our door awakened us.

"Coming!" said Julian, leaping out of bed and throwing his dressing gown over his naked body as he went to the door.

Nicolai was outside. I heard him say, "Don't wake Joanna, just come out for a moment."

When Julian came back in, he said, "The child has disappeared. They're afraid she's been kidnapped. I'm going with Nicolai and the other men to search for her."

Quick as he could be in putting his clothes on, I had never seen him do it so fast as he did then.

"Can I come with you?"

"No, you'd be too much of a responsibility."

"Isn't Lucrèce going?"

"Nicolai didn't say . . . but she knows the mountains and you don't, and she has a right to go if she wants to."

He was gone before I could ask any more. Five minutes later I too was dressed, and looking for someone to tell me what had happened. The house was breathlessly still. The door of Lucrèce's studio was ajar, and so was that of her bedroom. She had probably gone with the men. But where were the other women? As I walked through the silent house, my own footsteps muted by soft-soled shoes, I half expected to come upon Marioara creeping out of a closet or a chest, taking advantage of everyone's absence to leave her hiding place. Cissy had frightened the life out of us once by hiding in a big trunk and pretending not to hear when we called her.

I went to the kitchen. If I didn't find anyone there, I could at least make some tea for myself. It would steady my nerves. The kitchen was as deserted as the rest of the house, but a wood fire was alight in the great cooking range, and an iron kettle was already singing on top of it. I was looking around for the tea, and a pot to make it in, when Marie came in from outside. She had been in the church. A Mass was being said for the child's safe return. All the women were there, except for Lucrèce, who had gone with the men to search for the child, and Miss Godwin, of course, who was in her room—asleep. That was why Marie had left the church sooner than the others. She had been afraid that Miss Godwin might wake up and find everyone gone and get into one of her

162

rages, though the master had given her some sort of medicine to calm her down and send her to sleep....

Marie was too upset to be coherent, and I was too nervous to question her intelligibly in Rumanian, but bit by bit I managed to piece together what had happened.

Miss Godwin, it seemed, had awakened very early, as old people do, and had looked into Marioara's room, which was next to her own, and had found the child's bed empty. Believing that Magda had taken the child into her own bed, which was strictly forbidden, Miss Godwin had burst into Magda's room ready to scold the pair of them. But Magda was fast asleep by herself. Miss Godwin had then gone muttering off to Lucrèce's room, to scold *her*—"Imagine that!" said Marie. "The old witch!" But she had found the door of Lucrèce's studio locked, so she had gone, followed by Magda, to Nicolai's room and had found that door locked too. But Nicolai had been aroused by the commotion and had come out immediately, to be confronted by bitter complaints against his sister. He had told the old woman to be quiet and had taken her back to her room, with instructions to stay there. Half an hour later he had awakened everyone in the house, except Miss Godwin, with the news that Marioara was nowhere to be found— he and Lucrèce had looked for her everywhere, all over the house and grounds, in all her favorite hiding places: in the stables, in the cowshed, even in the church, whose door was always unlocked for the only things there that would interest Gypsies—the gold and silver vessels and candlesticks—were kept locked up in the crypt.

Gypsies. We had been warned to keep a sharp eye on Pip and Cissy, never to let them out of sight—even in the park—because of the Gypsies who would steal pretty children and maim them and make them beg. We had thought these were old wives' tales, but now Marie was telling me that a band of Gypsies had been encamped near the village recently, and it was possible that Marioara had been stolen away by them; just before dawn was the time they chose to prowl around the villages, looking for chickens and geese....

"But what would Marioara be doing in the village at dawn?"

"Oh, she likes to run away by herself—what do you expect with that old witch always scolding her?"

And then, of course, she might have gone into the woods to

look for wild flowers and got lost, or Tomaso the bandit might have found her there and carried her off for ransom. Had I heard of Tomaso the bandit? He was young and good-looking, just the sort of person a lost child would follow—and it was easy to lose your way in the woods, and your life too . . . there were bears, and wild boar, and some poisonous snakes, and waterfalls dropping hundreds of feet into bottomless pools . . . and the prettiest wild flowers always grow in the most dangerous places. . . .

I thanked Marie and went out. The undisturbed quiet was not the peace of Sunday. It was the stifling, premonitory stillness of an evil about to strike. I was drawn in spite of myself to the edge of the forest, from where I could hear the distant calls of the searchers. I walked for a mile or more along the rutted track, and then, as the sound of the voices grew fainter and fainter, I made my way back to the church. The priest was on his knees, chanting a sort of litany, with three or four women murmuring the responses. I knelt down with them on the stone floor. Every now and then one of them would get up and leave and someone else would come in and take her place.

The monotonous chanting, the discomfort of kneeling upright and unsupported on the hard stone and my determination to bear it, to forget it altogether, eventually put me into a state of half-trance in which I was not aware of myself at all, and I might have ended by fainting but for the sudden, firm grasp of my arm by Magda, who had come in and knelt down beside me without my noticing. She led me out of the church. The fresh air revived me and brought me back to reality. The church clock struck eleven; I must have been on my knees for a couple of hours.

Marie had prepared a caldron of *mamaliga*, the cornmeal porridge that was the staple diet of Rumanian peasants. Everyone who came into the kitchen was fed. I had no desire to eat, but Marie insisted. I asked if Miss Godwin was all right. She was still asleep, they said—at least she was quiet, and they had thought it better not to disturb her. But I thought she had been too quiet for too long. I offered to take her a cup of tea. It would be an excuse for going in.

Before going in, I knocked. There was no reply. I knocked again. "It's Mrs. Crest," I said. "I've brought you some tea—may I come in?" This provoked an unintelligible mumble that I chose to interpret as permission to enter. Miss Godwin was lying in bed with her eyes wide open. When she saw me, she raised herself on one elbow to reach for her false teeth, which were in a glass of water on the table beside her bed—an old-fashioned brass bedstead, probably brought from England to please her. The top buttons of her nightgown were unfastened, and one withered breast hung out like a wrinkled pear left on the tree all winter. Her yellow-white hair was unpinned, exposing bald spots on her skull. Her almost lashless eyes were gummy with sleep.

The sight of old age ungirt, undone, should have aroused my pity, and would have in the case of any other old woman; but I sensed in Miss Godwin a malignancy, a cancer of the soul that aroused only revulsion. It was an effort to approach her and ask her politely how she was feeling. Before she answered, she put in her dentures, which restored some of her dignity without making her any more lovable.

"I am perfectly well," she said.

"I thought you might like some tea."

She looked at me keenly, as if she had never seen me before. "Are you the new nursery maid?"

"I'm Joanna Crest. My husband and I are staying here for the weekend—don't you remember?"

But she had already lost interest in me and my identity. "Where is the brat?"

"If you mean Marioara, she's . . . playing somewhere outside."

"And where is her mother?"

"I don't know where her mother is. Her father has gone for a long walk in the mountains—with my husband."

A silence ensued while she drank the tea. When I took the empty cup from her hands, she lay back on the pillows, mumbling. I thought she might be hungry. "Is there anything else you would like, Miss Godwin? Some toast . . . a boiled egg?"

"No. Nothing." She shut her eyes. I stood for a moment, looking down at her, trying to feel some compassion for her, and failing.

"Well, what are you waiting for?"

I was halfway across the room to the door when she said sharply, "Come back!"

I stopped and turned. "What is it that you want?" I asked without moving.

"Don't be impertinent! Do what I tell you! Come here at once! *I will not have disobedience*—do you hear?"

She seemed so enraged that I feared she might have a stroke if I defied her. So I went back.

"Sit down on that chair!"

Still humoring her, I obeyed.

"How long have you had the honor of knowing Prince Nicolai Aman?"

"We first met the prince and princess two years ago."

"There is no Princess Aman. Lucrèce is the Devil's daughter."

"I was under the impression that she and the prince were twins," I said mildly.

"They *are* twins—who said they weren't? I should know. I was present at their birth. They were born within a few minutes of each other. Lucrèce came first. The midwife handed her over to me to hold while Nicolai was delivered. If only I had known then . . ."

She brought her ridiculously small white dentures together with a click, like a snapping fox.

"If only you had known . . . what?" I asked after an interval of silence, hating my own curiosity.

"That's none of your business, young woman. What are you sitting there for? Be off with you!"

I was only too pleased to be off. But once I was safely outside the door, I waited, listening. The bedsprings creaked. She was getting up. I heard her using the chamber pot. The bedsprings creaked again. A heavy movement or two. A breaking of wind. Then quiet. But it was only when she began to snore that I went away.

It was now about one o'clock in the afternoon, and I already felt so exhausted that I didn't know how I was going to get through the rest of the day. I wished that I had insisted on going with Julian—anything would have been better than this interminable waiting, hoping, inaction. An hour's sleep might have helped me, but the mere inclination to go to my room and sleep made me feel guilty. I went once more to the edge of the forest. I could hear no human voices. Nothing but the twittering of birds and the rushing of water over rock. I returned to the house. I would get a book, I thought, and try to read. I had noticed a lot of English titles on Nicolai's bookshelves.

The folding doors between his study and his bedroom stood open. The divan that he used for a bed had not been restored to its daytime appearance. The whole room was in the disorder created by emergency, by the need to find equipment or clothing not in regular use and to leave in a hurry. It was on the shelves in this room that I found the kind of book I wanted: a recently published novel that had been well reviewed in *The Times*. I decided to take it with me to the grassy slope beyond the church, from where I would be the first to hear the voices of the returning men, and where I could see, and be seen by, the women coming and going between the farm and the church, so that if they had any news from another direction they would know where I was.

At first I had to force myself to concentrate on the novel. I found myself reading the words without grasping their sense. But I persisted, and gradually the fictional characters and events took over, blotting out reality, and I surrendered to them as one surrenders to sleep after setting an alarm clock that can be relied on to go off at the right moment.

An alarm clock did go off at the right moment. But it wasn't an exterior sound; it rang in my subconscious mind. The sun had already gone down, and I was almost at the end of the book, when I heard, or felt, that extraordinary alarm. No voices came from the forest. None of the men appeared. None of the women called to me. But I knew, I was absolutely certain, that the search had come to an end.

I ran down the slope to the church and entered it just as the priest was rising from his knees. After bowing to the altar, he turned to the little knot of kneeling women and raised his hand in blessing. "Go home now," he said. "The litany is over. God's will be done."

The women left, but I stayed. The priest came to me. *"Il y a des nouvelles?"*

I shook my head.

His eyes, ringed with fatigue, continued to question me. All trace of the jolly, worldly priest who enjoys a good meal had gone. His pale, black-bearded face was like that of a suffering Christ. At last he said, *"Vous êtes mère?"*

*"Oui, mon Père."*

Another long, scrutinizing look. A deep sigh. Then, *"Priez pour elle. . . . Je n'en peux plus. . . ."*

He swayed as though he were going to faint. I took his arm to steady him, and he allowed me to lead him to the only seat in sight, the carved priest's chair inside the sanctuary. *"Pardonnez-moi. Je suis exténué. . . ."*

I advised him to put his head down between his knees. He obeyed me like a child.

After a while he raised his head. *"On devient vieux. Dans le temps, j'étais capable de rester à genoux toute la nuit. . . ."*

At that moment, Marie came into the church. She was out of breath, as if she had run all the way from the house. The priest got up, but he was still unsteady, and he leaned on my arm for support as he stepped down from the sanctuary to the nave. Marie told us that Lucrèce had just returned alone. She had walked past the waiting women as if she didn't see them, and had gone into her studio and shut the door. She had looked . . . but I didn't understand the word that Marie used to describe how Lucrèce had looked. The priest interpreted, *"Désespérée . . . Elle avait l'air désespérée."*

He disengaged himself from my supporting arm as if the confirmation of his intuition of what God's will might be had given him back his strength. He dismissed us with a blessing, which we knelt to receive. As I turned to go, he said again, *"Priez pour elle."*

It was now so clear to me that Marioara was Lucrèce's child that I was astounded at myself for not having realized it before. Both Julian and I had swallowed Nicolai's simulated frankness, his protective fiction, hook, line, and sinker. Yet now it seemed so obvious that that was just the sort of quixotic thing that Nicolai would do, perhaps that any affectionate twin brother would do, in such a case. The truth, I thought, would confirm Julian's faith in Nicolai's basic decency, but it would shatter his romantic image of Lucrèce as some sort of vestal virgin. Which might have been a relief to me under other circumstances, for it did not shatter my image of her as a strong, self-contained woman. If anything, it enhanced it. But all I felt at that moment was pity.

My thoughts were interrupted by Julian's voice calling my name. He and Nicolai were walking together along the rutted track. I told Marie to go on to the house and I turned back to join the two men. But they separated at the door of the church.

"Nicolai wants to tell the priest," Julian said.

"Where did you find her?"

"Not very far from here—at the bottom of a ravine, a sort of flume, but accessible only from the top. Nicolai had to let himself down with a rope. He decided to do it only after we had given up all hope of finding her alive. Actually, it was Lucrèce who suggested it. Have you seen her? As soon as Nicolai's signal came up, she rushed off into the woods. I ran after her. But when I caught up with her she asked me, quite calmly, to leave her alone—she was all right, she was going back to the house."

"No, I haven't seen her. But she's at the house. Marie saw her come in."

He took my hand and held it very tightly. We sat down on a bench in the garden. We were both of us thinking, *It could have been Pip or Cissy.*

Presently Nicolai appeared. He came up to us and embraced us, putting one arm around Julian's shoulder and one arm around mine. "My friends," he said, "I am going to ask you to leave now. One of the men will drive you into Brasov in time to catch the evening train to Bucharest."

We went together into the house. "Can you be ready to go in about twenty minutes?" Nicolai asked. "I am going now to Lucrèce. And then I'll find someone to drive the car."

Julian and I packed our things in silence. We both felt stricken and useless. It was terrible to think that the only thing we could do to help was to leave our friends alone with their grief.

Nicolai was waiting by the car when we came out. Magda's young man, Peter, was at the wheel.

"I would like to see Lucrèce for a moment," I said, "do you think . . . ?"

"I think she would like to see you, and you too, Julian. But knock very softly, in case she's asleep. I gave her some bromide."

I wanted to see Lucrèce alone. As we went to her wing of the house, I whispered to Julian, "Do you mind if we go in separately?"

"No. It's better that way."

She was not asleep. Someone was in her room with her, talking. At the studio door we paused, uncertain of whether or not to interrupt. "It sounds like Miss Godwin," Julian said.

169

It was Miss Godwin. Her voice suddenly rose on a high note of biblical denunciation. "God is not mocked! God chastises the sinner! God crushes the fruit of whoring and incest under His heel. . . ."

"Did you see her?" Nicolai asked.

"No," said Julian. And I added, lying in the hope that Nicolai would not go back to her now, would never put two and two together, "She didn't answer our knock, she must have fallen asleep."

## IV

We were aware that incest was not uncommon in that part of the world; but to come to terms with it emotionally in connection with two people whom we loved and respected, with whom, in fact, we were more than a little in love, was very different from the purely intellectual acceptance of it as an ethnic deviation from our own sexual taboos.

Everything we admired in Nicolai and Lucrèce, and in their lives, not only their personal rectitude, but everything—their political ideals, their efforts to create a utopia, their religious faith—was devaluated for us, contaminated by a sin against nature that both of us had been taught to regard with horror. And the contamination extended to us, affecting our relationship with each other by inhibiting sexual desire in Julian, as though the sin of Nicolai and Lucrèce had tainted all sex with its strange, seductive evil.

There were moments when I thought that our strongest bond had been irreparably weakened, perhaps broken. And in one sense, it had been. We were never again to make love with such joyous freedom, such pre-serpent innocence and delight in ingenuity as we had done, miraculously, for the first eight years of our married life. Evil had changed overnight from an intellectual concept to an emotional reality. We could no longer assume, as we had, as I certainly had, that whatever we did with each other, with love, was pure.

Yet, in the final analysis, that notion, the notion that love purifies everything, was deep-rooted enough to stop us from repudiating our friends. That, and the romantic appeal of great sinners. For the incest of Nicolai and Lucrèce was sin on a grand scale; neither pitiful, like the half-hearted "mistakes" of Old Browne, nor tawdry, like the family games of the Gavriolescos. And the death of the child had conferred on it the grandeur and inevitability of Greek tragedy.

In the first terrible wave of revulsion and disillusionment that had temporarily blotted out all other feelings, we had decided to cancel our summer reservations at Sinaia. But subconsciously, I suppose, we both knew that this was only a shock reaction. For Julian didn't write the letter and I didn't remind him to do so. In fact, we said very little to each other about the situation. It touched each of us too deeply, too personally, for open discussion. Our change of attitude was arrived at silently. We watched each other go through successive phases of feeling, recognizing them, without comment, as mutual reflections.

Nicolai kept his promise to write, but only after several weeks had gone by, which was just as well. He wrote:

My friends, I wish I could see you both, but for the present I can't leave here. That night, just after you left, poor Nana had a stroke. She is paralyzed all down one side and unable to speak or do anything for herself. Lucrèce looks after her. In a sense our whole household has had a stroke—it's as if the springs of our communal life had been broken. When are you coming to Sinaia?

This letter arrived in the middle of June, a few days after Sybil had shown me the obscene ring, which symbolized a relationship so degrading that the forbidden love of Nicolai and Lucrèce seemed noble by comparison.

Julian wrote and told Nicolai that we would all be in Sinaia on the first weekend in July.

We expected him to drive over to see us that weekend, and the prospect of meeting him, and taking up our friendship with him and Lucrèce again in the light of our new awareness, and in the shadow of their tragedy, was more dismaying now that it was so imminent. "I've been thinking," Julian said, "and I don't see how we can possibly take up the friendship again on the same footing as before."

"Obviously not."

"What I mean is, we can't lie, and allow them to go on lying about something so important, and still be friends."

"If they choose to go on lying, it seems to me that we have to accept the lie."

"We can lay *our* cards on the table."

"I can't."

"I can," Julian said, "and I will—even if it means never seeing them again afterward."

"Which we probably won't," I said. "They're far too proud."

But Nicolai didn't come that weekend, or the next. Nor did he write.

At the end of the third week, on Saturday evening after supper, Julian and I were strolling through the park on our way to the Casino when we saw Nicolai and Lucrèce coming toward us, outwardly unchanged, outwardly as serene and regal as ever. In the few seconds that elapsed between our first sight of them and our actual meeting, I panicked. When I was a young girl, one of my mother's friends lost her only child, and afterward, whenever she came to see us, she would talk about him and weep. How would Lucrèce behave? What should *we* say and do? What would *they* say and do?

They did what their breeding made inevitable. They greeted us as if nothing had happened between their goodnight to us after the Easter celebration and this meeting. Lucrèce, in particular, gave the impression of having achieved a state of mind in which it was possible for her to start again with us from that point, relying on us not to mention the passion of Easter Sunday—and unaware, of course, that we knew their secret.

Knowing what Julian was determined to do, I trembled inwardly. For the moment, however, he took his cue from them, and we engaged in a sincere-sounding but totally artificial conversation about the weather, the people staying at the resort, the concerts at the Casino—about nothing, in short. It was Nicolai who suddenly sounded a more serious note, but still not a wholly true one.

"We intended to come over and see you as soon as you got here. But we couldn't because of poor Nana. She had a second stroke, then pneumonia set in . . . and that was the end. It was, of

172

course, the best thing that could happen for her, and indeed for all of us. But she was part of our lives. . . ."

While Nicolai was telling us this, I glanced covertly at Lucrèce. Her expression was grave and composed; it betrayed nothing of what she must have felt. In the face of this reserve, to lay, as Julian put it, our cards on the table would be nothing short of brutal. No friendship could survive such an act. But sooner or later he would do it, I knew that.

"We were wondering," Nicolai said, apparently casual, "whether you two would like to come back with us to the farm—and stay overnight."

I left the decision to Julian. He paused before answering. His hesitation was so noticeable that Lucrèce said softly, "Don't come if you would rather not—we understand."

"Oh no," Julian said grimly, almost savagely. "Oh no. You *don't* understand."

I put my hand on his arm. "Julian . . . "

"We'll come," he said more quietly, but with a concentrated bitterness that even I hadn't suspected him of feeling. "We'll go back to the pension now and get our things and tell Fräulein—unless you would like to dance for a bit at the Casino, first."

Again I said, "Julian . . . "

"In this country," Nicolai said, "it is not the custom to go to public places of amusement when one is in deep mourning, even if one feels like it. Which we do not."

For a moment he and Julian looked at each other with the pain and surprise of close friends who have somehow come to the verge of hating each other. Then Julian said, "I'm sorry, old chap, I shouldn't have said that."

"We'll wait for you here," said Lucrèce.

We left them sitting on a bench near the bandstand. As we moved away, the band struck up a Viennese waltz. Julian's expression was set and grim. I foresaw an unbearable scene. I said, "Do you hate them? Because if you do, we'd better not go."

"We have to go. We have to resolve this bloody situation even if it means doing violence to them and to ourselves. You know that."

"I'm not so sure. If we let Lucrèce think she was right—that

173

we'd rather not go to the farm because it would remind us ... because it would be painful ... our connection with them would die a natural death. And it won't be long before we're out of the country."

"It's you who should be the diplomat," Julian said, "not me. I'm not cold-blooded enough."

The look he gave me was hostile. I felt included in his bitterness and disillusionment.

Nicolai and Lucrèce must have been watching for us. While we were still at a good distance from them, they got up and came to meet us. We walked together to their car without saying anything.

Julian and I sat together in the back, and Lucrèce sat in front with Nicolai, as on the last occasion when the four of us had driven through the forest together at night—on our way to the tavern at Brasov. We had all been silent then; but our mutual silence now had a different quality. The tension then had originated with Lucrèce; and Nicolai, sensitive to her moods, had reflected it. Now there was a powerful tension among the four of us, and between me and Julian; a tension so explosive that the only safety lay in total silence.

Although it was only about ten o'clock when we reached the house, all the lights were out, as if in mourning for the old and the young dead. I had forgotten how early people went to bed in the country.

The night was soft and warm. Lucrèce suggested that we should sit out-of-doors. The big courtyard, which we had seen only in spring and fall, was transformed now into a bower of roses and honeysuckle. A few folding chairs, the hammocky deck chairs of striped canvas that one saw lined up at the English seaside or in Hyde Park, were grouped at one end around a low wicker table.

Nicolai brought out a flagon of wine and four of the Bohemian glass goblets, and Lucrèce opened a tin of Huntley and Palmer's mixed biscuits. Then Nicolai turned off the terrace light, leaving us in a perfumed darkness made faintly luminous by the moon, in whose light forms were discernible but faces and expressions blessedly invisible.

The wine relaxed the tension between us just enough to allow us to talk more or less naturally about impersonal subjects.

Nicolai filled up the goblets a second time. He emptied his very quickly and refilled it. I got the impression that he was bracing himself to tell us something. Finally he said, "Lucrèce and I are thinking of going away."

"Going away?" repeated Julian with surprise. "For how long?"

"Forever," Lucrèce said.

"You can't be serious!" Julian cried. "What about your people?"

"I'll see to it that they don't suffer," Nicolai said.

Julian took two or three turns up and down the length of the courtyard. Then, in answer to a gesture from Nicolai he refilled his own goblet with wine. "So that's why you asked us to come here tonight—to say good-bye."

Lucrèce said very quietly, "You did not want to come, did you?"

"No," Julian said.

"Then why did you come?"

Julian hedged. "That question is more difficult to answer than you realize, Lucrèce."

The silence that fell now among the four of us, and our physical stillness, was so profound that I could hear the petals of a blown rose falling on the flagstones beside my chair. A small nocturnal animal came out of the bushes and sat motionless in the moonlight within a few feet of us, to scurry away only when an owl hooted in the distance.

"It began a long time ago," Lucrèce said very low, as if talking to herself, "when we were about fifteen. It seemed the most natural thing in the world. Natural, and beautiful, and inevitable."

"It began before that," her brother said. "It began before we were born."

There was another long silence.

Then Nicolai went on speaking, but in a different tone; objective and unemotional, as if he were arguing a point of law.

"In a purely physical way it happens quite often in our society—Rumanians are not so puritanical about sex as the English are. Sex between adolescents, even between siblings, is looked upon as a natural phase in the process of growing up.

"But with us it was something much deeper than that. It was the physical manifestation of our fundamental oneness, our *total* oneness."

He paused, and raised his head, as though looking to us, the unseen jury, for signs of comprehension.

"The usual change, the turn outward, the normal sexual attraction to others, never took place. Instead, we grew more and more involved with each other, more and more satisfying to each other. For either one of us to turn elsewhere for physical love would have been for us an adultery far more serious than what we saw and despised in the lives of the grown men and women around us.

"If our parents had had any inkling then of what was happening, they would probably have diagnosed our condition as prolonged adolescent romanticism, and separated us for a year or two. But they didn't see anything. The fact that we were twins blinded them, I suppose. It was natural for twins to be inseparable companions. As for Nana, she disapproved of Rumanian morals, and she was very suspicious of what Lucrèce might be up to, but she never looked in the right direction. Such a suspicion was beyond Nana's imagining. And we were naturally secretive—about everything. For our determination to belong only to each other, and in the fullest possible way, wasn't our only deviation from the norm. We were revolted by, and in revolt against, the inequalities of our feudal society.

"But at seventeen, although we were on fire with revolutionary idealism, we were intelligent enough to know that we were still too young to pit our values against the values of the society of which we were a product. Even at twenty-one we were still too young to do that. And even now, at thirty, we haven't done it openly."

"But at twenty-one I wasn't too young to want a child," Lucrèce said, again as if talking to herself, explaining herself to herself. "For me that was the logical progression in our relationship. It seemed to me that a love that didn't produce a child was like a fruit tree that doesn't bear fruit—it soon ends up on the fire. What irony . . . ."

"Christ Almighty!" Julian leaped up from his chair and strode off into the darkness. A minute or two later, he came back and sat down. "Sorry," he said, "but I find all this bloody hard to take."

176

"It is for us to apologize," Nicolai said. "Our only excuse for submitting you to this ... to such ... embarrassment is that we thought you would want to clear things up, to know whether what you overheard was the truth."

"It was not only that," said Lucrèce. "We, too, wanted to clear things up. To be honest with you. To tell you what we believe to be the truth. To be understood."

They had turned the tables on Julian, and he hated to lose the initiative in any situation. He reached for the wine. "I may be able to understand you better if I get drunk."

The flagon was empty. Nicolai said, "I'll fetch another one," but Lucrèce said, "No, let me get it."

When she was out of hearing, Nicolai said, "She is on the extreme edge."

I wasn't sure what he meant, but before I could ask he put up a warning hand, and a moment later she reappeared, reminding me of another occasion when her approaching footsteps had been inaudible to me but not to him. Julian had caught the drift of Nicolai's words quicker than I had. "Forgive me," he said, when she filled his goblet, "if I sounded brutal. I didn't mean to be, the last thing I want to do is hurt you. I love you both."

He held out his cigarette case to Nicolai, who took a cigarette from it as if accepting a peace offering. Lighting it, he smoked for a little while in silence. Then he said, "Do you want me to go on?"

"Yes. I won't interrupt again."

"We were nearly twenty-two when our mother died. And after our period of mourning, my father, who had been trying to marry Lucrèce off ever since she was eighteen, began to suggest possible 'good marriages' for me. Of course he didn't get anywhere with either of us. But the real reason seems never to have occurred to him. He didn't seem even to realize that our preoccupation with each other was abnormally exclusive. He simply thought we were hard to please. When we said that we wanted to go and study in England for a couple of years, he thought it a good idea. Perhaps he hoped that the English would prove more attractive to us than our compatriots.

"He gave us introductions to everyone worth knowing in London, from his point of view, and at first we went out a lot—for form's sake. Then we gradually dropped out of the social round, on the pretext of being too busy with our studies, and entered another world altogether—the world of Socialist politics. It accepted us very simply on our merits—one of which was, I am sure, that we spoke such good English. And although we were foreigners, our musical-comedy country *had* been an ally during the war. Needless to say, we dropped our title. Nobody asked any questions about our private lives. We were just two students with the right political opinions."

He paused, as if in recollection of incidents that mattered to him, but that were not strictly relevant to the story he was trying to tell us.

"Our daughter," he said finally, "was born in a South London hospital. On the birth certificate the father's name and profession were listed as unknown."

He paused again, and took a little wine before he went on.

"When she was six weeks old, we came back to Rumania and brought her with us. Not directly here. We left her with foster parents in another province, where we were unknown. We brought her here only after our father's death a few months later, when our mourning made it possible, necessary, in fact, to withdraw entirely from society for a year. After that the people who had been invited here when our parents were alive had got used to not being invited, so none of them ever saw Marioara, or realized that we had a child living with us.

"As for our people here, we let it be understood that she was the orphaned child of some distant relatives. Which they accepted for what it was, a conventional fiction. No one believed it. Everyone took for granted that she was my illegitimate child—which was quite natural, all the masters had illegitimate children."

Julian said, "May I ask you a question?"

"Yes, of course."

"What would you have done about the child if your father had not died when he did?"

"I don't know. I think that to have her with us I would have told him that she was my child. But the decision was never ours to make. Everything was decided for us. By our initial revolt we had set in motion a mechanism that controlled us."

Out of the darkness came Lucrèce's beautiful, somber voice. "We aroused the vengeance of God," she told herself.

Nicolai went over to her and knelt down beside her chair. Her hands were clasped in her lap. He took them in both of his and pressed them against his cheek. The gesture was extraordinarily tender, and touching in its openness. "My dearest," he said, speaking very soothingly, as to a sick child, "my dearest, you mustn't forget God's mercy."

Again the four of us fell silent.

It was Lucrèce who spoke first. "Perhaps we have said enough. Perhaps we are asking too much of friendship. We have lived with all this for so long that we cannot judge its effect upon others. Only the priest has heard it. But priests are used to hearing such things. Like God."

"Between friends," Julian said, "there can be no half measures. Only the whole truth will do. It may hurt, but at least it makes a clean wound."

"Even a clean wound can be fatal," Nicolai said.

"We came prepared to take that risk," Julian told him.

"I know now," Nicolai said, "Lucrèce and I both know now, that we should have come back from England prepared to take that risk with our father. The wound that killed him was not a clean one."

I recalled the first secretary telling me as we danced together at the legation party that their father had been killed in an accident—a car crash. Was something concealed here too?

As if he could read my thoughts, Nicolai went on, "It's true that he was actually killed in a car crash, but we don't know whether it was really an accident."

"Whatever it was," said Lucrèce, "we were the cause."

"But we didn't know it at the time," Nicolai said. "I told you once, Julian, that I couldn't help feeling guilty for using the money and the property that I had inherited from my father in the service of an ideology to which he was bitterly opposed, and you told me that I had no reason to feel guilty on that account. I think you were right. But it would have been a very different matter if I had done what I did knowing, or believing, that I was guilty of his death—or at least morally responsible for it. As it was, the project had been started long before we found out what had happened on the day of his—accident. We were still unaware of it when we first met you. In fact, our enlightenment came only after we had met you for the third time—at Lucrèce's show."

"It changed our lives," said Lucrèce. "It changed us. The next time we were together with you, at your house, *you* were the same, but we were different people."

"When the coroner returned a verdict of accidental death, due to momentary loss of control of his car on a dangerous curve, there was nothing to make us doubt the truth of it. And Nana kept silent. She kept silent for four whole years—until her hatred of Lucrèce grew too strong for her to contain."

"Sooner or later she had to speak. She acted as God's mouthpiece."

Nicolai moved restlessly, as if he wanted to contradict Lucrèce but dared not, for fear, perhaps, of pushing her over that edge which might, I thought now, be the edge of madness. He stroked her hair, silently humoring her. After a few moments he took up the story again.

"It was after the memorial Mass on the fourth anniversary of my father's death. Lucrèce had just returned to the house. . . ."

"She must have been watching for me at her window. She must have seen me come in. She was there in my studio, waiting for me, and I thought she had gone mad. She cursed me, she cursed the day I was born. She asked God to strike me dead. She called me terrible names. She accused me of causing my father's death and my brother's damnation. Then she started to slap my face—and I screamed for Nicolai."

"When I came, I, too, thought that Nana had lost her mind. Lucrèce was lying face down on the floor with her hair all unpinned and her dress half torn off, and Nana was whipping her savagely with one of her own leather sandals.

"I dragged Nana away forcibly and locked her in her room. Later, I gave her a sleeping draft. She slept for twenty-four hours. When she woke up, she tried to pretend that she didn't remember anything about what had taken place. But she couldn't keep up the pretense—she hated Lucrèce too much, and she burst out against her to me, in the vilest terms.

"Faced, for the first time, with her naked avowal of hatred for the one person in the world I loved the most, I lost all love for Nana. All pity, too. I cross-examined her as I would have cross-examined a hostile witness in court, and I broke her down. She finally told me as much of what had happened on the day of my father's death as she herself knew.

180

"This is what I pieced together from her half-hysterical admissions. On that day, my father was here alone. Lucrèce and I had gone to Bucharest in my car, and we planned to spend the night there, in our town house. Nana took advantage of our absence to go into Lucrèce's rooms. In the course of her prying she found, in Lucrèce's trinket box, two keys. One of them opened Lucrèce's secretary, which she always kept locked, and the other opened an inner drawer in which there was an envelope containing Marioara's birth certificate and a package of letters I had written to Lucrèce on different occasions, including one that I wrote to her after the birth of our child, while she was still in the hospital.

"The English birth certificate made it perfectly clear to Nana that Lucrèce had had an illegitimate child by an unknown man while in London. The letters, in particular the one celebrating the birth, revealed that I was the father. They were written in Rumanian, but after twenty-five years in this country Nana understood the language much better than she chose to admit.

"She took the certificate and the whole package of letters to my father—she believed it to be her duty, she said. After he had looked at the certificate, he asked her where she had found it, and how. She told him the truth. He took the keys from her, and made her solemnly swear that she would never speak of the birth certificate to anyone. She was to completely forget its existence. She had not dared to tell him what the letters revealed, and the package was still unopened when she left him—she was, if I know my father, ordered by him to get out of his sight.

"A couple of hours later, he took his car and drove off without telling anyone where he was going or when he planned to return. On the road to Bucharest, at one of the sharp curves near Sinaia, his car hit a tree and turned over. The doctors said that he must have been killed instantly."

Now it was Nicolai who got up and began to pace up and down the courtyard. It had become extremely dark. The moon had gone down behind a mountain and the dawn had not yet come up.

When Nicolai ceased pacing, he did not resume his seat. He stood before us, once more addressing an unseen jury. His voice, which had broken when he spoke of his father's death, was even, and his tone impersonal, as he summed up the evidence.

"One significant fact, the only one that we have to help us conjecture his intentions, is that before he left here he put the certificate and the package of letters back where Nana had found them, locked both the drawer and the secretary, and replaced the two keys in the trinket box.

"The unanswered question is, Did he restore the damning evidence to its place because he wanted to see if his children would tell him the truth without being confronted with it, and in his distress of mind took a dangerous curve too fast? Or was his disappointment in us and his sense of besmirched family honor so great that he decided to kill himself? But in such a manner, and after taking such precautions, that unless Nana talked, we would have no reason to believe that it wasn't an accident. Either course of action was in keeping with my father's character."

"Whatever it was, we caused it," said Lucrèce again. "We killed him."

This reiteration of guilt suddenly made me angry with Lucrèce. I admired her for her strength, and it didn't make much difference to me whether she was a strong sinner or a strong saint.

"Anyone would think that you *wanted* to be guilty!" I said. "Your actions may have been the indirect cause of his death, but Miss Godwin was the direct cause of it. In fact, *she* was guilty on three counts. She set out to destroy you, Lucrèce, and in the process she destroyed your father and your child."

A peculiar silence followed this tactless outburst. Then Nicolai asked, "Have you any special reason for thinking that?"

I wished now that I had kept quiet. "No tangible reason. It's no more than an intuitive guess, I suppose." Then I told them what I hadn't yet told Julian: of the incident between me and Miss Godwin on the day of Marioara's disappearance; of my dislike for the old woman, my fear of the evil, the will to destruction, that I sensed in her, and of my feeling that her hatred was directed not only agaisnt Lucrèce but against Marioara too. She was probably jealous, I told them, of any female, whether mistress, sister, or child, whom Nicolai loved. And since then, I said, I had wondered whether her confusion of me with a maid or a child had been genuine, or only a cunning attempt to make me think her senile and not responsible.

"So all this time you've been quietly analyzing the situation," Julian said with a mixture of bitterness and respect. "I didn't know that you had it in you to be so secretive. Or so analytical. But you still haven't explained what connection Miss Godwin had—or you think she had—with what happened to Marioara."

Before I answered, I looked at Lucrèce. It was getting light. I could see her face quite clearly, and the grayness of the light made it look like stone. Her expression was grave, serene, composed as ever, and now I saw this serenity as unnatural, a mask—like a death mask. I looked from her to her brother. He said, "Tell us, Joanna."

Challenged, my intuitions seemed so farfetched that it would be better not to voice them. But I knew by the waiting silence that I was not going to be let off now, I had already gone too far.

Reluctantly, disjointedly, I told them, "I think Miss Godwin spied on Lucrèce. Somehow or other she must have found out where it was that Lucrèce went all by herself every afternoon, and told Marioara—Marioara admitted that, herself. And I think that for some obscure reason she led Marioara to believe that Lucrèce would go there to see the sunrise on Easter morning. . . ."

Lucrèce started to scream; terrible, piercing screams that rang in my ears long after her brother and Julian had carried her between them into the house.

We were driven back to Sinaia by the same young man who had driven us to the railway station at Brasov on Easter Sunday. He was as impassive and silent now as he had been then, yet both then and now he conveyed the impression of not being surprised by what had happened.

Julian said, "We shall never come here again."

I knew what he meant. It wasn't that he had decided against coming here again, but that he felt, as I did, that it wasn't in the cards. Professional nomads quickly acquire an infallible sense of whether or not they will ever return to a place they are leaving. But I was sure that Nicolai had meant it when he had said on taking leave of us, "I shall come over and see you as soon as it is possible," for I was sure that he still needed us, needed to further unburden himself. The whole story hadn't been told yet.

There was the usual long interval of silence, however, and our stay at Sinaia was almost over when he finally appeared. He found me alone. The sudden illness of a colleague had obliged Julian to give up the last few days of his leave.

Nicolai arrived, without any warning, one day after lunch, when the children were having their naps and I was lying in a deck chair on the sunny balcony onto which all the front bedrooms opened. I was trying to sleep, but the old lady who had recently come to stay in the room next to mine wanted to talk about her daughter, who was in such favor with the royal family that she had a personal key to one of the doors of the Summer Palace. I didn't believe it, but when the chambermaid came to tell me that Prince Nicolai Aman was waiting for me downstairs, the old lady gave me a knowing look that was almost obscene.

Although I had been expecting Nicolai every day for more than four weeks, the announcement of his arrival threw me into the same kind of panic that I had felt on encountering him and Lucrèce in the park—the panic of the moment preceding an unavoidable experience that can turn out to be at either extreme of the emotional spectrum.

Yet now, as soon as I saw him, I told myself that the buildup of emotional expectation, or fear, was all in my imagination. And our first half-hour together, sitting on the terrace of the hotel drinking *spritzl*—white wine and soda water—seemed to bear this out. Nicolai, though a little drawn and anxious-looking, was back again in his urbane, Anglicized persona, which, now that I knew how false it was, I could no longer tolerate.

Struggling to achieve the real contact with him that I wanted, even though I dreaded it—and that he must want, I thought, or he wouldn't have come—I realized that he was actually harder to communicate with on a personal level than was the more obviously uncommunicative Lucrèce. His apparent frankness was in fact the most impenetrable of all screens, tightly woven as it was of carefully selected fictions into a perfect forgery of truth. Even, I thought, on that night of harrowing confession, we had glimpsed the real man only for a moment. His moment of open tenderness to Lucrèce.

We were getting nowhere. He had said, "Lucrèce couldn't come," and I had said, "I'm sorry. How is she now?" and he had avoided answering. We finished our *spritzls*, and Nicolai called the waiter to bring us more. But I said I had had enough, I felt like taking a walk.

One only had to walk a few hundred yards from the hotel to be in the forest. Nicolai and I went up the winding road to the Summer Palace, which was as far as the average strolling visitor ever got, and I told him what my next-door neighbor had said about her daughter, who could let herself into the palace whenever she liked. "That must be Magda Lupescu," he said.

A little farther on, we left the road at his suggestion and followed an upward path through the woods. After climbing for half an hour or so, we came to a little waterfall and sat down beside it to rest. I dabbled one hand in the ice-cold water, then rubbed it dry on the pine needles. Nicolai covered it for a moment with his own hand, pressing it lightly. "Dear Joanna . . ."

I said, "Dear Nicolai . . . Please tell me about Lucrèce."

He hesitated. "Lucrèce is ill. Very ill."

There was something in his tone that alarmed me, conveying an impression of the worst left unsaid, like the telegram that tries to soften the final truth by implying an already nonexistent hope.

"Her illness is not physical. She's been split in two. And she thinks that the lightning that split her in two, and split us apart, is the vengeance of God. . . ."

I waited for him to go on. Instead, he lay back on the bed of dry leaves and pine needles and closed his eyes, recalling a similar gesture of withdrawal on the part of Lucrèce. I let him be. To put him at ease, I too lay back and closed my eyes. We were very near to each other, but it was just as if Pip were lying beside me—I felt maternal toward him, protective.

When his even breathing told me that he had fallen asleep, I opened my eyes, with the feeling that I had to watch over him while he slept. His blunt-featured, Slavic face, which had been so sensually attractive to me, now appealed only to my compassion. He had said that his relationship with Lucrèce had begun before they were born. Looking down at him now, all his weakness exposed in sleep, I understood. I could see them following an inevitable destiny; curled together in the same womb, and in life refusing to be uncurled; forging bonds that they thought were indestructible, only to have them destroyed by a flash of Divine retribution.

Nicolai sighed in his sleep and stirred. I didn't want him to wake and find me lying so close beside him, so I slipped off my sandals and waded to a boulder a few yards distant from him, still keeping a watchful eye on him while the water swirled achingly cold around my ankles. He awakened suddenly, sitting up with a jerk and rubbing his eyes as if he didn't know where he was or how he had got there. Then he saw me. "Excuse me," he said. "I fell asleep." He knelt down by the pool and dipped his whole head in it, shaking the water out of his blond hair afterward like a dog, then drinking from his cupped hands.

"For a moment," he said, "when I first woke, I was confused. I haven't been here for years, but Lucrèce and I used to come here as children, when our parents were visiting at the palace."

So that was why he had been unable to go on talking about Lucrèce—here, in these nostalgic surroundings, it was too painful. Yet it was he who had suggested coming here. Perhaps he had thought that it would help him to talk about her and had found out that he was wrong. I wanted to help him now, but I couldn't think of any opening remark that wouldn't sound either banal or prying. So I said nothing. In silence I dried my feet and put on my sandals; in silence he watched me. Then I asked, "Shall we go on up?"

His answer came from behind the screen. "There is nothing I'd like better, but I'm afraid that I have to be getting back to the farm . . . at this time of year we are pretty busy, and my right-hand man, Marie's husband, is temporarily immobilized with a broken leg. . . ."

With every downward step we were getting farther away from the accomplishment of his purpose in coming to see me. And it might well be the last opportunity. In two days' time, I was leaving for Bucharest, and a few weeks later we would sail for South America.

The turrets of the palace were already in view when I finally cried, in desperation, "Nicolai! Why can't you tell me the truth? Why can't you ever tell the whole truth about anything?"

## V

When I said good-bye to Nicolai that afternoon in Sinaia, I knew that we would not meet again. The moment of truth between us had been too painful. I had succeeded in breaking through the screen, and in doing so I had wounded the pride of the man behind it.

Julian, who knew nothing of this, expected to see Nicolai, if not Lucrèce, or at least to hear from him, before we left for South America. But he let us go without a word. It was years before we heard from him again. But I think that this is where I should record the letter, or testament, that he began to write on the anniversary of Marioara's death, but sent to us, in care of the Foreign Office, only after two more Easters had come and gone. Here it is:

Easter, 1927

My friends,

I do not know when I shall send you this—perhaps never. But it must be written. I must write it to save ... what? My soul? My sanity? I am not sure that I haven't already lost them both, irretrievably. In any case I must make an effort to set down the truth. The whole truth.

When I saw you last, Joanna, you accused me of never telling the whole truth about anything, of constructing a screen of plausible falsehoods to hide behind, which was such a successful counterfeit of truth that I myself could no longer distinguish between the two.

This accusation shocked me because it was true.

For years, for all of my adult life, I have been my own counsel, constantly manufacturing a watertight brief for the defense of my sister and myself. So deep-rooted a habit of dissimulation is hard to overcome, and my effort to overcome it may not succeed. But I shall try to be honest with you, I owe you that much at least for your decency to us (that English schoolboy word is the only one that fits), and as an apology for our exploitation of you.

I said *our*. That is untrue. It was I alone who did it consciously. Lucrèce acted, as always, in good faith. She reached out to you sincerely, impelled by a deep need; and if you had not learned the truth about us by chance, she would have ended by telling you. It was she who insisted on asking you over to the farm to hear our "confession," and she who also, characteristically, offered you the opportunity to decline—as she once told you, she doesn't like to put her friends in a position where they have to make an excuse.

Let me say now, and unequivocally, that Lucrèce is a noble person. Everything that she does has grandeur.

As for me ... my only claim to nobility lies in my worthless title. Nana was right in thinking that I was dominated by Lucrèce, but wrong in imagining her to be my evil genius. On the contrary, what she tried to do was to elevate me to her own high spiritual plane, to exalt me beyond my capacity. The weakness that had been left out of my sister's character had been added to mine; it was the penalty of our spiritual oneness and our physical separateness that we lacked the balance usual when opposing qualities are embodied in two separate physical organisms. And *my* life, at any rate, has been a perpetual struggle to overcome the difficulties of being one soul in two bodies—not of the same sex.

Lucrèce, as a woman and an artist, was able to live a cloistered life, but I had to face the world. Therefore the screen. One has to deal with the world in terms that the world understands, you know that, Julian. And for me, whose whole way of life and thought were diametrically opposed in every aspect—emotionally, idealistically, politically—to that of my world, such terms could only be counterfeit.

But to keep silent—worse, to lie for years on end about one's deepest beliefs—is unbearable. And it is equally unbearable to have to keep silent, or lie, about one's deepest personal feelings. That was why, when I heard about Julian from my father's old friend in your legation, I wanted to meet you. I thought I might find in Julian, at least, someone with whom I could be myself.

But I was like the fabled captive whose long imprisonment in the dark destroyed his ability to see by the light of day.

It was unfortunate that the first opportunity to meet you was provided by the Gavriolescos. Maximilian's shady reputation, and our relationship to Micu, could have prejudiced you against us from the start. And I was ashamed of using their not very creditable interests with regard to you to further my own, even though they were relatively innocent. Nothing could alter the fact that I was involving myself in a thoroughly distasteful situation, in which Sybil and Maximilian and Consuela and Micu and I (but not Lucrèce) were all exploiting one another in order to exploit you for our separate, personal ends.

At that time we were not conscious of needing anything more than congenial intellectual companionship. The notion that outside friendships might be complementary to our intimate relationship—and even necessary to its preservation—had not yet entered into our conscious minds.

No. That's not true; it had entered mine. But it was only when we met you for the second time, at the legation ball, that Lucrèce felt the first intimations of an emotional experience on another level that might coexist with ours. These intimations arose from undertones that anyone less sensitive than Lucrèce, and even Lucrèce herself in a less receptive state, might not have perceived. In any case they answered an un-acknowledged, or, rather, an unrealized, need in her, and as a result she invited you to the opening of her show.

There you passed a peculiar test. And with flying colors. You were willing to pay an absurdly large sum that you could not easily afford for a relatively insignificant little drawing that Lucrèce values above all her other works. But there was more to it than that. She knew, intuitively, that the deeply personal nature of the drawing, the love it symbolized, had aroused in you deeply personal responses, which gave her a joy hitherto unknown to her—apart from me: the joy of achieving emotional communication through her own particular medium of expression.

She was so moved by this experience that she would have accepted your invitation to dine intimately at your home even if nothing had happened in between to change her. For the change in our lives resulted from the change that took place in *her*, which was the result of a revelation in every sense of the word: Nana's disclosure, and the realization that what she had seen as a unique achievement, the integration of the different aspects of love into a single perfect relationship, was the unforgivable sin—the sin of Lucifer himself.

You may wonder how either of us, and especially Lucrèce, whose faith was stronger and more profound than mine, could ever have reconciled our incestuous union with our religion. But we had done so, right from the start—and with a burning sincerity on Lucrèce's part that quelled any sneaking doubts on mine. And this was precisely where she believed herself to have sinned most grievously. Incest, as such, was only a variation of the human sexual frailty to which we were accustomed, but in exalting it as a purer and more comprehensive form of love between man and woman than that sanctioned by God through His church, she had defined her own code of good and evil, putting herself, like Lucifer, on an equal footing with God.

The priest convinced her that her claim to having committed the unforgivable sin was in the same category as the sin itself, and compounded it. He enjoined reparation by self-denial, atonement by penance, but before all and above all, humility. Which involved hope, and faith in God's infinite mercy. He commanded us both to live without sin, as true brother and sister, leaving it up to us to accomplish this as we saw fit.

We persuaded ourselves that our total separation by distance would be wrong. That by living separate lives we would be depriving our child of the one thing that we could give her in compensation for our crime in conceiving her, and allowing her to be born—our combined love. and attention. We decided on the only alternative: We would stay together, but apart. We would give each other the distilled essence of love, unsullied by what Lucrèce now saw as unnatural lust. And we would achieve this with the aid of solemn vows—not only of chastity with regard to each other, but of total celibacy.

The vows were kept. But I had my private temptations, as Lucrèce had her private penances. Every night for me was a purgatory. Every day for her was a *via crucis,* and her calvary was a cross carved by her in memory of our father on a rock near the edge of the precipice where Marioara fell to her death. Lucrèce went there every day, winter and summer, to pray and meditate on her guilt.

It could be argued, and I could make as good a case for the prosecution as anyone, that there was no real virtue (in the biblical sense of the word) in anything that we were doing; that our decision to stay under the same roof was motivated by weakness rather than by concern for Marioara, that our vows of chastity were dictated by fear of hellfire and our vows of celibacy by possessiveness, and that our recognition of friendship as a good was really a sexual need, born of frustration. And even Lucrèce's innocence of any such conscious motivations could be construed as a subconscious escape into madness.

A question that tortures me is, When did that madness start—if madness it is; was it caused by the child's death, or was the child's death the result of it?

Lucrèce is not mad in the ordinary sense of the word. She is perfectly rational. She carries out her duties as mistress of the household as competently as ever. She is painting even better than before, though now she chooses predominantly mystical subjects. Her life is austere, disciplined and devout as the life of a nun, but that in itself is not a sign of madness, or even of religious mania.

Yet I must believe in her madness. I *must.*

I have to believe in it if I am to keep sane myself; for I know that I shall never cease to love her, as I always have loved her, a thousand times more than anyone else—alive or dead.

She did not shed a tear, not a single tear over Marioara's death—at least not in my presence or to my knowledge. Even at the funeral, when I was crying like a fool, she was absolutely calm. Abnormally calm. I consulted a physician in Bucharest about it, presenting it to him as the case of a tenant's wife. He said that such calm was a not uncommon symptom of shock and that sooner or later something would happen that would touch the right nerve and provoke a healing crisis.

You touched the right nerve, Joanna. But the crisis you provoked benefited Lucrèce only by releasing a monster to torment *me*. When she came to herself after the storm and the deep sleep that followed it, her unnatural calm had been replaced by the sort of sunset tranquillity that one sometimes sees on the faces of old nuns. But I had lost all hope of achieving tranquillity.

It was not long after this that I realized with a shock that I no longer had any idea of what was going on in the mind that had been like an open book to me all my life; and, with a second shock, that *my* thoughts were my own for the first time in my life. The power of reading each other's thoughts had left us.

When I came to see you in Sinaia, it was, as it had been whenever I made an effort to reach you, because I needed you. I felt that I could not go on any longer without confiding in someone. And you were the only people to whom I could speak. I wanted to examine what was tormenting me in the light of your detachment and sanity.

Yet when you offered me the opportunity, Joanna, I failed to take it. But the fact that you cared enough about me to get angry with me and castigate me for moral cowardice, was enough in itself to strengthen me, and it was then that I made the decision not to transfer any part of my torment to you while you were still so close. Even now, with time and distance between us, this letter may seem to be only another mistaken effort to share an intolerable burden with you; but in fact it is more in the nature of a testament.

But, as you see, I am finding it hard to come to the heart of the matter, to explain the source of my anguish and fear. Why?

I know why. It's because Lucrèce is me and I am Lucrèce; and despite the door that has closed between our minds I am unable to separate her acts from mine—or even to distinguish between them.

It is two years since I wrote the last paragraph, and it made the whole letter up to that point seem dishonest; or, at best, special pleading—valueless as a bad confession.

So I put it away in my desk.

Last night, I took it out and reread it. And I saw that through my very inability to be wholly truthful, the truth emerges, and is merely confirmed by the final paragraph. It is in the light of the final sentence in that paragraph that you should consider the implications of what I am now going to tell you in a very few words.

My torment derives from the juxtaposition of two utterances: one made by the priest on the morning of Marioara's disappearance, and the other made by Lucrèce in the delirium of her breakdown.

When I first learned from Nana and Magda that Marioara was not in her room, I thought that she had just run out into the garden, and I decided to go and find her myself, without disturbing Lucrèce. I encountered the priest on his way back to the church after taking the Blessed Sacrament to a sick woman in the community. I asked him whether he had seen Marioara, and he said that he had not. "When I was leaving the church," he said, "about an hour ago, I saw Lucrèce come out of the woods and cross the meadow to the house, but the child was not with her." He knew, of course, about her "calvary"—the place where she went every day to pray and meditate—and it did not surprise him that she should have gone there to greet the Easter sunrise. Nor did it surprise me. And I thought no more about what he had said until the night when Lucrèce broke down and complained against God for demanding the ultimate sacrifice of her child.

"Where was Your angel? Why did You send me no angel?"

Those were the words she repeated over and over, weeping.

Nicolai

At first, Julian didn't grasp the significance of Lucrèce's words. But I did. I had been brought up on the Bible, and I knew the story of Abraham and Isaac by heart.

# 5

# Amanda

Julian had been attached to the embassy in Rome for six uneasy months when Amanda wrote to me from Venice, where she and Whitt were staying with Nelson Garth, the American consul.

She needed more than ever to see me, and talk to me, she said, but it wasn't possible for her to come to Rome. Nelson was all alone, his wife had had to leave unexpectedly for the States—her mother had suffered a heart attack—and having them there with him meant so much to Nelson that they couldn't curtail their visit. But Nelson would like to have us come to Venice for the weekend if we could possibly manage it. He was writing to invite us by the same mail.

We had known the Garths in Bucharest, and Julian took Nelson's invitation in the same way that he had taken Old Browne's invitation on the day of our arrival back from South America—as a proof that he still had some friends. But the circle was narrowing. In spite of his promise to me that day to "be good" in his new post, he was already in trouble because of his too openly expressed antifascism, and his generally "difficult" temperament, which was not improved by the whiskey to which he was turning more and more often for consolation.

For our first evening in Venice, Nelson had invited people in, which made any private exchange between me and Amanda impossible, but gave me an opportunity to observe her and Whitt and the way they acted toward each other. They seemed to be getting along extraordinarily well. Her manner was kinder to him than it had been, and she looked even younger and prettier than she had in the spring. If she hadn't told me herself that she wanted to divorce Whitt, I would have thought that he had taken some lessons in what to do in bed to keep a wife happy. But I knew that Whitt wasn't responsible for her new radiance, her heightened good looks; and although I didn't know just who was, I strongly suspected Granby-Smith.

After the party, plans for the following day were discussed over a nightcap with Nelson. "Joanna and I plan to go off on our own for a few hours," Amanda announced. "I want her opinion on the tablecloths and the glassware we're thinking of ordering, and that marvelous antique chest—did I tell you, Joanna, that we took over poor Adrian's lease?"

"Whitt was just telling me," Julian said.

"Yes ... the man who replaced him didn't want such a big place—he's a bachelor, and we felt cramped in our apartment, so we made an exchange. And now I'm shopping madly for things to fill it up."

I wasn't sure quite what to believe. But the shopping trip turned out to be genuine. And it puzzled me that Amanda should spend so much money, and so much care, on furnishings for a home that she was secretly planning to abandon. Or was she more practical, and less gullible, than I thought; were her purchases an insurance against the possible failure of her lover to live up to his promises?

For lunch, she took me to a little restaurant on a small canal where, she said, we were not likely to run into our menfolk. "When we went past it yesterday with Nelson, he said it was quite well known as a place that women frequent when they go out together—and that's just what we want, isn't it, Joanna?" It gave the impression of being some sort of club, but nobody questioned our membership, and a table was found for us in a quiet corner of the room, at Amanda's request. "I want to be where we can talk undisturbed," she told the waiter.

When he had taken our order and left us alone with aperitifs and antipasto, she said, "I guess I'd better begin by telling you that the man I'm in love with is Charles Granby-Smith. Does that surprise you?"

"No. I thought it might be him."

She looked at me rather sharply. "What made you think so?"

"I knew that after you left Rumania he agitated to get himself transferred to Brussels, and I put two and two together."

"It's true that he asked for Brussels to be within reach of me, but he had another reason for wanting to leave Bucharest. Do you recall one afternoon at the country club—we'd been playing tennis—when he had an English girl with him, and he'd seen you in a café earlier on with Sybil Gavriolesco and asked you who she was?"

"Yes. I clearly recall that afternoon."

"You do? Well—*she* was the reason why he asked to be transferred."

I pretended to be obtuse. "The English girl?"

"Why, no! *Sybil!*"

"Really?"

"You don't sound very surprised."

"Nothing surprises me anymore."

"You've changed, Joanna. You didn't use to be so cynical."

"Tell me why Granby-Smith. . . ."

"Please call him Charles! Granby-Smith sounds so distant, and hostile—as if you didn't like him."

"Calling a man by his surname is a British habit. It has nothing to do with likes and dislikes. Tell me why it was so important to him to get away from Sybil."

"She was making his life intolerable, that's why. 'Hell hath no fury' is right. That day when he noticed her in a café—she was so flamboyant no one could help noticing her—she must have looked pretty closely at him, for she lost no time about making his acquaintance. She attended one of those benefit tea dances organized by the British colony in aid of something or other in the hope that he'd be there, of course, and he was there, doing his duty, and she got someone to introduce him to her, and from then on she never let go."

"He must have said or done something to encourage her."

"He was polite to her, nothing more. He asked her to dance. And on one or two occasions after that, he ran into her and talked with her. He found her amusing. But he *never* gave her any reason to think that he was seriously interested in her. And as soon as he realized that she'd fallen for him, he did everything he possibly could to shake her off."

"How do you know that?"

"Why, because he told me so himself! Charles doesn't lie to me, he knows he doesn't have to. He's been absolutely honest with me about his life and the women he's been involved with."

"I don't think that men are ever absolutely honest with a woman about their relations with other women. They're too vain for that—they tell only what puts them in a good light."

"You certainly have become cynical."

"I've got over my romantic idealism, that's all."

"Then maybe you'll believe me when I tell you that your friend Sybil acted like a real bitch. Why, she even tried to blackmail Charles!"

The Bible story of Potiphar's wife suddenly became suspect—the fabrication of a male narrator who despised women.

"I can believe anything of Sybil ... except that she lost her head, like an infatuated schoolgirl, over a man who was no more than commonly polite to her."

"So you can believe her capable of anything.... Yet you're taking her side against Charles."

"I suppose I've caught Julian's habit of supporting the weaker side, right or wrong."

"I don't think Sybil's a weak person."

"She's in a weak position. But aside from that, we were friends."

"It was always a puzzle to me how you could be so friendly with her—and I find it even harder to understand now."

Since I couldn't give the true reason why I was on Sybil's side against Granby-Smith, I said nothing. Amanda, misunderstanding, touched my hand. "Forgive me, Joanna. I don't have any right to criticize your choice of friends."

At this moment our waiter appeared, bringing scampi and a bottle of wine. His manner was obsequious and condescending at the same time.

"I don't like that waiter," Amanda said. "I don't like the way he looks at us—it's a conniving sort of look. Who does he think we are?"

"It's not a question of *who*," I said. "It's *what*."

She stared at me, then turned very red. "You mean that he thinks we're...."

"Who cares what he thinks? We'll never come here again."

"We certainly won't! You know, Whitt won't even take me to a nightclub because he says the hostesses are all whores and he won't have his wife sitting in the same room with women of that sort, and now his wife and her best friend are being taken for a couple of them. . . . Boy! Would he be mad if he knew!"

I could imagine his horror if he knew what sort of a couple we were really being mistaken for. "If I were you, Amanda, I wouldn't say anything about our having come here for lunch."

"I'm not planning to." Suddenly she laughed, a little stridently. "A whore off duty—what do you know about that!" Then her face clouded, and she fell silent.

I wanted to ask her what had happened to Maximilian Gavriolesco. But she spoke first. Her train of thought had taken her back again to the Bucharest country club. "It's amazing that you should recall that afternoon at the club so clearly, after almost three years. But since you do, I'd like to know whether you noticed anything—what I mean is, did you guess then that Charles was in love with me?"

"No, I didn't dream. . . . Were you . . . lovers?"

"Oh no! Just in love. We didn't sleep together until the last week before Whitt and I left Bucharest, and then only once—I mean, there was only one occasion. You see, Joanna, being unfaithful to one's husband isn't so easy the first time around. It wasn't something I could do lightly. I swear that's the truth, Joanna. I was deeply involved with Charles emotionally, but I didn't want to get involved with him physically so long as there wasn't any hope of marrying him—and there wasn't until he finally broke off his engagement to that English girl, Lady Betty . . . Lady Betty . . . I can't recall her second name, honestly I can't. That's very Freudian, isn't it?"

"His engagement? That does surprise me. I thought Lady Betty—I can't remember her name, either—was just an old family friend."

"Just an old family friend is exactly what she was. He hadn't announced their engagement officially because he had doubts— even before he fell in love with me—but the understanding had always been that they would marry. Their families had adjoining estates. They rode and swam and punted and played tennis together, they had the same friends, the same set of social values—you know the sort of thing, all the ingredients for a suitable marriage except love, the right kind of love. At least on his side ..."

I interrupted her to ask what she meant by the right kind of love.

"It's not so easy to define, Joanna. It's what I *don't* feel for Whitt. I guess it's a combination of the physical and the romantic."

"What do you feel for Whitt?"

"Boredom. He's so dull. I know that sounds cruel, but it's the truth. He's a good man, and I respect him as a person. But he bores the hell out of me! In bed, out of bed, all the time—oh Joanna, you can't begin to imagine how much my husband bores me!"

I could. I could also imagine that if Granby-Smith were ever to become her husband, it wouldn't be long before he was saying the same thing about her.

"I guess you're wondering why I ever married him in the first place. It was pretty simple, really, and rather simpleminded. I was flattered to have a man of his age—he's fourteen years older than I am—with a fine position in the Foreign Service, crazy about me, a mere kid, still at college and having a hard time not to flunk out. And then, aside from a little kissing in cars, I had no sex experience—Whitt would have died rather than touch me before we were married—and it never occurred to me that sex could matter so much, or that there could be so much difference between one man and another in bed—but I had to sleep with Charles to find *that* out.

"Don't get me wrong, Joanna. Sex isn't the only reason I want to marry Charles, I swear it isn't. I enjoy just being with him. Just going places and doing things with him along. Golf with Whitt was tedious, and even tennis, except when we played you and Julian—that was always fun because Julian got so mad if we won—but now, when Charles comes for a weekend and he and I and Whitt go to the club together, I enjoy everything—why, I've even learned to play poker!"

"What about Whitt, how does he feel?"

"He's perfectly happy. He enjoys Charles's company, and as

I'm always in a good humor when Charles is around, it all works out fine. He doesn't suspect a thing. And he doesn't have any cause to when Charles is visiting in our home. I'd never let Charles make love to me while he was Whitt's guest. I couldn't do that to Whitt."

"Then where . . . when?"

"Mostly in his apartment, whenever I can find an excuse for going to Brussels alone, which isn't nearly often enough. Imagine being madly in love and only being able to go to bed together once every four or five weeks! It's driving us both nuts," she added with her wide, frank smile, "but it's worse for me because *I've* got to go to bed with Whitt in the meantime."

I wondered who Granby-Smith was going to bed with in the meantime.

"Well, why go on like that? If you're quite certain you want to leave Whitt and marry Charles, wouldn't it be more honest to ask Whitt for a divorce now instead of playing around and buying things for a new home and pretending you're looking forward to moving into it with Whitt?"

"I'm afraid of what Whitt might do. It would be an awful shock to him."

"I can't imagine Whitt doing anything violent. If I were to tell Julian that I wanted to leave him and marry another man, there's no knowing what he would do, but Whitt's not the man to beat up his wife or shoot his rival."

"You don't understand. I'm not afraid of his being violent. I'm afriad of his doing what Adrian did . . . there *are* similarities," she added with a rather touching honesty. "Whitt trusts Charles. He looks upon Charles as his best friend."

As if in answer to a summons, the ghost of Old Browne came dripping out of the sea to stand beside our table, portly and naked; a warning for both of us in his drowned eyes.

We finished our meal in silence. Then Amanda said, "Let's get out of here and go have an espresso somewhere else. Being taken for a whore doesn't seem so funny anymore."

Idling gondoliers at the quayside vied with each other with offers of trips at bargain prices. One man suggested a trip across the lagoon to the Lido. "Let's do that," Amanda said. "Let's hire his gondola for the whole afternoon. We still have so much to talk about—nothing's resolved yet in my mind, and this will be our last opportunity."

That night we were going with Nelson to a performance of *Tosca*, and by noon next day Julian and I would be on the train to Rome.

While the gondolier sang, to please the so obviously rich foreign ladies, the talk continued. "Do you mind if I ask you a very personal question, Amanda?"

"That's okay."

"Has Granby-Smith . . . oh, all right, Charles, has he asked you in so many words to get a divorce from Whitt and marry him?"

"Yes . . . well, he's said that he wants to marry me. But there mustn't be any scandal—because of his career. He'd never get to be an ambassador if Whitt cited him as a corespondent, and even without that, even if Whitt were to let me divorce him for incompatibility, or whatever, it would go against Charles if people thought that he was the real cause of our divorce."

"If you marry Charles, people are bound to think that. You can't prevent a certain amount of scandal."

"Oh but we can! We have it all planned—but the carrying of it out doesn't depend only on Whitt, it depends on me too, on how strong I am. To start with, I'd either have to tell Whitt the truth, and rely on his goodwill toward both of us, which is asking a lot of Whitt, I realize that, and hurting him about as badly as it's possible to hurt a man—through both his love and his friendship—and risking a reaction like Adrian's, or I'd have to keep my mouth shut about Charles and make Whitt believe that I really do want to leave him simply because we're incompatible. Which wouldn't be easy. For one thing, it wouldn't be easy to convince him that there wasn't someone else—I've done too good a job of playing the happy-wife role." She sighed. "But Charles would like it better that way, he would prefer not to figure in the divorce, even privately."

"I imagine he would prefer that," I said, dryly enough for Amanda to give me a quick, suspicious look. "But weren't you ever happy with Whitt—was it all playacting?"

"Not at first. There were times when I really was happy with Whitt—and even now I can't honestly say that I'm *unhappy*.

Actually Whitt is a kinder person than Charles. But he's so uninteresting."

After a little silence, she went on. "Anyway, whichever course I take, for the sake of Charles's career we couldn't come together for a couple of years. I'd have to go to the States—ostensibly on a visit to my parents, though of course I wouldn't go near them—and not come back. I'd go to Reno, or Mexico, or wherever, for the divorce, and then, after an interval of a year, Charles and I would meet again, 'by chance,' and renew our old acquaintance, and end by getting married. And no one could say a thing against it. Although Charles says there are still people in England who would disapprove of his marrying a divorced woman."

"Is this your own plan—or did Charles suggest it to you?"

"He made me see the necessity of keeping away from each other for a time. Of course, we *would* get to see each other after I've gotten the divorce, he promised me that, but without anyone knowing. It's important that our names shouldn't be linked too soon."

Her naiveté astonished me. I had always imagined American women to be more sophisticated than English women.

She said, "Why are you looking at me with that superior smile?"

"It's not a superior smile," I said. "On the contrary, it's rueful, if anything. I'm thinking how terribly old I feel compared to you—how old are you, by the way?"

"Twenty six. How old are you, Joanna?"

"Twenty-nine, in a few weeks I'll be thirty. Does that give me the right to talk to you like an older sister?"

"You may talk to me any way you like—I've come to you for advice because I don't have a sister. I don't have anyone to confide in."

"What about your parents?"

"My mother would be on Whitt's side, she adores him. My father would say, 'I told you so'—he always thought Whitt was too old for me. And they would both be dead against a divorce."

"Are they Catholics?"

"No, they're strict Methodists, like Whitt's folks. Whitt's more religious than I am. I broke away when I first went to college.

But I still have inhibitions. I guess that's why I had so much trouble over going to bed with Charles for the first time—I couldn't help thinking of it as terribly sinful. But the funny thing is, Joanna, that although my conscience gave me hell, the idea of its being a sin made it twice as exciting."

Poor Amanda, I thought, even if Granby-Smith loved her, he would never marry her. He was too ambitious. Sooner or later he would go back to Lady Betty—if he had ever broken with her, which I doubted—and make the loveless marriage that would eventually lead him to an ambassadorship. If Amanda broke up her marriage on account of him, she would end up with nothing, like Sybil.

"What are you thinking about now, Joanna?"

"About Sybil Gavriolesco. I'm wondering what it was that happened to Max. . . ."

"That was a real horror show—I'm surprised that you didn't hear about it. I should have thought she would have written to you herself."

"We don't correspond. We sent each other Christmas cards the first Christmas after I left, and that was it. I don't correspond with anyone in Bucharest, and neither does Julian."

Our gondolier made the gondola fast to a candy-striped post. I gave him some money for wine and told him that he could sleep for an hour, we were going to have an espresso somewhere and take a walk.

We found a place on the almost deserted waterfront, so much pleasanter without its wall of cabanas and carpet of bodies, where we ordered coffee and continued our conversation. Amanda tried to start in on her own problem again, but I brought her back to Sybil and Maximilian—whose fate was entangled with hers whether she liked it or not.

"Maximilian is dead," she said. "But it was the way he died that was so awful. It seems that they kept some savage hunting dogs, boarhounds, at their country place—did you ever see them?"

"I saw them once, being exercised."

"Well—they killed Maximilian. They tore him to pieces, the way hounds kill a fox."

"Oh my God!"

Everything swam before my eyes. I thought I was going to

faint. I took a swallow of the strong coffee, emptied the cup and ordered more, chiefly to distract Amanda's attention from myself.

I said, finally, "From whom did you hear about this . . . this terrible thing?" I had almost said, "this murder."

"Whitt's former secretary, who knew that we were acquainted with the Gavriolescos, sent us a newspaper clipping about it—it was front-page news. And then Charles got a hysterical letter from Sybil."

"Did he show it to you?"

"No, but he told me what was in it. He wrote back. I advised him not to, I thought he would only be encouraging her to pursue him all over again, but he said he had to write to her and try to calm her down. Anyway, if she married Max for his money—and I can't imagine her marrying him for any other reason—she didn't get it. He left everything to his daughter and her husband—who kicked Sybil out of the house."

"Poor Sybil . . ."

"I'd have more sympathy for her if she hadn't been so bitchy with Charles. I do pity her, of course, but I can't help feeling that she got what she deserved. I know that you feel differently about her, Joanna, but you saw a different side of her. I just can't help seeing her through Charles's eyes."

Now it was I who said, "Let's go."

The wind from the sea had suddenly cooled, and we had to cross the lagoon. I was torn between a need to hear the exact circumstances of Maximilian's death, and the revulsion, the physical nausea, that all thought of it produced in me. It was only when we were back in our gondola that I could bring myself to ask Amanda how it had happened. "Dogs don't usually savage their master."

"All the newspaper said was that he got up in the night and went outside—apparently they have outside plumbing. . . ."

"Yes, they do. Go on."

"Okay, so he went out, half asleep, and the dogs had somehow got loose, and they evidently mistook him for an intruder. It was all over before anyone could get to him."

"Where was Sybil?"

"Out somewhere—she had a little car of her own, she made Max buy one for her, said she wanted to be independent. She got back about half an hour after it happened, and her fool of a stepson-in-law let her see what was left of Max and she went into shock."

"The bloody little rat!"

"What's that? What did you say?"

"I said the bloody little rat!" My voice rose in spite of myself. I felt my control slipping. Tears came into my eyes.

"Why, Joanna! You're crying!"

"It's so . . . so *brutal*. Life's so brutal. . . ."

She tried to calm me down, she thought I was crying over Max. "He's not worth it, my dear. He would have died soon anyway, he was over seventy, and sick—Charles says he was syphilitic. And he was an old crook, you know that. Charles says"—and she lowered her voice to a whisper—"that he ran a chain of expensive whorehouses!"

There was something in the way that she imparted this that restored my sense of humor. I dried my eyes, and told her that I wasn't crying for Max, but for Sybil.

"She'll be a lot better off without him, even if he did cut her out of his will. And if I were her I wouldn't want such dirty money."

"Have you any idea what she's doing—has she gone back to England?"

"Nobody knows where she is—she just disappeared from view. Charles tried to find out. She didn't write to him again, and he got worried."

"I suppose he was worried that she might turn up in Brussels."

Amanda had to admit there might be some truth in that. "But I think he was more afraid that she might have taken her own life—you see, she was pretty desperate, in her letter she begged him to come and take her away from it all, and to marry her. Of course he had to say no—imagine the scandal! And there never had been any question of his marrying her. It was all in her mind. But just because she was so wacky anyway, he feared the shock might have finally sent her around the bend."

I thought that even if I were to tell Amanda the truth about Sybil, and her relations with Granby-Smith, she wouldn't believe it, any more than the visitor at a mental hospital believes what the inmates say. I said, "Let's not talk about it anymore. It's too dreadful, it doesn't even bear thinking about. Let's not talk at all for a while, do you mind?"

We were three-quarters of the way across the lagoon when she held up her hand. "Please, téacher, may I speak now?"

"You have my permission, Amanda Elliott."

"Look, Joanna, you have a pretty good idea now of how things stand between me and Whitt and Charles. Will you tell me just what you think I ought to do? I won't promise to do it, but I do respect your opinion, and I'd like to have it."

"Very well. First of all, and most important, I think that you shouldn't talk to Whitt about divorce at this point. Second, I think it might be a good thing for you to get away from both Whitt and Charles for a time. You could tell Whitt that you want to go to the States for a while—give him any plausible excuse that he'll accept—and tell Charles that you have to get things into perspective, and you can only do that if it's impossible for you to see each other. If you decide that you really do want a divorce, you can write to Whitt about it—but first to Charles, of course—and if not, if you make up your mind to stay married to Whitt after all, you can come back to him, and no harm will have been done."

"Thank you, Joanna. I know that's sensible advice. I may not follow it, I may not be able to follow it. But I'll keep it in mind."

Next morning, before we left, she found an opportunity to tell me that she had come to a decision and had spoken to Whitt about going back to the States to visit her mother. "Mommy has a heart condition, so he thought it quite natural that I should want to go, seeing what happened with Mary Garth's mother. In fact he seemed rather pleased, and said he'd try and book me a passage on a boat sailing next week."

On the train back to Rome, I told Julian what had happened to Maximilian Gavriolesco, and what I believed might have been Sybil's part in it. After we had left Bucharest, I had felt free to tell Julian something about Sybil's horrible marriage—the ring, her loathing for her husband, her wish that he would die—and now he thought that I might be right in seeing a sinister connection between the manner of Maximilian's death and the episode with the dogs that we had witnessed on our first visit to the House of Pavilions.

"But we mustn't jump to conclusions, Joey. Motivation alone

is not proof of guilt. Even if Sybil was up to no good with those dogs, someone else may have triggered the fatal action—Micu, for instance. He was almost certainly in debt, and Consuela probably knew that she would inherit her father's money—or most of it."

"But Micu didn't have the courage to go near the dogs, he was terrified of them—you saw that yourself."

"There was no need for him to go near them. All he had to do was give an order. Or the dogs may have got loose by accident—a gate not properly fastened, a weak chain. . . ."

"Their attack on Max was no accident."

"Granted. But the man who lays in a stock of arsenic with his mother-in-law in mind may be a murderer in the sight of God but he's not yet a murderer in the eyes of the law."

"The law . . . do you think that Sybil's in danger of being accused . . . ?"

"Not if she dances to Micu's tune. But God help her if she doesn't."

He took out the hip flask of whiskey that he always kept with him, and held it out to me. "Have a drink?"

"No, thanks."

"Well, if you don't need one, I do. A stiff one."

Now was the time for me to divert him, to tell him something amusing. But before I could think of the right thing, he brought something up himself that did more than merely divert me.

"Want to know what old Whitt told me?"

"Yes—what?"

"That silly bitch Amanda is having an affair with our friend Granby-Smith."

"Whitt told you that! When?"

"Last night. He and I stayed up and got drunk together after you and Amanda and Garth had all gone to bed."

"But . . . but how *could* he tell something like that about his wife to another man?"

"The poor devil had to tell *someone*. And I'll bet she told you—that's why she wanted you to herself, wasn't it? Come on now, admit it."

"All right. She told me. But she thinks that Whitt knows nothing about it—that he hasn't got even a suspicion."

"Whitt's no fool. He believes the affair will die a natural death if he doesn't force any issues, so he's keeping quiet about it. Granby-Smith has a long leave coming up very soon, and rumor has it that he's going to get married while he's on leave—to some girl in England, someone he's known for years. He's also due for promotion, so the chances are that at the end of his leave he'll go to a new post. And that will be that."

"But Whitt looks so happy, and satisfied, and in love with Amanda—doesn't he care that she's sleeping with his best friend? Old Browne killed himself when the same thing happened to him."

"That wasn't the same thing. Whitt's not in love with Granby-Smith. And he's a realist, where Old Browne was a romantic. Whitt knows that he doesn't satisfy Amanda in bed, he knows she'll have other affairs, but as long as she doesn't want to leave him he'll ignore them."

"Could *you* do that?"

"Hell, no! I'd beat the bloody daylights out of you and knock the other fellow's block off. But it won't ever happen with us."

"What makes you so sure?"

"For one thing I keep you well. . . ."

"All right—*all right!*"

"And for another, you're not the sort of girl who cheats on a man. If you ever fall in love with someone else, you'll leave me before you sleep with him."

"I'd better—if I don't want a couple of black eyes."

After a moment of silence, he said, seriously, "I wouldn't lay a finger on you if you were honest with me about it. Amanda isn't being honest."

"She's more honest than you think. This is her first affair, and she didn't enter into it lightly. She respects Whitt and doesn't want to hurt him, but she does want to leave him. She's genuinely in love with Granby-Smith and wants to marry him, and she imagines that he intends to marry her if Whitt will agree to a divorce."

"Then she's an even bigger fool than I thought she was. Granby-Smith will never do anything that might spoil his career. I know his kind. They always ditch unsuitable women—after they've had them. I wouldn't be surprised if it was Granby-Smith who ditched Sybil. If so, he's got a lot to answer for."

"He *is* the fellow who ditched Sybil," I said. "And we don't know yet just how much he may have to answer for—he's afraid she's killed herself."

"That's typical of his vanity. And of course it would be very convenient. But Sybil's not the kind to commit suicide for the sake of a man. She's more likely to stay alive come hell or high water just to get even with him—and there's Micu to get even with too."

He took out his flask again and drank all the whiskey that was left in it. Then he shut his eyes and slept, while I looked out of the train window at the cypresses marching past like a moving frieze, black on azure, as once, an eternity ago, the ships and cows and windmills of Holland's flat meadows had loomed up to meet us out of the fog. We had traveled a long way since then, and it seemed that our travels had led us more deeply into other people's lives than our own. But perhaps it was just that other people's lives were more clearly perceptible to us than our own, as was their corruption.

# Interlude

Three excerpts from the diary of
the Hungarian poet Anthony Keres
Budapest—1936

January 7

It is six o'clock in the morning, and I have not slept yet. I have only just got home after a very strange experience. So strange that I want to put it down before it has time to undergo the sea change that memory and imagination, especially *my* imagination, work on everything.

Last night I had supper with Bibi. She called to ask me if I remembered what day it was, and when I said, Twelfth Night, she reminded me of what I would rather forget, that it was also the anniversary of our wedding day, and begged me to spend the evening with her—for old times' sake.

Each time I see her, it is more difficult to believe that she is the same woman with whom I was once so passionately in love. Each time, her deterioration of body and soul seems to have progressed a step further; a horrible process of spiritual dissolution seems to have set in before physical death.

Last night our meeting was even more painful than usual. She wants to come back to me. She has conceived the insane idea that to live with me again as my wife would give her peace. Or so she says; and the kindest view I can take of that is that she does not recognize her own motives for what they really are. But whatever they are, I will not, I *cannot*, live with her again, *ever*. It was almost unendurable to be with her for even a few hours, and I was barely able to swallow without vomiting the food that she had prepared for me. Does this mean that I am without compassion? No doubt it does, for true compassion involves love, is a form of love. And I am unable to revive in myself the slightest feeling of love, in any form, for Bibi. Pity, yes, that I have. But pity is a form of pride.

It was almost midnight when I succeeded in getting away from her, but I was not in the right frame of mind to come straight back here. The peace that I have achieved in this solitude is, like all states of peace, fragile; and even Bibi's talk about coming to live here again was enough to disturb it. In eight years of living and working alone in this place, I have exorcised its ghosts, swept it clean of my own paltry memories, good and bad, and replaced them with visions created by other men—greater men than I, who speak to me through their writings and their music. But my reconstructed paradise is not invulnerable, and I feared to carry back to it the seeds of corruption if I did not first purge myself of the cynicism and bitterness aroused in me by Bibi's destructive desire to share it with me, and by her jealous reminder that I cannot share it with any other woman, any new love, as long as she refuses to set me free.

In this mood, B. would have helped me more than anyone else—he and his cello together have an almost Godlike power to restore peace to the soul. But since that was out of the question, I went to Zoltán, and found him still up, studying a brief, and alone—Margit is away, visiting her mother. Zoltán said what he always says, that I should not allow myself to be emotionally blackmailed, that I should be more ruthless with Bibi. But that is the lawyer talking. As my good friend he knows that I am not ruthless by nature, and that to act strongly with Bibi I would need a powerful incentive—the love of a woman who would make the fight worthwhile.

We talked until four o'clock in the morning, and Zoltán took for granted that I would sleep on the divan in his study until the trams had started running again and the taxis were back on their stands. But to his amazement, and my own, I said no, I had to get home. I would walk. I would like to walk. And that was the beginning of the strangeness. Because I didn't want to go home, and I certainly didn't want to walk there; I wanted to lie down and sleep on the divan. But it was as if someone else's will was imposing itself on mine, in the way that my mother used to impose her will on mine when I was a small boy, deciding when it was time for me to go home, and saying good-bye for me whether I liked it or not.

Zoltán told me not to be ridiculous. I, or rather the voice that was speaking for me, assured him that I meant what I said and would he please not insist. At that point he must have got the idea that I didn't intend to go home, but to some woman's apartment in Pest, for he suddenly laughed and called me a rogue.

When I found myself out in the street, dead tired and faced with a long, lonely walk at the darkest and coldest hour of a bitterly cold night, I felt like a fool. I could not imagine what had possessed me, and I decided to go back and tell Zoltán that I had changed my mind. But the directing voice said, *No. Don't go back, go on, and hurry, there isn't a moment to lose.* Possessed now by an irresistible urgency, I began to run. The streets were utterly deserted—not even a stray cat was to be seen.

When I entered the arctic circle of the bridge, I was assailed by an overpowering sense of desolation, and stabbed in the chest by a knife edge of wind cutting along the half-frozen surface of the river and piercing my winter garments as if they were made of paper. For a moment recognition was paralyzing: this cold was more than a purely physical sensation, this desolation more than the absence of living creatures; this was the chill and the desolation of the presence of death.

I was a little more than halfway across the bridge when I perceived a dark object a few yards ahead of me on the footpath; at that distance it looked like a sack propped up against the parapet. As I drew closer, it assumed the contours of a human figure. When I reached it, I saw that it was the figure of a woman bundled up in a hooded sheepskin coat. She was leaning against the parapet, facing the water. Her folded arms rested on the deep layer of frozen snow that topped the parapet, and her bowed head rested on her arms. She was absolutely motionless. Rigidly still. I believed her to be dead. I looked at her with a feeling of sorrow, of grief, as if she were not a stranger, but a friend to whose rescue I had come too late.

I addressed her, "*Assonyom . . . Assonyom . . . ,*" not expecting any response. And there was none. None whatsoever. Now I asked myself what to do, and the obvious answer was, Don't touch her, go and get the police. But I had only gone a few steps when the inner voice that had been directing me all along stopped me—not commanding this time, but pleading, *Don't leave me, I am the reason you are here.*

I turned and went back. She had not stirred. Now I asked her, as if she were alive, if there was anything I could do to help her. She made no answer. I repeated my question more loudly—as though that were all that was needed to wake the dead. She stayed silent. Then I touched her shoulder, lightly at first, then pressing a little to get the feel of the body under the heavy coat, and although she did not respond to my touch, I knew now that she was alive. She had to be aroused. I took her by the shoulders and shook her. Then she said in English, faintly but distinctly, "Go away."

Addressing her now as *Madame*, I told her in English that it was dangerous to remain still in such cold, she could freeze to death. She muttered something about that being what she wanted, and I told her that we do not always know what we really want. She allowed me to turn her around and draw her away from the parapet, and I had the impression of a young face, but it was no more than an impression, for the moon was down and the nearest streetlight was not near enough to illuminate her features, and after that I avoided looking at her directly—despair has a right to anonymity.

She was docile, resisting only questions. When I asked her where she wanted to go, she said, "Nowhere." When I asked her where she resided, she said, "Nowhere." I had no right to demand her identity card, so I told her that I would have to take her to the nearest police station. Then she said that she lived in Buda. She was so numbed with cold that she could not walk without assistance. I had to support her by putting my arm around her shoulders. It was like supporting a child, she was so thin and small, and she trusted herself to me with the simplicity of a child.

On the Buda side we encountered a policeman. He stopped me, polite but curious; he had seen the young lady go up on the bridge quite a while ago, more than an hour, and had thought there might be something wrong. I showed him my identity card and told him that I would look after her. He was satisfied. One advantage of being a university professor is that it guarantees one's respectability in the eyes of the police.

Now I had to find out in what district of Buda she lived. She was still reluctant to tell me. She said she could go on alone. But when I insisted on seeing her safely home, she gave in, and told me that she lived on the Vár, not very far from the Matthias church. We set off up the hill, linked like a pair of lovers; I kept my arm around her and held her close to my side, partly to help her along, partly to provide her with animal warmth, and partly in the hope of giving her a little human comfort. We did not speak at all.

Outside the British legation on the Batthyany utca we met another policeman. I had the feeling that he recognized my companion, though he did not acknowledge it with any salutation. On the little square where poor Uncle Bandi used to own a villa, she stopped, and I was not surprised when she pointed to his former home and said that was where she lived—I had heard that its new owner had leased it to foreigners. She gave me her hand and thanked me for what I had done for her. I understood that she did not want me to go any farther with her.

In taking leave of each other, we looked at each other directly for the first time. We were standing under a streetlamp, which allowed us to see each other's faces quite clearly, but I think that she was too frozen—in every sense—to really see me. I don't believe that she would recognize me if she were to see me again. But I would recognize her anywhere. Her face made a deep impression on me. Why? It was by no means the classical "tragic mask" that gains in beauty when grief turns it to stone; it was a small, rather flower-like English face of the type that unhappiness mars. Her only real beauty lay in her eyes, large, deep-set, and brilliantly blue even in that pale light. Marvelous eyes. Unforgettable. Again, why? Perhaps because of the unconscious appeal in them. But even more, I think, because of what I saw behind their brilliance, behind their appeal—the ice fields, the wastes, the frozen sea . . . but I must beware of too many metaphors, too much symbolism.

I watched her cross the square, open the garden gate, and disappear into the darkness. But I stayed, watching, until I saw a light go on in one of the upper windows of the villa, and long after that—until the light went out again, and I felt intuitively that she was safe, that her life-and-death crisis was over.

Well, those are the facts. What do they prove? My presence on that bridge at that particular moment saved a life, that is certain, and it is equally certain that it was not entirely fortuitous; that is to say, that I performed the actions that ultimately took me there against my inclinations and in response to an irresistible compulsion.

What was the origin of that compulsion? Does it go to prove the existence of a God who cares for the fall of each individual sparrow? Or was it an example of an as yet unproved scientific phenomenon—a kind of "wild" telepathy, cries sent out at random by one mind to be caught at random by another, and be responded to, or not, depending upon the power of the cry, or the quality of the receiver? Or responded to only when the thousandth chance causes a message to be picked up by the one and only receiver capable of decoding it?

I am too tired now to think about this.

January 12

. . . She is constantly in my mind—I could almost say that she *inhabits* my mind. I am unable to work. Even when I am lecturing to my students her image interposes itself between them and me. And I think that she is herself responsible for this possession—not consciously, I doubt if she thinks of me consciously, I doubt if she has any conscious memory of me as a person. I believe that she is holding onto me subconsciously—as a symbol of survival. . . .

January 15

. . . I have found out who she is. Her name is Joanna Crest, and she is a married woman. Her husband is connected with the British legation. They have two children, a boy and a girl. Zoltán, who knows them socially as well as in his capacity of legal adviser to the legation, says that the eldest, the boy, is sixteen or seventeen years old. This doesn't seem possible. My mental image of her, the impression left with me by that one long look at her under the streetlamp, is that of a very young woman, little more than a girl.

But in any case, I am now in a position where a moral choice has to be made. The question that troubles me—quite apart from the movement of my own heart—is how far "morality" justifies the refusal of help. If I force her out of my mind for the sake of her family, won't it be like dislodging the hand of an exhausted swimmer from the edge of a boat for fear of its overturning and endangering those already aboard?

# Part Two

# 6

# Fricka

## I

The embassy at Rome had had all it could take of Julian and his too outspoken antifascism by the time he had been there a year, and for the next five years he was handed gingerly from one head of mission to another as explosive material. Back and forth we went, all over the map of Europe, with brief, uneasy halts between journeys.

The scenes of these painful sojourns have all run together in my mind like inkblots, and the gloomy, northern country in which we were halted when Fricka came to live with us is no exception. Its remembered landscape is featureless, blurred by perpetual rain; even the city we lived in has imprinted only one sharp image on my memory: that of the boulevard on which our rented house was located.

It was a wide boulevard, lined with trees and divided in the middle by a grass-covered strip with a footpath where pedigreed dogs were walked on the leash and pedigreed babies promenaded in low-slung prams. Smug and respectable, it created in me a nostalgic longing for the poison-ivied banks of the Calea Victoria. But from time to time its complacency would be shattered by the roar of Julian's motorcycle; his winged horse, the power that offered him release, and that he used only for release; conserving it as one conserves any precious power, any last resort.

He had bought it without saying anything to me. He had ridden it home along the boulevard, brand-new, powerful, shining, and parked it in the side entrance to our house without explanation. No explanation was necessary. I knew why he had bought it. I knew what it stood for.

Luckily for Julian, he had one good friend at the Foreign Office. Thanks to this man, Julian had not yet been asked to resign from the service. Instead, he had been transferred from post to post in the hope that eventually he would encounter a superior who would bear with him. And he seemed, at last, to have found one. But there had already been an "incident." This time the row had been with one of the underdogs that Julian championed. He had lost his temper with the man, who claimed he had been assaulted. "Only with words," Julian said. He was believed—his verbal impact when he was angry was notorious. But he was officially warned to refrain in future from "employing in the line of duty such words as may produce an illusion of physical violence."

"Bloody pussyfooting bastards," he said. "One day we'll show them what real violence is. Where's the whiskey—I need a stiff one."

"Don't drink now, Julian. In half an hour you have to be back in the chancery."

"Fuck the chancery."

"Julian, listen to me, *please!* You're going to have to make a choice, they're forcing it on you. Either you resign from the service of your own accord, or you stop providing them with valid reasons for getting rid of you."

"Whose side are you on—mine or theirs?"

"Yours, of course. I'm simply pointing out that you can't go on like this. It's an impossible situation."

"Do you think I don't know that? If it weren't for you and the children, I'd clear out tomorrow . . . there's a revolution brewing in Spain, and I'd like to be in on it."

His pause before mentioning Spain wasn't lost on me. Spain was an afterthought, an alternative that he couldn't be counted upon to choose. His present chief, a fatherly man, was doing his best to prevent him from committing professional suicide, but he didn't know, as I did, how often Julian's thoughts dwelt on physical suicide as the only possible alternative at this point of what he believed to be his wasted life.

He said now, "That German woman is arriving this afternoon, isn't she?"

"Yes. Her train is due in at three-thirty. Pip and Cissy are coming with me to the station to meet her. I must tell them to get ready, it's nearly three now."

"Go ahead. I'm not stopping you."

"Your appointment is for three o'clock, Julian."

"I know that."

"If you don't go now, you'll be late for it."

"And you want to be sure that I leave the premises sober—that's it, isn't it?"

"Yes, Julian."

He got up, and I held my breath; it was fifty-fifty whether he would go to the cabinet where the whiskey was kept, or to the hall, to put on his hat and raincoat.

He came over to me and gripped my shoulders. "I don't *want* to drink," he said. "I don't even like the taste of the bloody stuff. But my life's intolerable without it. Even you, and I love you, Joey—I may not seem to sometimes, but I do—even you can't make this life tolerable to me."

But for the moment I had won. I went with him to the door and kissed him good-bye before he went out into the perpetual drizzle that kept the boulevard green and my spirits at zero.

Julian had been of two minds about engaging the "German woman," Fredericka Friml, as a resident governess for Cissy and tutor for Pip, because now he was of two minds about Germany. As a boy he had been to school there, and had lived with a German professor's family, who had taught him to love and respect their culture. In the Kaiser's war he had felt that he was fighting not against a people that he loved, but only the madness of a military caste.

But the rise of Nazism was another matter. Fascism, for Julian, was more than a political principle contrary to his beliefs, it was an absolute evil, a poison that infected all areas of the human spirit. Fräulein Friml was of Julian's generation, so her education dated back to the period that he knew, and remembered as golden. But had she been able to keep herself untainted by Nazi ideology? It was just possible. She had lived outside Germany for more than a decade, teaching the children of foreign diplomats, all of whom had praised her to the skies.

As I walked with Pip and Cissy through the wet streets to the railway station to meet her train, I had my own particular doubts and fears, and I knew that the children had theirs. Pip, who had outgrown female authority, was afraid of having to defer, noblesse oblige, to that of a middle-aged woman with a university degree, and Cissy was afraid that she might not come up to the standards of learning set by such a personage.

My feelings were mixed. A different breed from the nursery governesses of the past, whose position in the household had been on a kind of hierarchical mezzanine, just above the domestics and just below the master and mistress of the house, Fräulein Friml would live with us as a full-fledged member of the family. This worried me. I was afraid of admitting anyone into the family on an intimate footing. Thus far, although I couldn't conceal the more violent scenes of our private life from the domestic staff, the intangible barrier between the household levels allowed me to act as if they had never taken place. It was like living on the other side of clear glass and pretending that it was a brick wall. The new governess would be with us on our side of it. There could be no pretending with her. Yet I needed someone with whom I could be honest, with whom I didn't have to keep up the kind of perpetual false front that I had condemned in Nicolai.

"How are we going to identify her?" Pip asked. "Did you tell her to wear a green feather in her hat, or something?"

"No. We've got her photograph to go by."

Pip mistrusted photographs, he had found them misleading; when the real person turned up she was never as pretty or as young as her picture had made her out to be. But the snapshot that Fräulein Friml had sent us showed a woman who looked her age, which was thirty-nine, and had no pretensions to beauty, though if she had been a man she could have been described as handsome. As a woman she was too spare, too lean for an epithet that suggests female opulence. Pip had remarked that she looked like a nice horse. And he was the first to recognize her among the crowd of passengers pouring from the train. "There she is! She hasn't seen us—she's going the wrong way," he said, dashing off to intercept her.

They came back together, smiling and speaking German. Tall, long-legged, with a long face and neck and big, prominent eyes, she looked just like her photograph, and in the sense that all human beings have their prototypes in the animal world, hers was undoubtedly equine. But she had a thoroughbred air, the indefinable quality known as "class."

"This is my mother," Pip said, with the proud inflection in his voice that always touched me.

"And this is my daughter, Cecelia," I said. "We call her Cissy."

Cissy executed the polite bob taught her by earlier preceptors.

"Am I permitted to call you Cissy?" Fräulein Friml asked her in German.

*"Bitte schön, Fräulein."*

"But your accent is fabulous!" Fräulein Friml told her, winning her in one sentence.

We took a cab home, and by the time we got there, Pip and Cissy were so subjugated by the new governess's charm that they vied with each other for the privilege of carrying her bags upstairs and showing her around.

Julian called from the chancery. "Well?"

"She's here. And she's got the children in her pocket already."

"I hope she keeps them there. Do you like her?"

"Yes . . ."

"You sound rather doubtful."

"No. I do like her. It's just"—I tried to formulate a vague feeling of uneasiness—"just that she seems almost too good to be true. But you'll see for yourself at dinner."

A family dinner that night was to be the official inauguration, so to speak, of the new Friml regime. As a rule Pip and Cissy took their main meal in the middle of the day and had a light, early supper together in the schoolroom. Julian and I had to go out a lot, and in any case the children didn't enjoy having dinner in the evening with their father. We never sat down before eight o'clock, and by that time he had usually had more than a few drinks and his temper was uncertain. But this evening he came home from the legation in a better mood than he had been in when he left. His appointment had gone well, thanks to his abstinence, and his interest in what I had to say about the new member of the family kept him from drinking too much before dinner.

"So she seems almost too good to be true, does she? Well, at least that's a change, that last French slut was almost too bad to be true. But what is it about Fräulein Friml that is so exceptional?"

"It's her whole personality. She's somehow . . . distinguished. Not at all the sort of woman you'd expect to choose a subordinate position in someone else's house—particularly when she has the qualifications for teaching at a university."

"She may have tried it and found it boring. Spinster teachers can live bloody lonely lives. In a family she has companionship, and with diplomats she gets a chance to travel and practice her languages. Is she anything like her photograph?"

"Yes. Though she's rather better-looking in real life. She has nice hair, a sort of chestnut color, and nice teeth—when she smiles she looks quite young. And she's well-dressed, in a rather mannish way."

She appeared at dinner in a severely but elegantly cut black dress with a little round collar of white lawn; a symbolic note that called up an image that was to exert a powerful influence on my feelings for her; a combination of the nun image and the mother image that were already linked in my mind by precisely this little symbol. Nuns wore white next to their pallid faces, and my deeply religious mother had done the same; everything she wore had touches of white at the neck. And everything Fricka wore was surmounted by an always immaculate little white collar of linen or lawn, which was in effect her governess's badge, and which became for me, by association, the outward sign of an inward grace, like Lucrèce's halo of braids.

The dinner celebrating Fräulein Friml's arrival turned out to be the pleasantest family occasion we had had in a long time. She lost none of her self-assurance in Julian's rather aggressive company, and her ease of manner with him seemed to give Pip and Cissy more confidence. Very soon after they said goodnight, she tactfully excused herself to do her unpacking. "I like her," Julian said. "I think she's going to fit in."

She fitted in with the deceptive skill that appears to be effortless. And little by little the unpredictable tempo of our lives became less erratic—as if she were somehow regulating it. Which in a way she was, simply by being there.

Before she had been with us a month, she asked us to call her *Fricka*. The extreme personal reserve that surrounded her like a moat made this request seem like a mark of favor, a lowering of the drawbridge seldom offered. Once accepted, the favor had to be returned in like manner. But the verbal intimacy was never abused; Fricka kept the same scrupulous distance as had Fräulein Friml. Discretion didn't spell indifference, however. If she witnessed a scene between me and Julian, or heard him raising hell when he had had too much whiskey, she would take no notice, say nothing. But later she would show me some little extra attention, or Cissy would come in and hug me, and I would know that Fricka had told her that I was unhappy.

Pip didn't have to be told; he was old enough to know that I was chronically unhappy, and why. He was unhappy too, and he spent as much time as he possibly could out of the house.

But although Fricka demonstrated her awareness by acts of tacit sympathy for Pip as well as for me, she showed no disapproval of Julian's behavior, and no sign of hurt feelings when he was surly with her.

Until she came, I had dreaded evenings alone with Julian as much as I dreaded having people in—which almost always ended in embarrassment. Fricka's cool presence changed the whole atmosphere of evenings at home. Intelligent, aware of the situation but emotionally detached from it, she could ward off trouble as I, tense with love and anxiety, was no longer able to do. And she did it as if she were playing a game, whose object was to score as often as possible against the whiskey bottle. With a masterly touch, she would produce just the right challenge, or reminiscence, at just the right moment to make Julian forget that he wanted another drink. She could also cunningly steer him away from subjects she didn't like—notably German politics.

She and I were seldom alone together. We each had our special responsibilities and duties, and mine involved going out a lot socially. But I was always aware of her as an unobtrusive source of moral support where before there had been none. She helped me in countless small, practical ways too. Little tasks that I had put off doing would be quietly done for me, walks with Cissy would be combined with errands, something Julian had asked for, some delicacy, perhaps, would be obtained and brought back to me for him.

She had been with us for about three months when I got my first glimpse of the woman behind the paragon. Julian had gone out after dinner to play chess with an American colleague, and

Fricka and I were left alone together for the evening. We sat by the fire like two old friends, Fricka with some knitting and I with my sewing, but our talk was not the personal talk of old friends; we were still a long way from intimacy. We had been listening to excerpts from Wagner's *Parsifal* on the radio, and pursuing my own train of thought, I remarked on the basic human need for saints and heroes.

"That's not a basic human need," Fricka said. "It is only a sickness."

"Then it is your national sickness," I said.

She flushed. "Possibly. But at least *I* do not suffer from it."

"Don't be too sure. Whatever you like to call it, it's indigenous to the human race. Since the world began, mankind has invented gods—heroic figures by definition."

Though to be precise, I thought, the human need was not only for gods; I myself, although I believed in a male God, invented goddesses, and my candidates for canonization were always women. I admitted this, with a laugh, to Fricka.

"It is good that you are so sensible," she said in her most ironic tone.

"I would probably be more sensible not to canonize anyone," I said. "Unfortunately, I feel a basic human need. . . ."

Fricka didn't laugh.

The radio, diffusing an all-Wagner program, was now playing the *Liebestod* from *Tristan and Isolde*. Half teasing, but curious too, I asked Fricka, "Have you ever been in love?"

"Like *that?*" Fricka said scornfully, jabbing a knitting needle in the direction of the radio. "No! The men in my family, my father, my uncles, my brothers, were a vaccination against *that* sickness— *Gott sei Dank!* To love a man is to be a slave."

The front door opened and shut. Julian was back. Fricka hastily rolled up her knitting and said goodnight. I could understand that she would rather not confront Julian in my presence so soon after what she had said—which made her attitude to him seem hypocritical. Was it a holdover from a masculine-dominated youth that made her so conciliatory with just the kind of dominant male she didn't like? Or was she doing it for my sake, trying to make things easier for a poor female slave, a weak sister?

228

If this was the case, and I liked to think that it was, then I had found a friend.

Julian was in an exceptionally good mood. He had won three out of four games of chess. "Where's old Fricka?" he asked.

"She's gone to bed."

He didn't get himself a drink, he sat down beside me on the sofa and told me about the chess games and what a good fellow his American colleague was. "No hard feelings at all about being beaten—we've got a return match lined up for next week." He put his arm around me and nuzzled the side of my head. "It's amazing, Joey, your skin smells just the same now as it did when I kissed you for the first time—like hay."

If only he could always win, I thought.

It wasn't very long after this that Julian discovered a hidden side of Fricka, or believed that he had.

Fricka's maneuvers to ward off talk about politics didn't always succeed. Failing, she would become silent, letting Julian express his opinions and keeping her own to herself. But at any mention of Hitler, she would say, "Please! Let us not speak of him." His broadcast speeches were of political interest to Julian, who would put up with the hysterical oratory for the sake of what he might learn. But as soon as that rasping voice with its incantatory rising rhythms abraded the air, Fricka would ask to be excused and leave the room.

Yet one day we surprised Fricka rapt in front of the radio, listening to Hitler making a big political speech. She was so enthralled that she didn't even realize we had entered the room until Julian said, "What's this? I thought you couldn't stand that fellow's ranting!"

Startled, Fricka turned off the radio. "I was listening only because I was curious," she said. Then, reverting to German, and staring at the now silent radio as if it were Hitler himself, *"Er ist unheimlich."*

"Does that mean that you've let him hypnotize you as he's hypnotized most of your compatriots?"

"I am not so easily hypnotized," Fricka said. "Please! Let us not speak of him."

But now Julian was not so easily put off. "If she can listen to Hitler," he said, "she can listen to what I think of him and his damned *Politik*." And that evening at dinner, her plea fell on deaf ears. Her reaction to Julian's furious attack on Hitler and all his works was a noncommittal silence. But watching her as she listened to Julian's polemic I got the impression that she was having a hard time keeping silent—though there was not the slightest indication in her expression of what she was burning to say. She left her food almost untouched, and excused herself as soon as the meal was over, refusing coffee. It was the first sign of disapproval, or of wounded sensibilities, that she had ever allowed to surface.

"Well," Julian said, "I got her on the raw, all right. She's not been honest with us, there's no doubt about that."

"She doesn't have to tell us everything about herself."

"Not about her private life, no. But she's hiding more than that. She's altogether too damn guarded about her opinions. I'd respect her more if she had the courage to admit that she's a Nazi."

"Oh no, you wouldn't. You'd fire her on the spot."

Maybe Fricka had been less than honest with us, but there were possible reasons for her lack of candor that were just the opposite of the conclusion that Julian had jumped to. Had he forgotten our year in Mussolini's Italy? How most of the Italians we knew had been cautious in their behavior, and guarded in their speech, to the point of paranoia? And Fricka may have had personal reasons for her interest in Hitler's broadcast speech; at the moment when we came in, he had been in the middle of a diatribe against the Jews. "For all we know," I said, "she may be Jewish, or part Jewish."

Julian shook his head. "Fricka's not Jewish."

"But she could have Jewish friends—whose fate depends on Hitler's policies."

"I doubt that."

I recalled her bitter words about the men in her family. "She could have fanatical Nazi relatives who would denounce her if they thought she was disloyal to the Führer, and who may have suggested that she listen to his speeches—she gets letters from Germany. In fact, a difference of opinion between her and her family that she daren't admit may well be her reason for living abroad with foreigners instead of teaching in Germany."

"Warm in her defense, aren't you," Julian said. But he conceded these possibilities. I could see that although he wasn't convinced, he would like to be—if only because Fricka was such a good governess. But to me she meant more than that. Confronted by the possibility of losing her, I realized in how many ways I had learned to depend on her.

I said, "I think we should go by what we see. She couldn't do more for me if she were my own sister."

We didn't pursue the subject then—we had to put in an appearance at a charity affair at the British Club, at which Julian had too many drinks and was rude to the manager of a British bank.

Later, in bed, after lying awake for a long time in silence, staring at the ceiling, Julian said, "I'm willing to give Fricka the benefit of the doubt about what she hasn't told us—for your sake. Living with me is hell most of the time, I know that, and you need a woman friend. Don't imagine that I don't know what's happening to our marriage. It's going on the rocks, but there's nothing I can do about it."

"That's not true, Julian. If only . . ."

"I know, I know, if only I would drink less, if only I wouldn't be rude to pawky bank managers, if only I would kiss the collective Foreign Office arse! Well, I can't, and I won't. Goodnight."

Now I lay awake, tormented by the truth of what he had said about our marriage.

Julian began to thresh and moan in his sleep. Suddenly he sat up, flailing his arms as if he were trying to beat off an assailant, and gasping for breath. I thought he was having a heart attack. Then I realized it was a nightmare. I switched on the light. "Julian, Julian! Wake up! You're dreaming. . . ." He clutched at me, sobbing. I tried to calm him. "It's all right. . . . It was only a dream. . . ." Then he opened his eyes and said, as if he had not yet separated dream from reality, "You were just in time, Joey. She was strangling me."

"*She?* Who?"

He seemed not to hear. "Julian, tell me, who was strangling you?"

Without answering, he got up and went into the bathroom. I could hear him running the water in the basin and dowsing his head in it. When he came back to bed, he lit a cigarette and smoked it in silence. The distant look in his eyes told me that he was reconstructing the dream and trying to interpret it, but for himself, not for me. When he had finished his cigarette and stubbed it out, I switched off the light. After a moment, I reached out and touched him. It was a gesture of reassurance more than anything else. His response to it was totally unexpected. He turned to me with an access of passion that took my breath away, and led us into a jungle of savage delights untasted for so long that I had almost forgotten their existence. It was years since we had made love like that—with no holds barred.

In the early hours of the morning, Julian fell asleep from sheer exhaustion, his body still entangled with mine. I was exhausted too, but I couldn't sleep. I felt ravaged, as by a fearful storm, and my mind was demanding explanations as to its origin. I could only think that the murderous dream had given rise to it, that it was Julian's response to the threat of annihilation by a hand other than his own, a mustering of the vital forces that sex represented for him.

Whatever its cause, that night's flare-up of sexuality brought us together as nothing else could, though in a curious way. It was a renewal, but of a phase in our emotional lives that had in itself been an attempt at renewal: the phase of conscious sexual experimentation that we had entered into after our first long period of spontaneous desire for each other—which had needed no conscious arts to keep it going—had been brought to an end by Nicolai and Lucrèce.

Reentering it now gave us the odd illusion of having an illicit affair with each other. We took every possible, and impossible, opportunity to go to bed together, and the more unsuitable the time or the circumstances, the more exciting it was. Fricka must have sensed a change in the atmosphere and felt threatened by it, particularly as it had followed immediately on the radio incident. She became silent and withdrawn. "She feels guilty," said Julian. But to me she seemed merely forlorn, and *I* felt guilty because for the moment I did not need her.

The moment was short-lived. Our flaring, almost demoniacal

Indian summer was brought to its end by a blast of cold reality from the outside, a warning that death was not so easily thwarted. Julian's benevolent chief died suddenly of a heart attack.

Julian wept. "I loved the man," he said. "He was damned good to me."

After the funeral services, Julian went out for a long ride on his motorcycle. But I had no fear that he wouldn't come back. This was an act of mourning. And of contrition.

When it was announced that Granby-Smith was coming to take the dead man's place, Julian went out for another long ride on the motorcycle. Now I did feel afraid. But again he came safely back—violating the sleep of the boulevard at four o'clock in the morning. This had been an act of defiance; not defiance of bourgeois complacency, but of Granby-Smith's power to destroy him.

Soon after their arrival, the Granby-Smiths invited us to one of those legation luncheon parties that dispose of secondary social obligations without wasting a whole evening on them. Julian was virtually ignored by his probably very reluctant host. But his hostess, the Lady Betty of whom Sybil had rightly been jealous and whose power Amanda had sadly underestimated, was so nice to him that I knew she was trying to make up for her husband's calculated coldness. Her kindness made me look at her with a sympathetic eye. She had none of the glow of sexual fulfillment, licit or illicit, radiated by Almira and Amanda. But she had something else, something more touching. She knows her Charles, I thought; she knows, or intuits, that he betrays her whenever he gets the chance, but she stays faithful to him, she accepts him as he is. Acceptance was in every line of her pleasant face.

At lunch I was not placed next to Granby-Smith, but I was close enough to him to overhear what he was saying to the women who sat on his right and left, and it was like listening to an old record. Afterward, over coffee in the drawing room, he singled me out for his flattery.

"Mrs. Crest, what is your secret? I would give anything to know it."

"What secret?"

"The secret of how to cheat time. Here you are, looking as

young and beautiful as you were when I last saw you in Bucharest, seven years ago. And here I am. . . ." He raised his hands in a self-deprecating gesture that I was meant to contradict.

"Thanks for the pretty compliment," I said, "but I saw you more than a year after we left Bucharest."

"Really? Where was that?"

"At the house of Almira and Adrian Browne. We had just arrived back from South America, our boat had docked that morning, and you had come down from Brussels to spend the weekend with the Elliotts."

"Ohh . . . yes . . . I believe I did spend a weekend with the Elliotts while I was in Brussels. Well, well . . . I'd forgotten all about that." He laughed a little uneasily.

"We had some hours to wait before going on to Rome, so we looked in on Adrian Browne and he invited us for cocktails."

"Ah! Rome! Now, I wouldn't mind being posted to Rome. Marvelous place. Betty and I spent a month there last autumn. Mussolini's done a lot for Italy—he's turned it into quite a civilized country, good roads, good trains, palatial railway stations, good hotels. Even the Venice canals don't smell as bad as they used to."

Poor Old Browne. Not worth mentioning, are you? Or maybe he has forgotten who you were and what happened to you. We'll see. "I haven't had any news of Almira Browne since Adrian's . . . accident. Do you know where she is now?"

"Yes, indeed. Betty and I saw her only the other day. She's living in Paris, in rather a nice house on the Left Bank. She's become a patroness of the arts—and a bit of a bohemian herself. My wife doesn't quite approve. She thinks that Almira's being taken advantage of by the young artists she sponsors—painters, dancers, musicians, she calls them all artists. And they're all impecunious, of course. But Almira seems to thrive on being taken advantage of."

Earlier, he had wanted to know how to cheat time. But even if I could have told him, it was too late now. Time had been ruthless with him. In the past six years he had put on a lot of flesh, and lost, along with his elegant figure and some of his hair, a good deal of the charm that had so endeared him to women. His vanity, his shallowness, his egocentricity were all more nakedly apparent now than they had been, as if the inner man were coming to the surface with the deterioration of the outward mask. Yet there must be, I thought, some core of genuine feeling in him to keep the love of a woman as good as Lady Betty. And Sybil and Amanda had both loved him. Did he ever think of them? Or had he simply erased them, as he had erased Old Browne?

Less than a week after the lunch party, Betty Granby-Smith called and invited me over for tea at short notice. I found her alone in her private sitting room, and I thought I was in for what had so often happened to me before. *May I give you a word of advice, Mrs. Crest.... I'm sure that your husband's career is important to you.... We women can do a lot to help, you know.... May I suggest....*

But Betty Granby-Smith said none of these things. She said, "I'm so glad you could come. I found that I had a little time for myself this afternoon, and I called you on the off chance that you would be free too. In our situation life is so filled with people that persons get crowded out—haven't you found that?"

I certainly had. But she had entered our common situation later in her life than I had, and on a different level, at the point in her husband's career when the overwhelming tide of "people" was almost at its peak—only in the coveted embassy could it rise any higher.

"I was brought up in the country," she said, "where one has a few good friends and they are as much a part of one's life as the family furniture. Charles and I have known each other since our nursery days. We had our first lessons together. Our families have been friends and neighbors for generations."

Which meant that she and her husband must be about the same age. When I met her in Bucharest, not long before their marriage, I had thought her a girl, and she probably had been a girl in the sense of being virginal. There was still something virginal about her, virginal and wise at the same time, as if thwarted sexual flowering had been compensated for by the acquisition of spiritual grace.

She remembered meeting Julian and me at the Bucharest country club. "Did you like living in Rumania? Charles hated it. It intrigued me—of course, I was only there for a short time—but it gave me an odd feeling. I felt ... I wonder whether you felt anything like this—I felt like a child reading a book that is full of allusions to things that he doesn't understand."

"It took me the best part of four years to grasp the meaning of some of those allusions," I told her.

"Charles drove me up to Sinaia for a weekend, and from there we went for long hikes in the mountains. Such marvelous forests! But eerie. One felt that werewolves and vampires might really exist there. Yet I felt more comfortable there than I did in the city. I understand country people and country ways."

Would she have understood Nicolai and Lucrèce? No, I thought, no . . . but she would have forgiven them.

She asked about Pip—"I understand he goes to school here"— and about Cissy—"How do you manage about her education?"

I told her about Fricka. "How lucky you are," she said, "to have found someone like that!"

So the talk moved desultorily from one thing to another; nothing of any consequence was said, no confidences were made by either of us, but I left feeling warmed. Julian was back before I was. "Where have you been?"

"Having tea with Betty Granby-Smith."

"Oh. Fraternizing with the enemy."

"She's not an enemy, Julian."

"Actually I agree with you. In fact I think she quite likes me. She's much too good for that bastard—I wonder what she sees in him."

"I think she's the kind of woman who wants to be needed—and he probably needs her."

Julian looked skeptical.

"I don't mean sexually, Julian. There *are* other ways of needing a woman."

"Are there?"

For a week or two, the cold war between Julian and Granby-Smith stayed cold. But with Julian, wars never stayed cold for long. It was only a matter of time before the gunfire began.


A puppet theater company was in town. Fricka and I went with Cissy to see it. It was raining harder than usual when we left the theater. We couldn't find a taxi, so we had to take the tram, and we didn't get home until six o'clock, making me late for a cocktail party at the legation, where I had agreed to join Julian at five-thirty.

I was changing my clothes when Pip knocked on my door. "May I come in, Mother?"

"Not just now. I'm in the middle of changing, and I'm in a hurry—I was supposed to be at the legation half an hour ago."

"Mother . . . please, I must speak to you. It's important."

I put on a wrapper and let him in. "What is it?"

"It's Father. He's gone out on the motorcycle. He left about four o'clock. I think something had happened . . . something bad."

"Did he say anything?"

Pip hesitated. "Only that he wasn't coming back."

My whole body started to tremble.

"I tried to stop him from going, Mother, but he didn't take any notice of what I said—he didn't even swear at me. He simply shoved me out of his way. He was like someone walking in their sleep."

"Had he been drinking?"

"No, I'm sure he hadn't. He was just terribly upset about something."

I couldn't stop trembling. Pip stood there, looking down at me. He was tall, as tall as his father, but still a boy, slight and awkward. He felt for me because he loved me, but he couldn't feel with me because he didn't love his father.

"I'm sorry, Mother. I shouldn't have told you what he said. He'll come back . . . he always does."

There was more bitterness than reassurance in Pip's tone. But it braced me. "Have you said anything to Fricka?"

"No."

"Then don't. Will you do something for me? Will you call the legation and give whoever answers a message for Lady Betty. Say who you are and that I've asked you to call and apologize for our absence and explain that owing to . . . owing to . . ."

"Unforeseen circumstances?" suggested Pip.

"Yes, that's it. Be very polite."

"Of course, Mother."

But he still stood there, looking at me helplessly. "Mother dear . . ."

I pulled his head down and kissed him. "Don't worry. I'm all right. I'm going to try to rest for a little while."

At eight o'clock Fricka and I sat down to dinner without Julian. I longed to confide my anxiety to Fricka; but I felt that to voice my fears might bring about their fulfillment, and the special silence that we both observed regarding my personal life had not yet been broken between us. But of course she knew that something was wrong. I hardly spoke, I ate almost nothing, and I offered no explanation of Julian's absence. After dinner, I said I had a headache and went to my room. And there I waited, as I had waited on that Easter Sunday morning at Brasov; keeping my fears out of the forefront of my mind by reading, but with my senses all alert, and listening.

At two in the morning I put down my book and went to sit by the open window. It was still raining hard, but the air was mild. The boulevard was deserted and absolutely quiet. I was so tired now that my mind was a blank. I didn't think of anything. I simply waited and listened.

The clock of a neighboring church had just struck three when I heard what I was waiting for. Seconds later the roar of the motor came to a crashing stop and was replaced by the blaring of the horn. It went on and on without stopping. A terrible, lonely sound. It aroused Fricka, who followed me out of the house, and together we ran through the rain and the dark to answer its mindless summons.

The police informed the legation. When I got back from the hospital, Fricka told me that Granby-Smith had been trying for hours to get me on the phone, and she had told him that I would call him as soon as I got in. I didn't want to. But I had no choice.

His agitation was extreme. "Mrs. Crest! Oh, thank God you've called! What news? How is he? The hospital wouldn't tell me anything."

"They don't know anything—yet. He's still alive. . . ."

"Thank God! Thank God!"

"But he's unconscious."

Granby-Smith knew as well as I did what that might mean. "But there's reasonable hope . . . isn't there?" he said, repeating, as if the hope were primarily his, not mine, "Isn't there?"

"I must go now," I said.

"Mrs. Crest! One minute, please! There are things I have to

tell you . . . not over the telephone. I have to talk with you. When can I see you?"

"I don't know."

"I'll come to your house—at any time."

"I don't know when I'll be here. I'm going back to the hospital now. I just came here to see the children and get some things."

"I must see you, Mrs. Crest. I *must*. . . ." There was an almost hysterical note in his voice. "You don't know what I have been through since I heard."

I told him that I would go to see him. I couldn't say when it would be. I would call him.

"At any time of the day or night," he said.

Late that night, the doctor told me to go home. They would let me know if Julian regained consciousness. I called Granby-Smith. He said he would send his chauffeur to the hospital with the car. But it was Betty who came. She embraced me with tears in her eyes. On the way to the legation I told her how things were with Julian, how obscure the hope. Before we went in, she put her hand on my arm. "Don't be too hard on Charles."

It was startling to see Charles Granby-Smith, who had been so callous with Sybil and Amanda, so undone now by his conscience, so stripped of his masks and defenses. He took my hand and looked into my eyes, and I noticed the dark rings under his. "I am sorry. Truly sorry. You must believe that, Mrs. Crest. I acted too hastily . . . my wife. . . . May I explain? Are you willing to hear me out?"

"That's what I've come here for," I said, refraining instinctively from telling him that I knew absolutely nothing.

Granby-Smith paced the room while he talked. I sat perfectly still on a straight chair, listening, saying nothing, not even making the appropriate sounds when he looked to me for responses.

"Your husband and I have never got along very well, I assume you're aware of that. . . . I confess I wasn't very happy to hear that he would be a member of my staff here . . . no doubt he felt the same about working under me. He had a record for being troublesome, difficult—but of course you know that. . . . I mention it only in explanation—in slight mitigation, perhaps—of my own conduct. . . . With anyone else I might have been more patient. I was impatient before I called him in, I admit that, and I came

239

down on him harder than the circumstances warranted, I admit that too. But when I reprimand a man for an error of judgment, I don't expect him to fly off the handle and insult me. Your husband insulted me *personally*. No, even now, I don't think I'm to blame for losing my temper with him at that point—his insolence was more than any man could take calmly, and more than a man in my position should take calmly. But I shouldn't have acted so precipitately. I should have given him a chance to apologize."

I could have told him that Julian would never have apologized. But to tell him that wouldn't help now. What mattered, if Julian lived, was how far Granby-Smith would, or could, undo the damage that he had evidently done.

But he was preoccupied with his own guilt to the exclusion of everything else. "If your husband dies," he said in a very low voice, "I shall be responsible for his death . . . and I shall never be able to forget the look on his face when I picked up the phone and asked to be put through to the Foreign Office. He said I could save myself the trouble, he was going to clear out . . . and I told him to go ahead, but that I wasn't taking any chances."

Granby-Smith suddenly sat down and buried his face in his hands. We both sat there in silence for a long while. Then he raised his head and said without looking at me, "That's all. That's what I had to tell you."

I remained silent. He looked at me as if my continued silence was beyond his comprehension. "Have you nothing to say to me?"

"What is there to say?"

Did it occur to him then that he was thinking only of himself? Perhaps. Now he was silent for a long time. Finally, he said, "Tell me what I can do?"

But it wasn't for me to tell him that. I advised him to ask his wife. "She will know," I said. "She will tell you what you must do."


When Julian came out of his coma. the first person he set eyes on was Fricka.

Day and night I had watched by Julian's bedside, forcing myself to remain awake. I was on the verge of collapse when the doctor ordered me to go home and sleep, as he had done once or twice before. This time I refused; I became, I suppose, hysterical;

crying, and insisting that whatever happened to Julian, I must be there with him when it happened. The memory of my mother's illness and death was still unpurged.

The doctor called Fricka, who was well known to him by then—she came so often to inquire about Julian—to bring Cissy to see me, to strengthen and cheer me. He asked her to come and take me home and put me to bed; but she came prepared to watch beside Julian in my place, and brought Pip with her to take me home. She persuaded me to go with him in a taxi. I wept uncontrollably all the way. Pip didn't know what to do with me. He was at the age when emotion in adults is embarrassing. He no longer believed that he could comfort me with a cup of tea, but as yet he had nothing to replace it with.

Worn out, I slept for fifteen hours. And the first person I saw when I awakened was Fricka. Fricka smiling. Fricka holding her hands out to me as if she was bringing me a gift.

"Julian?"

"He has come back!" she said. "He begins once more to live!"

But his full return was slow and reluctant, as if his will were not in it. It was unlikely that he had recognized Fricka when he had opened his eyes and seen her sitting beside his bed. I was not sure that he recognized me, when I went back to him. And even when recognition was definitely established, memory still seemed uncertain, incomplete; as if he had left a part of his being behind in whatever depths and distances he had wandered through during his absence. His bodily injuries, serious though they were, were less disquieting than this.

Nine weeks went by before he could be moved from the hospital to our house on the boulevard. It was a period full of tormenting fears, of unanswerable questions, in which Fricka was a pillar of strength—friend, mother, sister, all rolled into one. Thanks to her, I was able to spend the greater part of each day with Julian, in his hospital room, where he lay silent hour after hour, in great physical pain but singularly uncomplaining. At the end of the day, I would take a tram back to the boulevard, blessedly certain of finding all well at home, the children and the household kept on an even keel by Fricka's capable guidance.

Alone with her after dinner, I would confide anxieties to her that I didn't want to admit to the children, but needed to talk about. Fricka would listen with attention, turn the light of her common sense on them, and put them into proper proportion. "What on earth would I do without you, Fricka?" "*Ach!* You would manage. No one is indispensable."

But she was making herself indispensable to me, and I recognized that in so doing she was fulfilling a need in herself; she and I had been brought together, I thought, at just the right moment for both of us.

When Julian came home from the hospital for a convalescence so long drawn out that I began to despair of his ever getting well, he appeared to have forgotten his suspicions concerning Fricka. Trained in first aid, she was as skillful in changing dressings and rewinding bandages as she had been in diverting bad moods, and he accepted her ministrations with the same passivity and childlike gratitude that he had shown to the nurses in the hospital.

Performing these practical services for Julian seemed, rather surprisingly, to give Fricka satisfaction. She was more than efficient, she was compassionate. Watching her, helping her, I had no doubt at all about that; touch. is revelatory, the presence or absence of compassion shows itself in the touch. She is beginning to like him, I thought; pity has changed her attitude, truly changed it. She doesn't see him as a male brute anymore but as a male child, hurt, and dependent on women for help.

Julian said nothing about what had happened between him and Granby-Smith, nothing about the suicidal motorcycle ride, nothing about his future. It was impossible to determine how much he had forgotten and how much he simply didn't want to think about. "Don't prod his memory, leave it to work on its own," the doctor said, which I used as a reason to keep Granby-Smith away. But Julian's other colleagues came to see him, and the junior members of the chancery staff were clearly impressed by the apparent tranquillity of the man who had so recklessly ruined his career by telling the head of the mission some nasty home truths—for the row, it seemed, had been heard all over the chancery.

I wrote to our friend in the Foreign Office. He replied, in a personal note, with sympathy for me and best wishes for Julian's recovery. *As to his future, we will see about that when the time comes.*

In the meantime he was officially on sick leave, and we lived within the strict confines of the present.

The present was, perforce, without sex. I felt the distance that the absence of sex, its suspension, always put between us; but now, perhaps because it was more absolute and beyond our control, I also felt a curious self-containment, a sense of personal independence, of belonging wholly to myself for the first time since my marriage.

One night, half undressed, I was brushing my hair in front of a long mirror that also reflected Julian in his bed. He was looking at me as if he had never seen me before, as he might have looked at an unknown woman who attracted him, whom he wanted; and I felt the small electrical shock that such a look from an unknown man produces—if the man is sufficiently attractive. I reached for my robe. "Don't put it on," said the unknown man in the mirror, urging me with his eyes to take everything off.

Naked, I stood facing him in the mirror until, at last, he closed his eyes with a little sigh.

At the end of four months, limping, scarred, his right arm still in a sling, Julian was pronounced fit to take up his duties again. He received the news with indifference, the indifference of a man who no longer controls his own fate. An official dispatch informed him that it had been decided in view of his serious accident, and on further examination of the events that preceded it, to put him on probation. Where he would be posted would be determined after a personal interview. This was accompanied by a handwritten memo from our friend:

Dear Crest, Please arrange to come and see me in London as soon as possible.

"You go and see him, Joey. If I go I'll only blow my chances," Julian said, with the first indication of caring about his fate that he had shown since the accident.

"That won't work. He'll insist on seeing you sooner or later."

"Well, at least you can try it. Don't write first. Just go, and call him up when you're in London."

"I don't like leaving you."

243

"I'll be all right. I'm capable of looking after myself now. And Fricka will take care of everything else."

Fricka urged me to go. She knew what was at stake. "I will take good care of everybody," she said, "I think you can trust me, no?"

On the morning that I left for London, she came with me to the door, where a taxi was waiting. It was early, and Julian was still in bed. Although a farewell handshake was an understatement of my feelings, it was what came naturally to me. It was Fricka who broke our unspoken convention by embracing me, and kissing me on both cheeks. Deeply touched, I returned the embrace.

I waved to her from the taxi. She stood in the arch of the door out of the rain, watching and waving until my taxi turned a corner.

Our friend at the Foreign Office fell in with my pretense that I just happened to be staying in London for a few days. He asked if I could find the time to come and see him—he may have been glad of an excuse to put off the confrontation with Julian, to whom he would have to say so many hard things.

Granby-Smith, it appeared, had been driven by his conscience, or persuaded by his wife, to modify in his written report of the incident what he had said in anger over the telephone. He admitted to having lost his temper and acted and spoken too hastily. But he had evidently given our friend the impression that Julian's state of mind at the time was influenced by alcohol, which was double-edged, like an insanity plea in a criminal case. The period of probation granted Julian was now a final chance on more than one count. As to his posting, there were two possibilities: London, a desk in Whitehall, which I doubted that Julian would survive for long; or Budapest, where an unexpected vacancy had occurred, owing, by coincidence, to a near-fatal accident.

"*Budapest!*" I could hardly believe my ears. "Did you say Budapest?"

"Yes," our friend said, slightly annoyed. "Any objection?"

"Good heavens, no! I've been longing to go there for years!"

"Really? May I ask why?"

His tone was cold. I was making a mess of things. I didn't know why I so desperately wanted to go there. But I had to give a convincing reason. "Why? Because it's the wickedest city in Europe!" I said. And I knew by the way he laughed that I had said the right thing.

Less than two weeks later, we were traveling once again on the eastbound Orient Express, on our way, this time, to Budapest, the capital of Hungary.

## II

Getting off the train at midnight in the murky glass-domed depot at Budapest was more like a dream than the fulfillment of one. We had to cross the river to Buda, and the city of dazzling light that rose up before me when the river came into view was a continuance of the dream. Bridges of light. Ships of light. Spires and towers and crenellations of light. All singing, singing in the dark over and on and beyond the river.

Early next morning, I awakened to the light of the sun, invisible and almost forgotten in the sodden weeks of premature winter on the boulevard. I stepped out onto the stone balcony to bathe in the streaming gold of a Hungarian autumn.

In the garden below, her footsteps crunching on fallen leaves, Fricka was gathering gold in the form of flowers, filling her arms with sheaves of tawny and yellow chrysanthemums. I called down to her softly, so as not to wake Julian, "Fricka . . . Fricka . . ." She looked up. The sparkle of the early morning sunshine caught the chestnut lights in her hair and made an aureole of it. "Isn't this wonderful? I'm coming down—I'm dying to see the garden."

We had subleased the villa just as it was from the man whom Julian was replacing—which suited both sides since neither could be sure of the future. It was a rambling old place, with balconies and terraces overlooking what had appeared in the moonlight to be a very large garden. The house had so many bedrooms that we each had a choice. Fricka had asked for the only one on the ground floor, a guest room that had its own bathroom as well as a terrace. For himself and me Julian had chosen, had insisted upon, two rooms—next to each other with a communicating door, and French windows opening onto the same balcony, but still separate; a choice that was one more sign of the change that had taken place in him since his accident.

When we had gone to bed on the previous night, the communicating door had been open. Now, it was shut. I turned the handle quietly and looked in. Julian was lying outside the bed covers, wearing his dressing gown, as if he had got up in the night and had been too tired to get back in between the sheets again.

His face, slack and furrowed in heavy sleep, was somehow unfamiliar, as though it had been made up to give him the appearance of age and a deathly weariness. It affected me painfully. I had to get away from it. Slipping a coat on over my nightgown, I ran downstairs and out into the garden barefoot—I wanted to step into heaped-up gold and feel it crackle under my bare feet.

"No shoes! You will catch a cold," Fricka said.

"That's what my mother was always telling me as a child, but it never happened. Oh Fricka! How glorious it is here! It's a different world."

"It's only a different climate," said Fricka.

"Which makes it a different world. All this gold ... it's magical."

"Fairy gold," Fricka said. "An illusion that vanishes when you try to grasp it."

I believed that Fricka's apparent cynicism was a mask that concealed a deep need for affection. She was a lonely woman, and in an odd way she was proud of it. Her attitude toward friendship in general was a mixture of exaltation and disillusionment: A friend was a beautiful thing, but very few people knew how to be one, and her implication was that she had yet to find one.

This morning, my euphoria, my sense of a new beginning, was so strong that I wanted to communicate it to Fricka by making her feel that in me she had found a friend, someone who truly cared for her.

Strolling along, thinking how difficult it was to tell anyone how much you cared for them, I began timidly, "Fricka ... there's something I want to say to you...," then paused, at a loss for words, and became aware of a painful tension emanating from her. What did she think I was going to say? To reassure her I slipped my arm around her waist. I could feel her shiver at my touch like a nervous animal.

"I have told you many times," I said, abrupt because I too was nervous, "how grateful I am for all your practical help. . . . But I've never told you how much your friendship means to me. How very fond of you I am. How very glad I am that you were able to come here with us."

She said nothing. I thought I had embarrassed her. "Well," I said, "I just wanted you to know how I feel, that's all." Needing an excuse to remove my arm from around her waist, I stopped to pick a solitary late rose. Then we both moved on without speaking.

The garden descended in terraces planted with grapevines. On the lowest level were fruit trees—apple, cherry, peach. Below a retaining wall, the hill, encrusted with villas and gardens, sloped down to the river. On the other side of the river the flat city of Pest sprawled in the sunlight, still sleeping because it was Sunday.

There were apples on the ground. I picked one up, and bit into a worm.

Fricka laughed.

"Look at those marigolds," she said. "They would be nice for the dinner table—if you want to cut some of them, here are the scissors. I have all the flowers I can carry. I shall go back to the house now and put them in water."

"I mustn't stay out much longer. Julian doesn't know where I am—he was still asleep when I came out."

"Well?"

"He might need something."

"If he asks for you, I shall tell him where you are, and if he needs something, I shall get it for him. Stay out as long as you wish."

I watched her tall, straight figure ascending the steps from one level to another with affection mixed with pity for the solitariness of the outsider in a family, giving, but not belonging. Then I wandered on through the orchard, intoxicated by the beauty of the morning.

Taking a different path upward, I came, very unexpectedly, on a kind of miniature swimming pool. An oblong stone bath, like a Roman bath, it was about three feet deep and full of greenish water with golden leaves floating on its surface. It was completely hidden from view, and I had an impulse to bathe in it. I shed my coat and nightgown and stepped in. The water was cold and stagnant, but like everything else in that garden that golden morning, it had a magical quality, as the waters of baptism have for those who believe in it.

The bells of many churches began to ring for Sunday morning services. Differently toned and timed, overlapping each other, they formed an aleatory peal. One of them was close by, in the church of Saint Matthias, whose floodlit spire had been at the apex of last night's city of light. I sat in the sun, listening to the bells, until I was dry. Then, full of light, I went back to the house, which I entered cautiously; I didn't want the maids, whom we had taken on with the villa, to catch their new mistress wandering around barefoot and in her nightgown.

Somewhere I could hear Fricka talking in a low voice. Then she laughed. I thought I had never heard her laugh so happily. Maybe what I had said had pleased her. She was on the upstairs landing, talking with Julian on his way to the bathroom. "Your husband would like his breakfast—I shall order it now, no?" she said as we passed on the stairs.

"Thanks. I'll have mine with him. Are the children already up?"

"Since a long time. Pip has gone for a walk, and Cissy has been washing her hair."

My first knock on Cissy's door went unanswered, a second elicited a muttered "Come in." She was combing her newly washed hair, which she tossed back from her face without looking up at me. "Good morning," I said.

"Oh, it's you, Mummy, I thought it was Fricka."

I started to tell her about my exploration of the garden. "Yes," she said, "I know. I saw you down there with Fricka." Her tone was impatient to the point of rudeness. I said nothing more. Cissy looked ashamed. Suddenly, almost violently, she threw her arms around me and hugged me. I was touched and surprised. For the past few months she had been extremely remote; absorbed, I supposed, in the dreams and conflicts of adolescence. With her face hidden against my shoulder, she said in a muffled voice, "I hate Fricka, Mummy."

"But . . . I don't understand, darling. What happened?"

"Nothing. I just hate her. I could kill her!"

It occurred to me then that Cissy was probably jealous of my friendship with Fricka. I said, "That's not very kind of you, Cissy—and not very reasonable."

Cissy disengaged herself from my arms and started combing her hair again, covering her face with it to conceal her expression, but exposing her nape, that eloquent little hollow that can excite both pity and passion in the beholder. I touched it lightly with my lips. "If you like, darling, we'll go for a walk after breakfast and explore the Vár."

"Without Fricka?"

"Just you and I together."

I took my breakfast of tea and toast with Julian. We sat in the sun by the open French doors of his room. He looked younger again, and less used up. But he seemed tired. If he had so little vitality that the simple effort of bathing and shaving was enough to tire him out, how would he stand up to the psychological demands on him that would begin that afternoon with tea at the legation and an interview with his new chief?

With the old Julian, the answer would have been easily predictable: Sooner or later there would be a fatal explosion. Now, that was unlikely. He was moody but controlled. His temper no longer flared at the smallest provocation. He had given up drinking. The desire for alcohol seemed to have left him. All desires seemed to have left him. All enthusiasm. All passion. The fires had gone out.

We talked idly about the house and garden, and the unpacking that had to be done, and the entertaining that we would have to do as soon as we were settled, and the arrangements that had to be made for Pip to enter the German *Gymnasium*, which, owing to the difficulties of the Hungarian language, was the only school Pip could attend.

"What are you going to do this morning?" Julian asked.

"I promised Cissy that I'd go for a walk with her—after that I'm going to start unpacking."

"Could you unpack some books for me before you go out? I'd like *Ulysses* if you know where to put your hand on it."

Since the accident he had taken to reading novels. I got out the copy of *Ulysses* that we had obtained from Paris and brought it to him. "Anything else before I go out?"

"No . . . well . . . I'd like the radio, but after you come in will do for that. When do you think you'll be back?"

"I don't know . . . in about an hour, I suppose." I kissed him. He accepted the kiss without returning it.

Downstairs, Pip was trying to find his belongings among the piled-up cartons. "If you want to do me a favor, Pip, unpack the radio and take it up to your father."

"I'll unpack it, but I'd rather not take it up to him, Mother."

"All right. Ask Fricka to take it up to him."

Outside on the cobblestone square more gold was drifting down. The Sunday quiet was like that of a country village. No cars were parked on the narrow streets; there was no traffic, only a few pedestrians going to and from church, missals in hand.

Cissy tucked her arm confidingly under mine. She was nearly fourteen, half child, half young girl, but with none of the bodily awkwardness of transition; physically, she was progressing from one state to another as gracefully as a musical phrase. Her classic profile, I thought, looking at her sidewise, was more like Julian's than mine—Julian's when he was young and glowing with idealistic hopes for himself and the world. She held her head high, her chin tilted with the hauteur that in Julian annoyed people, but that in her was charming.

She said, "You like Fricka very much, don't you, Mummy?"

"Yes, I like her very much."

"She's your best friend, isn't she?"

"She's a family friend. She's equally fond of us all."

"I don't think she is," Cissy said.

So that was it. She was jealous of Fricka's fondness for me—not of mine for Fricka. This hurt a little. I waited for her to tell me why she thought that Fricka cared less for her. But Cissy gave no reasons. Finally I said, "I'm sure that you're mistaken, Cissy. Since your father's accident, Fricka has taken on a lot of extra work and responsibilities in order to help me out. But now that everything's going better she will have more time for doing things with you."

Cissy said nothing. The open, passionate child had become a maddeningly self-contained adolescent. I said nothing further, I just pressed her elbow affectionately against my side.

On the Fisherman's Bastion we stopped, and stood looking down through its white arches at the great sweep of the river that reflected the blue of the sky. What a heavenly place to live in, I thought. "We're going to be very happy here, darling, happier than we've ever been anywhere—I just know it."

Cissy gave me a very grown-up look, absurdly but touchingly superior and protective. "Dear little Mummy . . ."

How old one is at fourteen, I thought.

When I got back to Julian, he was listening to the BBC news

on the radio. "Pip unpacked it and set it up for me here, with an aerial wire to the roof. Rather decent of him."

The family Sunday dinner, suspended since Julian's accident, was today being formally reinstated. All together around the dinner table for the first time in months, we were ill at ease, and I found myself describing what we had seen on our morning walk like a voluble guide. The cook had got in the supplies for this first meal on her own, and had played it safe with English roast beef. It was tough, and Julian still had difficulty in using a knife. I offered to cut his meat up for him if he would pass me his plate.

"I can do it," Fricka said. "I am nearer."

Julian ignored us both. He pushed his plate over to Pip. "Cut this up for me, there's a good chap."

Pip flushed, but did as he was asked.

"Thanks, old chap," Julian said.

Fricka lowered her eyes, but not before I had caught the shine of a wildly improbable tear. The long silence that followed lasted until the dessert was brought in. Julian was the first to break it. He asked Pip how he felt about attending the German school. "They'll try to cram Hitler down your throat, of course, but they can't force you to swallow him. And if you can avoid being contaminated by their beastly propaganda—and you will if you're my son—you'll get a valuable education."

"Thank you," said Fricka.

Julian went on without taking any notice of her interjection. "We must learn all we can about the Nazi mentality, about fascism in the form of Nazism, if we are going to be able to fight and destroy it when the time comes."

Now Fricka flushed, but Julian was looking at Pip. "And that will be *your* task, my boy. The bloody crusade of your generation."

This was the first positive statement concerning political ideology of any kind that Julian had made since his accident, and I wondered if it was an indication of a reviving interest in life. But it was only a tiny, isolated spark of the original fire that died immediately.

Apparently it was enough that Julian should keep quiet on the subject of politics, and control his temper, for his colleagues to accept him. Everything seemed to be going well for him in the chancery, and for the first time in his career I didn't feel that I had to be forever smoothing things over socially.

Yet, although Julian's new personality made life much easier, it disturbed me. It wasn't a deliberately assumed, protective persona; it had assumed him, fallen on him like snow to bury him. All the time I was going the social round with him at my side, quiet, polite, indifferent, I felt as if I were linked to a dead man. Alone with him at home, it was the same thing. There were moments when I found myself wishing for the old storms again. Our marriage hadn't gone on the rocks; it wasn't going anywhere, it was becalmed. And the sexual love that for years had been as indispensable to me as air and light was gradually being replaced by what I believed to be the asexual love of friendship, as I became more and more attached to Fricka.

Then an icy wind came up from an unexpected quarter, and the false security of the dead calm was gone in a moment.

We attended a Thanksgiving dance at the American embassy. Although it was frustrating for Julian, who loved to dance and hadn't been able to since his accident, there were compensations. With his limp, his stiff right arm, which he kept in a sling to rest it, his scarred but still handsome face, and his melancholy expression, he was a romantic figure, and when I was dancing it seemed that some pretty woman was always waiting to take advantage of my absence from his side. That evening, an American divorcée named Miranda, whom we met everywhere, sat out three dances in a row with him, while I went on dancing with a dull partner rather than give her the idea that I didn't quite trust her with my husband. Which I didn't.

That night I went to Julian's room uninvited. Since his accident he had tacitly forced me into taking the initiative in our rare lovemaking. He made room for me beside him, rather grudgingly, like a passenger in a bus making room for a fat fellow traveler. He accepted my kisses with the passivity that was part of his new personality, but when I reached out to caress his body with my hand, he gripped my wrist. "No," he said, "none of that if you don't mind."

I felt as if he had struck me in the face, hatefully, in cold blood. For a full minute neither of us spoke. Then he said, "Would you mind going back to your own bed? I want to sleep."

I left his bed with as much dignity as I could summon. I despised myself for crying, but I couldn't help it. He said, "There's nothing to cry about. I'm tired, that's all."

"No," I said, "that's not true, that's not all. You've never been like this with me before—never cold like this. For some reason you've turned against me. You hate me ... and I want to know why."

He remained silent. My sense of being shamed, shamed and hurt, gave place to indignation, to anger. I wanted to hit him, to beat some response out of him. But something warned me that the violence that once would have brought us together might now be dangerous. The effort to suppress my feelings was almost more than I could manage. Finally I said, with a coldness that equaled his, "Go on, tell me. I have a right to know."

He said slowly, "I'll tell you if you promise not to make a scene. I can't take scenes. You may have noticed that I don't make them anymore. I know I can't take them."

"I won't make a scene."

"All right, then. I don't hate you. I simply don't want you. There's someone else. I'm sleeping with another woman, a woman who gives me what I want and whom I don't intend to give up. I should have told you before, but somehow I couldn't. I hoped that you'd guess without being told."

"So it's been going on for some time."

"Yes."

This jolted me even harder than his admission of infidelity. The deception it involved was so unlike him. How systematically he must have lied to me, how many official engagements he must have invented, to be able to keep a regular liaison going!

But when I questioned him he remained stubbornly silent.

Finally I asked him outright if it was Miranda.

"I'm not going to tell you who it is."

"I think I have a right to be told."

"And I think that the other woman has a right to be protected."

"Very well. Be a gentleman. Don't tell. I'll find out for myself."

He said then, "In fairness to Miranda I can't let you imagine that she is my mistress when she is nothing of the kind. You have no reason whatever to be jealous of her. In fact, you have no reason to be jealous of anyone in our social circle. And that's all I'm going to tell you. And now will you please let me sleep. It's almost five, and I have an important appointment at nine-thirty."

"Damn your appointment!" But I left him to sleep—if he could. I couldn't. My hurt was like a hard knot in my stomach. The insistent visual image of Julian coming alive at the hands of another woman, achieving resurrection in another woman's body, made me physically sick. There had been something in his tone that made me believe him about Miranda, but not that it wasn't anyone in our social circle. He had said that, I thought, merely to throw me off the track.

On the following night, late again, after one of our endless evening engagements, I said, "I must talk to you, Julian. Don't worry, I'm not coming into your bed. I'll sit here."

"I'm sorry I was brutal to you last night," he said, "but it seemed to be the only way."

"The only way?"

"To convince you."

"So you meant what you said about that woman . . . about not giving her up."

"Yes."

"Then I suppose you want a divorce." It was so incredible that I should be saying this that I had the feeling I was hearing someone else saying it.

"No. I don't want a divorce."

"I don't understand."

"I don't want to marry her."

"But you want to go on sleeping with her."

"I intend to go on sleeping with her."

"But . . . what about me?"

"There hasn't been any real sex between you and me since my accident."

"I'm not to blame for that."

"I know. I'm not blaming you. I'm merely stating a fact."

"So what you want is to keep her as your private wife and me as your official one. Is that what you're asking me to put up with?"

"Is it so much to ask? People are doing it on the quiet all the time."

"Not very long ago you would have thought it a terrible thing to ask. I don't know you anymore, Julian. You're not the same person anymore."

"No. I'm not the same person. I've become what you always wanted me to be. Negative. I don't get drunk. I don't lose my temper. I don't preach socialism. I don't insult my colleagues. I don't shout at the children. I don't shout at you."

"And you don't love me anymore."

"You can't have it both ways."

"But you love someone else . . . and that's positive."

He sighed. "I refuse to play at quibbles with you. This conversation is making me tired. It's late and I have a lot to do tomorrow, and when I get overtired at night I can't think straight next morning."

This sort of thing went on between us night after night. I would resolve to say no more. To leave him alone. But I couldn't. I would drag myself through my inescapable social obligations in a paranoiac daze, speculating constantly on the identity of the woman who had taken Julian from me, suspecting every attractive woman we knew—not always excepting Miranda—and seeing each one, while I exchanged pleasantries with her, naked with Julian. And at night I would say, "I know who she is, Julian, I've guessed," and I would name this one or that one and beg him to give her up and make a new start with me, and always he said, "I'm not going to tell you who she is, and I'm not going to give her up, and now I'm tired. . . ."

I avoided the children. Since we had come to Budapest I had been so much happier that they couldn't fail to notice that something had gone wrong, and I didn't want Cissy, with her growing feminine perceptions, to start guessing at what it might be. And I didn't want to spoil Pip's improved relationship with his father. As to Fricka, I badly needed her moral support, but I was reluctant to admit to her that my husband was unfaithful to me and that I was suffering on account of it; so I avoided her too.

But eventually I realized that I was losing my sense of proportion, and with it whatever power I still had to regain Julian's love and retain the respect that I felt he still had for me in spite of what he was doing. One afternoon, when lessons were finished for the day and Cissy had gone out skating with Pip, I sought Fricka out in the schoolroom. She was sitting at the table, correcting Cissy's work. She said, without looking up, "Cissy has written an excellent German composition on the Faust legend—would you like to read it?"

"Later. I'll take it with me and read it later. I want to talk to you now, Fricka."

She closed the exercise book and looked up. "Is something wrong?"

"I'm terribly unhappy."

"*Aber warum?*" And then, when I didn't answer, couldn't, because I wasn't sure of my voice, "Is it something with Julian?"

"Yes. It's Julian. . . ."

"Well?"

"He's fallen in love with another woman."

She made a little contemptuous gesture. "*Ach was!* He will fall out of it again—men are always falling in and out of what they call love. This can't be the first time it's happened to Julian in eighteen years of marriage."

"He's been attracted by other women, of course—he may even have had a passing affair or two when he and I were separated for some reason—and I've been attracted by other men—though I've never slept with anyone else. But no one has ever come between us until now. This is serious."

"He still loves you more than anyone . . . that is easy to see."

"You're wrong, Fricka. He doesn't love me anymore. That's what hurts. And he doesn't care how much it hurts."

Fricka gathered together the books that were scattered over the table and put them one by one into their places on the shelf. With her back to me, she asked, "Do you know who this woman is?"

"No."

"Have you asked him?"

"Oh yes, I've asked him. He won't tell me. But there are several possibilities—we meet a lot of attractive women, and some of them are at loose ends. She's probably been a guest in this house more than once. How blind can one be?"

Fricka shrugged. "It will pass. If I were in your place, I would take no notice of it. Just give it time to wear itself out."

"That's common sense, I know. But love and common sense don't go together."

Fricka was silent.

"You've never been in such a situation, Fricka. You can't really understand how I feel."

She sharpened two pencils before she spoke again. "If you think that I cannot understand, why did you come to me?"

"Because you're my friend. And because I needed a dose of your common sense."

It was getting dark, and the temperature was dropping. Fricka switched on a light and went to close the curtains. "You are taking this affair much too seriously," she said, "and you are not being realistic." She came back into the circle of light, frowning a little, as if she were considering how best to explain a mathematical formula to Cissy. "Shall I tell you what I think you should do?"

"Yes . . . I may not be able to do it, but tell me."

"You should let someone else make love with you. You have been faithful to one man for too long—you wouldn't eat exactly the same food for dinner every day for eighteen years, would you?"

"Fricka! What an extraordinary thing for you to say . . . you, of all people! It's as if . . . as if a nun were to advise me to go and commit adultery."

There was a sudden clatter of young voices in the hall. Pip and Cissy must have brought friends back for tea.

"I am not a nun," Fricka said. "I am only an old maid."

After this conversation, I got the impression that Fricka was avoiding me. When we did see each other it was never alone, and she acted as if I had told her nothing—certainly nothing of any importance. But one morning she came to my sitting room. She wanted to talk about Christmas, to make plans.

"Christmas?"

"It's only two weeks away! Shall I help you address those cards?"

In front of me on my writing desk was a pile of Christmas cards that I hadn't been able to bring myself to sign and send off.

"I have to write in them first."

"Well, you write in them, and I will put them in their envelopes and address them."

"I can't. . . ." Tears came into my eyes against my will. I bowed my head over my desk to conceal them.

Fricka was silent. A minute or two went by. Then she came up behind me, put her hands on my shoulders, and drew me back against her.

## III

Julian took to locking the door between our two rooms. He said I bothered him and he had to get his sleep.

The locked door gave rise to terrible dreams. One night, early in January, I had one of my recurring nightmares. I was wandering up and down the corridors of a vast hotel whose name I didn't know in search of a room whose number I had forgotten, along with my own name. In this dream there was always a moment when I would feel the imminence of some unspeakable horror, from which I would escape only by awakening. This time it was heralded by a strange sound, halfway between a groan and a cry. I woke up with a violent start, and sat up in bed, sweating and trembling, the cry still echoing in my ears. Had it come from behind the doors of my dream or from behind the real door that separated me from Julian?

There was not the slightest sound or suggestion of movement in the next room. But it was precisely in that silence and stillness that the horror might reside. I went out on the landing. There, too, all was quiet. Pip and Cissy were sleeping peacefully; listening at their doors I could hear their even breathing. No sound came from the floor above, where the maids slept. Downstairs, in the hall, the tick of an antique clock accentuated the surrounding silence.

I sat down on the top stair. The peculiar solitude of a sleeping house became in my dream-haunted imagination the solitude of the dead. Awake in this isolation, I was afflicted by the same ghastly sense of nonexistence that my dreaming self suffered in the face of the locked doors. My need for a human response that would prove me alive was so great that I couldn't resist the urge to go and awaken Fricka.

But at Fricka's door the nightmare became a reality. The amorphous horror took shape, revealed itself as the known and loved, its cry a double obscenity, blaspheming both love and friendship.

And setting me free.

My only thought was to get away as fast as possible. Winter wraps and boots were kept in a hall closet. I pulled on my snow boots, wrapped myself in my sheepskin coat, and left the house by the garden door. The snow in the garden was deep, untouched, purifying. I plunged into it with a sense of purification.

Out on the square I started to run. Instinct drew me toward the river, but in search of darkness, not light; the illuminations were switched off, the city of light had vanished. At the chain bridge, instinct divided, to pull me in two directions: up the steps that led onto the bridge, or still farther down, to the lower quayside, the dark edge of the water.

Whichever way you go, my divided instinct told me, the choice will be irrevocable.

The finality of this choice that I had to make immobilized me. I waited for a sign of some sort—for how long I don't know. It came in the form of a policeman. He emerged from a side street, stopped a few yards distant from me, and stood quite still—waiting, I suppose, to see what I would do. I remained where I was, waiting for him to make my decision for me. If he goes away, I said to myself, I shall go down to the water, but if he challenges me, I shall pretend that I am on my way over to Pest. After a while, he came toward me, and I moved away from him up the steps onto the bridge.

I didn't look back or stop walking until I knew that he couldn't see me anymore, or even hear my footsteps. I was halfway across the bridge before I felt I could safely stop. The isolation was total; the hour, and the intense cold, had made of the bridge a no-man's land between the sleeping cities. I leaned over the parapet, resting my arms on frozen snow, and looked down at the water, swift and black between floating masses of ice. On one of these sat Old Browne, like a Buddha on a lotus, promising me nirvana.

I hid my face on my folded arms and gave myself up to the creeping, narcotic cold. All feeling left me.

When I heard the policeman again, he seemed to be coming from the Pest side. But I no longer had the energy to move. He stopped, and said something in Hungarian. Then he went on.

Then he stopped again and came back. I heard his footsteps in the way that a patient going under before an operation hears the anesthetist's questions. Now the policeman seemed to be asking me questions, which I was powerless to answer even if I had understood them. Then I felt his hand on my shoulder, physically forcing me back into consciousness, arresting me, forbidding me to escape from my pain. "Go away," I said. "Go away."

Now I heard him telling me in English that I was in danger of freezing to death.

*And if that is what I want?*

*We do not always know what we want. Sometimes we think we want death when what we really want is life—a different kind of life from that which we have.*

Question and answer both seemed to be only in my mind. I felt myself pulled very gently away from the parapet. "Let us walk." My legs buckled under me. I was held up, supported. "Now, which way? Where do you wish to go?"

"Nowhere."

"Where do you live?"

"Nowhere."

These questions and answers were spoken. He tried again. "Nowhere." "Then we shall go to the police station." That brought me to my senses. "I live in Buda," I said.

His arm was around my shoulders. He propelled me forward. "We must walk very fast to make your blood flow again." When my blood began flowing again, my mind cleared. I felt angry with the policeman for not letting me die, and at the same time I was grateful to him.

On the Buda side of the bridge we met the policeman from whom I had escaped. He asked a question. My policeman showed him a card. A few words passed between them that I didn't understand, then they each said "*Jo ejszakat*," which I knew meant "Goodnight," and my policeman said, "And now, which way, Madame?"

I told him that I was all right now, that I could go on alone—but I didn't really want to, I was afraid of being alone. He said he couldn't allow that, he must see me safely home. So I told him where I lived. On the long walk up the hill he kept his arm around me, helping me forward, and warming me. We stopped at a little distance from the villa, under a streetlamp, and I saw now that he wasn't dressed like a policeman. He was a very tall man, wearing an ordinary long overcoat and an astrakhan cap with earflaps. Looking at his face for the first time I got the impression that I wanted above everything else at that moment: the impression of immense gentleness and kindness.

I said, "Thank you for what you have done for me. I shall be quite safe now—I live in that villa, over there."

"I shall wait here until you are safely inside," he said.

I crossed the square and went through the gate in the garden wall and on into the house without once turning my head. If I had done so, I think I would have run back to him and asked him to take me home with him.

When I thought of him again, I could not recall his features, or even whether his face was young or old. I remembered only its immense kindness.


I didn't get up at the usual time. I didn't get up for three days. I said I had caught a chill. I said to leave me alone. I said all I wanted was peace and quiet. I kept everyone out of my room but the housemaid, who did her work silently, padding around in felt slippers while I feigned sleep. But I slept hardly at all, and the chill was not in my body.

At first the unhappiness that kept me face to the wall in my shuttered room was general; an all-over misery, an ache of the whole being. Whichever way my thoughts turned they encountered a jab of pain. Then these multiple stabbings consolidated into one concentrated agony, with Fricka at its center. The pain of Julian's betrayal had already been accepted, and by acceptance dulled. What I had to come to terms with now was the metamorphosis of a friend, with a nightmare Fricka, obscene as the frenzied nuns of Loudon.

On the afternoon of my third day of solitude, Cissy came timidly to ask how I was feeling and would I like some tea.

"I'm better," I told her. "I'm going to take a bath now and get dressed. I'll have tea downstairs in my sitting room. Are lessons finished for today?"

"Yes. I have homework to do, of course, and my piano practice—that is, if you're really and truly feeling better, Mummy. Fricka said I shouldn't disturb you with the piano while you were sick."

"That was thoughtful of Fricka. But it won't disturb me now. Will you ask her if she will have tea with me while you're practicing?"

Cissy looked disappointed. But I had to see Fricka alone.

When she came into my sitting room, looking her usual ladylike, straitlaced self in a plain gray dress topped by her insignia, the immaculate little white collar, I found myself questioning my own sanity. Was it possible that jealousy and a dream had deluded me into imagining what had never actually taken place, into hearing utterances that had never been made?

She was smiling. "So! You are better—*Gott sei Dank!* But you still look pale. You must take care—the grippe can be followed by a pneumonia."

"Do you think I had the grippe?"

"But of course! There is an epidemic."

The housemaid brought in the tea, and a plateful of open sandwiches. "I ordered these especially for you," Fricka said. "I thought you would be hungry after living on nothing but tea and broth for three days."

"Thank you. But I am not hungry—you eat them."

I poured the tea into the Herend china teacups that were part of the equipment of the villa. When Fricka took hers from me, her hand shook a little, and two thoughts entered my mind simultaneously, *These cups are too fragile for daily use,* and, *Her hands are guilty*—as if her hands, her capable, compassionate hands with their healing touch, were separate entities, with the power to remain innocent regardless of what she did with the rest of her body. This sudden conviction of their guilt, their degradation, their disloyalty to me, was so unbearable that it brought tears to my eyes and broke my control. "How could you!" I cried, reproaching them rather than Fricka herself. "How *could* you?"

She said much too quickly, "What do you mean? I don't understand what you are saying."

"Please don't lie anymore, Fricka. You've lied enough."

Now she was slower to speak. At last she said, "So Julian has told you."

"No. I . . . heard you together."

Now her silence seemed interminable, unendurable.

"Say something, Fricka . . . for God's sake, say something!"

She raised her hands in a little helpless gesture and let them fall again into her lap. "What shall I say? What do you want me to tell you?"

"The truth. You must be honest with me. We must be honest with each other. It's the only hope—don't you see that, Fricka?"

Her only response was an enigmatic little shrug.

"You're not just 'another woman,' Fricka. You're not just my husband's casual lover. You're my friend."

With a sigh, she said again, "What do you want me to tell you?"

"Everything. The whole truth about what happened . . . about how it ever came to happen . . . about your feelings for him. And for me."

"What good will that do?"

"It might salvage something."

"It will only cause you more pain. There are some things it is better not to talk about."

"Nothing that you could tell me now could hurt me more than you have hurt me already by lying to me."

"So . . . When you first found out that your husband was unfaithful, when you brought your suffering to me, when you asked for my help as a friend, should I have helped you by telling you that he was unfaithful to you with me?"

"Yes."

"*Ach!* You deceive yourself."

In the next room Cissy was playing her scales in the systematic manner taught her by Fricka: C major straight, three times. C major in thirds, three times, in sixths, three times. C minor . . . up and down, up and down, up and down . . . Her fingers were amazingly flexible. Fricka was a good teacher.

"Fricka . . . I want to know when it began."

"What does it matter when it began?"

"It matters a lot to me. Please tell me."

"*Ach, Gott!*"

"Tell me." I could hear my voice hardening against her unwillingness. "Go on, tell me."

"*Also* . . . if you must know . . . it began when you were in London, when you went to see your friend at the Foreign Office."

Now I was stunned into silence, appalled by the first cost to myself of the honesty I had demanded from Fricka. One can bear the destruction of the present, I thought, as long as the past is left intact. My mind supplied me ruthlessly with one image after another defaced by her words, with a whole bright structure of illusions wrecked in the name of truth—gone even the gold of that golden first morning.

Now Cissy was practicing her arpeggios: one octave, two octaves, right hand, left hand, both hands together, up and down, up and down, up and down. How much does Cissy know?

The slam of the front door, the thump of a full school satchel on the hall table, Pip's voice interrupting the arpeggios. "Who said you could make that row?"

"Mummy. She's better. She's having tea in her sitting room with Fricka."

"Oh."

"You'd better not go in. They're talking."

"I have no intention of going in."

How much does Pip know?

A rustle of music sheets. The ripple of a Clementi sonatina. What am I going to do? What ought I to do? This isn't just between me and Fricka.

When Cissy had finished the sonatina she closed the piano and left the room. The silence she left behind her threw Fricka and me into isolation, forced us to come to grips with the unresolved situation that both divided us and united us. But before we could do that, I thought, we had to reach a much deeper level of understanding; I had to find out how much she cared for Julian; she had to realize what she had done to me, where the real injury lay.

Until this moment I had avoided looking directly at Fricka. It was too painful, like looking at the dead. Yet when she finally broke the silence that enclosed us, it was the deadness of her voice that compelled me to look at her. "I shall go away," she said. She was leaning back in her chair with her eyes closed. Her face, gone gray as her dress, was desolation itself.

"I shall go away," she repeated, as if to strengthen a weak resolve. "I shall take the night train to Berlin. My passport is in order. I have only to pack my things."

Two warring voices started to shout each other down in my

mind. One said, *Let her go, this is your chance to get rid of her quietly*, and the second said, *No! She must stay!*

The second voice won; it had won long before it ever started to shout. It had whispered incessant sophistries to me during my three days of solitude. *Don't be a fool. Come to terms with this situation. Julian needs her. His need for her is part of his sickness. What will he do if she goes? And what will happen to her? Didn't you vow to be a good friend to her? That she has failed you is no reason why you should fail her. You expected too much of her, you set her on too high a pedestal. . . .*

I said now, "I'm willing to try."

"I don't understand."

"I'm willing to try going on as we are."

"Is that possible?"

"I don't know, Fricka. But I'm willing to try if you are."

Tears trickled out from under her closed eyelids. She fumbled in her pocket for her handkerchief. I looked away. She loves him, I thought, she has changed places with me, she is the slave now.

After a little while she came over to me and stood looking down at me with eyes that still glistened with tears. Then she put her hands on my shoulders, and immediately I believed again in their innocence. "I did not want to hurt you," she said. "I lied to you only because I did not want to hurt you. Is it possible that we can live so without hurting one another?"

"We can try."

Then she kissed me lightly on the lips, as if to seal the agreement. "In the end," she said, "I shall be the one who suffers most."


Julian seemed pleased to find me up and dressed when he came in, and not unfriendly. I ordered a fresh pot of tea for him and offered him the untouched sandwiches. He echoed, unconvincingly, Fricka's insincere supposition that I had had an attack of grippe.

"No, Julian," I said, looking him in the eyes, "it wasn't that. It was nothing physical. I think you know what it was. It was shock. The shock of a bad dream . . . of cries in the night. But I'm out of it now. I'm cured."

A spasm passed over his face like the flicker caused by a twinge of physical pain. I perceived it with detachment. Now, for the first time, I had an inkling of what the bad dream had done to free me, to finally cut through the tenacious sexual bonds that his verbal admission of infidelity had strained but not broken. In my relationship with him, as in Fricka's, a shift of power had taken place.

"I have come to a decision," I told him. "I have decided to let things be as you wanted them to be. I have told Fricka."

"So you and Fricka have got together and divided me up between you."

"Isn't that what you asked for?"

He was silent. For the second time that afternoon I was at a crossroads, and, as before, the choice of direction was momentarily mine. But, as before, the decision had been made in advance; like most decisions that appear to be sudden, it was the product of a long, slow process. I no longer had the will to say the words or make the gesture that might, at that moment, have brought Julian back to me; a realization that carried with it a profound sadness as well as a sense of release.

I said, "Do we have an engagement for tonight? I've forgotten."

"It's our night for the opera—if you want to go. They're doing *Carmen.*"

We had a series subscription for the opera. "Do *you* want to go?"

"Not particularly. I'd prefer a quiet evening at home."

"I'd rather like to see *Carmen.*"

"Pip could take you. He'd enjoy it."

I felt tested. To agree without demur would be a proof of my sincerity with regard to the new arrangement.

"That's a good idea," I said. "I'll go and ask Pip now."

Julian looked as if he wished I hadn't agreed so readily. I said, "Are you quite sure you don't want to come?"

He shook his head without speaking. I sensed a mute appeal, and felt threatened by it. If he had put it into words, asked me outright to stay at home with him, I would have done so. I waited for a moment or two before leaving the room, to give him a chance to speak, and when he didn't take it I felt absolved. Though not without pain.

Pip was studying in his room.

"How would you like to take me to the opera tonight. It's *Carmen*."

"I'd love to! But . . . what about Father?"

"He suggested it. He doesn't feel like going out tonight."

Pip still seemed uneasy. I could guess why, but he expressed it in the form of concern for my health. "Are you sure that you're well enough to go, Mother? It's awfully cold outside."

"I'm quite well—you know how quickly I recover. And anyway, we'll go by taxi—I have to dress up, our seats are in the orchestra."

"What shall I wear?"

"Your dark suit and a white shirt."

He was very sweet to me, proudly assuming the role of the protective male escort, treating me as if I were, miraculously, one of the young girls with whom he sometimes walked home from school but who, still bound by a rigid conventional code, would never have been allowed to go out alone with him in the evening. But I wanted more than the rather touching solicitude of a seventeen-year-old boy for his mother; more than any mother could ask from her son. I wanted moral support, reassurance that what I was doing was right, understanding, and, above all, tenderness.

In the foyer, between the acts, we ran across the Hungarian lawyer who was legal adviser to the legation, Zoltán Orsagh, and his wife Margit—one of the attractive young women whom I had so mistakenly suspected of having an affair with Julian. Assured now of her innocence in this respect, I greeted her warmly, and she asked whether Julian and I would be free to come to a party at their place on an evening about three weeks later. I accepted the invitation, thinking that if Julian didn't want to go I would go by myself. But when I told him that, he said of course he wanted to go.

# 7

# Joanna and Keres

## I

At the Orsaghs' party, Julian and I were the only English people present, and we were made so much of that I suspected Margit of having arranged it especially for us. None of the other guests was known to us, they came from professional and artistic circles outside the usual range of the "diplomatic set." Hungarian names were hard to catch correctly on first introduction, but Margit was adroit in letting me know whether I was meeting a music critic, a novelist, or whatever, and I had learned the trick of linking appearance with profession in my mind, so I usually said the right things to the right people.

Julian was asked to make a fourth at bridge, and he went off to play in another room. It was an old-style apartment whose lofty rooms—none recognizable as bedrooms—were connected with each other by double-winged doors, now opened wide, allowing the guests to disperse for talk or music, cards or flirtation. I chose talk. But the conversation begun in English for my benefit ended up in Hungarian, and I found it a strain to follow what was being said. I excused myself to go and watch Julian's bridge game.

Instead, attracted by the sound of music, I strayed into a small, dimly lighted room where the pure notes of a string quartet were issuing from a radio turned on low. Beside it a man sat listening with his eyes closed. He gave no sign of having heard me come in. I sat down quietly near the door. I was only just out of view of the group I had left, but I felt as removed as if I had stepped not only into another room, but into another world.

The radio musicians were playing the slow movement of a late Beethoven quartet. The listening man appeared to be totally absorbed in the music. He sat with his head tilted back, and the wan light from a green-shaded lamp, the only light there was, fell directly on his face, which I recognized as that of a man I had mentally classified as "crumpled poet." But it had some other, more elusive association for me, a resemblance . . . but to whom? I had no conscious memory of having seen him before this evening. I looked again at the still face, which somehow reflected the heavenly peace of the music, and impressions that my conscious mind had failed to retain slowly surfaced, until, with a growing, marveling certainty, I became aware of when I had seen him before.

When the quartet came to an end, he opened his eyes and looked across at me. "I don't think we want to hear anything else after that, do we?"

I shook my head, and he switched the radio off. "The musicians are my good friends," he said. "Especially the cellist—we even make music together occasionally. May I offer you a cigarette?"

His manner was so free of constraint that I thought he could not have recognized me. Then I realized that he could not possibly be the first to show recognition. Once again it was in my hands to direct the course that my life would take, and once again I had the feeling that I was merely ratifying a decision already made. I said, "Please forgive me, but I don't know your name, I didn't catch it when we were introduced. I am Joanna Crest."

"My name is Anthony Keres," he said, "and I am not surprised that you did not catch it. Margit forgot to turn it around, and said it in the Hungarian form—*Keres Antal.*"

I repeated it after him phonetically. "Keresh Ontal."

"You pronounce it well," he said, smiling. "The second *a* could be a little rounder, but you have a good ear."

I remembered now that Margit had called him *Professor.* I said, "May I ask you something, Professor Keres?"

"But of course . . ."

"This may seem strange. But I am curious whether you have any recollection . . . whether you have an idea that you may have . . . spoken with me before, under different circumstances?"

After a pause, he said simply, "Yes."

"Do you recall the circumstances?"

"Yes, I do recall them."

I feared that I was being indiscreet. "I am sorry. I am embarrassing you—please forgive me."

"There is nothing to forgive. It is entirely in your hands whether or not we shall speak of that previous encounter."

The words were formal, but I felt that they signified an unwillingness to intrude rather than indifference. "I thought you were a policeman," I said. "It was only when I saw you in the light of the streetlamp, near my house, that I realized I had been mistaken. Even so, it didn't seem possible that you should be that man—I had to ask you before I could be sure. And meeting you here tonight is an almost unbelievable coincidence. . . ."

He looked at me in silence, as if he was trying to make up his mind about something. At last he said, "It is not a coincidence. I knew that you were going to be here tonight, and I came because I wanted to see you again. I could not forget you."

His words gave me a feeling of such intense joy, such comfort, that I was almost afraid of it, of the need it revealed, the emptiness. Zoltán's sudden appearance, summoning us to supper, was a relief.

The bridge players said they were famished after playing four rubbers. "How did your game go?" I asked Julian. "Pretty well," he said indifferently. "Your husband was the all-around winner," one of the others told me. In the past, Julian would have been crowing with delight. Now he didn't seem to care whether he won or lost. "What have you been doing?" he asked.

"Listening to music with Professor Keres—you two have met, haven't you?"

"Briefly," Julian said. "I understand, sir, that you are a writer, and that you lecture on English literature at the university."

"That is so. I fell in love with England and English literature when I made my studies there as a young man."

Zoltán took me into the supper room. Keres followed with Julian. The buffet was laden with exotic delicacies for which I had no appetite. Zoltán kept pressing them on me in the hospitable Hungarian manner. "But Madame! You eat like a bird!"

On the other side of the table, Julian was saying to Keres,

"What do you think of that fellow Joyce? I've just been reading *Ulysses*."

Zoltán said to me, "I am glad you and Keres got a chance to talk. He's a fine poet—and he's one of my oldest friends."

I sensed in Zoltán an amiable curiosity. His friend must have expressed a wish to meet me, and he must be wondering why. "We didn't talk much," I said. "We were listening to a quartet on the radio—some friends of Professor Keres were playing."

"Ah! The Székely Quartet—they are excellent. Have you never heard them before?"

I confessed that I hadn't. "We must remedy that," he said. "They have a concert coming up soon, we might all go to it together, and get Keres to come along."

"I'll suggest it to Julian," I said.

Julian and Keres were now discussing D. H. Lawrence, and *Lady Chatterley's Lover*, which Julian had been lent by someone at the legation. I would have liked to hear what Keres had to say about it, but Zoltán's curiosity made me cautious.

For the rest of the evening I stayed away from Keres, but tried to keep him in view. I didn't want him to misunderstand, and leave before I had a chance to speak with him again. Finally, when I was alone for a moment, he joined me.

"I have to go now," he said. "Tomorrow is one of my early days at the university. On Mondays and Thursdays I lecture first thing in the morning. But I leave early. And in fine weather I usually walk home."

I thought I understood, but I wasn't sure.

"If you should ever feel like walking some of the way with me," he said, "it would make me very happy."

I said nothing.

"Near the bridge, on the Buda side, there is a church. I reach it at about noon, and I usually stop and go in for a minute or two. It is very close to the bridge."

I had no need to ask him which bridge he meant.

Private communication between me and Julian had almost entirely ceased. It had depended, I realized now, on the intimacy of sharing the same room and the same bed. In our overpeopled existence, only the nights had been ours alone. But now the nights were Fricka's. Under the old circumstances, our evening at the Orsaghs', the people we had met there, would have been discussed in bed before we slept. Now, I went upstairs alone, and it was only the next day, in Fricka's presence, that Julian said, "I rather liked that writer. He had some interesting ideas. I wouldn't mind meeting him again."

"Why not invite him here?" Fricka said.

"That's a good idea. Put him on the invitation list, Joey."

A sudden rage flared up in me. This wasn't the first time that Fricka had encroached on my sphere of action. "I'll think about it," I said, with my mind already made up. If Julian wanted Keres to come to our house, he would have to issue the invitation himself. I never would.

Keres had been in my mind all day. At noon, I had imagined him going into the church, half-expecting to find me there, waiting a little, then realizing, because he was sensitive, that I wouldn't come so soon, that time would have to pass. But just to imagine him there, to picture him striding up the steps to the church door, wearing his long coat and fur cap, as when I had seen him first, supplied a frame of reference in which to place him—for I had no other. I couldn't picture him lecturing to his students because the ambience of a university was unfamiliar to me, and I had no idea what his home was like, or even where it was.

I knew nothing about his life. But in saving mine he had entered it at a very deep level. With that single act he had come closer to me than anyone I had ever known. And because this meant so much to me I was afraid of it.

I let pass two more opportunities to be with him, days of brilliant, cold sunshine on which he certainly must have walked home. But when the second Monday came around, sunless, with new snow getting ready to fall, I took the darkening skies as a warning not to let fear and mistrust keep me away. An hour before noon, I put on the sheepskin coat in which he had first seen me, and walked down to the bridge that I had avoided since that night. Now I saw it as a symbol of resurrection.

A few flakes of snow started to fall. It was twenty minutes to twelve. I went into the church. The only person there was an old sacristan, pottering around replacing burned-out candles and votive lights. I thought of Nicolai and Lucrèce, and I set a votive light burning before the shrine of the Virgin—but whether for them or for myself I wasn't sure. Then I sat down to wait near the entrance.

After a while I looked out. The snow was falling now in big, fluffy flakes. He won't come, I thought. But I waited.

The church clock began to strike twelve. On the eleventh stroke he walked in, shaking the snow from his fur cap, his shoulders covered with snow. Coming in from the whiteness outside, he didn't immediately see me, but my eyes were used to the semidarkness and I could see his face clearly enough to perceive the disappointment on it and the way it lighted up when he finally saw me. He came and sat beside me without saying anything, and at once the fever of uncertainty and self-mistrust that had kept me away from him until now left me. I felt completely at peace.

The church clock struck the quarter, and Keres said softly, "Shall we go now?"

I walked beside him through the heavily falling snow without seeing where I was going, without caring. He stopped at a low, arched entrance. His home? No. A little café. "Let us go in here," he said. "We can sit here as long as we like—they know me, I come here often."

The proprietor asked if he wanted his usual table, and Keres said yes, and ordered tea for us both. The table was in a corner beside a window. Keres hung up our coats, and we sat down, facing each other. In the bleak daylight that filtered through the snow-encrusted window, he had more reality for me than he had had heretofore. I was seeing him now, I thought, as he really was; divested of whatever might have lent him illusory qualities—the projection of my own desperate need, the pervading spirit of Beethoven's music—but in no way diminished by their absence. This unassuming, rather rumpled man, no longer young—I judged him to be in his middle forties—with a sensitive, intelligent, but deeply lined face, and kind eyes that looked straight into mine, was inhabited by an extraordinary spirit of his own, no doubt about that, a spirit so limpid that it put all subterfuge to shame.

"I should not have waited so long," I said. "There was no need, I see that now. I should have come when I wanted to, the very next day."

"Why didn't you? I hoped you would. I waited for you."

"I was afraid."

"Of me?"

"Of myself. Of making another mistake."

"In the course of my life," he said, "I have made a great many mistakes. But that did not stop me from risking another one."

"Do you mean when you suggested this meeting?"

"Earlier than that. Consciously, it was when I took steps to find out who you were, and to see you again. Unconsciously, it was when I answered the call for help that you sent out from the bridge."

"Call? Did I call for help?"

"Not verbally. Not even, perhaps, in your conscious mind—but from depths in which you knew better what you wanted than you did on a conscious level."

"And you heard me."

"Does that sound insane to you?"

"No. No, it doesn't. Because it's something that has happened to me. I have experienced that kind of hearing."

"It had never happened to me before, and I did not understand it."

"But you were influenced by it—you allowed it to direct you."

"I couldn't help myself."

"So that was what brought you there."

"Ultimately, yes. But there was a chain of circumstances. . . ." He smiled. "I am not usually out in the streets at such an hour."

"Neither am I."

There was a little silence. I was not yet ready to offer any explanation because to this man it would have to be nothing less than the truth. He said, "That morning, I lay down to sleep at the time when I am accustomed to start getting up. But before I slept, I wrote down what had happened in my journal—like most writers I keep a journal. I wanted to put it on record before my memory, or future events, had time to modify it. It seemed to me then, it still seems to me now—even more now—to prove the existence of"—he hesitated—"of some force we don't yet understand."

Whatever force it was that had brought us together had, I thought, been at work for longer than he imagined. I said, "If you believe that you really got a call for help from me, where were you when it reached you—and how did you become aware of it?"

"I was at Zoltán's. I had spent the earlier part of the evening very painfully, with a woman who was once dear to me. The woman to whom I am married, but with whom I no longer live. When I left her it was nearly midnight, but I felt too sad to go straight home, so I went to see Zoltán and we talked until four in the morning. He wanted me to stay, and sleep there, but something told me to leave—made me leave, against my inclinations, because I was very tired and the night ... well, you know how cold it was. When I found you on the bridge, I knew that the message had come from you. Yet when you actually spoke to me, you said, 'Go away'—do you remember?"

"Yes. I remember. Down on the river, on one of those floating pieces of ice, there was a drowned man. He was talking to me. Inviting me to come down to him."

In Keres's silence I sensed an unasked question.

"He drowned a long time ago, in the sea. He was not my lover, nothing like that. He was just someone I was fond of. Someone I pitied. Someone whose death I wept for after it happened—but didn't fully understand until that night."

"We have a lot to tell each other," Keres said, as if it was quite natural to assume that we should have the time and opportunity, and the desire, to exchange our life histories.

The snowstorm was turning into a blizzard. The other habitués of the café were leaving, afraid of being snowbound, and Keres thought he should call a taxi for me while it was still possible to get one.

At home, my return went unnoticed. Julian was lunching with a colleague, Pip was at school, Fricka and Cissy were busy in the schoolroom. I went up to my room, lay down on my bed, and almost immediately fell into the first dreamless sleep that I had had since Julian's door had been locked against me.

I began now to live for the hours I spent with Keres; and not only *for* them, but also *by* them. And like the devout Catholic who lets nothing keep him away from the Mass that is the source of his spiritual sustenance, I arranged my days, juggled my obligations, so that nothing should keep me away from the meetings that sustained me, from the man who gave me back the self-esteem that I allowed to be filched from me daily by Julian and Fricka. But Keres knew nothing of that. All Keres knew was

275

that something in me had been broken, and with unbelievable patience and insight he undertook to mend it.

The word *love* was never mentioned between us. And I didn't think of him as a lover. I thought of him as a friend. I knew now that what Old Browne had given me, and wanted from me in return, was neither love nor friendship but something in between— companionship, linked in his imagination to a romantic, unrealizable dream. Keres was the first, the only man who had ever offered me true friendship, or believed me capable of a serious intellectual exchange that rose above sex.

All the same, our meetings had to be clandestine. The openly shared pleasures of friendship, such as concerts and art galleries, were out of the question. Obviously, we could not meet at my home, and the privacy of his could have endangered our relationship in another way, and in any case he didn't suggest it. We spent our time together sauntering through the less frequented streets and alleys of Buda, or sitting in little cafés where I was unlikely to run into anyone who knew me.

But we were soon to feel less confined; the blizzard that had cut short our first rendezvous turned out to be the last snowfall of the winter, and early in March the headlong Eastern European spring unfolded the world around us as abruptly as the winter had folded it in. Within a few days of the first thaw, the smell of the melting snow on the Buda hills was mixed with the pink fragrance of almond blossom, the wind blew soft and wild, the river ran free, the cherry trees in our garden burst into bloom overnight, and the ground was starred with narcissus. But the garden was a lost paradise, a fool's paradise, in which I no longer wanted to walk. Instead, I went farther afield with Keres, up countrified roads past other private Edens, whose iron gates could not keep in the intoxicating breath of lilacs and syringa, until finally on a summer-like afternoon at the end of April, we stopped at the gate of a garden so full of both that they almost concealed the house they surrounded, a little whitewashed villa with blue shutters.

"This is where I live," Keres said.

It had taken us more than ten weeks and twice as many meetings to reach this gate together, and I still hadn't told Keres about Fricka. It had seemed to me that the mere utterance of her name would be enough to cast an evil shadow between us.

Julian's name, on the other hand, cast no shadow at all, as if it belonged to a man who had lived in the distant past. There was no death so final, I thought, so devoid of illusions of immortality in another world or hope of resurrection in this one, as the death of love.

But these things troubled me only when I was away from Keres. When I was with him my mind was freed from its distresses, so I never wanted to speak of them, and neither did he want to speak of his. We escaped together, but more as teacher and pupil than as equals, into that untroubled region where poems conceived in conflict and pain are brought to birth in a tranquillity that they absorb and contain in themselves and impart, even centuries later, to those who know how to read them.

I had got to know Keres unframed, detached from any physical ambience. And he had got to know me detached from mine—of which Julian had in the past been such a dominant element that I had been visible, even to myself, only in relation to him; the frame had overwhelmed the picture. But now, unframed, I found it hard to see myself at all, to believe in my own separate existence, in my own value as a woman. And until I could achieve that, I could not give myself to Keres—I had no self to give. He understood this without being told anything, and little by little, by his recognition of me as a spiritual and intellectual being, he was giving me back the self I had lost.

But that was not the sole reason Keres had taken so long to bring me to his little house with the blue shutters . . . he had to be sure that I would not destroy it. I realized that the moment I stepped inside its white walls. Although I knew no more about his personal life than he knew about mine, I recognized in him a pilgrim, one who had traveled along much the same paths as myself, but who had already attained a summit from which I was still very far.

The interior I had imagined for him had been austere, but much less so than the reality. Knowing that he had been married, and to a woman whom he had loved, I did not expect to find him in surroundings as totally stripped of a woman's influence as a monastery—what had she done to him that he should have expunged her so utterly? Here, as in a cloister, the asceticism was linked with serenity; and just as the gentleness in Keres's face transcended everything else, so now the serenity of his house transcended its lack of adornment.

We entered a stone-flagged hallway from which a steep flight of uncarpeted stairs led to an upper floor, and passed through a very small room containing a table, four straight chairs, and a cupboard, into a much larger one furnished chiefly with books which were stacked up on the floor as well as on the shelves. There was a piano with a bust of Beethoven on it, surrounded by piles of sheet music, a couple of worn armchairs, and a desk buried in papers. It was all in the apparent disorder peculiar to writers and scholars, who have their own private notion of order based on the principle of keeping within reach anything they are likely to need while at work and knowing exactly under which pile of papers to find it. But the visible surfaces were speckless; the bare wood floors, the whitewashed walls, the windows, all gave the impression of being thoroughly dusted, washed, and polished every day. And in this, and in this only, I saw a woman's hand.

The rooms had the soft greenish light, the cool, underwater atmosphere of a place surrounded by trees. Keres threw open the casement windows, letting in a flood of warm air and spring scents, and a bee or two. In a sunlit part of the garden, a sturdy old woman was preparing a plot of earth for planting. "That is my housekeeper, Kati *neni*," Keres told me. "She likes to grow tomatoes."

Standing there with Keres at the window of his house, I had the same sense of a miraculous arrival shadowed by an imminent inevitable departure that I had once had on a long sea voyage, when the ship had put in for a few hours at an island that seemed to be part of a mythical archipelago of the blest, and that I was not likely ever to see again. The repetition now of that pang of intense but fleeting joy was like the fulfillment of a prophecy, a confirmation of the myths that my mother had lived by. I could hear her plaintive voice telling me that the Isles of the Blest may be glimpsed at certain moments by the unblest but never inhabited by them. And I felt a great sorrow for my unblessedness that, aside from everything else, would bar me from ever inhabiting this isle to which Keres had brought me.

He said, "Why do you look so sad?"

I was unable to speak. I felt like weeping, but I was unable to weep. It was as if when I sealed the pact with Fricka I had sealed off the source from which tears flow.

Then Keres said the words that broke the seal, and broke my heart at the same time, because I knew that a final departure was inevitable. Yet it was those heartbreaking words that, coming from Keres, made me whole.

"I love you," he said, and again, "I love you."

What I wanted more than anything in the world then was to stay there with him, to progress quietly, without any break, from the rites of friendship to those of love. But I had an appointment with Julian that had to be kept.

Keres said he would walk with me down to the main *Korut*, where I could get a taxi. But today I didn't want our parting to be in a public place. In the stiff little dining room, the spotless little refectory, he took me in his arms, and we kissed for the first time. But after that one long embrace he let me go. He knew that I had to go.

"There is something I want to give you," he said. "It is more symbolic than anything else. But there is something else . . . do you remember when I asked you that night where you lived and you said, 'Nowhere?' "

From a drawer in the cupboard he took two keys. "The big one unlocks the gate," he said, "and the little one opens the door of the house."


The appointment with Julian had to be kept punctually; it was semiofficial. We were required by protocol to assist at a legation reception for a visiting British dignitary, and it was essential to Julian's precarious position that I should not let him down on occasions of that kind. I no longer loved him, but I was still his wife. I owed him my allegiance in his professional life—and I suspected that he would soon be badly in need of it, for it was obvious that he was getting closer and closer to some unpredictable crisis.

I was to join him in the chancery, and we would go up to the reception together, being certain to be there at least a quarter of an hour before the guest of honor was due to arrive. When I got back to the villa, I saw that I had exactly twenty minutes in which to change my clothes and get to the chancery. The day was so warm and bright that I decided to wear a cream-colored summer dress and a wide-brimmed leghorn hat. On my way to the chancery I met Pip, coming back from his school.

"Mother! How perfectly beautiful you look!"

"Thank you ... but don't I always?"

"Well," Pip said, with the brutal honesty of the young, "You haven't been looking up to much lately ... I don't mean your clothes, you're always well-dressed, it's just ... just that today you look younger and jollier than you've looked for a long time."

I blew him a kiss. "I must fly, your father and I are on duty as official receptionists to Sir Edward. ..."

*Jolly* was hardly the word to describe how I felt. But Pip's admiration of my appearance was reflected in varying degrees on the faces of the chancery staff. Julian was waiting for me alone in his own office, sitting idle at his desk, staring out of the window. He took no notice of me until I said, "Julian ... I think it's time to go upstairs."

"Oh," he said, "is it? Very well."

As we walked through the outer office, clerks and typists, locking their files and getting ready to leave, bade us a polite good evening, but I felt in them a constraint that had not been there when I had passed through alone a few minutes earlier.

That afternoon I discovered for myself that the basis of the cliché that all the world loves a lover is that the lover loves all the world. I found myself looking kindly on everyone, being warm and attentive even to bores, even to the pompous Sir Edward, without the least effort.

Afterward, on the way home, Julian said, "Well, I must say you turned on the charm very effectively." The bitterness in his voice made it a reproach rather than a compliment.

"I wasn't consciously 'turning on' anything."

"It looked as if you were," Julian said, "particularly with Sir Edward. I was rather sickened."

"Were you? I wonder why. Even supposing that I was making a deliberate effort to be nice to him—which I wasn't—it couldn't do you any harm. It could only help you."

"I don't want your help."

Was it my imagination, or did he ever so faintly emphasize the last word? We walked on in silence. We had never had very much to say to each other; our means of communication was more primitive, and with that gone we were like two strangers with only a word or two of a common language. When we got home, he went upstairs to his room without a word and locked himself in.

Our duties were not over. There was to be a formal dinner party at eight-thirty. Before facing that, I too needed to be alone for a while—but nowhere near Julian. I went to my sitting room at the back of the house, slightly above the garden level. On its little balcony was a deck chair and beside it was the book I had been reading before I had gone out to meet Keres at noon. I took off my hat and my high-heeled shoes and subsided into the striped hollow of the hammocky chair. Down in the garden, Cissy and Fricka were playing badminton. Trees hid them from view, but I could hear their voices. Pip was probably out playing tennis with his friends; he despised badminton, and he preferred to go out, for although Julian no longer got angry or violent, his silent presence was inhibiting, and when he was not there, the idea of his possible unannounced return and withdrawal behind locked doors was even more so.

I reopened the book, which Keres had lent me the last time we met. It was a collection of medieval Latin verse, with translations by an English Latinist, a woman, for whom Keres had a high regard. A translator himself—from English into Hungarian—Keres knew the difficulties of translating poetry, the "almost impossibilities," as he put it. It was an art, he thought, in which women, with their intuitive powers, their ability to tune in to other minds, to sense what no dictionary could tell them, were better suited than men. Yet he could not cite very many women translators of poetry, and I told him that the reason was probably that a woman couldn't afford to expend her talent on someone else's work, she had to fight too hard for recognition of her own.

I had not yet had time to read through the whole collection. I had dipped into it, reading a poem here and another there, wherever my attention was arrested, and it was arrested first, and powerfully, by the opening lines of an Easter poem, written in the ninth century by one Sedulius Scottus, that touched a chord of memory long quiet and set it vibrating like a bell: *Last night did Christ the Sun rise from the dark, The mystic harvest of the fields of God. . . .*

Every poem I read seemed to speak directly to me. An unknown poet who wrote in the thirteenth century ... *The golden sun has fled our world, Snow falls by day, The nights are numb* ... spoke to me of *my* fall, *my* winter, and the scholar of Benedictbeuren rejoicing ... *The fields are green again* ... *Love is reborn* ... sang of *my* spring.

Keres had told me that he wanted me to read the works of those ancient poets because he believed that their love of nature, their identification of joy and sorrow with the different seasons of the year, would find a response in me, and, above all, because they were a celebration of life. But now, the last poem in the book, whose first line was faintly underscored in pencil, told me something else, made it clear that Keres himself was speaking to me through these long-dead voices; *Herself hath given back my life to me....*

I put down the book and closed my eyes.

From a great distance, Fricka's High German accents broke into my reverie and made me aware that dusk was falling and with it a heavy dew. "We shall stop now—no? It gets dark."

"Too dark for me, I can't see a thing," Cissy said, her accent a perfect echo of Fricka's.

It was usual for them to speak German together; in fact it was a rule that they should. But overheard like that, it gave the most banal remarks an intimate flavor, and made me feel shut out; a feeling that wasn't dispelled when they appeared, sauntering along the path arm in arm.

I called out to them, "Who won?"

Startled, they looked up. "Fricka won," Cissy said. "Fricka always wins."

The dinner party at the legation broke up early; Sir Edward was going on to a reception elsewhere that Julian and I were not expected to attend. On our way back to the villa, walking through the sweet-scented April night side by side but completely cut off from each other, we met Fricka.

"I could not bear to stay indoors on such a beautiful night," she said. "I am going for a walk around the battlements—why not come with me?"

I objected that my evening shoes were not comfortable for walking. "What about you?" Fricka asked, appealing to Julian.

It went through my mind that she wanted him to go with her as a form of open recognition. Julian stood mute, apparently unable to make up his mind. I had the feeling that he was waiting for me to help him by saying something more decisive. For an instant, I saw the three of us objectively, as characters in a play, caught by a camera at a moment of suspended action—when destiny is hanging on a word.

Then Fricka laid her hand on Julian's arm, animating him as if she had touched a spring. They went off together in the direction of the battlements on the other side of the Vár while I went on alone in the direction of the villa. But instead of going in, I followed the road down to the main avenue, where I picked up a taxi and gave the driver Keres's address.

At the corner of the lane that led up to the cottage, I let the taxi go. I wanted to approach my love quietly, unheralded; I wanted my coming to be a surprise. I had not planned to come, I had acted on impulse, but I had no regrets. On the contrary, I was filled with the sense of release that follows on a right decision. As I walked up the lane overhung with trees, all in early leaf, I felt in a state of pagan grace; at one with the spring night, tuned in to the almost inaudible music of growth and emerging life.

The keys that Keres had given me were in my bag; when I had changed for the evening, I had transferred them from one bag to another because I wanted to have them always with me. I fitted the big key into the gate. It turned easily and silently. I entered and relocked the gate without arousing anyone; no lights went on in the windows facing the lane. Cautiously as a thief, I crept around to the other side of the cottage. There, in Keres's study, a light was burning. My footsteps noiseless on the heavily dewed grass, I approached the unshaded windows, closed against a fluttering army of night insects, and looked in.

To look into any lighted room from the dark outside is to see it touched with mystery, endowed with a charm that it may not actually possess. But for me this was already a charmed room, charged with mystery, and the magical qualities of the lighted window merely served to bring into focus what was already there.

Keres was sitting at his desk, with his spectacles on his nose, writing in a book that I assumed was his diary. He had changed into a shabby velveteen jacket, and his shirt was unbuttoned at the neck. He smiled as he wrote. Was he writing about me? I hoped so. I loved him so much, so much. Too much, it was madness to desire the unattainable with such intensity.

Between the two windows was a door, an ordinary door without glass. I tapped on it very softly. Keres looked up with a startled gesture and listened, clearly puzzled as to what the sound had been and where it had come from. I knocked again, as softly as before. Keres said in Hungarian, "Who is there?" I made no answer. Then he opened the door.

The look on his face when he saw me standing there was indescribable—it transfigured me in my own eyes. Never before had any man looked at me with such profound emotion, such wonder and joy.

"You have come to me . . . ," he said. "You have come to me!"


## II

Lying awake in my solitary room, watching the sun come up, I was filled with happiness of a kind that I felt could never be taken away from me no matter what the future might hold.

My window was open, but the only sound coming in from outside was the waking twitter of birds. Then the peace was suddenly shattered by a cry. High-pitched, anguished, it came from somewhere down in the garden. I heard my name called loudly, urgently, twice . . . and once again, on a falling, fainting note.

I ran from terrace to terrace with the gravel of the path cutting my bare feet, "Julian . . . Julian . . . Julian . . ."

I found him slumped over the stone rim of the sunken pool with his arm hanging down in the stagnant green water that was rapidly turning to crimson. My cries brought Fricka running, her hair hanging loose, her feet bare like mine, and together we tried to staunch the crimson flow with strips torn from our nightgowns.

At the moment of his return to consciousness, Julian's eyes rested on Fricka, as had happened once before. But this time he recoiled from her as he would from a poisonous snake. His agitation was so great that the doctor gestured to her to leave the room.

I laid my hand lightly on Julian's damp forehead, and he grew calm again. After a while, bandaged, made comfortable, he slept.

"He must be kept very quiet," the doctor said, "very calm. It would be best if he were to see no one but you, Madame."

I asked him to explain that to Fräulein Friml—she was so anxious to be of help. He said he quite understood.

"The patient is confused," he told her. "He probably mistakes you for someone he feared in his childhood. It would be better to stay away from him until he is himself again."

Fricka looked from him to me and back again. "I understand," she said.

Arrangements were made by the legation for us to leave for London as soon as Julian could safely travel. At the same time, Fricka would go home to Germany. She went about performing her last services for us with her usual efficiency, going further than ever beyond the call of duty. Taciturn, gloomy, disfigured by private weeping, she checked the inventory, replaced broken objects, settled with tradesmen and servants, and packed our belongings for us, while I kept continual watch over Julian.

On the afternoon of our departure, she asked me if she might see Julian for a few minutes to say good-bye—the Berlin train left earlier than the Orient Express. Julian was up and dressed, sitting listlessly in a low chair, staring at his wrists.

"Fricka wants to say good-bye to you—will you see her?"

"No."

"Not even for a minute?"

"No."

"She's desperately unhappy."

His hand reached for mine. I took it and held it. He said, "Don't plead for her, Joey."

"I can't help feeling sorry for her."

"She doesn't deserve your pity."

"Nor yours?"

"Nor mine. She's a snake."

There was a knock on the door. Julian's grip on my hand tightened. "Don't let her in. . . ."

"All right. I won't let her in."

I went out and shut the door behind me. "I'm sorry, Fricka, but Julian doesn't feel well enough to see you—he asked me to say good-bye to you for him."

"How can you be so cruel?" she said, turning away.

I left Pip with Julian and sent a message to Fricka, asking her to come to my sitting room.

She came in dressed for her journey—wearing, in fact, exactly the same things that she had been wearing when I first saw her. Then, she had been smiling. Now, her face was stony. I took two envelopes from my writing desk. One contained her salary. She put it in her bag with a curt *"Danke."* "And this," I said, "is a letter. . . ."

"From him?"

"It's a letter of recommendation—to have with you in case you can't get in touch with us later."

"Is it from him?"

"No. It's from me."

She turned it over in her hands as if uncertain what to do with it, accept it, return it, or tear it up. Then I told her a second lie. "He has read it, and approves of it," adding more truthfully, "He is in no condition now to write anything himself."

She put it away in her bag without opening it. When I had asked her to come and see me, it had not been only for this. I had believed that we still had something to say to each other, and that the saying of it might help to clarify my complex feelings toward her and purge us both of bitterness. But now I realized that there was nothing more to be said.

I held out my hand. "Good-bye, Fricka."

But she would not shake hands with me.


Sleepless on the train, my head throbbing to the rhythm of the wheels that were taking me farther and farther away from Keres with every turn, I felt momentarily reprieved when the rhythm changed and the train slowed down. The engine exhaled deeply and came to a stop in the middle of nowhere, as it habitually did once or twice during its journey across Europe—as if it needed a rest. In the short interval of silence, I listened for Julian's breathing, which was so light it was almost inaudible. I leaned over the edge of my upper bunk and looked down at him. He lay on his back, quite still, with his bandaged wrists limp on the coverlet. His face was pallid in the blue light, and utterly calm, as if the sleeping drug I had given him had carried him down below the deepest of dreams, and even below their source.

Silently, smoothly, the wheels began turning once more, and

within a few seconds I was again at the mercy of the inexorable rhythm of separation, which gathered speed and with it a swaying motion that finally rocked me into an uneasy half-sleep. As soon as it was light, I got up. We were nearing a frontier station, and when the officials boarded the train I wanted to be out in the corridor armed with the diplomatic passes that would keep them from disturbing Julian. By now he had risen to the upper levels of sleep, and my movements caused him to stir and mutter, "Don't let her in. . . ."

I whispered close to his ear, "She can't come in—she isn't on the train." After he had quieted down, I opened the door to the next compartment. Cissy was still asleep, but Pip was awake, reading. "I must cope with customs now," I told him. "Will you keep an eye on your father?"

"Yes, Mother."

He did whatever I asked of him without hesitation. But a distance had sprung up between me and my children. They didn't know what to think, and I didn't know what to tell them—or what Fricka had told them before she left.

Pip was giving his father tea from a Thermos flask when I returned to the compartment. "Thanks, old chap," Julian said. He looked at me with a wordless appeal in his haunted eyes, and held out his hand to me; a heartbreaking gesture that moved me to inward tears every time he made it, which was often; he liked me to hold his hand all the time.

We were nearing the end of our journey when I wrote this letter to Keres.

April 30, 1936

Beloved,

This is to say good-bye. I am writing it on the train, and I shall post it in London. I wanted desperately, oh so desperately, to see you before I left. It was agony to go away without having been with you, heard your voice, felt your arms around me one more time. But there was no possibility. Absolutely none. Everything happened too fast.

Yet now . . . now that the inevitable leap into the dark has been made, I think that perhaps it was better to part like that—with our last memory of each other one of pure happiness. If I am to keep my footing in the darkness around me and ahead of me, I shall need a constant light;

not a flame that can die of too little air or go out in too strong a wind, but a steady radiance, emanating from somewhere deep down, like the light of the earth itself. And the memory of our perfect night together is that kind of a light.

You will probably hear from Zoltán Orsagh that Julian tried to take his own life. It is not public knowledge. The official story is that the discovery of a grave physical condition resulting from his accident necessitated his immediate return to England for an operation. But Zoltán knows the truth. What he doesn't know is what lies behind it. Even I am not quite sure.

I never spoke to you about those things, my darling, because I didn't want to introduce any sadness into our brief time together, and because I wanted to keep untarnished the luminous world of the mind and imagination into which you led me further and further each time we met, and I think you felt the same way.

On that snowy morning, when we were sitting in the little café together, you said that we had a lot to tell each other. But you implied that we should have plenty of time for that in the future. A belief in our shared future has been implicit in everything you have said and done, and I have tried to believe in it, or at least hope for it. But at this moment I cannot see any possibility of a future together. There will be time enough and to spare for telling each other our life histories, but they won't be told in each other's arms, my darling, or while sitting together on winter evenings beside the tile stove in the white peace of your workroom. They will have to be set down on paper, in solitude. As a poet, you won't find this so difficult, but what about me? I don't know how to distill the past and make poetry out of its essence. I don't even know how to write a real love letter. I can only say, I love you. I love the whole of you with the whole of myself. I love you totally, body, mind, and soul—but that is too vague a definition. I shall try to tell you what it means to me in terms of little intimate things.

To start with, I love your bones, your big, loose-limbed frame and all its movements, your long stride and the way you measure it to fit in with my smaller steps, the incredibly gentle touch of your huge hands, the way you bend over me from what seems to me a very great height, the way you fold me into your body's shelter. I love your voice, and all its different inflections, the way you say my name, the way you say "I love you," the way you mutter curses in Hungarian when something won't work, the way you speak English—the little mistakes you make and your funny little smile when you realize you have made one. I love what you consider your imperfections—the gray in your hair, the deep lines on your face, your need to wear glasses for reading and writing. I love your contradictions, your untidiness, the disorder on your desk and the strict, strict order in your soul, the depth and intensity of your emotions and your absolute control over them. I love you for your tenderness to me and your kindness toward everyone. I respect your mind, and I love you because you respect mine, because you—so gifted yourself, so great— believe that I too am gifted, that I too have some greatness in me. I love you because you have taught me what loving means, what love is . . . and how to read a poem. . . .

The writing of this litany of love temporarily eased the pain of separation. I didn't know yet that this was the start of a repetitive cycle of feeling common to all separated lovers; the sense of contact that would last like a long-held breath until the letter should reach Keres, be briefly renewed while I imagined him opening and reading it, and give way almost immediately to an irrational anguish and uncertainty that would last until a reply brought relief. A tormenting cycle to which I had sentenced myself indefinitely by promising Julian never to leave him as long as he wanted me with him.

Now, as I started to help Julian put on his clothes and get ready to leave the train at Calais and board the Channel boat, I had an inkling of what that promise might mean when my resolve was no longer sustained by circumstances of high drama, when the noble gesture had crystallized into a permanent position, unalterable no matter how painful.

# 8

# Joanna and Julian

We met every day. He would wait for me in the early afternoon outside the gates of the sanatarium. It was a place without locks and keys. The patients were free to come and go as they pleased, on the theory that as long as they needed the security of the institution they would return to it of their own free will. Julian responded to this psychological form of control almost too well; he did more than surrender to it, he clung to its safety.

Our daily meetings took place outside any set framework, like my meetings with Keres; afternoon tea in little teashops, long walks over Hampstead Heath, no opportunities for intimacy—the parallels were painfully close. But with Keres I had been moving toward love, and with Julian I was moving away from it. Keres and I shared a dream. But I could never again share a dream with Julian. He must have sensed this, or feared it, for he kept his pathetic dreams to himself. It was as if his mind and spirit had embraced the same voluntary limitations that governed his actions. Yet within these limitations he seemed to have broken the shell of apathy in which he had been encased ever since his accident, to have turned outward again, but with none of his old intolerance. He spoke of his well-to-do fellow patients—crackups from all the professions—with a sympathy that he had accorded only to the poor in the outside world, and he would report the most insignificant demonstrations of friendliness to himself—a smile or a compliment from a nurse, a confidence from a fellow patient, a few friendly words from a doctor—as if they were momentous experiences.

He never spoke of Fricka, or of anyone we had known in the past. The fate of the masses had long since ceased to interest him, and so, apparently, had the fate of his own children. He never mentioned them of his own accord, and he received my news of them with indifference, as though it were no concern of his. When I told him that they had gone to stay in the country, he accepted the fact without asking where or with whom. Which saved me from having to tell him that I had communicated with the Crest family, and that Pip and Cissy had gone to stay with their grandparents.

Their absence left me totally alone, but I needed solitude. Every day I wrote long letters to Keres. They were not, strictly speaking, love letters. They were for me the timid beginning of a long exchange of ideas with Keres, the poet, that brought me closer to Keres, the man, and led me to creativity of my own.

I would sit by the open window of my top-floor flat with the sooty rooftops of London spread out below me and the smoke from their chimneys dusting the sill with grime, and visualize Keres sitting at his desk by the windows of his workroom, which opened onto a garden drenched with the sweetness of rain-washed grass and flowers. Or I would imagine him sitting at his piano, practicing Beethoven. He had written me that his friend the cellist had been there and they had played Beethoven together,

... the two magnificent last sonatas for cello and piano. One of them ends with a fugue that is far too difficult for me—but my friend only smiles when I make mistakes. I told him about you. I hope you don't mind. My way of telling him was to show him a series of poems that I am working on—they are yours, my Joanna, and when they are all finished I shall send them to you. After reading them through twice, he embraced me without speaking. Then he sat down with his cello and played the Bach suites for me. That was his way of celebrating what my poems had told him—for him there is something sacramental about the Bach suites....

Every day before going to meet Julian I would look in at the post office to see if there was a letter for me from Keres, who wrote to me poste restante. If there was one, I would put it unopened into an inner pocket, where I could feel it reassuring me like the touch of his hand, and communicating to me so much of his strength and gentleness that I was able to give some of it to Julian. But when a day or two went by without a letter from Keres I would feel emptied of even my own little fund of strength. At such times Julian would say, "You're not feeling ill, are you?" and a peculiar look of apprehension, almost of panic, would come into his eyes.

At the end of August it was decided that he should come home for a trial week in the outside world. But he didn't want to come to the flat. He wanted to go with me to the little hotel on the beach at Clovelly. Everything in me resisted the idea, but I could see no way out. Julian made the reservations himself—a display of initiative guardedly applauded by his doctor.

On the Devon and Cornwall Express, Julian and I, alone in a first-class compartment, sat facing each other on either side of a window, as we had faced each other in countless express trains. But now, on our way back for the second time to the place from which we had started out, I had the feeling of coming full circle.

When the trip was arranged, Julian had asked me to bring him one of his good suits, a silk shirt, and a pair of gold cuff links that I had given him at the time of our marriage. But he wanted to get a new tie for the occasion, and we went together to choose one. "You should get yourself something new to wear," he told me.

I got myself a whole new outfit. I took with me not a single garment that I had ever worn before, and the resulting sense of disguise enabled me to imagine myself a stranger to the man sitting opposite me in the train, and to see him, for a brief, illusory moment, as an unknown fellow traveler; a well-dressed, well-groomed man in early middle age, with the voice and manners of a gentleman—politely concerned as to whether I wanted the window open or closed—and a tired face, cruelly scarred but still handsome thanks to the kind of features that retain their distinction through all the assaults of life. But behind this noble facade, for noble it was, I glimpsed, by the flicker of a strange light in the windows, a smoldering ruin.

He spoke hardly at all. No doubt he was engaged in his own act of disassociation, an effort to break away from his psychological dependency and brace himself for his confrontation with reality.

Among other things, he had to face the fact that his career in the Foreign Service was at an end—for what was euphemistically described as "extended sick leave" was no more than a merciful period of delay before the sword fell.

We arrived at Clovelly just in time to wash and change before dinner. The proprietress of the hotel apologized for not being able to give us the room Julian had asked for—the one we had occupied on both previous occasions—but she had put us into the room next to it, which had the same view. It was smaller than the other, with only one bed in it, an old-fashioned fourposter, not very wide; but there was no bed in the world, I thought, wide enough for me to want to share it with Julian. Intellectually, I acknowledged that my promise never to leave him would sooner or later involve me in living with him again as his wife, and that he hoped for a sexual reconciliation at Clovelly, but I was not prepared for the violence of my emotional reaction against it, now that it was imminent.

I said, "There's not much room in here for two. . . ."

"That's all right," Julian said. "I'll take my things down to the bathroom at the end of the passage and leave you to change by yourself."

It was just what he had said on our honeymoon, when we had both felt shy. But it was only after several steps had been exactly retraced—after dinner we had strolled on the breakwater, at ten o'clock Julian had said, "Shall we go upstairs now?" and on the upstairs landing, "I'll smoke a cigarette out here while you get ready for the night"—that I recognized his conscious reenactment of the past.

I was lying in the dark, listening to the lap of the waves and measuring their intervals by my own heartbeats, when Julian came in and lay down beside me.

The bed faced the window—wide open to the sea with muslin curtains looped back to form a triangle of water and sky made faintly luminous by a veiled moon. More than anything else about this reconstruction of the past, it was this triangular opening on the night sea, and the harbor smells of seaweed and nets and tar, that revived the emotions of that long-ago night when Julian and I had lain naked together for the first time. But the past, reproachful, betrayed, was of no help now. The sensory memory of the sea wind blowing over my bare skin only made me shudder.

"Don't be afraid," Julian said. "I won't touch you if you don't want me to."

After a while, from under the dead weight of my silence, he asked, "Are you sleepy?"

"No."

"Then perhaps we might talk a little ... the night was always our time for talking, wasn't it?"

"Yes, Julian."

"There's a lot to talk over now—so many things that I want to say to you ... but I don't know if I'm going to be able to say them...."

He groped for my hand and took it in his.

"I've been through hell, Joey."

"So have I, Julian."

"I know that. Knowing it has been part of my hell. It makes me terribly afraid...."

His grip on my hand tightened. His fear communicated itself to me. "Afraid ...?"

"Of the future—of what I might do in the future. I can't be certain of anything anymore, myself least of all. I envy the madmen who imagine themselves sane—at least they're all of a piece. But I'm in two pieces, Joey. You have no idea, you're too normal yourself to have any idea of what it's like to be half-mad, and sane enough to know it. *Knowing* it, that's the awful thing, Joey. Knowing it, and not being able to do anything about it. It's like old age or some incurable disease whose course one can do nothing to stop. All I can do is try to come to terms with it."

I too was trying to come to terms with a change that had happened to me. But I said nothing.

"Joey ... Do you ever think of Nicolai and Lucrèce?"

The question took me by surprise. They were always at the back of my mind; but Julian hadn't mentioned their names for years, and I thought that he had forgotten them.

"Yes," I said, "I think of them sometimes. Why do you ask?"

"Because I have been thinking about them a great deal lately. I understand them better now than I did before, particularly Nicolai. I see an analogy between my state and his ... the only difference is that his mad self lives in another body."

A gust of wind billowed the muslin curtains. The waves slapped the pebbles with sudden force. A newspaper left on the table fluttered apart. The hasps of the casements started to rattle. "We'd better shut them," I said. "The tide's coming up, and the wind's coming up with it."

"All right," Julian said, "I'll shut them."

He relinquished my hand and went to the window. Holding aside the curtains, he leaned out, thrusting his naked torso against the wind like the prow of a ship breasting a heavy sea. The wind rushed past him into the room, the canopy of the bed filled and flapped like a sail. He leaned out farther and farther. Letting go of the curtains, he extended his arms up and out . . . "Julian!"

The sound of my voice arrested the flight. One self gave way to the other. The casements were closed and fastened. The voice of Ondine was shut out.

Shivering, Julian put on his bathrobe, lighted a cigarette, and sat down in the armchair beside the empty grate. "I wonder if it's too late to get them to make a fire in here. . . ."

"It's only eleven o'clock. Shall I call down and ask them?"

"No—I'll go down and speak to whoever's in charge, and dispense some half crowns if necessary."

While Julian was gone I got up and put on my robe and sat down in the armchair on the other side of the fireplace. His half crowns produced a jug of mulled cider as well as a bucket of coals and kindling. The sticks were dry and the coals were soon burning brightly, creating around us an illusory fortress of light and shadow.

Julian held out his hands to the blaze, exposing his scarred wrists. "This is something I've missed, living out of England," he said. "There's nothing in the world like an English coal fire—we'll have one in every room of the cottage."

"The cottage . . . ?"

"The cottage I want to buy. That's one of the things we have to talk over."

"Where is this cottage, Julian?"

"I can't tell you that . . . I'm not quite sure where it is. But it's somewhere deep in the country, all by itself at the end of a lane. I'll recognize it when I see it."

"What is it like? Describe it to me."

He stared silently into the fire for a long time. Then, speaking very slowly, with long pauses, as though the cottage were taking shape bit by bit in the glowing cavities of the coals, he began to describe it.

"It's a simple, whitewashed cottage with four rooms.... There's a kitchen and parlor downstairs—with stone floors. And two bedrooms upstairs. The bedrooms have board floors, uneven, sloping.... It's old—maybe a couple of centuries—and a bit dilapidated.... It's been empty for a while, and the owner hasn't bothered to keep it in repair ... that's why the price is so low. It needs a lot done to it ... and the garden has run wild, honeysuckle and lilacs growing all over the place...."

Involuntarily I said, "Oh ..."

Julian looked up like a dreamer startled awake by a sudden sound. "What's that? What did you say?"

"Nothing. I just said, oh. You were talking about the garden."

Searching my face for something that wasn't there, he said, "Would you ... would you be willing to live with me in a little place like that?"

"Yes ... if that's what you want, Julian."

"But it's not what you'd choose for yourself ... is it?"

I wanted so much to reassure him, but the irony was too cruel. It was all I could do to keep back the tears that were pricking my eyelids.

"No," he said, answering himself, "no, of course it isn't. Well ... I don't blame you."

The long silence that followed, a deep, human silence unaffected by the uproar of the elements, was weighted with the sadness of the resignation contained in his last words. And I could do nothing to lighten it, or break it.

In the end, Julian broke it himself, by holding out his hand to me. "I love you, Joey. I have never stopped loving you."

I could not say what he wanted to hear, but I got up from my chair and sat down on the floor beside him and took his hand. He intertwined his fingers with mine. I was like the stone balustrade that accepts willy-nilly the embrace of the vine that will eventually smother it.

I was well aware of the cruelty of the inanimate, of the eloquence of the unsaid. Without having uttered a single unkind word I had effectively destroyed Julian's dream—not deliberately; it was as inevitable and unwilled as his destruction of my love for him had been.

Together we watched the structure of glowing coals in the grate cave in like a burning house.

The room cooled and darkened. Julian was so quiet that I thought he had fallen asleep. But when I changed my position to ease my cramped limbs, he said, "Don't get up. Let us stay like this for a little while longer."

Drawing me closer to him, he put his hand inside my robe and gently stroked my breasts, then bent and kissed them, caressing my nipples with his tongue. They responded automatically, as leaves on a tree respond to a passing gust of wind that has no effect on the tree itself.

A few hours ago the prospect of making love with Julian had been abhorrent to me for many reasons, some of them based on fear, some of them dark and complex, but, above all, because of my feeling that a physical reunion with Julian would be a betrayal of Keres and the night I had spent with him. Now, on the edge of the act, I realized that whatever else it might be it was not that. In themselves the actions of the body were innocent; they were pure or impure only insofar as they were endorsed by the spirit.

Although I remained unaroused by Julian's caresses, I had no doubt that I could satisfy him. He had never been sensitive to the ebb and flow of desire in me, he had taken for granted both his power to arouse me and the validity of my responses. Why should he be able to distinguish now between the real and the simulated? But there was a reason. His confidence had been based on a constant that wasn't there anymore, and nothing could disguise its absence, or compensate for it.

We made love there on the floor beside the cold hearth. His approach was almost timid; he entered me like a nervous bride-groom afraid of hurting a virgin bride. His gentleness was touching, yet somehow frightening. It was not natural, it created the impression of being consciously assumed as a safeguard, a means of holding in check some savagery that could not be controlled if it should once break loose. He achieved his climax quickly and in silence, save for a few sobbing breaths.

Without the anesthetic of passion, I had felt the hard floor bruising my shoulder blades. Disengaging myself from Julian's arms, I got up. He caught at my hand. "Don't leave me!"

"I'll come back."

When I came back, he was lying on the bed, naked. He said, "Deep in your heart you hate me, don't you?"

"No," I said, "I do not."

I took off my robe and lay down naked beside him. Encouraged, he began once again to kiss and caress me—with more sensuality than before, but with the same unnatural constraint. I lay on my back with my eyes closed while he bent over me, exploring my body with his mouth hungrily yet cautiously as if it were unknown territory; not hostile, but neutral, yielding but not giving.

Eventually, realizing, perhaps, that he had lost the power to evoke the responses he wanted, he gave up the attempt. When I opened my eyes and met his, they were fixed on me with a look of inexpressible sadness. But the sorrow in them was mixed with something else, something dark and threatening that made me tremble inwardly.

"Don't be afraid," Julian said, "it doesn't want to hurt you. It loves you."

As though to reassure me, he moved away from me and lay back on his pillow. Closing his eyes, he lay without moving, without speaking; but waiting, wordlessly asking for the impossible. His still uncovered body challenged me to take the initiative that in the past he had always believed to be the ultimate proof of my love for him. But I was incapable of it. My limbs refused to obey me, refused to enact the compassionate lie.

Julian and I were separated now by a vast emptiness that was not to be bridged by a handclasp.

Sleep finally came to the rescue; falling between us like snow, and burying me so deeply that even the choking spasms of a nightmare failed to awaken me fully.

At the moment of my awakening in the morning, just before I opened my eyes, the memory of this nightmare hovered for an instant on the fringes of my consciousness. It vanished before I could capture it, but it left in its wake a haunting echo, Fricka . . . Fricka . . . Fricka. . . .

I had overslept. It was broad daylight, and I was alone. My

traveling clock showed half-past ten, but I still felt tired, and my head ached. Julian, I thought, had done well to let me sleep and go down to breakfast without me.

I dashed some cold water over my face, swallowed a couple of aspirin, threw on my clothes, and ran downstairs, expecting to find him in the lobby. But the lobby was deserted. I looked into the dining room. Breakfast was over. The waitress was setting the tables for lunch. "Good morning, Madam."

"Good morning. I know I'm too late for breakfast, but could I please have some tea?"

"Certainly, Madam. It will take about five minutes."

I went in search of Julian. The sitting room was inhabited only by two old ladies reading the morning papers. Out on the veranda facing the sea a young couple stood entwined. A flight of rickety steps led down to the shingle beach and the little harbor. Julian was nowhere to be seen. The wind had gone down, and the sun was shining brightly on calm blue water, but last night's storm had left a chill in the air. It was too cold for swimming, I thought, Julian must have gone for a walk.

Back in the lobby I encountered the proprietress. "Good morning, Madam. I hope you are well rested. Mr. Crest asked us not to disturb you. He left a note for you."

My dearest,

I'm going back to London. It's safer there. I apologize for what happened last night. It didn't mean to hurt you, it made a mistake, it thought you were Fricka. It loves you, Joey, but it doesn't always know what it's doing. That's why I'm leaving. But there's no reason why you should leave too. The hotel bill is paid up for the whole week, and you may as well take advantage of it to have a little holiday.

I love you. Don't forget that, Joey. I love you.

Julian

Had he really gone back to London? He had taken nothing with him, his suitcase was still on the stand, his clothes were still hanging in the cupboard.

I asked for a railway timetable. "What train did my husband take?"

The proprietress said that he had hoped to catch the seven-fifty express—but George, the porter, would know, he had taken some luggage up to the station for another departing guest. George, called in, said yes, the gentleman had caught the seven-fifty by the skin of his teeth. I asked for my bags to be taken up to the station in time for the next London train.

After packing the bags, I had more than an hour to spare. Waiting was intolerable. My head ached fiercely, my nerves were taut, my muscles tense. I decided to take the warm bath that I had not had time for earlier. It relaxed me a little, physically. Afterward, combing my hair before the mirror still foggy with steam, I thought I must have forgotten to soap my neck. But the dark smudges on my throat didn't come off. I wiped the mirror clear and looked at them more closely. They were bruises. Fingermarks.

Of the journey up to London I remember only the chanting of the train wheels as they repeated over and over and over the echo of the nightmare. *Fricka . . . Fricka . . . Fricka . . .*

At Paddington, I called the sanatarium. Julian was not there. They had not seen him. I went home to the flat. An hour later I called the sanatarium again. Julian was still not there. They would call me as soon as he arrived.

But when, at last, they called, it was to tell me, as gently as they could, that he was never going to arrive. That he was never going to arrive anywhere on this earth ever again.

They were kinder to me than Micu had been to Sybil. They didn't allow me to see what was left of Julian.

# 9

# Joanna

The October weather was clear and bright. I could see for miles across the city from the window of my flat in Belsize Park. But I felt as if I were drowning in a dense fog.

I was alone. Pip and Cissy were at boarding schools found for them by their grandparents, and the few relatives who had rallied to my side at the time of Julian's death had gone back to their own lives and left me to pick up the pieces of mine. And I had deliberately cut myself off from the one person who could have helped me—Keres. Since my return from Clovelly, I had not been to the post office to pick up his letters, nor had I written to him.

Early one morning, it was not yet eight o'clock, the telephone rang, which was in itself a rarity. When I answered, the quiet voice at the other end of the line, asking for Madame Crest, was so like Keres's voice that it almost stopped my heart.

I heard the voice saying, "I am the cellist of the Székely Quartet, and a friend of Anthony Keres ... a Beethoven concert ... tonight at Wigmore Hall ... I have a ticket for you...."

Sweat broke out on my forehead. Keres was holding out his hand to me, but I couldn't grasp it. I was paralyzed—even my tongue wouldn't move.

Eventually I heard myself saying, "But I cannot come ... I cannot come because I am in mourning."

"That is just why you should come," the quiet voice said.

I began to weep.

"All great music is holy." Strange words to hear from a stranger over the telephone.

"I will come," I whispered.

Afterward it seemed as if the whole conversation had taken place in a dream. But when the time came, I set out for the concert hall.

With the ticket, at the box office, was a note from the cellist asking me to come to the artists' room after the concert.

It was the first time I had been in a concert hall or a theater since I had left Budapest. The people around me, talking and laughing, seemed to come from a different universe than the one in which I was drowning. I closed my eyes and waited for the music to begin.

It began with an early work, full of youth and joy, an invitation to life. To me it was like the singing of birds in the morning, which enters one's sleeping consciousness without jarring it into too sudden wakefulness.

I opened my eyes and looked at the players. I could see the cellist clearly from where I sat. He was a tall man, as tall as Keres, and he had the same big hands with long fingers. He played with his head bent over his cello, glancing at the first violin, or the music, without lifting his head. The inward look on his face while he was playing recalled the look on Keres's face when he was listening. The words that had seemed so strange over the telephone, no longer seemed strange.

There were two short intermissions. I stayed where I was, with my eyes closed; shutting out the alien universe, rehearing the music in my mind.

The last work listed on the program was the *Quartet in A Minor*. It was the one I had listened to with Keres over the Orsaghs' radio. It had been like a benediction then, but now it was something more. It was a requiem.

When it was finished, I remained in my seat until there was no one left in the hall. Then I went to the artists' room, trembling as if I were going to meet Keres himself.

The artists' room was still full of people wanting autographs. I sat down in a corner. The cellist, guessing who I was, came over to me. I told him I was not in a hurry, he should finish giving his autographs. When everyone had gone, he asked me if I would go and have something to eat with him at a quiet restaurant close by.

In his long black overcoat and wide-brimmed black felt hat,

carrying his cello in a canvas bag, he looked like a personage out of a Gothic tale. We walked along together without speaking. He was clearly shy, and I was summoning up my courage to tell him that I would rather not go to a restaurant. "What I would like best," I said, "is for you to come back to my flat and have something to eat there. Is that asking too much?"

He said, "No. I will be happy to come."

We took a taxi. I felt no need to talk. What Keres had so often told me about this man was, I felt, the literal truth; music was his language, words were merely substitutes—to be used only when absolutely necessary.

We were halfway to our destination when I said, "That last quartet has a special meaning for me. I heard you play it on the Budapest Radio. I listened to it with Keres."

"Yes," he said, "Keres told me. But it was pure coincidence that it was on the program tonight."

I said, "Nothing is pure coincidence."

We did not speak again until we reached Belsize Park.

I left him sitting by the window, looking out at the lights of London, while I went to the kitchen to get supper. All I had was some cold meat and cheese, and a cherry cake. And I found a bottle of wine that someone had given me.

When I brought it all into the sitting room on a tray, the cellist was examining a Hungarian box, beautifully handcarved with a peasant design. "I got that in Budapest," I told him. "Keres helped me choose it. I keep all his letters and poems in it."

We sat down facing each other at the table. He was obviously hungry. I was not. But I took a piece of cake and a glass of wine to keep him company. I didn't know quite what I wanted to say to him—or what I would be able to say to him. But I knew what I wanted from him.

He looked at me once or twice, as if wondering what it was that Keres had seen in me to fall in love with. Then he smiled at me very sweetly over his empty plate. "That was very good," he said. "Thank you."

I brought him coffee, and he asked permission to smoke. Then I said, "I have a confession to make. I asked you to come here because I wanted you to play for me. Will you?"

"Nothing would make me happier."

He asked for a hard, straight chair, and I brought him one from the kitchen. I sat in the low chair by the window, watching him tune the strings, and thinking how much he resembled Keres. He had the same type of Hungarian face, long and thin, with high cheekbones and a slight Mongol tilt to the eyes.

Then he began to play the Bach suites.

As the power and purity of the cello's unaccompanied voice transformed the lonely room that had been my purgatory, I understood what the cellist had meant when he said, "All great music is holy."

Through this great music, through this musician's hands, I was being given absolution.

When he had finished, he put his cello away without saying anything. Then he came and took my hand and lifted it to his lips. It is I who should be kissing his hands, I thought. I took them both in mine and touched them with my lips. He seemed to be overwhelmed. I said, "I thought Keres had the biggest hands in the world, but yours are just as big."

He said, "Shall I tell him that?"

"If you wish—he will know what I mean."

"Is there anything else that you would like me to tell him?"

I didn't answer at once. He waited.

"Tell him," I said at last, "that the reason I have not written to him is that I love him too much, more than it is right to love any one person—and for that I must suffer."

"Must you make him suffer too?"

I picked up the Hungarian box and opened it. From under the pile of letters I took out the two keys that Keres had given me. "Ask him," I said, "to forgive me for making him suffer. And tell him that I still have these. He will understand."

"I will tell him everything," B. said.

# 10

# Sybil and Consuela

On an April morning in London, the postman brought a square envelope addressed to me care of the Foreign Office in a handwriting that I hadn't seen for more than ten years. Flamboyant, scrawling, I recognized it with a shock of surprise and joy—the joy of recovering someone given up for lost—as Sybil's. The note inside, brief as a telegram, took up a whole page of heavy cream laid notepaper, stamped in gold with the initial S, and an address in Knightsbridge. Loosely dated, April, 1938, it said,

Dear Joanna, it's been a long time, hasn't it? I thought you might like to know that I'm still alive and kicking. Next time you're in London come and see me.

Sybil

I was just leaving for work when the postman came, so I put the letter in my bag and reread it on the bus. I usually took the underground, but there was a summer-like haze in the air that made me feel like making the trip on the top deck of a bus.

My job had been found for me by Keres. An old friend of his, a writer who had once been one of his teachers at London University, was losing his eyesight, and needed a general amanuensis, and Keres had written to him about me. I had been working for him for about a year. I did typing, and research, and translated German and French texts, and read aloud to him. He was an old man, a gentle scholar living on a quiet South Kensington square; working with him in a disciplined, orderly way helped me to put order into my own life, and dealing constantly with literature developed in me the creativity that Keres believed in and encouraged.

At home, I was alone most of the time. Pip was at Oxford, and Cissy was studying the piano in Vienna. Their grandparents had offered to take care of their education, and I had accepted; there was no point in being quixotic at their expense. In my quasi solitude I had finally achieved peace of mind, but it was, as Keres had said of his own, like all states of peace, fragile, and I hesitated to go and see Sybil for fear of disturbing it by reviving past memories.

It was a Friday, and my employer was expecting his daughter on a weekend visit, so we stopped work earlier than usual. The hazy morning had turned into a warm, sunny afternoon. Instead of going home I went to walk among the daffodils in Kensington Gardens. I was moving toward Sybil whether I wanted to or not. Sybil's pattern had been separated from mine for a long time, but I had learned that there was no such thing as total separation from any figure in the arabesque, alive or dead. Physically or morally each figure was inextricably linked with mine. In a sense we were all one, all parts of one intricate design, and all equally flawed.

The Knightsbridge address turned out to be a little dress shop, the kind of expensive boutique that displays a single item at a time in the window. Across the glass of the door was painted in gold script lettering the name *Sybille*. It was almost six o'clock, and they were closing up for the weekend.

An elegant young woman in black came forward to ask me, in heavily accented English, what she could do for me. I thought I must be hallucinating; it was Consuela, as unchanged by time as if she were made of porcelain instead of frail human flesh. Coppelia in a dress shop. Myself unrecognized, I asked to see Madame Sybille. Consuela went behind a screen, and I heard her say in French, "A new customer wants to see you, but it's six o'clock already," and Sybil's unmistakable voice replied, also in French, "Never mind, I'll see her."

She came out with Consuela, and stopped dead when she saw me. "My God! It's *you!* Consuela, you idiot, it's *Joanna!*" She hugged me. "*What* a surprise! When I wrote to you, I expected

306

you to be somewhere on the other side of the world!"

After a few minutes of confused talk among the three of us, Sybil said, "Let's go up to the flat—it's just upstairs, we live on the second floor."

"I must change and pack my suitcase," Consuela said. "Monsieur doesn't like me to be late."

Sybil told her to go ahead. "I'll lock up the cash box and all that. It will only take a minute, Joanna. What amazing luck to catch you in London! I can't get over it."

We went upstairs. The flat was one of those inconvenient conversions of an upper floor in an originally inconvenient town house of which I had seen so many when I was looking for a place to live in London. But the disadvantages of a kitchen and bathroom crammed into what had been a narrow landing was offset by the size of the two main rooms. I wondered what Sybil had done with them. I expected something bizarre, and in relation to her, nothing could have been more bizarre than the chintzy turn-of-the-century room she took me into. Its clutter of antiques and bric-a-brac gave the impression of having been acquired by lot at an auction by someone who didn't know the difference between the worthless and the valuable.

"This room doesn't look much like me, does it?" Sybil said. "All this antiquated stuff came from the rectory. It's awful, I suppose. But it's mine—which Max's stuff never was. I suppose you heard about Max's death?"

"Yes." I didn't want to talk about that. Neither, apparently, did Sybil.

"When my father died," she said, "three years ago, I inherited everything he possessed, which turned out to be quite a lot. He'd been investing small sums in gilt-edged securities for almost thirty years, and letting the interest accumulate, so there was enough capital to buy the dress business, and more than enough furniture to furnish this flat."

She lifted a sleeping cat from a chintz-covered easy chair and invited me to sit down. "When I lived with all this in the rectory," she said, "I hated it. But now it does something for me. It's so respectable."

Consuela came in from the back room, looking very chic in

navy and white, and carrying a small suitcase. She turned herself this way and that before Sybil as if she were modeling a dress for a customer. *"Ma toilette te plaît?"*

"You'll do," Sybil said, rough but affectionate. *"Tu rentres dimanche, hein?"*

Consuela shrugged. It was exactly the same indifferent shrug I had seen her give as a young wife when asked where her husband was. *"Je rentre le plus tôt possible,"* she said.

The doorbell rang. "There he is," Sybil said. Consuela lifted her face to be kissed like a dutiful child. And it was in that spuriously childlike gesture that I perceived what life had done to her. It had left no marks on her perfect face, no lines, no trace of emotional experience, but it had taken something away. It had taken away the light.

Sybil kissed her on the lips and gave her a little push toward the door as the bell jangled again.

"And now, Joanna, what about a drink?"

Settled with a tall glass of gin and ginger ale, she said, "Well, you haven't told me yet what you're doing in London and how long you're staying."

"I'm living here now—in Belsize Park."

"So *that's* how you got my letter so quickly! I suppose Julian's doing time at the Foreign Office for his sins."

"I'm living alone."

"Alone? You're not divorced, are you?"

"No. Julian . . . died."

Sybil put down her drink and came over to me. "I'm sorry," she said. "I'm so sorry. . . ." Then she kissed me, lightly and tenderly, several times, like a mother trying to kiss away a child's hurt. The gesture, coming from her, bowled me over. But she had always been quick to retreat from the least lapse into sentimentality, and she did so now. "Look here, why don't you stay and have supper with me—I'll order a couple of dozen oysters, and we'll split a bottle of bubbly and tell each other everything—all right?"

I nodded assent. But I wasn't prepared to "tell her everything." I no longer had any desire to tell anybody anything. My need for a trusted friend had been filled by Keres. I lived a solitary life, but I wasn't alone anymore.

Sybil was tactful enough not to question me. Instead, as the champagne loosened her tongue, she told me something of what had happened to her during the lost years.

We were drinking our champagne out of exquisite crystal glasses. Sybil, twiddling the slender stem of hers between her fingers, said, "These, and the goblets we used for our gin and ginger, were part of my mother's dowry. I didn't know her. She died when I was born. My father never remarried—which was why, I suppose, he couldn't forgive me for leaving him. He was a funny old boy, a miser with a conscience that wouldn't let him alone—a dead wife can nag more than a live one.

"He didn't make a will, and at first I thought that was just negligence, but after talking to the lawyer, I realized that it was his way of compromising between his miserly instincts and his conscience. He couldn't bring himself to formally bequeath his money to anyone, least of all to me, yet he had to face my mother in the next world. So he made sure that I would get everything as his next of kin, but not easily and not quickly. It took two years.

"I was living in Paris when he died, but the lawyer had my address. I was managing one of Micu's little businesses, one of his little 'fronts.' Giving me a job was my price for silence, and carrying out his instructions was his price for silence.

"As soon as the lawyer told me that I was Daddy's only legal heir, I made a down payment on the goodwill of this business. I had some savings—it wasn't difficult to accumulate perks. Micu daren't employ an accountant, and he was too afraid of me to investigate my books himself. I knew too much. We had each other by the short hairs. Which is why he didn't raise hell over Consuela's defection to me. Not that he cares a damn about her, but she was useful to him. You know—or do you?—that Max didn't leave me anything in his will. Everything went to Consuela and Micu—in short, to Micu, because in that feudal country, whatever a woman inherits automatically becomes the property of her husband. In any case, Micu controlled the source. He was part of the ring, and had been ever since his marriage."

"But so were you."

Sybil laughed. "I wasn't thinking of *that* ring—but I might have got a legacy if I'd been able to keep it circular. . . ." She paused, and I regretted reminding her of a ring that she probably wanted to forget. But she went on quite coolly. "What do you hear of Charles? He's got what he wanted, I suppose."

"Not quite. He hasn't been made an ambassador yet."

"Is he married?"

"Yes."

"Children?"

"No."

"That's poetic justice. I believe in poetic justice—sooner or later we have to pay for everything. But of course Charles was right not to marry me. It wouldn't have worked for either of us. Where he was wrong was in making a promise that he had no intention of keeping. He did that out of moral cowardice, of course. All men are moral cowards when it comes to women. What is his wife like?"

"Long-suffering. A childhood friend who puts up with his weaknesses because she loves him in a maternal sort of way. She was the girl you saw him with that day."

"That day damn nearly did me in. Did you ever wonder how I managed to get more than five months along without Max noticing—especially with all those family games going on? Well, of course I didn't. Max thought Micu was the father, but that didn't bother him so long as he got the public credit. Micu probably suspected an outside lover, but that didn't bother him so long as he got the private credit—it would only make his position more secure. Consuela only shrugged. It was all kept quiet, of course, because Max couldn't be sure how it was going to turn out, and he didn't want to be made a fool of.

"I was as sure that I was pregnant by Charles as any woman can be on intuition. But there was always the sickening possibility that it was Micu. And it was that, even more than Charles's bloody moral cowardice, that drove me in the end to take the risk I took. Thanks to you, Max believed that I really had lost the baby as the result of acute appendicitis.

"In some ways Max was an old fool. Maybe it was senility, that loathsome disease eating away at his brain. . . . His end from that could have been even more horrible. . . ." A shudder passed through her. I recalled what Amanda had told me, and I too shuddered. But Sybil was too preoccupied with her own reproachful ghost to sense the presence of mine.

The cat came and rubbed against her legs, meowing. She seized on the diversion. "Hungry, lovie? Come along then, I'll give you your supper."

I brought the plates with the empty oyster shells on them out to the kitchen. Sybil produced some cake and made coffee. "It's funny, you know, to look back dispassionately to a time in one's life that was one big bloody mess of violent passions, and sort them out, see which were real and which were aberrations. For example, my hatred of Max was real. My love for Charles wasn't. It was a sexual aberration, a temporary reaction against women because of Consuela, because I didn't understand how she could comply so meekly with all the beastly things that Max and Micu demanded of her. How ridiculous all that jealousy and possessiveness of Consuela's body seems now!"

"You *did* love Charles, Sybil. For God's sake, don't deny that."

She understood me. It was not for nothing that we had both been brought up in a religious atmosphere. We had a common language that had nothing to do with the way we each talked, which was very different. "Do you really believe, Joanna, that love redeems acts that without it would be evil?"

"I think so. I hope so."

We both fell silent. God knows we both had enough to ponder on. We brought our coffee into the sitting room, and Sybil lighted a cigarette. The candles on the table had burned down, and the room was in semidarkness. A quick, light shower had cooled the outside air and sharpened the street smells coming in through the open window.

Presently Sybil said, "I'm not sure whether I know what love is. If I love anyone, if I have ever loved anyone, it's Consuela. I've been fighting to get her away from Micu for years, but I couldn't do it until I was free myself. We are necessary to each other. I need her and she needs me, and not simply because I can give her what no bloody man can ever give her—an honest-to-God orgasm. Consuela needs me like a child needs its mother. And I am as much her mother as her lover. That's the truth, Joanna. You don't believe me, do you?"

"I do believe you."

"But you don't understand how I can send her off for a weekend with a man—like a madam—if I feel like that about her. And I don't blame you. You've gained your experience of life in the *beau monde*—the world of high society—but I've gained mine in the *demi-monde*—the world of prostitutes and procurers, where this sort of thing is all in a day's work, and has nothing to do with one's feelings."

"I think I do understand," I said. "When my mother was dying she tried to tell me something. Her lips formed the word *love*, but she couldn't go on. That was sixteen years ago, and I knew so little about loving that I could only guess at what she wanted to say. But now I think I know. I think she wanted to make me understand that love is the only thing that matters."

We sat on in the dark, talking together with a deeper understanding than I would have thought possible.

I told her about Keres.

"But what if he doesn't get his freedom?" she asked. "Will you go on waiting forever?"

"No one could ever replace him," I said.

I had known that ever since the April afternoon, two years ago, when he had told me that he loved me. But now I believed with him that nothing could keep us apart. We were not waiting; we were moving toward each other.

# About the Author

Theresa de Kerpely was born and brought up in England, which she left more or less permanently by the time she was twenty years old. Living in numerous foreign countries, she acquired fluency in five foreign languages. Not unlike her heroine in ARABESQUE, Ms. de Kerpely's marriage to a well-known Hungarian musician took her to Budapest on the eve of World War II. There she remained throughout the war, experiencing occupation by the Nazis, a nine-week siege, and liberation by the Red Army. After the war, Theresa de Kerpely came to the United States with her family and began her writing career. ARABESQUE is her fourth published book. She has enjoyed fellowships at the Huntington Hartford Foundation, Yaddo, and the MacDowell Coloy. More recently she held for three consecutive years the position of Writer in Residence at the University of Massachusetts at Amherst.

# OTHER STEIN AND DAY BOOKS YOU'LL ENJOY:

|  |  |  | U.S. | Canada |
|---|---|---|---|---|
| 8064-1 | **ASSASSINATION DAY**<br>Kenneth Royce | | 3.95 | NCR |
| 8042-0 | **C.L.A.W.**<br>Richard Graves | | 3.50 | 3.95 |
| 8013-7 | **DIRTY TRICKS**<br>Chapman Pincher | | 3.50 | NCR |
| 8019-6 | **THE DUNKIRK DIRECTIVE**<br>Donald Richmond | | 3.50 | NE |
| 8084-6 | **FALLS THE SHADOW**<br>Emanual Litvinoff | | 3.95 | NCR |
| 8066-8 | **THE GAZA INTERCEPT**<br>E. Howard Hunt | | 3.50 | 3.50 |
| 8032-3 | **MAN ON A SHORT LEASH**<br>Kenneth Royce | | 2.95 | NCR |
| 8080-3 | **THE RED DOVE**<br>Derek Lambert | | 3.95 | NCR |
| 8028-5 | **THE RUN TO MORNING**<br>Jack Higgins | | 3.50 | 3.50 |
| 8052-8 | **SIEGE**<br>Edwin Corley | | 3.95 | 3.95 |

## OTHER STEIN AND DAY BOOKS

| | | | U.S. | Canada |
|---|---|---|---|---|
| | 8056-0 | **THE BOOK OF GHOST STORIES**<br>Peter Haining | 3.95 | NCR |
| | 8012-9 | **CASEBOOK OF A PSYCHIC DETECTIVE**<br>Dixie Yeterian | 2.95 | 2.95 |
| | 8044-7 | **FIFTY TRUE MYSTERIES OF THE SEA**<br>John Canning, ed. | 3.95 | NCR |
| | 8094-3 | **THE SIN EATER**<br>Elizabeth Walter | 2.95 | NCR |
| | 8047-1 | **STAR SIGNS FOR LOVERS**<br>Liz Greene | 3.95 | NCR |
| | 8018-8 | **THIS HOUSE IS HAUNTED**<br>Guy Lyon Playfair | 3.50 | NCR |
| | 8025-0 | **YOUR PERSONALITY AND THE PLANETS**<br>Michel Gauquelin | 3.50 | NE |

# The Celebrity Book of Lists

**Fascinating Facts about Famous People**

## Ed Lucaire

CELEBRITY BIRTHDAYS • CELEBRITIES REAL NAMES • CELEBRITY FIRST SEX EXPERIENCES • CELEBRITY NOSE JOBS • CELEBRITY TATTOOS • CELEBRITY TWINS • CELEBRITIES BORN ABROAD • CELEBRITY SIBLINGS • CELEBRITY "MILITARY BRATS" • CELEBRITY REAL ETHNIC ORIGINS • CELEBRITY TOUPEES • CELEBRITY EYE COLORS • CELEBRITIES FROM BROOKLYN • CELEBRITIES

# LIZ GREENE

# STAR·SIGNS FOR LOVERS

## is an explicit book.

It not only shows how to interpret your own and your
partner's astrological "signature," the subtle
patterns that form a personality, but also why your
choice of lovers could be dangerous to yourself if
you ignore what is now known—and wonderfully
rewarding if you put the same information to
good and fruitful use.

# Your Personality and the Planets

## MICHEL GAUQUELIN

*Your Personality and the Planets* demonstrates definite correlations between planetary positions at the time of birth and the careers that people choose and how well they succeed in them.

*Your Personality and the Planets*, a practical book, will enable readers to use Michel Gauquelin's research to assess their own character, including the occupations they're best suited for, and to predict what their children will be like when they grow up.

# PMS
# DPMS
# PMS

## What Every Woman Should Know About Premenstrual Syndrome
### Updated
### RENI L. WITT

- How to find out if you have PMS
- How to alleviate PMS bloating, food cravings, painful breasts, headaches, abdominal, joint, and muscle pains, and other PMS symptoms
- How to overcome PMS tension, depression, hostility, fatigue, anxiety, and other mood changes
- A 10-point plan to ease PMS without a doctor or without prescription drugs
- The very latest medical advances and new treatments

Plus:
- The truth about PMS, violence, and crime
- Why it's called the "male chauvinist's revenge"
- Newly discovered risks of progesterone treatment

# EATING TO WIN

### Food Psyching for the Athlete

## Frances Sheridan Goulart

Whether you are a weekend athlete or a professional, whatever your age or sex, *Eating to Win*, the *original* book about sports nutrition, will teach you which foods increase your strength and stamina—and which do not. What you eat can determine whether you win or lose.

*Eating to Win* tells you how to win through food. It is sure to be the most indispensable piece of sports equipment you'll ever own.